# Field of Schemes

# Field of Schemes

*a novel by*

Jennifer Coburn

## _Also by Jennifer Coburn_

The Wife of Reilly

The Second Wife of Reilly
_(part of This Christmas, a three-novella collection)_

Reinventing Mona

Tales from the Crib

The Queen Gene

Brownie Points

*In memory of*

**Alex Pogman**

and

**Howie Hawver**

Great coaches who left the field far too young

# Acknowledgements

During my daughter Katie's seven years playing club soccer, our family met hundreds of parents, kids, coaches, and referees. Our teams traveled hundreds of miles to small towns and big cities in broiling heat and freezing cold to watch half-pint soccer, often regarding it with greater importance than the Olympics. Most of the time club soccer was an absolute joy. On occasion, people lost their minds, myself included. This book is dedicated to all of the parents who give their time, energy and money so their children can enjoy the many benefits of participation in team sports.

Thank you to all of the parents who shared their stories about club soccer. I appreciate your candor and self-deprecation.

Before my daughter played club soccer, I spent two seasons coaching the recreational team, the Kickin' Chicks. I look back on those days with great fondness for the kindergarteners and first-graders who have all blossomed into beautiful high school students. And because I knew absolutely nothing about the game of soccer, I am eternally indebted to my terrific assistant coaches: Eric Williamson, Mike Poltorak and Marv Mittleman. All of our team parents were gems, always cheering wildly, creating winning banners, and slicing endless oranges.

I appreciate the good friends who read early drafts of this manuscript and offered feedback. Thanks to Edit Zelkind, Lisa Taylor, Joan Isaacson, Deborah Shaul, Rachel Biermann, Jacquie Lowell, and Matt Levy. And I would be sorely remiss not to acknowledge Christopher Schelling, this story's most tireless champion.

Suzette Durazo came up with exactly the front cover design I had envisioned and I am grateful for her artistic talent and endless patience. Thank you to Lisa DeSpain for her formatting expertise, and to Phil Lauder and Leslie Wolf Branscomb for their eagle eyes that caught most, if not all, of my errors.

As always, thanks to my wonderful husband, William O'Nell, the best choice I ever made. He is supportive beyond the call of duty and I love him more than a shutout against a premiere team in the final game of the State Cup.

Thank you to readers, bloggers, librarians and bookstore owners for supporting my work, telling friends about my novels and inviting me to your book clubs. I greatly appreciate the tweets and posts on social media. Without you, it is impossible to do what I love most.

# Chapter One

"Let go!" the sculpted brunette demanded as she tugged the sleeve of the soccer jersey stretched between us.

Staring at her with steely determination, I wrapped my fist tighter around the other sleeve and yanked back. "You let go!" I replied with volume that surprised even me. Softening a bit, I tried to approach the situation rationally. "I understand you want the jersey, but I picked it up first." Shrugging ever so slightly, I added, "Fair is fair."

"If you had it first, it would be in your hands right now," she growled through perfectly veneered teeth. She narrowed her eyes with pure unadulterated hatred for me. At first glance, this woman wearing Lilly Pulitzer ribbon-trimmed Capri pants epitomized the well-maintained suburban soccer mom. Her chocolate brown hair was perfectly highlighted with subtle auburn undertones, and pulled back by a puffy headband wrapped in the same ribbon that trimmed her pants. Her nails were slick with a fresh manicure, clean square tips dangling beneath a diamond tennis bracelet. When she opened her mouth, though, it was clear that there was no love in her game. "Let go, I said," she barked.

"No. The shirt is mine! It *is* in my hands!" I reminded her. It was clear she was not going to politely back down from our tug-of-war over the black-and-white German National team jersey, the last one on the table at Soccer Post.

"It's in your *hand*, singular," she snapped, "*and* in mine. If you'd taken full possession of it, you'd have both hands on it."

*Was this true? Was there some sort of two-hand rule?!*

Like synchronized swimmers, we each placed a second hand on the jersey.

This was crazy. Perhaps the store had another jersey in the back, I thought. At the very least, they could special order another one for this psychotic mother, and I could take mine home for Rachel today. This woman probably didn't need the jersey right away as I did.

At the very moment I opened my mouth to suggest we ask for an inventory check, Psycho Mom gave the shirt a little tug to assert her dominance. Her muscles flexed impressively, the sinewy biceps and forearms of a woman with free time. Since I was bound to lose the battle of the brawn, I tried to appeal to her better nature. "Look, this jersey is very important to my daughter," I said softly, aware of a few customers staring at the two moms caught between the taut German National Team jersey. "She's had a rough year and I want to—"

Yanking the jersey again, the mother snapped, "Not my problem. Now hand over the jersey and—"

"And what?" I demanded. A woman stopped and stared, alarmed, tapping her husband on the shoulder before he hurried off to get help. "And no one gets hurt? Are you threatening me over a soccer jersey?" Then, I had a glimmer of sanity. It was just a black-and-white striped polyester soccer jersey. Without the German team emblem, and player number on the back, it could've passed for a prison uniform, which is exactly what I'd be wearing if I made a habit of getting into retail brawls with other soccer moms. I decided to let go of the overpriced jersey, drop the fight and walk out of the Soccer Post with my dignity intact. Well, maybe half my dignity.

Just as I resolved to forfeit this petty battle, the insane soccer mom did something I never expected. She pulled the jersey with full force, causing me to fly toward her and lose my balance. I'm not sure exactly what happened next, only that somewhere on our way down to the floor, the two of us knocked over the clearance rack and a life-sized cardboard cutout of Mia Hamm. As we landed, I noticed two things. One, Mia was still smiling, even though she was on her back with her eyes completely covered by men's shorts. And two, neither Psycho Mom nor I had let go of the now-torn jersey. "Look what you did!" she shouted as we lay on the store's Astroturf flooring.

The clerk rushed over to us, nervously asking what happened. "She attacked me," said Psycho Mom as she pointed at me. "She wanted my jersey, so she jumped on me and started going nuts." At this point, at least a half-dozen sets of eyes were on me, waiting for an explanation. A four-foot boy with a military buzz cut and goalkeeper jersey shook his head as if to say he thought now, in his entire six years, he'd seen it all.

"That's simply not true!" I defended. As I stood up, I realized that neither Psycho Mom nor I had loosened our grip on the jersey. "I was holding the jersey when she came out of nowhere demanding that I give it to her."

The teen clerk looked at the two of us, then glanced at the small goalkeeper and joined him in shaming head-shaking. "Ladies, I've got plenty of German team jerseys in the back. It's not like this was the last one, y'know?" The clerk shook his head again. "Why don't I run back and get another one? What size?"

In unison Psycho Soccer Mom and I mumbled, "Small."

I never thought I'd be one of those parents who became overly invested in their children's lives, yet here I was with half of a torn jersey in my right hand and a clump of another mother's hair in my left fist. (I swear it was an accident. I needed to grab something as I tried to regain my balance.)

I've always been appalled when I heard news reports about Little League and hockey parents' fights. I cried when I read about the mother who shot a cheerleader so her daughter would have a better chance of making the squad. Then there was that French dad who drugged his daughter's tennis rival. When I say drugged, I don't mean that young Fifi started seeing butterflies and lollipops dancing on a rainbow. I mean the poor kid took a swig of her Evian and dropped dead. It was truly ghastly, yet here I was having my very own fight with another soccer mom over a jersey. This crazy bitch even bit me after we landed on the floor! Now she brushed her hands against each other as if the whole experience had sullied her.

"Yeah, uh, listen, ladies," the clerk said. "Someone's gonna have to pay for this ripped jersey here."

Our words toppled over each other's again. "Not me." For someone so completely unlike me, this Psycho Mom certainly was reading from the same script as I was.

"Why don't you ladies split it?" he suggested.

"Looks like they've already done that, dude," a spectator couldn't resist injecting.

"Who won?" the little goalkeeper asked.

"It was a tie," said the staring mother. "Nice example you're setting, *ladies*."

"Mind your own business!" Psycho Mom snapped back.

The clerk's placing a new jersey in her hands had a sedative effect on Psycho Soccer Mom. While she was hardly friendly, I no longer feared for my safety. "Why don't we just split the cost of this one and call it even?" I offered.

"Fine," she said.

I didn't have the energy to continue with this madness. Besides, in my very own hands was a brand new German National Team soccer jersey. I had mine, she had hers. All was right in the world. As we finished our transactions, both Psycho Mom and I walked toward the exit of the store, sporting Soccer Post shopping bags. When we reached the door, she pushed it open and held it for me. Though I secretly feared she was going to pull a Zidane and head butt me in the chest, Psycho Mom was surprisingly pleasant. She smiled and gestured with her hand that I should walk ahead of her.

"Thank you," I said tentatively.

"No worries," she said. "You have a great day now!"

I stood motionless in the parking lot, staring agape as Psycho Mom bopped toward her minivan.

*Have a great day? Did she really just tell me to have a great day just minutes after sinking her teeth into my left hand?*

How did this happen? What had become of me? I've always been one of those people who saw the world as having enough for everyone, even when it didn't. My husband, Steve, used to tease me about this, telling me that while everything isn't a zero-sum game, some things absolutely are. That is, if there's only one spot left on the fencing team, there's only one spot. They're not going to simply adopt my hippy dippy philosophy of creating one big, all-inclusive team where every nearsighted klutz is given a saber.

I just got bit by another soccer mom, but my overwhelming feeling was one of victory because I would be going home with a German National Team jersey for Rachel. Now she could impress Coach Gunther by dressing in sportswear from his homeland.

How did I get here? When did this happen to me? And more importantly, once a person crossed the line into the world of crazy sports parents, was there any way back to normalcy?

# Chapter Two
*Four Months Previous*

Rachel was having the game of her life. Granted, her life had only been an eleven-year stint, her soccer career even shorter, but I'd never seen her play like she did that crisp day in November. I don't know if it was the fact that her team was playing the undefeated Blue Kittens or that it was the final game of her first soccer season, but something lit a fire under Rachel's cleats.

She was the star of the Purple Sparrows from her first game of the recreational season when she ran onto the field and scored three goals. I wasn't surprised by her speed, but was a bit rattled by her intensity. When others had the ball, she was unrelenting until they unwillingly gave it up to her. If she had the ball, she was consumed with desire to keep possession of it until it was time for her to shoot. Rachel moved around other players as if they were no more of an obstacle than the orange cones that Coach Andy set up at practice. No one on the field wanted that ball more than Rachel. Her desire was overwhelming.

This came from Steve. My late husband was so competitive that when our doctor told us that Rachel weighed more than any other newborn at the hospital, he proudly declared her the "heavyweight champion of the nursery." When we got Rachel's

Apgar results, Steve immediately asked, "Ten's the highest score, right?" When this was confirmed, Steve made a victorious gesture with his fist. At times I wondered if this new side of Rachel was a result of his death, her way of keeping him alive. In college, I remember a girl in poetry class told me that she had her first sip of scotch at her father's memorial service because she wanted to keep his taste on her lips. She found the burn in her stomach comforting, knowing that this was the same sensation her father experienced when ingesting his nightly elixir. Though my classmate never quite liked the taste of scotch, it became her regular drink as the taste, smell, and fluidity of it kept a bit of her father in her daily life. There was no way I could ask Rachel if she was keeping her father alive through soccer. Even if this were the case, no eleven-year-old would possess the self-awareness to make such an observation. The best I could do was talk about it with her when and if I saw issues arise. The second best thing I could do was be aware of my own feelings when I saw glimpses of Steve through Rachel. It was a rich blend of comfort and pain.

At that first game, when Rachel stripped the ball from another player, I instinctively turned to my right and said, "We got a player!" Intellectually, I knew Steve was not there sitting by my side, but instinct is faster than rational thought, sort of like light vs. sound. It was a pleasant millisecond when I convinced myself that Steve was beside me and all was well in our world.

Though Steve had been gone for nearly a year at that point, I was still startled by the sound of Bobby's loud voice responding to me. "We sure do," he said between his hoots. Bobby is what I later learned is a pretty common strain of soccer dad: a loudmouth with few manners and a whole lot of attitude. He had coffee-stained, badly capped teeth and a collection of baseball hats. His leathery skin suggested he worked outdoors, and his volume told me that he was an avid sports fan, the kind who was prone to road rage after his team lost a game. I tried to focus my eyes on the field as I fought the marble rising in my throat. Half of my sadness came from the reminder of Steve's absence. The other half came from Bobby's presence.

Thinking I'd opened a conversation, Bobby continued. "Don't tell me she never played before, Claire," he said. "Come on, your secret's safe with me." Then he let out the labored laugh of an alcoholic who smoked. This was his routine throughout the season. After Rachel scored, Bobby would turn to me and ask if I was certain Rachel had never played before. I assured him that she hadn't, and he jokingly accused me of lying. This was immediately followed by a fresh phlegm chuckle. Each time it was the funniest thing he'd ever heard. For me it was stale the first time around. Yet this one-sided repartee had continued from our season opener against the Kickin' Chicks until this final game against the Blue Kittens.

The score was 2-0 and Rachel had scored both goals. A bouncy little girl from the Blue Kittens was dribbling the ball when Rachel sped up to her and pulled it away with her foot. Another Blue Kitten began chasing her, but she promptly lost her footing and fell.

"Good job, Layla!" a mom from the other sideline shouted.

"Good job?" Bobby snorted. "How's falling on your ass a good job?"

"She's just trying to encourage her daughter," I said curtly, hoping to end the conversation. I failed. How did I always wind up sitting next to this guy? No matter where I sat, he seemed to show up next to me—even after I moved away from him. I was adept at getting away from people and situations I didn't like, but could never quite shake Bobby. He kept coming back. Like herpes.

He continued. "Yeah, I get the whole self-esteem thing, but feeding a kid a bunch of crap ain't doin' her any favors. 'Member last week when Rachel scored on that Screamin' Demons' keeper, and all the parents were carrying on about what a good job she did?" He laughed at the memory. "Her *job* is to keep the ball out of the net. I mean, she tried her best and all, but if she did a good job, the ball wouldn'ta gone in, y'see what I'm sayin'?"

I looked at him with no expression. "Her parents should sell her on eBay."

"Nah, I'm not sayin' that," Loud Bobby continued. "But don't feed her a bunch of lies and tell the kid that failure is success, 'cause that's when ..."

*Why did he think I cared to hear his musings on sports psychology and parenting? How many different baseball caps does he own anyway? Is it some sort of white trash fashion faux pas to be seen in the same cap twice? Last week it was a Skoal cap and this week it's some joint called Freddie's Palace. What woman looked at this and said, "Yes! This is who I want to spend my life with. He's fascinating, he's funny, and he has such a wide assortment of hats!"*

"... so I always say to Cayenne, give it your best and if that's not good enough, we'll practice till y'get it right."

*Is this guy still talking?*

The referee blew his whistle and gave us a two-minute warning. I loved his World War II-era clip art look and earnest nature. Seeing him at games always made me want to wear a cardigan sweater and rent *It's a Wonderful Life*. "Come on girls!" the Blue Kittens' coach shouted. "We can still win this!" "Dream on!" Loud Bobby shouted across the field. While the referee was like something you'd see on Turner Classic Movies,

Loud Bobby was pure Fox TV. He was the kind of guy who won the stupid tricks contest at local bars by inhaling a silver chain up his nostril and pulling it out his mouth. "Dream on, Coach!" Bobby taunted again. *Was this guy physically capable of speaking below eighty decibels?!* I dropped my head into my hands for fear that someone might mistake me for his wife—or even his friend.

Rushed, the Blue Kittens' coach began shouting instructions. "Layla, Willow, Annabelle, Emma, push up! Defense, move up! Everyone's trying to score except Money. Money, you stay back on D. Everyone else, you're a forward now!"

"Give it up, Coach!" Bobby shouted again. "Nothin's gonna save y'now. It's all over, pal."

The coach glared in our direction. *Not me. I didn't say a word. Hell, I think Layla did a good job when she fell on her ass. I am so totally not with this guy.*

None of my telepathic apologies seemed to transmit. The coach muttered something to the referee, who then pointed at us and blew his whistle. As if in slow motion, every head on the field turned in our direction. Parents on both sidelines stared. Kids gawked. Even families who were passing by, on their way to a game at a different field, stopped to hear what the referee was going to say.

The long whistle stopped. "Warning!"

After a split second of silence, I sighed with relief. Then Bobby responded. "That's what I was tryin' to give 'em, Ref," he shouted. "He can throw the whole damn team up top, but if he leaves one defender back there, our girl Rachel's gonna blow past her and score on these suffocated kitty cats *once again!*"

*Our girl?! Our girl?! Do people think this jerk is Rachel's father?*

The referee held up a yellow card and announced perfunctorily, "One more word and I'm asking you to leave, sir."

Bobby held up his hands in mock surrender. Every girl on the field was staring at Bobby, bewildered and horrified. And little fall-on-her-ass Layla looked particularly devastated. Or not. "Ya jerk," she muttered at Bobby.

"Yeah, be quiet, y'big old loser," another Blue Kitten added.

As the referee blew his whistle to resume the game, I noticed a tall black man with ropy, muscular legs and a snappy royal blue Adidas warm-up suit. He held a clipboard and took notes with the interest of a doctor listening to the symptoms of his patient with a rare condition. I'd seen him at a few of our other games, but never really gave much thought to who he was or why he was watching our team. But as he gave a sidelong glare at Bobby, I wondered if he was from the Kix Soccer League, taking notes about which parents were naughty and nice. Maybe Loud Bobby would be banned from games for life.

The ball was deep in our territory. It looked as though the Blue Kittens were finally going to score as the cluster of newly appointed forwards scrambled for the ball. Good enough. Let the Blue Kittens score a goal and feel good about their last game of a successful season, I thought.

It became so crowded in the goal box that it was tough to see what was going on. It looked like a kicking riot. The parents of the Blue Kittens started shouting, "Shoot! Shoot!" Their coach frantically joined in. "Take the shot!"

Parents from both teams were on their feet, leaning their bodies toward the action as if it might help the outcome. Throwing his hands in the air and beckoning the soccer gods, the coach good-naturedly begged, "Someone take a shot already. One shot is all I ask."

A mother on the other team grabbed her husband's jacket sleeve and wailed, "They're gonna score, I can feel it!" I wished

Steve were here to grab onto. I wished I could borrow his sweater the way I always had on crisp autumn days. I never fully accepted the chill of fall, always clinging to the hope that Indian summer might continue into the holidays. Even though I was born and raised in Los Angeles, I chose to believe the movie version of Southern California where people walked around in swimsuits year-round. I never owned many sweaters, but was especially glad for this fact when I met Steve and started borrowing his. I loved the way his Shetlands hung down to my thighs. The sleeves needed to be rolled up so many times, it looked as if I had doughnuts around my wrists. I called the look "girlfriend chic," while my mother dubbed it "frumpy wife." As I wrapped my bare arms around my t-shirt, I had to accept that it was cold and I was alone.

"Ain't gonna happen," Bobby told me.

"It could," I returned. "They're very close to the goal." *Why did I even respond to this imbecile?*

"Close, nothin'," he said, disregarding my comment with a wave of the hand. "Look how they're all bunched up. Cayenne's gonna snatch that up, no problem."

As Bobby predicted, Cayenne laid her goalie gloves on the ball, ensuring that there would be no goal for the Blue Kittens.

"I love their banner," Celeste, our team mom, whispered to me as she gazed across the field enviously. Despite the efforts of five mothers armed with glue guns, our team banner placed second to the Blue Kittens' in the opening day parade. While ours was beautiful, it didn't compare to the elaborate extravaganza the other team put together. Ours had a purple sequined border surrounding an enormous blue felt sky with puffy white clouds. Fifteen fully feathered purple sparrows flew toward a soccer net in the heavens as they clutched soccer balls with their claws. Each bird held a Styrofoam sphere that was painted like a soccer ball, with the girl's name and jersey number printed on it in purple metallic ink. When the mothers unveiled their masterpiece, I was certain we were a shoo-in for the prize.

After I caught a gander at our competition, I knew we'd be also-rans. The other team somehow managed to get battery-operated blue fur kittens to dance to a rap song, *I'm Smitten by Kittens*, which the team sang and recorded. The music was actually produced in a studio by a mother who had connections at Sony. The kittens were brought to life by a father, an engineer who just so happened to have thirty hours to spare to make sure his kid won the banner medal. If that weren't enough, another mother designed jewel-encrusted jerseys and actual cleats to fit their little paws. The lunatics from the Kickin' Chicks made their banner three-dimensional, with a goal net built around a backdrop of Astroturf. "Birds are so hard to work with," Celeste continued as Cayenne's foot connected with the ball.

Our goalkeeper's punting was breathtaking. Often the ball went so far to the other side of the field, it looked as if she might score. This one sailed past the midline. It was our three forwards against their sole defender. Of course, I wanted Rachel to succeed, but I was sort of hoping she wouldn't score another goal. She'd already had such a great game, another goal wouldn't make any difference to her. These kittens, on the other hand, didn't need a third goal scored against them in the final seconds of their final game. Who needed that kind of letdown just hours before their team party?

I was absolutely mistaken in my assumption that one more goal wouldn't make a difference to Rachel. She charged to collect the ball and began running toward the goal as if these final seconds were the most important of her life. I guess no one told her that the game had already been won. She scrunched her face with determination and looked to her sides for a teammate to pass the ball to. Both were left behind, unable to keep up with Rachel's speed. It was Rachel against one defender in the Blue Kittens' territory with less than a minute in the game. She stepped over the ball and kicked it to her side in a fake-out move I didn't quite follow. Her feet moved faster than my eyes. All I knew was Money, the lone defender, was now behind Rachel and it was my daughter one-on-one with a nervous-looking goalkeeper.

Rachel leaned to the left as if she were going to shoot to that corner, then suddenly shifted her weight and shot to the opposite corner as the keeper was mid-dive in the other direction. It was stellar. When the ball made it into the net, our coach ran onto the field and put Rachel onto his shoulders. The other girls exploded into a screaming celebration and rallied around Rachel, cheering.

This was good. Whenever I second-guessed my decision to move to the suburbs, I would visit this mental snapshot. Here she had community. Here we could build a new life. Here we could sew together a patchwork family with good people, top schools, and kids' sports.

# Chapter Three

In my mind the season ended with that goal. As the parents formed a London Bridge-style tunnel for the girls to run through, Celeste handed out boxed Yoo-hoos and cookies frosted to look like soccer balls. She cheerfully reminded everyone that our team party was that evening.

I had closed the chapter on soccer until next season. My daughter and the man in the Adidas warm-ups, however, had different plans.

He was a bold presence, a physical specimen of ebony muscle making his way toward our cluster of parents. He had an official look about him, his clipboard and club logo embroidered on his chest.

"Who's that?" I asked a mom. Just then Rachel ran toward me, asking if I'd seen her goals. "Of course I did, Rachel! You were amazing!"

Though sports weren't really my thing, I tried to match her enthusiasm because soccer seemed so important to her. I didn't want to be like my own mother, an anorexic Popsicle who refrained from facial expressions because they caused wrinkles. Whenever I brought home exciting news, she would say, "I expect excellence from you, Claire." In her own way, she was being supportive, but I yearned for a mother who was supportive in my own way. A child simply can't understand the subtlety of presumed excellence. I could've used a high-five every now and then. Or at least a smile. I couldn't control the fact that I didn't get a mother who would meet me where I was emotionally, but I could control the type of mother I was to Rachel, so I bubbled over as she did. When she ran to me with her youthful buoyancy, I held her hands and jumped a bit with her. "Really awesome, Rachel. You've never played better," I told her. Satisfied, she scurried off to chatter with her teammates.

Margo answered my question. "That's Preston," she said. "From the club."

"Why do you think he's here?" I asked, already knowing that he was there to reprimand Bobby. I have found many friendships were formed by having a common enemy. Loud Bobby's asinine behavior seemed like a fun conversation starter.

"He's here for Rachel, silly," she answered.

My mouth fell open in shock. "What has Rachel done?" *Did she gloat when she scored goals and I just didn't notice it?*

She looked at me as if I were an imbecile. "Are you kidding? She's broken every record in rec soccer history. Haven't you noticed him out here for the past couple of weeks?"

"Yeah," I said sheepishly. "I thought he was here to discipline Bobby."

"Bobby? What did Bobby do?"

"Don't you think he's sort of a jerk at games?"

Margo dismissed me with a laugh. "No, I think he's *very much* a jerk, and not only at games, but that's not the kind of thing that's going to get Preston out to the field. He'd never have time to recruit if he spent his time dealing with every obnoxious parent on the sidelines."

As Rachel sped across the field, making her way back to me, Preston called out to her in his Caribbean accent. "Hey Number Nine. Your dad here today?"

I felt like someone punched me in the gut, but tried not to react. Rachel was going to have to learn to deal with these questions more and more now that we were in a new neighborhood where no one knew our history.

"No, but my mom is," Rachel replied. Rachel's pumpkin-colored hair sprang for a full minute after she stopped running. She inherited my lanky body and red hair and Steve's athletic prowess and competitive nature. What was completely hers was the untarnished innocence with which she viewed the world. Her eyes were bright with optimism, and the smattering of freckles on her nose gave her an even greater sense of freshness. "She's right over there," Rachel said, pointing in my direction. "You're Preston Sanford, right?" Not just an island accent, but a soap opera name too?

He flashed a smile and waved a hand before heading toward me. "Quite a little soccer player," he said as he and Rachel reached me. His hair was shaved so close I could see his skull. This accentuated his high cheekbones and full lips. Preston's eyes were like slits with long lashes draping both top and bottom lids.

"Thanks," I replied, not sure of what the protocol was for accepting compliments made about your child. "Rachel really loves it."

The team started trickling away, waving as they left. "See y'tonight, Claire!" shouted Bobby as he and Cayenne walked to their car.

"I'm Preston. Preston Sanford," he said, extending his hand. *Erica Kane*, I did not say. "Claire Emmett." We shook hands.

"Rachel's got a lot of talent," Preston said. "I like what I saw out there today. I want to see her at tryouts in the spring." Turning to Rachel, he continued, "I can't make promises, but you've got the raw material and you definitely have the desire. With proper coaching, you could go far."

"Thank you," Rachel said, unable to contain her fidgety excitement. She looked a little bit like she had to pee when she thanked Preston for the third time and told him how "honored" she'd be to play for the Kix Club. Really, she said *honored*.

"Tryouts?" I queried, handing Rachel her sweatshirt. The wind shook the green and brown leaves clinging to the trees so they looked like shaking pompoms cheering for my daughter. Turning back to Preston, I continued. "She didn't have to try out this year."

Rachel looked a bit embarrassed. She inhaled to speak, but Preston put his hand out as if to yield traffic. "She's been playing recreational soccer. The club is competitive," he explained.

*What? We always try to win.*

"So competitive soccer is different than recreational because—" I paused for him to finish the sentence for me.

"Rec is only for fun," Preston replied. "Club soccer is fun, but the players are at a higher level, commitment- and skill-wise. The coaches are all professionals, so they really know how to teach technical and tactical skills."

*Technical and tactical skills?*

This is the point where I was ready to say no thanks and grab a hot cocoa. Who needed technical and tactical skills at any age, much less eleven?

The next words answered my question. "That sounds like a tremendous opportunity," Rachel said. *A tremendous opportunity?* Who was this kid? I guess no one *needed* technical and tactical skills, but one eleven-year-old wanted them with every ounce of desire she possessed.

"When you say commitment level, are you talking about more practices or more money?" I asked, to Rachel's great mortification.

Preston smiled as Rachel rolled her eyes, trying to distance herself from her mother. "Yes and yes, but the money can be worked out if it's an issue."

"It's not," Rachel said hurriedly. She wanted this deal closed immediately. "We've got plenty of money, and I'm so totally committed to soccer, I'd be excited about the two practices a week and summer tournaments. And State Cup," she said, nearly sighing. "It would be a dream come true to play at State Cup."

Smiling again, Preston said, "Looks like you've been doing your homework, young lady."

"Kelly plays club, Mom," Rachel explained. Kelly Greer was Rachel's best friend and our next-door neighbor. I'd popped by the house to chat with her mother when we first moved into the house in July, but I hadn't been back since. I confess that my sole purpose in meeting her was to make sure Rachel wasn't dining with the Osbournes. I didn't really have any desire to make a new friend. When Darcy started chattering incessantly about her incompetent pool guy, I found her energy a bit overwhelming. She seemed sweet enough, but seven months after losing my husband, everyone else's problems seemed annoyingly petty. I felt as fragile as a light bulb and Darcy was like a Tasmanian devil wielding a hammer. After a few minutes, I had to get out of her house.

"Kelly Greer?" Preston asked.

"She's my best friend," Rachel said as if that might help her make the team.

"Tremendous athlete. Nice girl. Has she filled you in on club life?"

*Has she? How did this slip by me? Have I been so consumed in my grief that I haven't paid attention to my daughter's first love?*

Rachel giggled, affirming his suspicion.

"Anyway, Mrs. Emmett, we'll go through all the details at tryouts, assuming you're interested."

"Oh, we're interested," Rachel said. She was sooo not a Rules Girl.

"May I take your phone number and call you before tryouts?" Preston asked me. Handing me his business card, he told me to call him anytime with my questions. The white linen card had the Kix logo and Preston's private phone number. His title was simply "Player Acquisition." I gave him our phone number and prepared to turn around and go.

"Preston played on the Jamaican National Team when they qualified for the World Cup in '98," Rachel told me. Well, she pretended to tell me. The truth was that she knew very well that I could not care less about the World Cup. What she was really doing was trying to impress Preston with her vast knowledge of soccer, his career in particular.

And it worked. His eyebrows rose as he acknowledged, "Ah, you know the Reggae Boys?"

"Who doesn't?" she said, shrugging.

"Smart girl," he laughed. "I guess we'll see you in spring then?" He shook my hand again and reminded me to call him anytime with my questions.

As he walked away, Rachel said, "Have a great Thanksgiving. Happy holidays! Good luck in State Cup!"

*Did she want to wish him a happy birthday while she was at it?*

On the drive home, I asked the stupidest question of my parenting career. "So, you want to do this club soccer thing?"

"Totally!"

"Why?" I asked.

"Why do I want to play club soccer?" she returned with incredulity.

"Yeah, why not just stay in rec?"

"You're not going to let me try out?!" she cried.

"I didn't say that," I replied. "I'm just trying to understand this a little better. I mean, it seemed like you had such a good time on the Purple Sparrows. Why fix what isn't broken?"

I could understand running away from unpleasantness. In fact, for my entire life I've been guided by the three-strikes rule. If one bad thing happens, I locate my nearest exit. At strike two, I've got one foot out the door. By strike three, I'm out of there. But Rachel wanted to move on from recreational soccer when the experience had been a positive one. Who flees at zero strikes?

"I did have a good time," she protested. "I kinda feel like I could have a better time if the team was good. Kelly says rec soccer isn't even soccer; she calls it 'swarm ball.'"

"It is *not* swarm ball!" I said, mustering as much righteous indignation as I could fake. *What the hell is swarm ball?* "You guys just beat the Blue Kittens!"

"Come on, Mom," she scoffed. "The Blue Kittens? This is really important to me."

That's when she got me. I had absolutely no idea why playing for a professional coach who wanted to teach her technical and tactical skills held any appeal whatsoever, but she did and that's what mattered.

"Okay," I said.

"Really?!" she screamed.

"Yeah, Rachel. You can go to tryouts, but remember that Preston said he couldn't make any promises. Keep your expectations realistic."

"I cannot wait to tell Kelly about this! When I told her Preston was showing up at our games, she totally knew he was going to recruit me, but I kept saying, 'No way! It's my first season.' But she was like so sure, and she was right. Yes!" she cried, doing some crazy little dance of excitement. Rachel was experiencing the familiar exhilaration of scoring a goal, while I, for the first time, knew what a goalkeeper felt like when a ball slipped through her hands. What just happened here?

# Chapter Four

The Greer home was everything mine wasn't. I sensed that from the moment I rang the bell, before Darcy even invited me in. With its dark wood double doors and autumn wreaths of clustered miniature pumpkins, there was a finished feeling to the home. Though Rachel and I moved into our new house in July, we still had unpacked boxes in every room and hadn't hung a single picture. The family photos, I knew, would be the last box opened.

Darcy flung open the door wearing a coffee-colored turtleneck and Thanksgiving theme sweater, looking rushed. She had dark brown eyes and a full head of curly black hair pulled into a low pony tail. A thick-boned woman, Darcy reached just beneath my chin and had a slight underbite. She was exotically attractive, the type of woman who would be cast to sell plum wine rather than light beer in a television commercial. "Have I caught you at a bad time?" I asked.

"Yeah," she quipped, smiling warmly. "But if you want to wait for a good time, it'll be another ten, fifteen years, so come on in." Her frenetic energy wore easier on me this time. In fact, I found her candor disarming. Most of the women in Santa Bella looked so well sewn together, it was reassuring to find someone who seemed to feel as frayed as I did. "How are you settling in? Come on in."

"Good," I said, following her into the kitchen.

Darcy's ultramodern kitchen looked like something off the cover of *House Beautiful,* with dominant tones of light wood and brushed steel illuminated by a flood of natural light. The only place I'd ever seen more windows was in a greenhouse. The ceiling was covered in silver with multiple crisp wires suspending sleek halogen lights. The centerpiece was a wood and stainless steel island with a gas range and granite cutting station. Around the periphery was light wood cabinetry that sunk into the surface of the walls. A few family photos were perched on a mantle over a small fireplace. Everyone was smiling on a sailboat, Darcy beaming and her husband tan and laughing. The lighting was such that I couldn't really see her husband's face as he wore a fishing hat and sunglasses, but I could tell he was a handsome man by the way he held himself, the way he looked confidently into the camera. Steve also looked straight into the lens. I always turned a bit, as if hoping that a different perspective might make me look better. I never noticed this until Steve once asked me why I looked like I was hiding in photos. When he said this, I looked back at all of my pictures and noticed I'd been posing this way since I was about eight years old.

"Sit, sit," Darcy said, pointing to her table. "Can I get you something to drink? Coffee? Tea? Orange juice?" In the time it took her to make these offers, she'd made her way around her enormous, modern kitchen. I wasn't even sure what she was heading toward, since she never opened the fridge or a cupboard.

"No, thanks. I just had breakfast. I was hoping to talk to you about Kelly's soccer team."

"Are you sure? I've got water boiling anyway."

"Um, okay," I agreed because it seemed easier than refusing.

"What do you want to know about soccer?" she asked. *Was she ever going to sit?*

"Well, this guy Preston came to Rachel's game yesterday and asked her to come to tryouts for the club in spring."

"Great," Darcy said, wiping a clean counter.

"Rachel's thrilled," I said, pausing.

"You're not?"

"I'm torn. I mean, it's flattering that he thinks Rachel has talent, but what are we getting ourselves into?"

Finally, Darcy sat at the table, bringing a sugar bowl, honey and a variety of packaged artificial sweeteners. Stirring honey into her teacup, she answered, "It's definitely a big commitment, but Kelly loves it so we manage."

"That's what Preston said, but what does he mean by commitment?"

She laughed. "It means that after your first season, most parents are ready for a mental institution." Before I could react, she continued. "I'm exaggerating, of course, but it is different. I'd be lying to you if I didn't tell you that it's way more intense than rec soccer. Well, some of the parents are more intense. I always thought it would be a good idea for the club to invest in an on-site therapist who could run sessions for parents while the kids are practicing, 'cause left to their own devices for a couple hours, some of these folks can really stir the pot."

"What do you mean?"

"They start questioning the drills, the plays, basically second-guessing everything the coach does," Darcy told me. "I'm telling you, they need to find some way to occupy these folks during practice."

"We have to stay for practice?" I asked, not thrilled with the prospect.

"You don't have to, but many of them do so they can micromanage. But Claire, that's only some of them, and you can stay out of all the politics. Kelly's had a great experience, and Ron and I stay away from all the petty bullshit. He was the unofficial assistant manager last year, and even he never got sucked into the drama."

Knowingly, I recalled Loud Bobby. "We had a crazy parent like that on the Purple Sparrows this year."

"I guess that's the main difference as far as parents are concerned. In rec, you'll have one or two nut jobs. In club, half the parents are normal and the others are, well, over the top in their own *special* ways. Then there are the two practices a week, the longer game season and tournaments in the summer and winter. It's a lot more expensive too."

"Like—"

"Like two grand."

"Two thousand dollars?!" I gasped. "Rec is seventy-five."

"True, but if Rachel's serious about soccer, she's going to want a coach who knows more about the game than some random parent who volunteered for the job."

I paused to absorb what Darcy was telling me. Twice as many practices. Twice as many games. Way more money and more Loud Bobbies. It sounded less than inviting. As if she were reading my mind, Darcy added, "If Rachel loves soccer, this will be the best thing you ever did for her."

And with those words, I mentally withdrew the money from my bank account and resigned myself to it.

Darcy had remained sitting for our entire conversation. It seemed like craziness had to be somehow involved in our conversation. She could sit and relax as long as we were discussing other people behaving madly.

"So what's the worst thing I can expect?" I asked.

Darcy thought about this for a moment, glancing up to the ceiling to recall a story. "A few years ago, well, many years ago, one of the more—eh hem—*ambitious* team managers got herself into some hot water with the club for unethical recruiting practices, if you know what I mean?"

I didn't. I looked blankly, which Darcy mistook for horror.

"Am I scaring you?" Darcy asked. "You asked for the worst. It's been a great thing for Kelly and—"

"Darcy," I interrupted. "I'm not scared; I'm confused. What do you mean by unethical recruiting practices? Did she pay people?"

"Well, let's just say," Darcy dropped her voice into a sultry tone, "she took one for the team."

"What?!"

"Yup," she smiled coyly.

"You're telling me that a team manager recruited a player by sleeping with—"

"The player's dad."

"Whoa," I said, absorbing this.

"It's actually pronounced *ho*."

"And you feel the kids haven't been affected by any of this?"

"Completely clueless," Darcy assured me. "She didn't screw him on the field."

"But didn't people talk?" I asked.

"Are you kidding? They *still* talk about it, but not with their kids."

I thought it was a bit naïve of Darcy to think that kids were oblivious to the gossip of adults. On the other hand, I wasn't going to keep Rachel away from the game she loved to protect her from the corruption that was present in every other walk of life. I wouldn't keep her out of school because the principal was catting around with a school board member. In fact, our principal was such a nasty old geezer that I'd be likely to send the slutty board member a box of chocolates and a thank you note for helping Mr. Portmond take the edge off.

CR &SO

Santa Bella wasn't the wholesome suburban haven I'd hoped to find when I sold our place in the city and moved. At first I thought Rachel and I would stay in our old condo, but everywhere I turned I saw Steve. I couldn't look at a chair without seeing him in it. I kept smelling his pillow at night, refusing to wash it months after he died. I thought giving his clothes to Goodwill would help, but the empty closet turned out to be an even worse reminder. I tried to put some of my own things in it to fill the emptiness, but every time I opened the door, I tried to remember where his things used to be. It reminded me of the game of Concentration where kids try to remember which images are on the cards after they are turned face down. Whenever I opened Steve's old closet, instead of seeing my dresses and skirts, I immediately panicked to see if I could envision where his pants and ties once hung. If I could remember, at least part of him remained with me. It was like trying to catch steam.

It wasn't just inside our home, either. It was the aroma of the pizza place on the corner where we ate on Sunday evenings. It was knowing where the Speed Stick was shelved at Vons, but not needing to buy it. It was the sympathetic look on my dry cleaner's face when I picked up my lighter load. It was the nothings that were everything.

At first I clung to the pain like a placeholder, as if letting it go would mean that we could never reverse time. As months passed, reality usurped hope, and I realized there were no placeholders; there was only empty space where Steve used to be. My mother told me that this feeling would pass with time, but it didn't. Though she meant well, my mother took me on a bereavement shopping trip four months after Steve died. She isn't shallow. Rather, she honestly gets great comfort from the act of shopping and purchasing new clothing, shoes and hats. I gave it a try because it was easier than turning her down again, but I felt no better after our day at Neiman Marcus.

Since my mother's suggestions of time and retail didn't work, I decided to try distance instead, and listed the apartment with a realtor, whom I also asked to find us a nice suburban family home at least an hour from downtown. Through a small ad on Craigslist, all of our furniture was absorbed by strangers looking to cozy their homes with a tapestry Steve and I bought in Bali, the hand-carved headboard his parents gave us as a wedding gift and the funky chair we picked up at an art fair in Napa Valley. In eight weeks, escrow on both places had closed and Rachel was enrolled for the upcoming fifth grade session at Santa Bella Elementary School.

Looking around Darcy's house that day in November reminded me that it was time I decorated and made my house feel like a home for Rachel and me. If the whole point of our move was to give Rachel a greater sense of stability, I needed to unpack our boxes. Rachel was better about this. She had posters on her walls and stuffed animals perched on her dresser before the sun went down on our first night at the new house. From the time she was five, I sensed she was a stronger person than I, asserting her will as I struggled to make decisions. I missed discussing with Steve my concerns about raising a daughter who seemed to ground me more than I did her. He always assured me that our family dynamic worked and that the three of us complemented each other to create a perfect balance. Back then, I feared he was wrong. Now, I feared he was right.

As she dipped her teaspoon into her mug, Darcy assured me that, as scandalous as the adults in club soccer could be, the positives outweighed the negatives. "Trust me," Darcy said, calmer than she'd been during the entire half-hour of my visit. "I would not put my daughter into a world that was bad for her. There are drawbacks, to be sure, Claire, but Rachel will have a great time, she'll make new friends and learn a lot," she said. "The kids really blossom."

Moving to Santa Bella created a fresh setting in which Rachel and I could make a new life together. My mother and my sister Kathy characterized it as running away, and I suppose they had a point. But more than that, I was running toward something new. I just never imagined that our run would require cleats and shin guards.

# Chapter Five

Days after Rachel's recreational soccer season ended, the holidays descended, and in the weeks between Thanksgiving and Christmas, there were three strikes that sent me packing. At Thanksgiving dinner at Kathy and brother-in-law George's house, Mother surprised everyone with the news that she had eloped with her longtime "companion," Blake, who was also her business partner at *Garb* magazine, Mother's color glossy for senior fashionistas. (They rejected my title suggestion *This Old Thing*, and positively detested *The Hag Rag*.) My mother tapped her fork to one of Kathy's crystal wine glasses and gushed with her news of being the blushing new bride. This means she smirked. Immediately afterward, she insisted that Kathy had big news of her own to share.

"I was planning on telling everyone at Christmas," Kathy said, nervously glancing at me. She knew me better than anyone, and understood that I was in no shape to handle two strikes in one day. Kathy was four years older than me and always had a stronger relationship with my mother than I did. In fact, though my mother was the editor-in-chief at *Garb*, it was really Kathy who ran the show. I know that my mother loves us both, but she clearly has more of a friendship with her eldest. Kathy was perpetually caught in the middle, though, wanting to please

Mother without alienating me. "It's not a good time, Mom. Let's wait till Christmas," Kathy said, shaking her head.

"Nonsense," Mother protested. "You'll be showing by then. I can see your bump already."

I wished I was a better person. I wished I was more like Rachel, who bounced out of her seat and kissed her aunt and grandmother, congratulating them without a moment of hesitation. "Omigod!" she shrieked. "When's my new cousin due?" she asked her contemporary cousins. "You guys are so lucky!" She floated to her Uncle George, kissed him on the cheek, then made her way to Blake, a dead ringer for Thurston Howell III from *Gilligan's Island*. I think the look was quite purposeful, as he almost always wore yachting attire and spoke through a clenched jaw. Kathy and I did imitations of him calling our mother Lovey—not that he'd ever try that. Barbara Walden was Barbara. She wasn't Barb, she wasn't Babs and she most certainly wasn't Barbie. She wasn't Honey, Sweetheart or even Darling. She was Barbara, and anything else was just frivolous. She never laid down any such ground rules, but her tight black bun and ivory sheet of taut skin sent the clear message that if you messed around with Barbara's name, you might very well be the first recorded incident of death by glare. To Blake, Rachel asked, "So, do I call you Grandpa?"

Warmer than Mother, Blake agreed heartily, grasping onto Rachel's hands. "That would be smashing." Kathy and I shot each other a look and mouthed, "Lovey."

I wished I could feel the celebration everyone at the table was experiencing, but I couldn't fake anything more than a smile. "Congratulations," I mustered. I hated myself for this selfishness, but when the rest of the world went on living, getting married and having babies, it was affirmation that time was going on.

And if time was going on, Steve was really dead. I kept hoping that if we all stood still long enough, we could get back to the place we were at last year. Of course, this is wholly inconsistent with my packing up Rachel and moving to Santa Bella, but that's the thing about grief. The terms are fluid. One day I feel terrified of change, and the next day it was my escape hatch.

Sometimes, I enjoyed steady movement backward, if only in my mind. Almost every day, I played the game, "What were we doing a year ago today?" I took out my calendar and looked at the notes I jotted down. I smiled recalling the night we all went to see *Wicked*. Rachel's school choral concert will always go down in my memory as one of our sweetest family nights. I sat next to Steve as we watched Rachel's grade belt out nineties "oldies" that we listened to when we met in college. They followed the younger kids who did an absolutely scrumptious tribute to America. "Yankee Doodle Dandy" and "You're a Grand Old Flag" were cute, but nothing charmed us more than the little boy with Coke bottle glasses standing in the front row thoroughly transfixed with the spotlights overhead. Although the later dates were filled with less activity and more doctor appointments, I still pored over those calendar dates with nostalgia. Steve was sick, but we could still chat. Much to his credit, we could still laugh. When we went for a second opinion, the oncologist said he gave Steve three months. The first gave him six. "I should've stopped while I was ahead," he told the team of somber looking doctors. "Okay, no third opinions or I might find out I'm already dead." They laughed uncomfortably, not sure how to respond to him. I knew how they felt. There were so many times Steve had to remind me that he was still the same person I married. We could still talk about things other than his lymphoma. Terminal illness or not, Steve still wanted to go over every detail of the

World Series games with his buddies. He still wanted to hear about my new client, the Bagel Bastard, who lashed out at me when we had trouble securing a domain name for his bakery website. He still wanted to hear Rachel's book reports, then tell her how the teacher would be crazy if she didn't give her an A+.

The day after Thanksgiving, I got the third strike through the mailbox. I saw a bright red envelope with a familiar script and a yellow mail-forward sticker on it. Glancing at the return address, I saw that it was Maggie Jennings' annual holiday letter. They seemed to arrive earlier and earlier every year. How I would miss Steve's dramatic reading of her obnoxious, self-important "Christ-missives." Some families read traditional classics like *'Twas the Night Before Christmas*. Ours giggled uproariously at the Jennings' family letter with Steve's dead-on impression of Maggie's southern accent.

*Beloved Friends and Family,*

*As we reflect on the year that has graced us, we feel so blessed that all of you are part of our lives. Thank you for being part of the Jennings holiday experience. As our oldest friends (the gold ones!) know, our family chooses a theme every year and uses it as a guiding spiritual principle. Last year, the Jennings clan adopted the theme "Caring enough" and found that when we extended a hand to those who are less fortunate, we helped them reach greater heights. This year we all agreed that it was time to take our volunteer work to a new level. And boy have we done that in a big way! Jessica reminded us all that it was Jesus who said that if we give a man a fish, we feed him for a day, but if we teach him how to fish, we feed him for a lifetime. Since we are celebrating the birthday of Jesus, we decided to use his little motto for our* theme for the upcoming year. This year, I hope you will join the Jennings family as we urge others to "Grab your pole!"

As you may know, Maggie is a gifted wreath-maker. Imagine the joy she'll bring to the needy when she shows them how to make their very own festive door hangings! Through the community center, she will also teach poor mothers how to make hand-crafted velveteen stockings, with all the glitter and bells to show the world their unique sparkle.

Ed knows how important it is for young men to learn to golf so he's set up a special clinic for recovering gang members. As a reward for the boys who stick with the three-week class, Ed will take them to our country club where they can see what the future can hold for them. Many of these boys believe that their only way into a club is working as a busboy, but we believe that anyone can rise to the top if they work hard and adopt a can-do attitude.

Jessica and Jimmy continue to let their heartlights shine wherever they go. Their loving spirit is both our joy and our gift. Jimmy got a very impressive score on his SATs and the headmaster at his school says he cannot wait to see him start applying for colleges. Jessica is a true gem who makes her parents proud. She continues to excel in school and her rigorous figure skating competitions.

While we are proud of Maggie's record-breaking Junior League fundraiser, "Hats! Hats! Hats!" there's an even bigger announcement we'd like to make about our charitable giving. Recently, a dear friend of ours passed away after a brave fight with lung cancer. He didn't even smoke. While mourning, we talked about what we could really do to help Steve's memory carry on. In this spirit, we began the Steve Emmet Foundation for Non-Smoking Related Lung Cancer.

What?! I dropped the letter. Picking it up again off the floor, I reread it. Not only did she misspell our last name, she botched Steve's cause of death. He never had lung cancer.

I couldn't read another word, though the letter went on for three single-spaced pages, including color photos of the family's trips and events. I had to assume that Maggie was at her *Hats! Hats! Hats!* fundraiser in the photograph where she had the Eiffel Tower on her head, but one can never be sure with her.

I tore the letter with rage and threw it in the trash. Not feeling quite enough distance from it, I emptied my half-filled kitchen garbage, and counted the days until trash collection. Steve was *not* a close friend of Maggie Jennings. He could barely stand Ed, though he was always cordial to the senior partner. I absolutely loathed when people tried to sidle up to the deceased as if they were best buddies. It seems like such a cheap ploy for sympathy, a way to make the tragedy their own. It was sort of like people who have their pictures taken with celebrities, then hang them on the wall to show the world that they hang with Jay Leno. That I could understand. But this was like posing for a picture with a casket. Even worse was when people tried to one-up each other about how recently they'd been in touch with the newly deceased. They'd yelp, "What?! How could he be dead, I spoke with him just last night?" Obviously, he died after you spoke, imbecile, I thought, starting to get angry. It seemed that people were just showing off, as if they were saying, "Look how close I got to death without actually dying!" It's the adult version of riding a bike without holding the handle bar.

Maggie's letters had always been such a source of holiday amusement for Steve and me. Now, this woman, who hadn't even been in touch with us since the funeral, was exploiting my family's very real tragedy for her moronic Christmas letter.

CR SO

After a long, fruitless discussion with my lawyer, I resolved that the best course of action was not litigation, but flight. I logged on to Expedia.com and typed in the word Paris, whispering it like Citizen Kane calling out to Rosebud. Paris was one of my favorite travel locations because it reminded me of my first trip overseas with my mother and sister. I was six, Kathy was ten and my parents were "taking a break" from each other while Daddy stayed with a friend in Florida. Many women would have seen this as a sad time in their lives, but Mother flourished in her newfound freedom. I didn't understand the full context of our trip, only that our mother was uncharacteristically generous with her time and attention. On our first day in Paris, she bought Kathy and me matching Madeline pea coats with blue and red wool hats that had earflaps and a string tie. "Ah, my little ones," Barbara sighed as she left the store and spun around with shopping bags dangling from each arm. I remember thinking she looked like a kite as she flung her head back and began laughing. "It is absolutely impossible to be unhappy in Paris."

If I ever needed to test her theory, it was now.

# Chapter Six

On the plane to Paris, I felt torn about my decision to take Rachel away for the holidays. Admittedly, this was a bad time to second-guess myself, but as we flew above the Atlantic Ocean, I looked at Rachel sleeping and wondered if I was doing the right thing.

As we were packing, I thought about how lucky Rachel was to visit Paris at Christmastime, but when I was strapped in my seat, surrounded by the quiet breathing of slumbering passengers, I was forced to think about my choices. Was this a mother-daughter adventure, as I'd originally told myself? Or was it an escape, as Kathy and Mother suggested? Perhaps it could be both, I realized, simultaneously giggling at the sight of the snoozing supermodel drooling on her green cashmere sweater. People always talk about running away from problems as if it's an entirely irresponsible thing to do. I've always found that a nice vacation from reality could provide much-needed perspective on life.

I knew I wouldn't be able to face the memory of our last Christmas. Steve lay in a hospital bed in our family room with round-the-clock hospice care. He died seconds before the New Year, which made it all that much more surreal. Though he hadn't been conscious for four days, it was still horrifying to hear the steady buzz of the monitor letting us know that

Steve's system had shut down completely. We had perhaps ten seconds of complete silence followed by the sound of horns blowing and people cheering twenty stories below. Steve would have appreciated the timing. I could imagine his spirit rising, his hands overhead, head nodding feigning modesty. A transparent ghost of Steve would laugh and say, "Thank you, thank you very much, folks. Life, you've been great."

Death becomes real in waves. First, the sound of the monitor let me know he was gone. Yet less than a minute later, I opened my mouth to remind him of the time we were in New York for his birthday and the Yankees had just won the World Series. Taxi cabs honked their horns (more than usual) and people shouted cheers and hugged in the streets. Steve turned to me and said, "All this fuss over my birthday."

When Steve failed to renew his *Sports Illustrated* subscription, a telemarketer called to ask why. I almost renewed just to keep the magazines coming.

Sometimes I'd run into friends Steve and I hadn't seen in years and they'd propose that we all get together. "Oh," I'd stammer to their expectant faces, "Steve passed away." I'd catch another wave of reality as I watched their expressions fall and they scrambled for condolences. They'd promise to call anyway, but I knew they wouldn't. They weren't being callous, but they no longer had any idea how to deal with me, which was my own state of being most of the time.

Almost a year later, I'd still sometimes see a shirt that would look good on him before I had to remind myself that he was gone.

CR SO

In Paris, Rachel and I pretended we were American movie stars hiding from the paparazzi as we hurried along the streets, covering our faces with bright colored wool scarves. As we battled the cold on our way to the Metro stations, we turned to each other and lamented the loss of our privacy. "Just because we're famous doesn't mean we don't deserve a personal life," I said, shaking my head as we spotted a Japanese tourist with a camera.

"Really, how would they like it if we were always trying to take photos of them?!" Rachel huffed convincingly. We giggled mischievously and trotted down the Metro steps as we made our way to our next destination.

Rachel was entranced by the paintings at the Picasso Museum. I watched her looking at the fragmented shapes and wondered what drew her in to them. Did she feel fractured and jagged like the cubist pieces? Was our life like a puzzle that didn't quite fit? Finally, Rachel turned to me to speak. "Picasso sure liked goats," she said.

"Seems like it," I said.

"These are really weird," she said.

"Weird good, or weird bad?" I pressed.

Rachel scrunched her face as if she were trying to decide. "Neither, just weird."

"What else do you find weird, Rachel?" I asked, probing for her thoughts on life's oddities, inconsistencies, and injustices.

"Um, I guess that no one in America speaks French, but everyone here seems to speak English. That's kind of weird, too. Oh, and the fact that they have chicken sandwiches here, but not turkey; that's kind of strange, don't you think?"

That evening, as we dined together over candlelight at a cozy restaurant with a view of the city, Rachel told me she had the best Christmas ever. "You did?" I asked, hoping she'd elaborate.

"Yeah, totally," Rachel replied as she ate her last bite of chocolate crepe.

"Me too," I said.

Because we shared a hotel room, I had the chance to watch her sleep more than I did at home. I loved the smoothness of her fully relaxed face and wondered why I didn't stop into her room more often and look at her after she'd drifted off. Jetting off to Paris together gave me the chance to rediscover Rachel in a way that I couldn't—or hadn't—at home. There was always homework or email or the telephone. Getting away let us escape mundane distractions that interrupt intimacy.

CR ∞

As we were pulling into our driveway from the airport, I saw Darcy standing on a ladder, removing the holiday lights from her house. I'd changed my mind about her. I enjoyed her frenetic energy when we chatted, which was now a few times a week. Whenever we'd see each other, we got going for at least an hour. She had a more raw honesty and vulnerability than many of the other mothers I'd met. While so many mothers spewed clichés about the wonder of motherhood, Darcy seemed unafraid to admit she found it to be a grind sometimes. I remember the exact moment I decided she was going to be a good friend. About a week after our first discussion about club soccer, I ran into Darcy at the gas station, fueling her trash-filled minivan. Veronica, her six-year-old, was screaming about Kelly not sharing her juice with her. Then Kelly whined that she didn't want her little sister's "gross, snotty mouth" on her drink because she didn't want to catch her cold. Darcy rolled her eyes, exasperated. "Ya know how everyone says these years go by so fast?" Darcy asked me. Not waiting, she finished, "Today I feel like, meh, it could go faster."

Darcy waved from her ladder and shouted, "Can you believe I have to do this? Chivalry is definitely dead." I smiled and rolled down my window to ask if she needed help. "Welcome home. How was Paree? Come by and tell me everything. I'm alone again, naturally," she said with a pained grin.

A while back, Darcy complained that her husband's work hours were killing their marriage. He was a surgeon and worked more hours than anyone with a scalpel should. Still, she said, Ron always made time to be at Kelly's soccer games. He even coached Veronica's rec team so she'd be ready for club when she turned seven. It wasn't that Ron worked too many hours to have an outside life. It's just that he filled it with everything except Darcy. She once confessed that she fantasized about divorcing Ron and moving to the city to help her brother Ira run his textile business in L.A.'s Garment District. "I find the hustle and bustle of it energizing," she told me. She would. I went there exactly once with my mother and Kathy on a mission for *Garb* and got vertigo. "When Ronnie graduates high school, I'd love to go back to work," she said. "I was good at it. Damn good. Ira always tells me when I'm ready to leave this bum, he wants me back."

I wondered why Darcy had to leave Ron in order to go back to work, but didn't ask. Darcy was a smart woman. I didn't need to point out to her that she could do both. Plus, who was I to talk? When Steve took his medical leave, I let my website design business completely fall by the wayside. The Bagel Bastard wasn't unique in the toll he took on my reserves. Listening to small business owners talk about how they needed graphics that communicated their "corporate synergy" and "client-centeredness" seemed so trivial compared to what we were going through. As I listened to the manager of a podiatry office drone on about foot pronation, I dug my fingernails into my thumb just so I could experience a different type of pain. The last contract I had was for a yoga studio where the business manager kept telling me how sensitive they were to the individual needs of their clients. Hoping she would understand when I explained that I needed to cut short our forty-five-minute conversation in order to get Steve to chemotherapy, she replied, "Oh, right, that reminds me, we need to include info on our cancer rehabilitation program on the website. The classes are so healing."

When Steve got sick, we were in the process of upgrading our life insurance policies and changing providers, so we hadn't yet canceled our lesser one. He joked that having two life insurance policies would certainly cause him to go into remission. As time went on, he became more solemn in his gratitude of our timing. With two life insurance policies paying me upon his death, I would never have to work again. Frankly, I couldn't imagine wanting to. I even gave up my labor of love, jewelry design. Necklaces and earrings seemed so irrelevant when our family was dissolving.

"Why don't you come over to our place?" I shouted to Darcy through my car window. "I want to get unpacked and download our photos. Bring the kids, we'll order pizza and I'll tell you all about it."

"I hate you for being able to eat pizza," Darcy said. "How's six o'clock?"

"Perfect," I replied.

Many women hated me for being able to eat pizza, but the truth of the matter was that I had the sort of body that was only appreciated by hungry women and clothing designers. I never drew too many cat calls from construction sites, just a few unsolicited suggestions that I eat a burger.

Opening the door was a challenge because our mail came through a slot in the front. As I scanned the pile, I saw Christmas cards from Mom and Blake and from Kathy, George and their girls. Friends, thinking of us during the holidays. Steve's firm. My accountant. I stopped suddenly when I saw Lil's handwriting.

At some point I was going to have to talk to her. I hated myself for returning her phone calls only when I knew she'd be out, but I feared that as soon as I heard her voice, I'd start crying and might never stop. In fact, that's exactly the reaction I had every time we tried to visit after Steve died. Every time I looked at her face, I saw his, which was unbearable. I sobbed after she went home and until I fell asleep, then woke up the next morning with the vague sense that something was dreadfully wrong. This luxury lasted a few seconds before I remembered he had died, and began another day of mourning. Six months ago, I decided that I'd return Lil's phone call on the afternoon she regularly volunteered at Children's Hospital. It seemed like a good way to delay talking to her for a while, but it became a habit. I called when I knew she was at church, playing bridge and getting her hair set. I detested my selfishness, avoiding this woman who'd been so good to me over the years. And worse, keeping her apart from her granddaughter—and Rachel from her grandmother. Knowing Lil, there would be a message on the answering machine too. It would probably say the same thing it always did: "It's Lil, calling to send my love. Please get back to me when you're ready." She knew I was avoiding her. I could never fool Lil, which was what made her simultaneously wonderful and terrifying.

Lil's mistake was giving me the out. I almost wish she demanded that I call her, telling me how horrible and rude I was being. I wish she reminded me of how much I owed her, but that wasn't her style these days. When Steve and I were first married, and I had postpartum depression, Lil took charge and physically took me to a doctor. She insisted on babysitting twice a week and enrolled me in a jewelry-making class in Santa Monica, suggesting I take myself out to lunch afterward so I could see the faces of Los Angeles. After Steve died, she didn't have that kind of fight anymore. She left a series of weak messages telling me that I could call her when I was ready. God, I was awful for not calling this woman. Clearly she needed to connect with us and yet I could not face her.

# Chapter Seven

January turned into February and Rachel and I were kept rapt in the excitement of club soccer through Darcy's and Kelly's tales from the California State Cup. Parked in their driveway was their silver minivan with windows painted with white letters. "Go Kelly #3!" was the largest proclamation. Next was "Kix Girls Rock State Cup" with smaller script letters below that listed the names and jersey numbers of the team.

I found myself sucked into the drama as if Rachel's curiosity were contagious. Every time we saw the minivan pull into the Greers' driveway, Rachel asked if she could run over and find out how the team did. I told her to give the family an hour to unpack and settle in. Then I'd end up going over too, listening to Darcy's take on the weekend while Kelly offered Rachel a play-by-play of the games. Ron had always disappeared by then, and Darcy was starved for the good audience she had in me. After the girls went upstairs to Kelly's room, Darcy regaled me with tawdry gossip about the bad behavior of parents at games. Making sure I wasn't scared off by this, she always prefaced, "This is the minority, Claire. Most people are completely normal, but they're no fun to talk about."

"Okay," I said, assuring her that she wouldn't scare me away from taking Rachel to soccer tryouts.

"So anyway," Darcy smiled with delight, "one of the Conquistadors board members got in huge trouble with our regional league for selling the naming rights for their annual tournament."

"Will you sit down?" I scolded. "You're like a bee!"

"If I don't do this now—" she began to defend her sweeping.

"What, the crumbs will settle in and stain? Sit. Sit."

Darcy obliged. "Okay, so their attorney was able to get them out of the contract, but still, it was a huge ordeal for a few days. Apparently the guy penned a deal with Taco Bell. He said he didn't see the harm since it went with their Latin name. The board said that associating an athletic event with fart-inducing fast food was not the image they were trying to project."

I laughed. "That's good of them, I guess."

"Are you kidding? Turf just signed a deal with Sizzler and Hot Shots is in negotiations with Pepsi. What's the difference?" Darcy asked. "The problem was that he did this all on his own, without discussing it with the board. This is all about bruised egos and pride. I guarantee you that if this guy went to the board, we'd be playing in the Fart Cup next spring."

Darcy said California was a testing ground for corporate sponsorship of kids' sports, but that in ten years it would be the norm. Thirty years ago, stadiums bearing the name of disposable razors, florists and Post-it Notes were unheard of. College bowl games weren't sponsored by Tostitos, FedEx and Citibank. Now, no one thinks twice about it. Darcy predicted that by the time our kids played high school soccer, they'd wear jerseys decked out with logos from everything from fast food restaurants to cell phone carriers and play in stadiums built by Children's Motrin.

 CR Ᏸ

In late February, Kelly's team lost in the "sweet sixteen" weekend of the still-unbranded California State Cup. There was talk of foul play and bracket reconfiguration, the athletic equivalent of political gerrymandering. Darcy also complained that Turf had a goalkeeper who looked no less than sixteen, but when she complained to Kelly's team manager, she was immediately hushed because the Kix squad had snuck on a thirteen-year-old ringer using a doctored birth certificate. Darcy also cracked me up with her imitation of the Patriots' team manager choosing field side. Apparently the home team gets to choose the side of the field the girls play on while the visiting team selects which of their two jersey colors they'll wear. Waddling around her kitchen, Darcy smacked her lips together like the dumpy Patriots dad, then licked her finger and held it in the air. Imitating his voice, she said, " 'The wind's blowing this way, but the sun's gonna be in their eyes if we stay on the south side.' " I laughed. "Then he looked at his watch, and I know he was trying to figure out how much the sun would move by halftime. It was a big debate among their parents while we all had to stand around with our chairs all folded up until they told us where we could sit."

"They get to choose where the spectators sit, too?" I said, incredulous.

"We certainly don't sit on the same side of the field," she said.

CR ED

A few weeks later, we got the call Rachel had been anticipating all winter. "Yes, Preston, of course I remember you," I said, signaling Rachel that it was Him, with a capital H. She looked up from the notebook on our kitchen counter and dropped her pencil for dramatic effect. "Yes, Rachel is still very interested in trying out for the club." By now Rachel was pacing around the room, frantically fanning herself with her hands, a gesture I'd seen Kelly do often. She was silent, not wanting Preston to think her uncool by squealing with delight, though that is exactly what I knew she would do after the phone receiver was back in its cradle and she'd triple-checked for a dial tone to make sure I'd absolutely disconnected. "Yes, Wednesday at four o'clock. Diablo Field. Uh-huh, sure, no problem. Cleats, shin guards, water," I said. Rachel was now on her back, on the floor flailing her limbs like some sort of tribal dance worshipping the sky. Though in our case, it would be fluorescent lights.

As predicted, Rachel checked to see if the phone were really, truly hung up before jumping around the kitchen screaming in some foreign adolescent tongue.

୧୫ ୫୭

When the big day arrived, I confess to feeling equal parts excitement and fear. This cocktail is called anxiety. We drove to Diablo Field where we saw hundreds of girls clustered into groups from age seven to seventeen. The field is elevated, so we had to climb a flight of stairs. The bright green Astroturf appeared to rise like the sun at daybreak. Though the sky was blue and the sun shone unobstructed by clouds, it wasn't quite spring weather yet. The crisp air still made its way under jacket sleeves and kept younger siblings jumping in place to create warmth. The small children found each other within minutes and began playing their own form of soccer with a miniature ball.

Preston was surrounded by what looked like a meeting of the United Nations Security Council. It seemed like every nation on the globe was represented by a coach in blue Kix warm-ups. A matronly-looking woman named Francine beckoned the new arrivals, telling us that we needed to get the girls signed in for tryouts. Rachel and I followed her to a tent with three volunteers, all of whom looked like the ladies in Madge's Diner from the old Palmolive commercials. One was in charge of taking Rachel's birth certificate, another said she had paperwork for me to fill out, and the last slapped an envelope-sized sticker with the number 43 onto Rachel's shorts. She was branded like a cow and dismissed while I filled out legal liability waivers and a "short" questionnaire about Rachel's soccer experience. "Good luck!" I shouted to Rachel as she trotted off. She turned back, looking slightly embarrassed by my comment.

The questionnaire was four pages long, with multiple lines for me to fill out the names of camps, trainings and private coaches Rachel had worked with. Did the Purple Sparrows' coach count? Somehow I thought not.

I flipped to the second page where I was asked to list all of the teams Rachel had played on, what bracket they competed in and their standing. Next, Kix wanted to know about the tournaments she'd competed in and how her team ranked. Clearly we were going to fail the written part of this test. I glanced over at Rachel, who was running around the periphery of the field with several dozen other girls her age. How many spots were on the team? What were her odds? For Rachel this may have been a field of dreams, but for me it was a field of nerves.

When I returned the form to Francine, she flipped through the pages and said, "You didn't finish filling it out, dear."

Standing before her, I felt naked. "Rachel's new to soccer."

"Okay," she chirped, sounding like she was masking her real message: *These blank spaces don't bode well for her.*

"And this Purple Sparrow team?" Francine asked, looking at Rachel's application. "Where's this league?"

"It's a Kix team," I said. "On the rec side."

"I see."

I wasn't sure why I needed Francine to encourage me. She had no say in whether or not Rachel made the team. "Preston invited her to try out for the team," I explained anyway.

"Oh," Francine said, sounding impressed. "That's a good sign." Why did I need validation from the check-in lady? Why did I feel relieved, and in fact proud, when Francine turned to Rhonda next to her and added, "Her daughter was scouted by Preston. From the rec program." The woman raised her eyebrows with approval. Now I could move on, which was surely appreciated by the woman standing behind me in line.

I walked over to a cluster of parents gathered around Preston asking questions. Soccer tryouts were the first daytime kids' event I'd ever been to where there were just as many fathers as mothers in attendance. The coaches had dispersed and were with different age groups of girls, each taking notes on a clipboard.

"Today we're looking at their individual ball-handling skills," Preston said, clearly continuing after a parental interruption. "And at the callbacks on Friday, we'll do some one-v.-ones and a few game-related exercises." *Callbacks? There was more than this?* "Then, at the final callback next week, we want to see their chemistry so we can put together teams that work well together. Does that make sense?" I hated when people asked whether something very simple makes sense. Did he think we were idiots? Or was I just cranky because I realized that this stress-induced nausea was mine for another week?

A woman built like a potato asked, "Will all the girls get to come to the callback?"

Preston shifted his weight uncomfortably. "This is the part of club soccer I like the least," he said. "Some girls won't be at the level we need them at, so there's no point in bringing them back and wasting your time."

A skinny woman with red hair raised her hand. "What if our daughter is having a bad day today? Can't she have another chance?"

Oh God, please don't let Preston mistake her for me. We have the same features, except for the deep lines on her forehead, surely a result of years of asking questions from a position of powerlessness.

Preston sighed. I could see that he wanted to extricate himself from this conversation, but needed to stay put until the parents dismissed him. After all, if the club was going to ask these folks for thousands of dollars to let their kid play soccer, it had to make sure everyone felt heard, served, and validated. I wondered how the American customer service mentality and California New Age style seemed to a native Jamaican. We must have seemed like a high-maintenance lot, to say the least. Tryouts had started more than twenty minutes ago, but Preston was far from being released. "I'm sorry, but in order to evaluate the girls properly, the groups need to keep getting smaller," he explained.

This was Soccer Survivor.

Before Preston could excuse himself, a Latino dad in a Yankees wool hat and too-long windbreaker jumped in with another question. "Say you know today that you're taking Savannah. Do I still gotta bring her to all these callbacks?"

*Mighty confident, aren't we?*

"Good question," Preston said. It also annoyed me when people complimented others on the quality of their questions. It seemed so patronizing and disingenuous. Who fell for such empty flattery?

The more these parents asked about the tryout process, the more I realized that every one of them wanted their daughter to make the team just as much as I did. With that thought, my anxiety level rose. "We need them to come back to get a sense of their chemistry with the other girls," Preston said, his hands now in his pockets, his weight shifting from side to side. "Some of the girls from last year's team will be on this year's squad, so we want to see how everyone jibes. Does that make sense?" *Duh, no, could you explain it again, slowly?!*

A dad who was doughy in both color and texture chimed in. "Wait jest a minute here. You tellin' us that some of these girls who was on the team last year might not make it on the team this year?"

"No," Preston said. A group of parents, presumably of returning players, sighed collectively. "What I'm saying is that some girls from last year *definitely* won't make the top team this year. If they need development, they'll play on the second team."

*Second team?! What second team?*

I raised my hand, finally deciding that I could ask a question. "How many spots are on each team?"

"Good question." *Oh wow, thank you very much. My daughter asks good questions too, by the way.* "Each team has a roster of fifteen girls, so thirty girls will make the teams."

"And the others?" asked the petrified redhead.

"Will not," Preston finished.

*O-kay then.*

"This is news to me!" shouted Doughboy.

"Yeah, if they were on the team last year, they oughta get priority!" demanded another dad.

"We're vested!" shrieked a mother in overalls and socks under her sandals.

"Don't get all riled up now," Preston offered in an effort to quiet the brewing parent mutiny. I could just see our ship sailing across the Astroturf, flying a shredded Jamaican flag. "Why don't you relax until tryouts are over?"

*Because we want to avoid our children being heartbroken at all costs! Because we want to be proactive and get immediate assurances that our kids won't be disappointed. Because my daughter told me that she believes her dead father watches her play soccer and that making this team is step one in her destiny to become a professional soccer player. That's why! Does that make sense?!*

# Chapter Eight

I peeked at the field where I saw Rachel dribbling a soccer ball around cones and trotting through a rope ladder as a tall blond man timed her. When she finished, she ran to the back of the line and caught my eye. She smiled to say hello and raised her eyebrows as if to tell me it was going well.

Minutes later, a small Asian woman came to Rachel's group and the blond guy left for another. She threw a ball at them and each responded by jumping in the air and heading the ball to the ground. It reminded me of feeding time at the seal tank at Sea World. Rachel was keeping up well considering she'd never done any of these things before, but she was not the wunderkind the way she was on the Purple Sparrows. Not by a long shot. Other coaches passed by and made notes about players. "Just take her!" I wanted to scream. *Take her, take her, take her!!!*

We had another hour of this, and I was not doing well. No wonder so many people are on anti-anxiety medication. Their kids must play soccer.

Just as Rachel was starting to get the knack of heading the ball, the coaches changed and a Middle Eastern guy started the girls in a foot juggling contest. I thought this was an especially poor use of tryout time, especially after Rachel was the first to be eliminated after four juggles. How was this guy supposed to assess my child when she was standing around watching other players do silly circus tricks?!

*Dear God, just let them take her and I will make the Good Samaritan look like a hooligan. I will rock sick babies in the hospital. I will never use Easter Seals' return address labels without giving money again. I will call my mother-in-law and invite her to our new house, and try not to cry when she tells me stories about "Stevie" as a boy.*

This juggling contest was interminable! When would one of those little show-offs miss the ball and put an end to my misery already?

As the group dwindled down to five, I started sending telepathic "miss the ball" messages through my eyeballs. Apparently I have no supernatural powers because all of them kept bouncing their balls on their feet, gleefully mocking me with their skills. Thankfully, Rachel seemed unbothered as she stood watching the final five—oops, make that four girls. *Yes!* She was having a friendly exchange with another girl, seemingly unaware of the fact that this child was the enemy. *Get a grip, Claire!* I told myself. This little girl is not the enemy. No, she was also eliminated quickly. It's these other little bitches who are still juggling who are the real enemies!

So much for my resolution to be a better person.

Rachel really needed to stop chatting with this girl. It wasn't that I didn't want her fraternizing with the competition, but the coach might see her and think she wasn't paying attention. *They need focused players, Rachel! Stop talking and watch,* I said through more secret eyeball messages. *Better yet,* you *take notes as if you are going to incorporate their technique into your own juggling, which, I'm sorry to say, needs work!*

My descent began.

All right, my descent continued.

I decided to stop watching and take a walk and get some air. I was already outside, but figured if I was moving, I'd create a breeze and give myself more much-needed oxygen. All right, I was talking crazy now. *Oh look! Another one bites the dust! Excellent.*

As I watched the final three jugglers, I noticed one was Kelly Greer. I looked around for Darcy but didn't see her anywhere. Before I could ponder why she hadn't offered to carpool, a stout father with a reddish brown goatee and thinning hair sidled over to me and asked how old my daughter was. "Eleven," I replied. "Her birthday's in July so she's trying out for the Under Thirteens." Apparently that was the right answer because he perked up immediately.

"You don't say. Which one is she?"

I pointed to Rachel in her cheap purple jersey, a bit embarrassed that I hadn't researched the tryout process better. I should have asked Darcy what the girls would be asked to do, or at least what the dress code was. All of the other girls wore soft club jerseys with the logos of Kix or other local soccer clubs printed on them. No one except Rachel wore a rec jersey with her name printed on the back in white iron-on letters.

He nodded. "Not bad," he said. "I been watchin' and she's one of the better ones. What's her speed like?"

"I haven't clocked it for a while," I bluffed.

"Y'gotta keep on top of these things. Make sure they're improving. Trackin' the improvement. Chartin' it to see where they need work," he advised. Holding out his pale, beefy hand, he introduced himself. "Dick Merrick."

"Claire Emmett," I returned. "Which is your daughter?"

"I got three girls out here goin' for U13," he said. "They're with yours. See them with the green headbands?" he pointed to a chunky blonde, a vanilla brunette and an athletic black girl.

"Easier for me to keep track of 'em that way." Dick had a slightly off look about him with one eye bulging and a smile that showed every tooth, molars included. He was one of those people you could exchange a few words with before realizing he was only one fender bender away from being put into an inpatient mental facility. Like I was one to talk with my secret eyeball messages and negotiations with God.

"You have *three* daughters this age? Are they, um, adopted?"

"They're my *girls*, not my daughters! Maybe you didn't notice that I'm white," he laughed again. This really wasn't all that funny. His wife might be black, or he could've adopted an African-American daughter. "One's my kid. The other two I brought out here 'cause they're a package deal." I said nothing, returning my gaze to the field. Dick pressed, "Know what I mean, a package deal?"

"They're friends and they want to play together?" I looked around for Darcy—or anyone I could talk to instead of this wild-eyed soccer dad.

"Yeah, well, Tandy's kinda dead weight, but we can get her on a team if we tell these clubs that they ain't gettin' the other two unless they take all three."

I wasn't quite sure what he was talking about, but nodded anyway because I really didn't care. I began to walk away when he started talking again. "See, I shop the package to different clubs and see who'll offer us the best deal," he said, holding out his covered can to offer me a swig. I declined. "Beer?" he asked, nodding toward a cooler near his chair.

"No thanks," I said, keeping my eyes locked on the field. I'd hoped Dick would read my body language and move on to someone else, but I had no such luck. I waved at no one and excused myself. "I see a friend I need to catch up with. It was a pleasure meeting—"

"What do you know about this group?" Dick asked.

"Kix?" I asked.

"Nah, these girls," he said. "Who's in, who's out? I mean, you got any intelligence?"

*Apparently not if I'm still here talking to you.*

"Do I have any information?" I clarified. Intelligence sounded a little too CIA to me. I looked at Dick as he let out a satisfied exhale after he finished his beer, and realized that he was the end of the spectrum that I was slowly walking toward. Rooting for your child—hoping she'll make the team – was normal. Dick was what became of parents when hope slid into desperation, then plunged into obsession. Looking at him was just the slap in the face I needed to return me to my normal self. With the Italian accent of Cher in *Moonstruck*, my inner voice urged me, "Snap out of it!"

My inner voice was not heard by Dick, though. "Yeah, what do you know about these kids? I heard that they're cutting four girls from last year," Dick said. "One moved to San Diego and the other burned out and is playin' tennis now. The other two suck."

"Oh, gee, I really don't know. Well, Dick, it's been—"

"You remind me of myself four years ago," Dick said. "You gotta know what you're up against, Claire, or these fuckers will screw you upside your head." *Maybe that's what happened to his eye.* "First year we did club, we were total pussies." *Did he just say ... and that reminds him of me?!* "We took Kylie out to one club. They told us who they wanted, who they didn't. It was bullshit. We were totally at their mercy and guess what?" My eyes shifted around the field looking for someone—anyone—to rescue me. "They took Mariah and Kylie and sent Tandy back to rec. Now, I make sure we're in the driver's seat. We got leverage now."

As he cracked open another can of beer, covered in a foam jacket, I had the perfect opportunity to leave. I should have left. A normal person would have left. But I just had to know what he meant.

"Leverage?" I asked.

"I mean they're a package," Dick answered as if to question whether or not I'd understood a word he'd just said. "I'm like their agent, and when I shop 'em around to clubs, I tell these fuckers that they take all three or none. And I tell them I'm takin' 'em to five clubs in the county and if they want this package, they're gonna need to make it worth our while."

"You actually said this to Preston?"

"Not yet," Dick snorted. "I let 'em see what Mariah and Kylie can do out on the field first. The timing needs to be right on these things."

I felt better about my own sanity.

This guy was like a reality TV show without the commercial breaks. I knew that a man who characterized himself as an "agent" for eleven-year-old soccer players was an imbecile. I knew that his efforts to put together a package deal and leverage the players set the bar at a new high in parental stupidity. There was something sickly entertaining about it all. *Stop it! This man is an undiagnosed nut job. He is not here for your entertainment. Be the good person you know you can be and walk away from this guy.*

"Your daughter and her friend Mariah must be excellent players," I said.

"They rock," he said too loud. "I tell these other coaches their choice is to take the three girls or watch them kick your ass on the field this season. Y'ever hear the expression, 'The fear of loss is greater than the desire for gain'?" I shook my head. "Means these guys want Kylie and Mariah, but more than they want 'em on their team, they don't want to lose 'em to another club." He wiped his mouth with the back of his sleeve and said, "Yer kid's lookin' good. Can I give ya a tip?" *Package her with Kelly Greer and leverage it? I am so already on it, my friend!* "Bring her in a real jersey for callbacks. She'll look better, she'll feel better, they'll think she *is* better if she's not in that purple thing. It's all mental." *It certainly is. That is as clear as day.*

"Dick, it was a pleasure meeting you," I said in my *I'll be going now* voice. I went between deriding this man and taking him seriously, neither of which was a good choice. "I'm going to check on—"

"Claire!" I heard a familiar male voice booming. It was Loud Bobby swaggering onto the field as Cayenne ran to join the girls. "I see you met the guru of all things soccer." He gestured to Dick, who punctuated his introduction with a belch. *Yeah, uh, guru isn't the first word that came to mind.* "Truck broke again," he told us both. "How fucked am I?" *Quite, but it really has little to do with your truck.* Bobby reached into Dick's cooler as if he knew it would be stocked with alcohol.

"Slip this on," Dick said, handing Bobby a foam cover that concealed the Bud logo. Now it could pass as a Diet Coke, though neither of these tanks would ever be mistaken for weight watchers. Bobby wore a cap that read "Muskrat Love" and showed two rodents embracing as a heart floated between their heads. His hands were leathery and smelled like beef jerky, which was a disturbing thing to notice from such a distance. Dick patted his friend on the back and assured him he'd take care of it, gesturing to the Palmolive ladies. "You lemme take care of that. Make sure y'get her here on time Friday, 'kay? Only so much I can do."

The sky grew dark and the field would have been black if not for the temporary stadium lights that were rolled onto the field. It looked as if we were on a movie set.

It seemed odd that instead of simply starting the tryouts a half-hour earlier and finishing at dusk, Kix would go through the trouble of lugging huge lights for the last half-hour. I decided not to suggest this to Preston, though. I'm sure that Kix was a well-managed club that had already considered these organizational issues.

Dick continued. "So I see yer finally takin' the kid pro."

Bobby laughed. "Her mom kept puttin' me off about it, but I told her this is Cayenne's last chance to make the switch."

"Um, excuse me," I broke in. "Why is it her last chance?"

"Too old," they said in unison.

"What?! She's eleven."

"Yeah," said Dick. "After this she's too old to make the switch."

"She is? It's now or never?"

"Pretty much," Bobby said. "Don't sweat it, Claire. She was recruited. By Preston. She'll make it."

*She will?*

"Not necessarily," Dick added. "He brought six girls out last year and didn't take a one of 'em."

*How do you know that? Why would Preston do that?! Why am I listening to this guy?*

"Hey, it was nice meeting you, Dick," I lied. "Bobby, good to see you, but I need to go see my friend, um, Jane. See you later."

"See ya, Claire," Bobby shouted.

"Nice lady, but clueless as all get out," I heard Dick report as I walked away.

A few steps later, I heard Bobby shouting at Cayenne. "Get the lead out! I need you first to the ball every time. You're with the pack. Speed it up!"

# Chapter Nine

As we started our hike, the leaves crunching beneath our boots, I suggested Rachel grab her sweatshirt. "Last chance to get it from the car. From here on in it's you, me and the woods." She rolled her eyes and told me she didn't need it.

A few minutes into our walk, I told her that I was pleased with her spring report card. I had a definite agenda for us—refocus on things other than soccer. Since the first tryout, all Rachel wanted to talk about was soccer. All I could think about was soccer. As much as Rachel wanted to make the Kix team, I wanted it for her more. Not so much for the soccer, but because it gave Rachel such purpose. If she was a normal adolescent, this would be important. Considering she'd recently lost her father, soccer was a lifeline.

When we didn't get a call right away, I dialed Preston to see if Rachel was invited to callbacks. I tried to act cool and tell him that I was "just getting our schedule together" and wanted to see if we should block out time for tryouts, or do something else equally fabulous. Better, even. I'll bet I really pulled one over on him. He chuckled a bit, which I found a little condescending, and said he would have to check his notes. After an eternal few seconds, he said that Rachel was one of the girls they wanted to have a second look at. "Great," I said, then paused hoping for more. Nothing over the top. Just a little reassurance, like "Rachel is a naturally gifted player who will undoubtedly be an asset to our top team." No such luck.

When I took Dick's advice, I knew I'd gone off the deep end. I actually went to the Soccer Post to buy Rachel a nice, soft jersey from the women's United States National Team. Just a subtle message that Rachel was on her way to the World Cup, and Kix really should get in with her on the ground floor before she signed a Wheaties endorsement contract and forgot all about them.

"Thanks," Rachel said of my comment on her grades. "I got that 'good' in math up to an 'excellent,' " she reminded me. Rachel was her father's child. Tenacious, competitive and hard-working. Any soccer team would be lucky to have her. *Any school! Any youth orchestra. Any art class would be lucky to have her. There's more to life than soccer.*

"I noticed," I said. "You really worked hard at that. I'm proud of you, Rachel."

"Thanks," she replied. "When is Aunt Kathy supposed to have her baby?"

"Any day now," I said. "Are you excited?"

*So far, so good. Not a word about soccer.*

"Yeah. Babies are so cute."

"Aren't they? How are things in your Girl Scout troop?"

"Well, Natalie's super mad at Mindy 'cause she says she only started liking Josh after she liked him first, and everyone's taking sides."

"Oh, where do you stand?"

"I don't care about any of this stuff," she said. "Josh is a dork." After a few steps, Rachel continued. "Can I ask you a question?"

I smiled. This was the moment when she let me see her soft underbelly. She would ask me a deep, perplexing question that would open up a discussion about life. Let the bonding begin, I thought. "Sure, Rachel, you can ask me anything."

"Do you think I made the team?"

"Rachel," I sighed. "I thought we weren't going to talk about soccer."

"We weren't?" she asked. "How come?"

Oh right. I hadn't filled her in on my abstinence pledge. "I, um, well, it's just that there are so many other things to talk about. Like nature. Look at the beautiful bird that just flew into that tree. Did you see how the bottoms of his wings are blue, but the tops are black?"

"You want to talk about birds?" Rachel asked.

"It doesn't have to be birds. Look around at all of these gorgeous plants and leaves coming back to life."

"Okay," Rachel shrugged. "That one's pretty. What's it called?"

"The plant?" I asked.

"Yeah."

"It's a, um, I don't know."

"Okay, what about that bird? How come its wings are like that?"

"Its wings?" I repeated. "They ... they ... they're black on top so they can absorb sunlight to keep them warm. And, um, the blue bottoms are to, um, let their babies in the nest know that they're coming in for a landing."

"Really?!"

"I don't know, Rachel," I said, half laughing. "I'm just trying to get us to remember all the other wonderful things in the world other than soccer. I really don't know anything about nature. I'm from L.A., sorry."

Rachel laughed, forgiving me. I was so sorry that the parent she was left with was tearing at the seams. She prattled on, "So,

Lisa says that Brandy's older brother had a Harry Potter bar mitzvah and that—"

"A Harry Potter bar mitzvah?!" I shrieked. "What the heck is that?"

"They turn the place into Hogwarts and do a Triwizard Tournament and—"

"They transform a temple into Hogwarts?" I asked, appalled.

"Of course not, Mom. Just the reception hall."

I told Rachel I remembered going to bar and bat mitzvahs when I was a kid. Sounding like, well, a mother, I asked, "You know what the themes were? Bar and bat mitzvahs. Not Harry Potter!" Darcy told me that her family had been invited to a seventies-style disco bat mitzvah where invitations were printed on vinyl and slipped into a cover that read "Saturday Morning Fever." What remained of the Bee Gees actually showed up and gave one of their hits a Semitic spin—"Now You're a Woman"— for little Katie Cohen.

"Anyway, that's not what I wanted to talk about," Rachel said.

"Sorry, honey." *What was I doing? She wanted to talk about unkosher bar mitzvahs and I was going off on some ridiculous tangent.* "Go on."

"So, Lisa says that Brandy's older brother got thirteen blow jobs in the bathroom from girls in his class," Rachel said matter-of-factly. "I didn't want to ask her, but what's a *blow job?*"

As I coughed my tongue out from the back of my throat, I tried to regain my composure. I wondered if there was a city we could move to where I could shelter Rachel from all of this. Another country? Planet? A plastic bubble?

I took a deep breath and looked Rachel square in the eye. "I think you have a very good chance of making the soccer team."

"Really?!" she cried. "I hope so. I mean, I feel good about the tryout, but there were so many awesome girls there. I feel like why would Preston ask me to come if he didn't want me on the team? But he did say he couldn't make any promises, so it's not like he said anything's for sure, but still. I did do well on the shooting drills. I can't juggle, though. Did you see how many Kelly did? She was at, like, 250 before she missed. I can't believe they make girls from last year's team try out again. Doesn't that seem totally unfair?"

"I heard some of the girls from last year's team won't make it this year," I said, trying to segué into a discussion of playing on the B-team.

"I heard that too," Rachel said. "Not to be mean or anything, but it *does* make room for new girls."

*Okay, not the direction I was going.*

"And the second team is just as good, I'm sure," I said.

"No, it's not," she said. "That's why it's the second team. I want to play on the top team."

"I'm not sure it's the best place to start with club soccer," I said as we continued onto the incline of the trail. "There's something to be said for starting slowly."

"And what is that?" Rachel asked.

"You have to crawl before you walk."

"Daddy said that I never crawled," she said.

"It's an expression."

"He said I got up one day and started running."

I hated to debunk her father's mythology, but that was not at all accurate. "Your father was an exaggerator. I was home with you and I assure you, you crawled, then stood, then walked, *then* ran."

"You don't think I'm good enough for the top team, do you?"

"I didn't say that, Rachel!"

"When I play soccer, I feel better than when I'm doing anything else in the world. I *have to* make this team."

"I hope you do."

"Do you think I will?" she asked.

"I think so."

Later that evening, I decided to address the blow job issue with Rachel. She caught me off guard on our hike, but I decided that if this was a term floating around among her peers, I had to answer her question. The alternative was letting a bunch of adolescent girls provide sex ed for my daughter. I thought about what Steve would say if I brought this up with him and decided to ignore my husband's posthumous advice. I could hear Steve's voice clearly defining, "Tell her it's when I kick a boy's ass and call the convent!" Instead, I took a deep breath between bites of dinner and reminded Rachel of her question earlier.

"Oh right," she recalled when I revisited the term at dinner. "What does that mean?" When I Googled websites for parental advice on talking to preteens about sex, they all said to give kids the scoop in a very matter-of-fact fashion. One explained that if parents provide the info in a neutral way, we take away the emotional charge and give kids the assurance that we're not going to freak out when they come to us with tough questions. I rehearsed my casual response a few times in front of my bathroom mirror, and finally got the words out without choking on the fourth try.

"It's when a woman kisses a man's penis," I said, quickly, and somewhat coincidentally, shoving a piece of steak into my mouth immediately afterward.

Rachel looked incredulous. "That can't be right," she said. I shrugged and pursed my lips, nodding that I was, in fact, correct. "That's gross! Why would anyone do that?" *Shit, they didn't cover this on the website! Why, why?* "It's, um just something that adults sometimes do." I longed to talk about soccer again.

"I'm sorry, Mom, but you must have it wrong. That has nothing to do with blowing."

*Shit, what do I say now? Do I insist that I'm right or let it go?*

"Rachel, you know, things get more complicated as you get older. Like remember how you once saw Cousin Chloe's math homework and thought you'd never understand long division?"

"No," she said.

"Well, it was when you were in first grade and you were just learning how to add and subtract," I reminded her. "You were really stressed over the fact that you couldn't figure out her fourth grade equations. Your dad told you to concentrate on what you were doing in first grade because division wouldn't make sense until you mastered addition and subtraction, then moved on to multiplication." Rachel shook her head, letting me know she recalled none of Steve's words. "Well, he said that and he was right. If you don't understand this other stuff, it's because you're not ready for it yet. Give yourself a few years and it'll start to make more sense."

I could hear Steve yelling from heaven, "A few years? What's with this *few years* business?!"

Then, straight from the "suggested tips" section of the Planned Parenthood website, I thanked Rachel for coming to me with her questions about sex and asked if there was anything else she wanted to know.

"If there are four spots on the top team, do you think I'm going to get one of them?" Rachel asked.

*Oh, thank God!*

# Chapter Ten

At the Friday afternoon callback, Dick graced us with a sober arrival and held court on one of the sidelines. A group of parents new to club soccer gathered around him like he was Jesus delivering the Sermon on the Mount. But instead of multiplying fish and loaves, he pulled covered beer cans from his cooler. He was clearly insane, but Dick seemed to know what was going on and many of us were eager—okay, anxious—for information. The soccer messiah told a dozen parents everything that was going on at the other clubs in our area. "Hot Shots started their last season strong, but had some real personnel issues, if you know what I mean," he said.

I didn't, and by the quizzical looks on several faces, I was not alone. As I looked around, I noticed that the group of girls had dwindled to about forty. At this session, there were only eleven- and twelve-year-olds. Dick explained that they weren't going to rotate coaches to observe the girls the way they did the first time around. At this session, all twelve coaches would watch girls for the entire time. They would be evaluated and given a score between one and one hundred. Next week, the coaches would go to a meeting, discuss every player, then one by one vote them off the island.

"What kind of personal issues?" asked a vacant looking woman with long, straight black hair. She looked far too young to be anyone's mother, much less an eleven-year-old's. She wore a lingerie-style top that exposed her taut, indoor-tanned midriff. My maternal instincts kicked in before my jealousy did. When I first caught a glimpse of the scantily clad jailbait with her perfectly scooped boobs, I thought to offer her a sweater. Upon further examination, I saw that she was weighed down by a sparkling doorknob on her left ring finger. Trophy bride. Let her freeze.

"Person*nel* issues," Dick corrected. "Their leading scorer tore her ACL and was out for the season." Everyone shook their heads as if to say what a shame this was, though it was unclear whether they were lamenting the serious injury or the loss of the impact player. "Had to have surgery on it, then spent the rest of the season in rehab."

Gia, the trophy bride, gasped. "She was on drugs too?! They keep getting younger and younger." A few people snickered, but Nancy, an earthy mom who looked like she bought her brown rice from a wooden barrel, caught my eye and made a face as if to say, *What a piece of work.*

Dick guffawed, eating up his role of being parent-in-the-know. Let me rephrase: Guzzling down his role of being parent-in-the-know. "Physical therapy." He looked at Gia like the wolf in a porn version of *Little Red Riding Hood*. He may have actually licked his chops at one point.

"Whoa," Gia remarked. "That poor girl has *a lot* of problems." She started shaking her head ruefully, then seemed frustrated when she couldn't get a grip on her hair to pull it back into a ponytail.

"That's terrible," I said. "Is she okay?"

"That remains to be seen," Dick said, raising his brows. "No one's seen her play yet. After surgery, they're never quite the same, but she'll be strong, that's for sure. She was one of the top-ranked forwards in the state." A few people seemed as revolted by his response as I. Looking at the group, most of these parents looked imminently normal, except for Drunk Dick, Loud Bobby, Trophy Bride Gia and one guy who tilted his head far too much when listening with an expression of studied concern on his face. There was just something slightly unhinged looking about him.

Then there was the guy who was pure, unadulterated attitude. It was the same guy from the first callback who assumed that his daughter would be selected on the spot. He cultivated a purposefully ghetto look, which included barbed wire and graffiti tattoos, a silver-rimmed front tooth and a stocking on his head. "No way, man," he said when Dick described the hoops we'd all have to jump through before our daughters were offered a spot on the team. "You can't be *sivious,*" he muttered. It took me a few times to realize he was butchering the word "serious." Darcy told me that "dadditude" was a common problem in club soccer. Many fathers seemed to feel that they were above the rules and refused to comply with just about anything the club asked of them. These guys always had exceptionally gifted daughters, so the clubs gritted their teeth and dealt with the fathers who were exceptionally gifted at being pains in the ass. They were male versions of divas.

One elderly grandmother was wearing a black veil on her head and had rosary beads hanging around her neck. She looked so out of place, at first I didn't realize that she was here for the soccer tryouts until a little girl named Giovanna ran from behind the woman's long black skirt. At first I assumed she was one of those itinerant vendors who intrude on your dinner at a restaurant, selling flowers or key chains. I thought she was hawking rosaries at a soccer field. Hell, I would've bought one. We're Presbyterian, but I was willing to concede that maybe the Catholics had the answer. Steve's family was Catholic and he had a lot of sports trophies. If that rosary could crack the code, and get Rachel on this team, I was ready to learn the Hail Mary and go for it.

Okay, so characterizing *most* of the parents as normal may have been a little generous. Especially since I was walking the line myself.

Dick looked around for dramatic effect. "Rumor has it she's up for grabs."

"The knee girl?" Gangsta Dad asked.

Dick confirmed. "My source tells me she may show up here Monday."

*His source? He has a source?! What was this, Watergate?*

*Wait a minute, what did he mean "show up here Monday"? Someone new could show up on Monday?!* Even with my limited knowledge of soccer, I could see that Rachel wasn't a shoo-in for the top team. She picked up the drills quickly and performed well. Still, others were faster, more agile and had better moves.

I couldn't be near Dick any longer. I had to walk around the field and focus on something other than soccer.

As I passed another group of parents on the opposite side of the field, I couldn't help noticing a dad with wavy, slightly overgrown brown hair and a square jaw that screamed sexy. His broad build, squinty eyes and full lips were attractive, but what was really appealing was the way he carried himself. The way he chatted with the others, nodding his head slightly, laughing deeply. There was an indefinable something that pulled my eye toward him, and his toward me. After I passed him, my heart was still racing with excitement. Chemistry was invigorating, though slightly guilt-inducing too. This was the first glimmer of my sexuality returning and I was torn about it. It was magically delicious (so much more so than Lucky Charms). At the same time, if I was attracted to someone other than Steve, I was filling a void that his death left. I'd somewhat guarded my voids, painful as they were. Filling them was a denial of their existence, and it felt intensely disloyal to even entertain the idea.

Every time I passed the group of parents, my eyes locked with Sexy Dad's. I wished I brought my running shoes so I could go faster and pass him more often. What a sexy, sexy dad he was. I felt like going to Victoria's Secret and buying frilly pink panties and a matching bra.

*Stop it, Claire! This is probably someone's husband.*

I smiled after my fifth lap, only to say hello, really. He winked back.

*Maybe he was single after all. After all, I didn't see a ring on his finger.*

This man was a chocolate truffle cake with a thick coat of melted caramel holding petals of shaved chocolate onto the outside. I thought better of licking him, though it wasn't as easy to control the impulse as one might think. This group had its own resident Dick who was holding court, telling parents about what changes the team would be making. I heard snippets, something about fitness training. He said parents would have to stick around for practice this year, an idea that was met with a collective groan. I couldn't just stop and join a conversation among the veteran parents, could I? God, that father was sexy.

Finally, Preston blew his whistle and motioned for parents to come to him in the center of the field. I draped my arms around Rachel's sweaty body. "How'd it go?" I whispered.

"It was harder today," she whispered back.

"I want to thank everyone for coming out today," he began. "All of you girls should be congratulated for your efforts." *Rachel didn't want to be congratulated for her efforts. She wanted to be congratulated for making the team.* "We have some very tough decisions to make." The other coaches all nodded in agreement. "Every girl showed something special out here today. We're going to ask all of the girls to come back for a final look on Monday. This is different than what we typically do, but there's a lot of talent out here, and we need to look at all of them again because they were all terrific."

Rachel looked at me, beaming.

*This is* not *good!* Thankfully, she could not read my facial expression or see the thought bubble over my head calculating the odds. Forty girls were being considered for fifteen spots on two teams. There were thirty spots, which meant there was a twenty-five percent chance that she wouldn't make either the top or second team. The fact that they couldn't easily eliminate one of the girls here today was not a good thing. All Rachel heard was that she was good. It would take her a few minutes to figure out that Preston just gave the identical compliment to thirty-nine other girls.

"Hey, wait a—" Rachel started before I nudged her. She was quicker than I'd given her credit for. *Don't say anything. It's minus two points for being a pain in the ass.*

Thankfully, no one heard Rachel because a parent raised his finger and began speaking. "Monday is the Hot Shots tryouts," she said. "If you've already seen our girls twice now, do we still need to come back Monday?"

"Good question, Jessica," Preston said. The exchange had a planted-question feeling to it. He definitely wanted this issue brought up. "If you want your daughter to play for us, bring her here Monday. If you want to play for Hot Shots, go to their tryout. Every year, we have parents who bring their kids to three

or four different clubs, and it causes a lot of problems for us."
This elicited some grumbling from parents. I plastered a *sounds
fair* expression on my face and said nothing. "This year, we're
going to ask the girls to sign a letter of intent that says if we offer
you a spot on the team, you will accept it."

Dick whispered to Bobby, "Sign the fucker then do what
you want."

Preston continued. "And to make sure parents are dealing
straight with us, we're sending some of our board members to
other clubs to see who else is showing up to those."

"No way, man," said Gangsta Dad. "*Sivious?*"

"That's such an invasion of our privacy," snapped Whole
Foods Mom, the one who didn't care for our resident trophy
bride. "What next, wiretapping?"

"Let's not be dramatic, Nancy," Preston said. *So far, he's
addressed two mothers by name. I wonder if he remembered my name.
I should ask a question.* I couldn't contain my grin as I saw Sexy
Dad smiling at me. I even liked his shoes, black leather slip-ons
with rubber soles. They were reminiscent of Hush Puppies, which
you had to be mighty cute to get away with. Wearing nerd shoes
was a bold display of confidence, a way of telling the world, "I
don't need to depend on a pair of shoes to make me good looking."

Preston held his hands out, motioning for us to take it down
a notch. "Like I said, there are parents who take their kids to
every club in town. We want to know who's committed to Kix
and who's playing the field."

Nancy snickered. She leaned in toward me and whispered,
"I think he just called us soccer sluts."

"So yer sayin' that if we take our girls to other clubs, yer
gonna blackball 'em?" Dick asked.

"I wouldn't call it *black*balling them," Preston defended.

"Grayballing?" asked Bobby.

None of the coaches was smiling, least of all a Chinese woman the size of a cocktail nut. She raised her brow and scanned the parents so invasively that I felt like I was being frisked at the airport. She clipped, "What Preston is saying is that it won't be a deal-breaker, but it will not win them any points here."

After ten minutes, the parent questions were becoming redundant and Preston looked at his watch. I understood the desire to keep asking the same question until we got answers we liked better. For one, it kept him from walking away and leaving us clueless for an entire weekend. There was also the off chance that he might accidentally tip his hand and give us the insight we so desperately craved. Thankfully, others were asking the same questions I would have, or I might have opened my mouth and started begging them to take Rachel on the team. Either team, top or second!

As parents started dispersing, I told Rachel I wanted to speak privately with Preston. After all, he recruited her. He owed me at least a minute of his time and some feedback, didn't he? "Can you hang out on your own for a few minutes?" I asked Rachel.

"Can I get a ride home with Kelly?" she asked.

"Sure," I replied. "Is Darcy down in the lot?"

"Her dad's here," she told me. I hesitated for a moment, slightly uneasy with the fact that I still hadn't met the elusive Ron Greer, but if he was Darcy's husband, surely it would be okay to let Rachel drive two miles with him.

"Let me ask him if it would be okay," I said.

"Mom, he already invited me over for dinner. I'm sure a ride home's no problem."

I glanced at the growing line waiting to talk to Preston and agreed. I was just being overprotective. Though Darcy gave him a failing grade as a husband, she had nothing but praise for his parenting. "Rachel, I might not be home for a while," I said, gesturing to the size of the line. "If you want to eat dinner with the Greers, go ahead."

"Thanks, Mom!" she shouted, Kelly now by her side as they walked down the stairs of Diablo Field. Turning to me, she mouthed, *Find out!*

ᘓ ᘔ

I stood in line for thirty-five minutes before I even came close to Preston. I listened as he advised the four parents ahead of me. He seemed pretty forthcoming, checking his notes on every player. "Cressida's got speed, but she shies away from the ball," he told the mother. "She needs to be more aggressive and attack the ball more. We need to see her killer instinct."

"She's eleven," whimpered the mother.

The next father explained that his daughter had a tough season. "Things weren't easy for Brianna. I'm not making excuses, but I want you to take it into account," the father said. "She had a very hard year."

*Poor kid*, I thought. I hoped these coaches gave this girl a break. I mean, she obviously dealt with some serious issues at home or at school or at—

"I mean, you know how it is, Preston," the father said, hoping to ally the recruiter. "You played halfback, but you can imagine how rough it is on a keeper without a good sweeper." *What? That's their big tragedy? They lost their cleaning lady?* "You try and keep the ball out of the net with the weak defense we had last season. I promise, you get a decent sweeper in there and she won't let one or two goals go by all season."

Another father listened intently as Preston scolded him for not working with his daughter on her foot skills. "John, she looks exactly the same as she did at the end of State Cup. Who'd she train with in the off season?"

The father shook his head apologetically. "She needed a break from soccer," he explained. "They made it so far in State Cup, she played ten months straight without a rest. She's eleven, Preston. She needed a break."

"And now she may get one," Preston said.

"What are you saying? Are you cutting Taylor?"

"She may need a year of development on the second team."

The father took this news surprisingly well. "She'll be on a team, though, right? If not the top team then the B-team?"

"Yeah," Preston said. "We saw a lot of great players out here today. Our blue team's going to be strong."

*Blue team?*

"Thanks, man," the father said. "Blue team, white team, I really don't care. I just need to know she's on a team."

"John, she's been with us since she was seven. We'd never let Taylor go. Work on her foot skills this year. Don't get complacent with her."

"You got it," John said, walking away relieved.

I wondered if Preston got somewhat of a charge from having so much power over parents. Could he and his foreign colleagues help laughing at the spoiled American parents whose greatest challenge was that their daughters might be cut from a soccer team?

"Hi Mrs. Emmett," Preston said when it was my turn to talk to him.

"You can call me Claire."

He didn't. Instead he just looked at me for a few seconds and asked, "What can I do for you?"

*What can he do for me? What the hell does he think he can do for me, bring me a Happy Meal with a Coke? I need information about Rachel!*

"I wanted to see if I could get an idea of Rachel's standing."

He flipped through several sheets of paper until he found Rachel's page. I saw diagrams jotted down, notes in several different scripts and a series of numbers. I wanted to grab the clipboard from Preston's hand and bring it home to Darcy so we could pore over it all night. "Rachel is very talented," he said. "She's on the bubble for the white team, so if she doesn't make it, she'll definitely play blue."

"What bubble?" I asked, imagining Glenda the Good Witch of the North floating down into Munchkin Land.

"I mean it could go either way," he said. "Like I said, she'll make one of the teams."

"I see," I said, trying not to sound disappointed. "What can she do to improve her chances?" I remembered my first conversation with Darcy, and wondered if Preston thought I was propositioning him.

"Some things she won't be able to get past, like having never played club soccer before. I've got to be honest, it's a drawback. What we need to see from the late-starters is that they are fast learners. If Gunther thinks she's smart and can catch up, it'll help Rachel's chances a lot."

*Gunther? Who the hell is Gunther?* I didn't want to ask who Gunther was for fear it would make me look like a stupid mother who passed along her stupid genes to her stupid daughter.

"That makes complete sense," I said, showcasing my calm, intelligent nature. "Should I bring her report card for Gunther when we come back on Monday?" Preston shook his head and glanced at his clipboard. I was losing his interest. "Stanford-Binet IQ test?" He shook again.

"Nah, a good coach will be able to assess her intelligence by watching her play. Ultimately the choice is his, so he's the one to impress."

"Listen," I whispered desperately, causing Preston to look at me with concern. "Rachel wants this more than anything she's ever wanted in her life. She just lost her father and we're new to Santa Bella. She tells me that she thinks her dead father watches her play soccer and that it's the only time she feels complete. Making the white team means the world to her, so if you could give me any advice, anything at all that would help her, I would greatly appreciate it."

I couldn't believe it. I played the death card. Steve would have been so proud. He was quite annoyed with me when I self-righteously told him that I would never exploit his death to gain political capital. "Don't be so high and mighty, Claire. Everyone in this world uses what they've got to get ahead," he said. "If you've got a dead husband, use it for all it's worth." He softened and gave me a slight nudge. "Come on, Claire. I want to feel like I'm helping you even when I'm gone. I'm telling you, it'll work like a charm. People will feel sorry for you and give you whatever you want just to get you to stop talking."

Steve was right. Preston held his hands up in what looked like a gesture of surrender. He came closer to me and whispered, "Okay, you seem like a nice lady and Rachel's a good kid. Gunther played for the German National Team and is gung-ho on Germany, but says Americans don't know anything about his country. He says that all Americans know about Germany is the Nazis. If you showed a little love for Germany, I'm sure he would think you were very intelligent for it."

"Really?"

"Oh yes," Preston said.

"Danke schön!" I said.

# Chapter Eleven

When I finally got home that night, there were two messages waiting for me on the answering machine. The first was from Lil, who was just calling to say hello. My heart dropped. The second was from my mother letting me know that Kathy was in labor. I shouted with joy and dialed my sister's cell phone without thinking. Not surprisingly, the call rolled over to voice mail. I tried George, then my mother, then Blake, who actually answered. "Blake here," he announced.

"Am I an auntie yet?" I squealed.

"Hello, Claire. Not yet, but your nephew will be here very soon," Blake said.

"Is everything okay? I mean, no problems or anything?"

"My dear, I stay as blissfully ignorant as possible in these matters," Blake said. "There have been no problems, but after that, I neither have nor want any details of the delivery." *Well poopy doo to you.* "The ladies sent me back to the apartment to get some of Kathy's things she forgot. Do you have any idea what woolies are?"

I smiled remembering a teenage Kathy with the flu. She rummaged around the house, frantically searching for her wool socks, crying, "How can I be expected to get better without my woolies?!" She was completely dependent on her brown wool socks with the reinforced toe and heel, the kind they make monkey sock puppets with.

"Brown wool socks," I told Blake. "Check the top drawer of the armoire. If they're not there check—"

"Mission accomplished! Claire, will we see you tomorrow morning or are you going to come in tonight?"

"We're on our way."

❧ ❧

When Rachel and I arrived at the hospital on Friday evening, Kathy had just given birth and announced that she was naming her son Steve. She seemed so fragile and tired, I didn't have the heart to voice my concerns, but I was definitely upset by her presumptuousness. How could she not talk to me about this? She said that she and George had planned to name him Paul, but once they saw him, they changed their minds. She beamed this news to me as if she expected me to be thrilled. Rachel was delighted that her baby cousin bore the same name as her father, but I could barely hold back the tears.

"What's his middle name?" I asked Kathy, hoping that perhaps they'd call him by that instead.

"Emmett," she told me.

"Emmett? You named your baby Steve Emmett?"

"You're upset with me," she said holding her baby blue bundle. "Emmett means truth, Claire. I've always loved the name."

"So did I," I said, a little annoyed. My eyes darted toward the door. "Look, I know your heart was in the right place, but I wish you'd discussed this with me first."

"I thought you'd be happy," she said earnestly. "We wanted to honor Steve."

"Kathy," I sighed. "Think about if George died and I had a baby and named him George Fuller. What would you think of that?"

Kathy's eyes welled with tears. "I'd love it. Oh Claire, I'm so sorry. I never meant to hurt you. I thought we were—"

"It's okay," I said, knowing that my forgiveness would be the only thing keeping her from a full-on breakdown right there in the maternity ward.

"No, it's not," she said. "I'm sorry. I'll fix it. We'll give him a nickname. Forgive me, Claire. I thought it would, I thought it would honor him—fill a void for you." Clearly my sister's head was up her ass. How could she think that an infant by the name of Steve Emmett would fill the void left by the death of my husband of twelve years? It wasn't his name I loved; it was him. Now, every time I saw this kid do something I didn't like, I'd think, "You're no Steve Emmett."

⌘

By Sunday afternoon, Kathy was home, hosting a small brunch for the family. Her nurse helped place mini quiches on trays and set out a decanter of coffee. As Kathy sat in her pajamas, rocking in her chair, George thanked us all for coming on such short notice to welcome the newest member of the family. "Especially Oliver and Renée," he said, gesturing to my father and his wife, who had flown in from Miami yesterday. "As you know, we've named the baby after our late brother-in-law Steve, but decided that he'll go by Duke, so raise your glasses and join me in toasting our newest little cowboy, Duke Fuller."

"To Duke," everyone said in unison.

*Duke? Cowboy?*

My father and his wife mingled about the apartment as if they were a regular part of the landscape. As chilly as my mother was, I had to give her and Blake credit for maintaining a highly civilized relationship with my father and Renée. Anyone looking through the window would think we were all friends, not related by marriage, kids, and divorce. Whatever problems my parents had in their marriage were quickly packed away when he moved to his condo on the eighteenth hole of a lush Floridian golf course.

As Rachel and I rode the train back to Santa Bella Sunday afternoon, she told me she was disappointed that they weren't calling the baby Steve. "What kind of name is Duke?" she asked. I found this an interesting question from a child who was classmates with kids named River, Sage and Pandora. Looking out the window, Rachel said she wanted to run before it got dark outside. "Tomorrow's the final tryout and I need to be in shape."

I laughed. "It's been two days."

"Right, so now I'm two days behind the other girls."

*Now there was a child* named *Steve Emmett. And one who* was *Steve Emmett.*

I jarred with the realization that I'd forgotten to go to the Soccer Post to buy Rachel a German National team jersey. And that Nietzsche book I wanted her to read. Okay, truth be told I didn't need her to *read* it. As long as she carried it and Gunther saw, that was good enough.

*Note to self. Go to Soccer Post when it opens and buy jersey. Go to Barnes & Noble. Google facts on Germany and its national soccer team.*

CR ൈ

After heavy negotiations, Rachel agreed to walk instead of run, and let me come along. I could tell she was tired anyway, and I convinced her to conserve her energy for tomorrow. I treasured these walks because Rachel seemed more free to ask questions she wouldn't bring up at home. Of course, I would prefer that she never hear about bar mitzvah blow jobs, but as long as she did, I was glad she brought her questions to me.

I was always surprised at what she picked up on. For instance, I would have never imagined that an eleven-year-old would sense the marital strife in the Greer house. I never had the chance to watch Darcy and Ron interact, but Rachel was at the house often enough to sense the tension that I'd only heard about over coffee with my friend. "I think Kelly's parents are going to get a divorce," Rachel announced unceremoniously as we made our way into the woods.

"What makes you say that?" I asked.

"That's what Kelly says," Rachel told me, staring straight ahead. "They've got this tone they use with each other, like they're annoyed all the time. When I was there for dinner, Kelly's mom was totally nice to us kids, but then when her dad asked a question, she sounded way annoyed."

When I was Rachel's age, I saw adults as simply part of the infrastructure of kid world. I didn't fully understand that they had their own lives, their own relationships with people that were independent from us kids. Of course, I was sad that my friend Darcy was still struggling with her marriage. On an entirely selfish note, I loved our current set-up where the girls seamlessly traveled from house to house. I wanted the Greers' to be a second home for Rachel, not someplace where she witnessed parents sniping at each other.

After a few minutes, Rachel asked what was really on her mind. Stop the presses, it wasn't even about soccer! "Did you and Daddy ever fight?"

"We fought," I said with nonchalance. "But we fought fair. Every couple fights. The question really isn't *if* we fought as much as *how* we fought." Before she could ask her next question, I answered it. "We wouldn't have gotten divorced."

"Four kids in my class have parents who are getting divorced," Rachel told me. "It's weird. I'm the only one with a dad who died."

I wondered what she was getting at. Was she just stating aloud the facts? Was she curious about her parents' relationship because she was beginning to forget it? Did she simply want my assurance that we were as happy as she remembered?

I was certain that Steve and I would have grown old together as a happily married couple, but the entire truth was more than what I was willing to share with my child. There was a time early in our marriage when it looked as though we were heading for a break-up.

Though Steve was elated when I told him about my unexpected pregnancy, the reality is that having a baby right after college was stressful on both of us. He assured me that he would have proposed anyway, but it was sort of a let-down to have him pop the question in the bathroom of our campus rental as a blue EPT stick sat on the sink ledge. I'd always imagined something different. The truth was that I'd imagined most everything different. I always had a vision of myself as a peaceful nursing mother, lovingly coddling her sleeping newborn.

The reality was a stark contrast. Steve was working insane hours in the midst of layoffs at his company, and I was slowly losing my mind. As much as I hated to admit it, I did not love motherhood right away. Lack of sleep, lack of space and lack of money were chipping away at my peace of mind. It wasn't the run-of-the-mill fatigue; it was a sinking feeling that having a baby was a huge mistake. My mother suggested a new hat might cheer me up. Steve advised me to "shake it off."

When things didn't turn around, it was Steve's mother Lil who came to my rescue. She took me to her doctor, where I was diagnosed with postpartum depression. Lil got my prescription filled, then insisted on babysitting for Rachel twice a week while I did something for myself. "Who is that?! I don't even know who I am anymore," I sobbed with dramatic self-pity. "I can't leave you with this beast," I said of Rachel. "She never stops crying, and if she does with you, it will mean what I think it means—she hates me. She hates her mother!" With that I fell to the floor, defeated by the thought.

Lil picked up the phone and called her friend Caroline to ask for the name of her marriage counselor. She then dialed Steve at work and told him—she didn't ask—to choose one day a week when he could go to lunch and therapy with his wife. I assured Lil that the marriage wasn't the problem, and that I was only kidding when I barked that I wanted to shove Steve's face into the Cuisinart, but she asked me to humor her and go anyway. For several months, Lil was the mother of us all. And like a true mother, she took great pride in fading into the background when her work was done. Her accomplishment was obsolescence.

In our second month of marriage counseling, I learned that Steve resented me for having post-partum depression. "What's that saying about me, Doc?" he asked. *About him?! Did he just say he was insulted by my depression? How this egomaniac managed to make everything about him was beside me!* "This should be the happiest time of her life, but instead she mopes around like she can't stand Rachel or me." I refrained from picking up Dr. Rosenberg's couch pillow and assaulting him with it, and tried to "hear him." *Hear him, my ass! This was ridiculous.* I told him that if he weren't at the office seven days a week, he might be able to relieve me from the pressure cooker of motherhood. Even as I said these words, I knew it was an empty rebuttal. Lil helped me plenty. I had relief. What I wanted was my husband to understand that my post-partum depression wasn't a punishment to him, the center of the universe. It wasn't a reflection of how I felt about our marriage. It was a chemical imbalance for which I was not to blame. As soon as I actually believed this, it became a lot easier for Steve to. For one, I wasn't trying to convince him of this anymore. As soon as I bought it myself, I stopped defending his charges that I wasn't trying hard enough. And when I stopped being so defensive, he wasn't quite as offensive. He no longer told me how happy I should be. I stopped telling him how he should shut up and get a clue. Slowly, we stopped "shoulding" on each other and came together in a way we hadn't before. We were like veterans of the same war.

This is not to say Steve became a saint or I transformed into a perfect mother. He was still his narcissistic self, and I still checked for the nearest exit at the first sign of turbulence. "I won therapy today," Steve would joke as we waited for the elevator outside of Dr. Rosenberg's office. Then he'd smile and wink at me as he hadn't since we first started dating.

Lil also loaned us the money to buy our first condo, which turned out to be an incredible investment. More immediately, though, it gave Steve, Rachel and me a second bedroom, a bigger living room and a kitchen two people could be in at the same time. Owning a home also quashed my desire to move to the Pacific Islands and make seashell necklaces that Steve and I could sell to tourists on the beach.

If it weren't for Lil, our marriage may have very well eroded the way so many of our friends' had. Perhaps erosion isn't the right image. Our relationship was more like a lovely piece of furniture that had a layer of sticky resentment slathered onto it. Then a coat of blame. After a year, we couldn't see the raw material anymore and had to strip the whole thing bare to start over.

I hoped Darcy and Ron would be able to work through their marital build-up the way Steve and I had.

"Mom." Rachel's voice returned me to the present. "Earth to Mom, come in Mom. Do you read?"

"Yes, Rachel, I hear you," I said. "I was just enjoying a moment of quiet." I looked at my daughter. Her adolescent features marked time for me. It had been so long since Lil came to help baby Rachel, Steve, and me. I wondered what path we would have taken if she hadn't stepped in. I was so grateful to that woman that it made it almost unbearable to think of seeing her again. She would remind me of everything we had and lost.

# Chapter Twelve

*Have a great day?*

*Have. A. Great. Day?!* Did she really just hold the door and tell me to have a *great day* after attacking me for a soccer jersey? Psycho Mom breezed toward her minivan and drove away. Was this a typical Monday morning for her? *Have a great day?* How could it possibly be a nice day once you've been bitten by a rabid soccer mom?

Driving home, I glanced proudly at my purchase more than a few times. Maybe I went a little overboard when I used the seatbelt to strap my shopping bag into the passenger seat, but I wasn't letting anything happen to Rachel's new top.

I knocked on Darcy's door and asked if she wanted to catch the lunchtime spin class at our gym. "I hear congratulations are in order," Darcy said. *Did Rachel make the team?!* "Rachel told us your sister had her baby." *I suck.*

"Yes, a boy!" I said. "He's big and healthy and cute as can be."

"How nice."

There were a few minutes of awkward silence before Darcy spoke again. "Listen, Claire, I don't want to keep anything from you. Gunther called this weekend and offered Kelly a spot on the team."

"That's great!" I said while simultaneously calculating how many other calls he might have made.

Silence.

"Do you know how many other calls he made?" I asked.

"Sorry," Darcy replied. "You could ask Mimi tomorrow at the callback. Her daughter Cara was on the team last year and she's the manager. She seems to know everything. You know the type?"

"Did her daughter get a call?" I asked.

"Yeah, she did," Darcy said. "Ron's kind of her right-hand man managing the team, so she phoned him last night and they went on for over an hour about tryouts, callbacks, who's new, who's gone. Basically, he had to catch her up on everything that's been going on this last week while she was out of town visiting her father. But thankfully she's got Ron to keep her up to speed on all things Kix and the road to State Cup."

"You sound less than excited," I said. "Isn't State Cup like the Holy Grail?"

"I know I shouldn't make fun of her, but Mimi is sooo into the team that it can get a bit annoying at times. She does a lot for the girls, though, so I shouldn't complain. God knows I have no inclination to manage the team. Anyway, you'll meet her tomorrow. Ron's been driving Cara to tryouts while Mimi's been away, but apparently she got back in town Saturday."

༄ ༅

Later that day, as Rachel was dressing for tryouts, I knocked on her door and went inside. "I got you a present," I sang.

Rachel opened the Soccer Post bag and gasped. "It's awesome. So cool. Thank you." She hugged me, then grabbed her U.S. women's team shirt and pulled it over her head.

"What are you doing?" I asked.

"What?"

"What are you doing? I mean, why aren't you wearing the German jersey I just gave you?"

"I don't know," Rachel shrugged.

"Don't you like it?"

"Yeah, I love it. Thank you so much."

"Why aren't you wearing it?"

"I don't know, I figured I'd wear this one today. What does it matter?"

I shifted my weight uncomfortably. "It's just that you wore that last time. Don't you want to wear something new?"

"Nah," she dismissed. "This one's fine."

"Rachel, put on this German shirt, right now!" I snapped.

Her eyes widened to ask what the big deal was. "Mom, who cares what I wear?"

"If it doesn't matter to you then humor me," I said, holding the jersey out to her, practically forcing it into her hands. "Wear the shirt, Rachel. It'll go nicely with your eyes."

"Mom, it's black and white!"

"It'll bring out your eyes. I want to see you in the jersey. Put it on!"

"Jeesh," Rachel said grabbing the shirt. "You are, like, way stressed out, Mom."

*Breathe in, out, in, out.* "It looks great on you, Rachel! A perfect fit. Now, since you're wearing the German National Soccer jersey, you probably want to know about the team."

"Um, not really," Rachel said.

"Well, you should know a little something about the team whose jersey you're in," I said.

"Oh yeah, like did you know that the U.S women's team was the first to—"

"Not now, Rachel. We need to talk about Germany first."

"We do?"

"Yes. We do," I insisted. "Did you know that Germany has one of the best international records in soccer? They've won the World Cup three times and were vice world champions four times?"

"Okay," Rachel said, looking at me as if I'd lost it.

"It's better than okay, Rachel. It's amazing, and you'd do well to give Germany a little respect. The team has been in every World Cup and hasn't missed a European championship since 1972!"

"Mom, what's wrong with you?"

"I just like Germany, that's all."

"You're shaking your hands in the air like a maniac," she said. Lowering them, I inhaled deeply. "Sorry, I'm just a little passionate about Germany, that's all."

"Why?"

"Because they love soccer and I love you," I said. Before Rachel could ask what the hell that meant, I told Rachel I had another good luck gift for her. "A book. And I'm sure you'll want to start reading it on your way to the tryout."

"*Maze Runner*?!" Rachel asked, excitedly.

"Better," I said, pulling the book from my purse.

She took the book and looked at it quizzically. "The Portable Nie—Neitz—" Rachel struggled.

"Nietzsche," I said.

"It looks hard," Rachel protested.

"Give it a chance. When you get to the field, read a few pages and see what you think."

"You want me to bring a book to the soccer field?"

"Why not, it's portable?"

"Mom, I don't want to start reading a new book ten minutes before soccer tryouts."

"Fine," I sighed. "Will you just hold it then?" I placed the book in her hands, cover facing out.

"You are losing it, Mom!"

*How wrong she was. I'd already lost it!*

CR ᏰᎦ

As we ascended the staircase to Diablo Field, I watched a small group of girls juggling on the field. Three were wearing the same German jerseys as Rachel. *Would it have killed you to hold the Nietzsche book?!*

Drunk Dick and his package were nowhere to be seen, which I assumed meant he got a better offer elsewhere. That meant three fewer players in the running.

I asked Darcy if Kelly wanted to drive with us, but she told me that Ron enjoyed watching every possible minute of Kelly playing soccer. "He wouldn't miss a strategy session with the general," Darcy said.

"The general?"

"Mimi," Darcy shrugged. She made a face as though she was annoyed with this, but I could understand where he was coming from. Watching Rachel play soccer was fast becoming one of my favorite activities. I was going to search out this Mimi person and see if she had the inside track on Rachel's standing. If she had her finger on the pulse of this club, then I wanted to chat with her whether she was annoying or not. She could be Fran Dresher on crack; I needed to find and befriend her.

As soon as I placed my chair down, I scanned the field for Mimi. Perhaps it would have been a good idea to have asked Darcy what she looked like. All I knew was that she was a mother, which narrowed it down to about half the adults on the field. Well, half minus one if you counted the barely legal stepmother, Gia, who walked over to me and asked, "Is there room for me?"

*It's a huge field and you're the size of an action figure so I'd have to say yes.*

"Sure!" I said instead. "Grab a seat."

I wondered why she was cozying up to me. I've always found that women like her have a lot more male friends than they do female, simply because in order to be a cock tease one needs to be in reasonable proximity to them.

"So, is Mimi around?" I asked Gia.

"Oh, is she back?" she perked. "I need to call her." Gia looked as though she just got back from Barbados with her long hair in cornrows hanging over her tan face. "We just got back from a little weekend getaway," she said. "The whole family. Fun, but sad too."

*Boo hoo.*

"Aren't you cold?" I asked Gia.

"I'm always hot," she said. "Guess I'm lucky that way." *Among others.*

"So which one's yours?" I asked with my eyes locked on the field.

"Sapphire," Gia answered.

I resented that the trophy bride thought I should just *know* who her little gem stepdaughter was. "And which one, pray tell, is Sapphire?" *Don't be snotty. Breathe deeply and be nice to the woman-child.*

She giggled. "Oh right, you don't know the girls. Sapphy's the one with the sapphire earrings." Then she pointed at her.

*Sapphy?*

Sapphy was also the only one wearing a bright red jersey. She was the only one with tie-dyed socks. She was the only one with yellow shorts, and yet Tropherella thought I'd first and foremost pick up on the earrings. Brilliant.

"She already made the team," she told me casually. "How 'bout your daughter? Did she get the call yet?"

"No," I replied, trying to mask the utter dismay I felt.

"No worries. The only girls Gunther's called were from last year's squad."

*Why did you mention it then? Shut up. Shut up and don't say another word to me, you Bo Derek wannabe.*

Not picking up on my telepathic messages, Gia continued. "I heard that some of the girls from last year didn't get the call and you know what? They're not going to. They're getting dropped to the blue team."

*Really? How many are getting dropped? Is it true that two girls didn't come back to tryouts this year? How many spots are left? How many girls are in the running? Do you have any real information in that thimble-sized head of yours?*

I looked back at the field where Rachel and her group were now playing a game on a small field. "Did Sapphire enjoy playing on the team last year?"

"Totally," she said, extending the word for emphasis. "I'm so stoked that Gunther's the coach this year. He's the best."

"Really, who did they have last year?"

"Oh my God, this totally great guy from Morocco. Toumi. He was the best too."

"Sounds like it's been good for you guys. I've heard some horror stories about club soccer."

"Oh yeah, they're all true," Gia laughed. "It's good and bad, though. I'd say fifty-fifty, mostly good." Noticing me watching the field, Gia gave a sympathetic nod. "Stressful?"

"A little," I lied.

"Totally reminds me of my pageant days," Gia said. This was my cue to ask her about her dippy little beauty contests as if I cared. How would she feel if I hijacked the conversation and made it about me and my vile interests? *I really need to look into a prescription for nice pills. I was out of my mind today! Where is this Mimi person? Is she carrying some official looking team manager bag? Maybe I should call Darcy and get a description of her.*

"Oh, there's Mimi," Gia said, pointing behind me. *Finally!* When I turned around, I expected to see a high-strung, slightly butch soccer enthusiast who held the answers to my questions. I was more than a little surprised to see what Mimi really looked like.

Our eyes met in a moment of recognition. I tried not to shudder, but instinctively braced myself in case she decided to attack again. It was Psycho Mom, and standing beside her side was Sexy Dad. She was anything but masculine in her royal blue sweat suit with two low hanging brown pigtails sweeping across her shoulders. She may have been mentally unstable, but she certainly was pretty, which is undoubtedly how she landed that delicious husband of hers. Sexy Dad walked beside her, the two engaged in an intense, albeit pleasant, discussion. Happy couples give me a twinge of jealousy. This one assaulted me with both envy and fear.

I glanced at her in horror, then refocused on Sexy Dad, who gave me a quick wink. *Oh God, please don't let her have seen that. If she was willing to bite me over a soccer jersey, imagine how possessive she'd be about her husband!* Mimi swatted Sexy Dad. "What?" he replied like a mischievous little boy caught with his hand in the cookie jar.

"What are you doing here?" Mimi spewed.

Sexy Dad snorted a little laugh. "Gosh Meem, who can imagine, with all that's going on here today," he said, gesturing to the rest of the field, occupied only by young girls in soccer gear and their parents.

I liked his bitter sense of humor, and the fact that it was directed at his miserable excuse for a wife. I was also saddened by the fact that Sexy Dad was definitely unavailable, not only for a real relationship, but now for sexual fantasies too. I knew myself too well to even go there. I wouldn't even get to have an imaginary kiss with him before Mimi would enter the scene, fangs glistening. No, Sexy Dad was definitely bad news. Married, dangerous bad news. Sexy, though. Lamentably friggin' hot.

"Are you coming?" Mimi asked her husband.

"Nah, bring me back something," he dismissed.

Mimi looked irritated as she stood with her hand on her hip. "Cream and sugar? Venti?"

"Surprise me," he said, still looking in my direction. "Something different."

"Cool, you going to Starbucks?" Gia asked. "I need to caffeinate something serious. Mind if I tag along?"

As Gia stood from her seat, Sexy Dad answered for Mimi. "Sure, g'head, Gia."

Mimi muttered annoyedly. I couldn't say I blamed her. I wondered what came first, the bitchy wife or the wayward husband. Was she a bitch because he was a jerk, or did it work the other way?

As the two women left the field, I sat next to Sexy Dad in a cloud of delicious tension, keeping my eyes focused on the girls. Finally, the silence became too awkward. "So, I'm Claire," I said, extending my hand.

"I know," Sexy Dad said. Our eyes locked in mutual attraction as we willed the corners of our mouths to stop rising. "It's about time we met, don't you think?" I nodded, afraid that the next words out my mouth might be wildly inappropriate. "I'm Ron," he said.

There was little to add other than that it was nice to meet him, which, pathetically, I did three times. "So, Germany did a great job hosting the last World Cup, don't you think?" *Oh shit, that's my Gunther script.*

Ron laughed slightly, seeming to enjoy my nervousness as it confirmed what he already knew—there was chemistry between us. "Do you think Rachel's going to make the team?"

*He knows my name. He knows my daughter's name. This man is a seasoned flirt.*

"I hope so," I replied. "It would mean the world to her, but the competition is so tough. I hear Gunther's already made offers to some of the girls."

"Word is he's got thirteen commitments," Ron answered. "He needs two more girls, a halfback and a fullback."

"There are so many girls here!" I fretted.

"She'll make it," he assured me, though clearly he was just saying this to be kind. "She's better than some of the girls he took from last year, and she's sure as hell better than the one from that Hot Shots trio."

"What?" I shrieked. "He took them?" Ron nodded. "Gia said Gunther only made offers to last year's players. Why aren't the three Hot Shots here?"

"Don't know, but they committed to Gunther over the weekend. Maybe they figured they didn't have to come back like the rest of us. There's one arrogant son of a bitch every year, Claire." *God, my name sounded good coming from his lips.* "It's not like we all didn't have something else we could've been doing instead."

"Oh, so your daughter made the team too?" I asked. Then I remembered Darcy telling me that Gunther had also called Mimi's daughter, Cara, over the weekend.

He furrowed his brow. "Yeah, I thought you already knew that." *Yep, there's always one arrogant son of a bitch.*

"Which one's your daughter?" I asked, wanting to see what gorgeousness Sexy Dad and Psycho Mom had created. Yes, she was crazy, but much to my regret, I had to admit she looked a lot like Angelina Jolie with her full lips, soulful eyes and powerful presence.

"Claire?" he said, laughing. "*Kelly* is my daughter."

*What? That doesn't make any sense. Your kid's name is Cara.*

Slowly, reality began to penetrate.

*My neighbor has a daughter named Kelly. Her father is also named Ron. Kelly is on this soccer—Oh. My. God.*

*This is Ron?!*

*This is Ron Greer?!*

*Nooooooo!!!!!*

"You're Darcy's husband?!" I said, sounding far too horrified. "I mean, Kelly's father? That's so great." *Shut up.* "So great." *Silence. Lips together and stop.* "So completely great." If I weren't afraid of leaving Rachel an orphan, I would have dug a hole and jumped into my early grave right there and then. But I didn't have a shovel and the field was Astroturf.

"Yeah, Kel told me about Rachel being scouted," Ron said, clearly enjoying his social upper hand. "I was on the lookout for you guys." He smiled. "I liked what I saw." *Bitter chocolate. This man is still flirting even though he knows I'm his wife's best friend.* "She's got a lot of passion. She get that from you?"

"No," I replied crisply. "Her father." I could not have been more clear in my contempt for this man who flirted with his wife's friends at kids' soccer events. That was the end of it.

*Three.*

*Two.*

*One.*

Oh God, why wasn't that the end of it?! Why didn't my attraction flat-line with the discovery that this man was the worst kind of trouble? Even in light of this news, my heart never stopped racing at the sheer thrill of being in his presence.

Having an extremely self-contained mother had its advantages. I could hear her voice sternly advising me that while I could not control my feelings, I could most certainly control my actions. And control them I would as I maintained laser-like focus on the field until the end of tryouts. When Ron asked a question, I gave him a cool, one-word reply without even glancing his way. Rather than being deterred by my coldness, he seemed amused, as if it confirmed that I was fighting my feelings.

I remember seeing a therapist on *Oprah* who said people could reprogram their feelings by creating a new association for them. I would do the same for Ron. Every time I saw him, instead of thinking about the tasty block of fresh milk chocolate he was, I would imagine him in an unflattering light—say, clipping his thick, yellow helmet toenails as he sat on the toilet in constipation. Then I'd imagine him standing and, in addition to the ring around his ass that came from sitting on the can too long, he'd also have a minefield of butt zits. Ugh! It was working. I looked at Ron and shuddered with disgust.

*Three.*

*Two.*

Oh God, it was so not working! As the whistle blew, Ron looked at me and gestured with his arm—his beautiful, muscular arm. There was absolutely no evidence of ass zits or bulletproof toenails. "Come on, Claire. We need to bring it in."

*Do we ever!*

As we walked toward Preston and the girls, Mimi and Gia reappeared. Before they made their way to the group, Ron asked if I wanted to take the girls for a quick bite to eat at Pixie's Diner. "To celebrate the end of tryouts," he said.

"No way," slipped out.

He looked stunned, though we kept walking and I started backpedaling. "What I meant was that I need to talk to Gunther. I want to see what he thought of Rachel."

"No problem," he said, shrugging. "How 'bout I take the girls to dinner while you take care of what you need to do? The girls earned a treat, don't y'think?"

"Oh, sure," I said. "That'll work."

Of course he wasn't inviting *me* to dinner. His offer was for Rachel, not her mother.

Rachel ran to me as we all gathered around Preston, who thanked us all for coming to tryouts. "We'll have teams formed by the end of the week and you'll get a phone call over the weekend," he said. *The weekend?! It was Monday!*

"There's no way I can make it through the week, Mom," Rachel whispered.

*I hear you, girlfriend.*

"I'll see what I can find out from Gunther," I whispered back. "Go to dinner with Kelly and her dad and I'll stay back and talk to him."

"You rock," Rachel said. "Oh, by the way, Gunther said he liked my jersey."

"He did?!" I whispered, trying to be discreet. I didn't need the other parents thinking I was some sort of hyper-competitive lunatic.

"Yeah," Rachel said. "He looked at my jersey and asked if I was a fan of Germany."

"And you said yes, of course, right?"

"Yeah, then I told him all that stuff about the national team you told me today. He sounded impressed."

*Yes! This was so worth getting bit!*

# Chapter Thirteen

"Welcome parents," she smiled, smugly holding a clipboard. "And congratulations girls for making the Girls Under Thirteen soccer team that's going to take the California State Cup this year!" Parents clapped and girls cheered wildly as Mimi Shasta made her enthusiastic introduction. We had not mended fences over the last week. In fact, I got a definite vibe that she didn't like the idea of my being a regular part of her life. It might have been the way she greeted me at the front door. After pouring on the charm, hugging and welcoming Rachel at the front door, she sneered at me and mumbled, "I thought you were the fat girl's mom." *I'm 5'8" and 116 pounds with my hair wet. I can see how you'd make that mistake.*

"Nope, I'm Rachel's mother," I said cheerily for my child's sake.

"Mmmmnnn," Mimi dismissed. "Oh well, it's all about the girls."

*Golly, Mimi, you mean we're not going to brush each other's hair and trade secrets about cute boys later tonight?*

As nasty as she was to me, I had to admit that Mimi had star quality. When she started the team meeting, she stood in her family room with everyone's rapt attention. Everyone, that was, except for Gunther, who looked as if his mind were elsewhere as he stared out the window as if he were waiting for the nice crafts lady to take him to make pictures with macaroni. Our coach looked like a lobotomized Bam Bam Rubble.

Darcy told me that Mimi, in addition to being beautiful, is the heiress to her family's import business. Life was sometimes so unbelievably unfair that I wanted to scream. If I did, though, the enormous house would have mocked me by echoing my cries.

The entryway to the Shasta house looked like the set of *Dangerous Liaisons*, with white marble floors and a table with elaborate, swirling gold and enamel designs on the legs. A cobalt blue sphere with tiny inlaid gold stars was at the center of a crystal chandelier that looked as though it would take days to clean. At the top of the horseshoe staircase was an enormous and ornately framed portrait of Mimi and her father. A short man with a thick neck and heavy eyebrows, he looked outclassed by his surroundings. I could see him betting on horses at the track or sitting at a high rollers table in Vegas.

As Rachel and I passed through the foyer, Rachel commented on the oversized vase filled with lush, exotic blooms. We passed a country kitchen where two uniformed cooks chopped vegetables as they spoke to each other in Japanese. Then we passed a dining room done in an Asian theme, with a black table that was so slick it looked like water, and a red tapestry hanging from the main wall. Around the room were impressive pieces in jade and ivory. Finally, Mimi led us into the family room, which was decorated modern funky with large red couches and a Frank Stella painting hanging beside a Piet Mondrian. I'm sure a decorator told her that an eclectic mishmash would give her house an offbeat, well-traveled feel, but I found the style jarring. It was as though she were warning visitors never to get too comfortable with one particular style. Mimi adopted this philosophy in her wardrobe as well, dropping the Lilly Pulitzer look for a decidedly hipper, more urban look now that she was introducing herself to the preteen girls. She wore purposefully shredded jeans and a t-shirt with rhinestones emblazoned over the words "Soccer is Life."

The girls cheered wildly as Mimi sounded utterly convinced that our team had already won the State Cup. Sapphire wrapped her arm around Rachel and pulled her into the huddle of giddiness. It was funny how one's priorities changed as a parent. It used to take me a long time to determine whether or not I liked someone. I'd weigh dozens of factors, reserving final judgment for weeks. As a mother, things were simpler. If a person was kind to my child, I liked her. When Sapphire reached out to Rachel, I became her instant fan. I also decided to cut the Trophy Bride a break. How could I begrudge a woman helping to raise the benevolent Sapphire? "Yeah, baby!" shouted Dick when Mimi made her proclamation. He high-fived Bobby, who hooted in the only way he could, loudly. "State Cup, yeow!"

The team parents were a mixed lot. Some looked normal and low-key, and others were clearly posturing, trying to establish their identity in the group. An anthropologist would have a field day observing us. Dick and Bobby immediately adopted Leo, the Puerto Rican guy with major daddiitude, and Raymond, the father of Violet, the Hot Shots shooter with the rehabilitated ACL.

I wished Darcy understood that I don't follow sports. When she referred to Raymond as "Earl Woods," I had no idea that she was making a joke and comparing him to the over-the-top father of Tiger Woods. Simply leaning toward me and whispering, "Oh no, we're stuck with Earl Woods this year," wasn't enough of an explanation for me. I had to find out who Earl Woods was the hard way.

Raymond gave me a puzzled look when I called him Earl, which I mistook as a signal that I needed to address him more formally. "I'm sorry, Mr. Woods. It's a pleasure to meet you. I'm Claire Emmett."

"Mr. Woods?" Raymond questioned. "You calling me Earl Woods?"

"Isn't that your name?" I asked.

He said nothing and turned away indignantly. I heard him muttering to the other dads about the "white bitch" who thinks all black people look alike. They all turned to look at me, and Leo made a clicking noise with his mouth before exclaiming, "Snap, that's tight."

I didn't think it would help matters to explain that Raymond was nicknamed Earl Woods because of his intensity, not his skin color.

"Earl Woods is dead!" Loud Bobby barked.

I thought Paulo, the Italian biker, would be a natural fit for the dad clique, but the fat four didn't adopt the insanely fit father of Giovanna, the little girl who came to tryouts with the elderly mafia widow. In fairness, Leo wasn't fat as much as he was doughy. He looked as if he could be in fighting shape after about eight doughnut-free weeks of working out. Ray looked pregnant, but also had bony elbows and hollow cheeks. Dick and Bobby were simply lard mountains from their chins down. Paulo wore his bicycling shorts and a bright yellow Tour de France shirt, looking as if he'd just finished biking fifty miles with his team.

I whispered to Darcy, "Why don't you think they've taken this guy under their wing?" She shrugged. A veteran of club soccer, Darcy was not nearly as interested in the parent culture as I.

After Mimi gave her rallying speech, she told the girls that they could go downstairs to the media room and watch the new Coerver training DVD, or play video games, air hockey and ping pong. She told the girls that the parents needed to go over the "boring details" and stuck her tongue out to the side as if to tell them that they got the better end of tonight's deal. She was the brand of mother who wanted to be friends with her daughter and her peers, the kind who might let the girls drink beer or turn a blind eye when boys showed up at Cara's slumber parties in a few years.

When the girls were gone, Mimi suggested we go around the room and introduce ourselves and talk a bit about our daughters' experience and expectations. She would then tell us about the team and club structure and how our season would play out. I always wondered why people asked about our expectations if they already had a program in place.

Nancy, who I came to know as Whole Foods Mom, introduced herself and told us that her daughter left the Turf club because it was too intense. "I want Deborah to grow as a player but also as a person, and I found the coach to be far too focused on soccer," she said.

*Her soccer coach was too focused on soccer? What did she want him to focus on?*

Mimi raised her eyebrows and said, "Okay, well welcome. I hope Kix is more what you're looking for."

Gia brought her husband Tom and her boobs with her. Daddy Warbucks thanked the team for their amazing support and friendship, and said that if Sapphire's experience was as positive as it was last year, he'd be happy. Wow, he was incredibly undemanding. I imagined him sitting in a smoke-filled boardroom, pounding on a table, shouting that if things didn't improve, heads were going to roll. The other thing that surprised me about Tom and Gia was their utter lack of sexual chemistry. I mean, sure, most twenty-five-year-old pop tarts are hardly growling with lust over their geezer grooms. But the husbands are usually a little more attentive to their playthings than Tom was.

Our team had three Katies, who were coincidentally mothered by two Jennifers and a Jessica. They all seemed to go to the same hairdresser, the guy who cuts a straight line across the shoulders, blows it under and flips the bangs under a little too tightly with a curling iron.

From the looks of Darcy and Ron, they were the perfect couple. No one would ever suspect Darcy resented the hell out of her husband, or that Ron flirted with soccer moms at tryouts. Maybe he wasn't flirting with me. Maybe I was projecting my attraction onto him. It's been a long time since I've had to use my vibometer. Perhaps it was on the fritz. They sat together smiling as if they were posing for their holiday card.

Like the compulsion to pick at a scab, I couldn't help looking at Ron to see if I was still in heat. Would he look like the constipated guy on the toilet, or the hot fudge sundae? *Shit! Hot fudge sundae!* I couldn't understand why the realization that he was Darcy's husband—and completely bad news—didn't kill my attraction for him. I had *never* been into bad boys. Brad Pitt went down a notch when he stole Geena Davis's money in *Thelma and Louise.* Even now, so many years after he played the rogue character, I look at him and think: *Those girls really needed that money!* Not to mention the whole heartbroken Jennifer Aniston thing. Why couldn't I turn down the heat on this real-life taboo?

I introduced myself and told the group that we were thrilled to have my daughter on the team because Rachel loved soccer and we recently moved to Santa Bella, so this would be a good opportunity for her to make new friends.

Mimi immediately jumped in. "I need you to understand, Claire, that this is a serious team, not a social outlet for your family."

"Oh, um, I know that," I stumbled. "I just meant that it'll be nice to get to know all of you throughout the season."

"Right," Mimi interrupted.

Dick spoke for his package, saying that his girls moved from Hot Shots because the coach didn't know what he was doing and the team's record wasn't what it could've been. "We're here to win State Cup, plain and simple. The younger my girls win at State, the more they get used to the idea they're champions. I'm always tellin' parents colleges are looking for skills, but they also need to see confidence, and nothin' gives a player that winnin' feeling more than kicking ass on the field. There's only so much scholarship money out there and I want my kids at good colleges."

*College scholarships?*

"Amen to that," Raymond said as Leo nodded emphatically.

"Straight up," Loud Bobby added.

When we got to Mimi, she stood in the red carpet pose, held her clipboard and flashed a wide smile. "Most of you know me. I'm Mimi Shasta, the team manager, and my daughter is a returning defender. Like the shirt says, soccer is my life. I played in college, so I absolutely love this game and congratulate you all on your choice not only in sports, but in clubs. Kix is simply *the best* soccer club for girls in Southern California." She paused for Dick and Bobby to end their side conversation, then continued. "Girls who play sports are more likely to do well in school, stay away from drugs, delay sexual activity and reap a whole host of other social benefits." *Wow, I didn't know that!* "Eighty percent of the women CEOs at Fortune 500 companies played sports in their youth," she added. *Really?!* "That's why I am all about girl power. Girls playing sports is the single most effective way to keep your daughters on the right track in life," she said. Parents nodded their heads. *Thank God Rachel made the team,* I thought, shaking away the image of my crack-addicted pregnant little dropout turning tricks on the corner of El Camino and Via del Mar.

Pointing at our mute coach, Mimi continued. "You all know how lucky we are not only that your girls made the team, but to have Gunther as our coach." *Was he going to speak?* "A lot of excellent players were cut from the team this year to make room for new girls—" *Did she just glare at me?* "so Gunther's got a big job ahead of him getting our rookies in shape, but he knows what he's doing, so I'm sure everyone will be fine." *Is she talking about Rachel? Didn't Gunther think she was in shape if he took her on the team? Why wouldn't she be fine?* "I'm sure you already know that Gunther was the youngest player on the German National Team and scored more goals in the World Cup than any other single player *in the world* in two decades." *Whoa! Okay, the guy wasn't a talker, but clearly he was a shooter.* "Say hello, Gunther," she said, nudging him slightly. *Please dear God, do not let him reply, "Hello, Gunther."*

"Hello team," he said. *Oh. My. God! He sounded like a robot. This guy was some sort of German lab experiment. No human had such a monstrous voice. He sounded like he was operated by hand crank.*

Mimi continued. *That was it from Gunther?* "Okay, so what I need you to understand about the team structure is Gunther needs to be all about the coaching. If you have questions about practice, game time, anything like that, I need you to call me." We nodded. "So, let's say it's the night before a game and you don't know where the field is, who do you call?" She stood waiting for a reply. "Okay, this is *not* a good sign, folks," she laughed and shook her finger at us playfully. "Let's try again. Who do you call?"

"You," the group replied half-heartedly.

"Who?!" she shouted like a cheerleader.

"You!" we all shouted.

"That's right. You call me. Gunther is all about the coaching. I am all about the management. Oh, and the fitness, but I'll get to that in a minute." She flipped through her notes. "Practices will be on Tuesdays and Thursdays at Diablo Field from 4:30 to 6 p.m., so make sure you adjust your schedules, move dance classes or what-not you have on those days. This year I'm going to need at least one parent from every family to be at every practice. Except for Mariah and Tandy, who are represented by Dick." *Maybe Rachel needs an agent. Not.*

Last week when we got the call from Preston, I felt like my equilibrium had returned. I was no longer the lunatic who got into brawls over German jerseys. I was level-headed Claire again. As soon as I heard Preston's voice say those magical words, "We'd like Rachel to play halfback for Gunther," the crooked horizon straightened. Now that Rachel had made the team, we could get back to normal.

Mimi flipped another sheet. "We need parents to be fluent in Gunther-speak," she said in response to a parent's concern about her being able to attend practices. *Gunther-speak?* "When you talk about games, tactics and strategy, we need you to be speaking the same language as we are at the club." *We're supposed to talk about these things at home?* "Because I was a college athlete, I'm familiar with the type of fitness training the girls need to excel at in soccer. Gunther asked me to be the fitness trainer for the team. If we're serious about taking State Cup, these girls are going to need to be in top physical form, especially our rookies," she said, looking at me again. Flipping onto the next page, she continued. "We'll play in eight weekend tournaments this summer before the regular season starts, which will give us a serious edge over the other teams." *Eight tournaments? There were only ten weeks of summer vacation!*

Dick and Bobby hooted, while Leo asked how much this was all going to cost. "If money is an issue, I need you to talk to me about it afterward," Mimi said. "We have a very generous foundation that provides scholarships for our families with limited means." A few people laughed at Mimi's reference to the foundation, though I wasn't quite sure why. Darcy later filled me in that Mimi's family funded the foundation. "Okay, so I also believe that in order to win as a team, we need to bond as a team, so I'll have the girls do homework here before practice and run—and I mean run—them over to Diablo Field and get them started on their fitness regimen." She sighed and flashed a megawatt smile. "Okay, I've done a lot of talking. Who has questions for me?"

One parent asked about game schedules, which Mimi said she would email to us as soon as the league got it to her. "We usually won't get our game schedule until a few days before the season starts. Men run the league, what do you expect?"

I raised my hand. "Who makes the banner?"

She looked at me as if I was a pitiful little purple sparrow hit by an eighteen wheeler on the freeway. "We don't make *banners* in club. Okay, so any other—"

"When do the girls choose their team name?" I asked.

Impatiently, she explained to the others, "Rachel comes to us from the rec side of Kix, so we're all going to need to bear with a few of these types of questions until Claire gets oriented. Claire, we don't name the teams after little plants and animals in club. Our name is Kix Girls Under Thirteen White."

*Yeah, girl power right back at you, Mimi.*

Ron leaned toward me. "I'll fill you in on everything later."

"Thanks," I said, nodding perfunctorily. *He smelled yummy. Why wasn't my constipation visualization working?!*

"Okay, so we need to talk about legacy numbers," Mimi continued. "Gunther and I discussed the matter and we both agree that returning players should have first pick at their old jersey numbers." *Yawn.* "Some of you have already called me with your requests, and I'm thrilled to tell you that they've *all* been accommodated." *Who wouldn't be thrilled?* "Dick was fast to grab numbers for his girls, which only leaves us with a few."

"You got number two?" Leo asked, or as he would pronounce it, *axed.*

Mimi checked her oh-so-official looking clipboard once again and nodded. "You're in luck. Do you want number two for Savannah?"

"Yeah, number two 'cause she's the shit," he said, laughing.

"How about you, Claire? I know this being Rachel's first year on a club team, she hardly has a *legacy* number, but is there one she's fond of?"

"Well, she was number nine last year," I said.

Mimi looked at me as if I were a moron. "That's Mia Hamm's number. Every girl in America wants to be number nine."

*Wow, I thought it was cool because it was the title of a trippy Beatles song.*

Mimi continued, "Kelly Greer's been number nine since she was three years old."

*I am so embarrassed. Not.*

"How 'bout number one?" I asked. A few people giggled. Ron patted my leg and whispered, "Goalkeeper's number."

"Why don't you tell the new people what numbers are available?" Ron suggested.

Mimi glared at me. *What the hell did I do?* "We've got numbers seven and thirteen left and—"

"Violet wants number seven," Raymond said. "Lucky little number seven."

"Okay, then, that's settled," Mimi said. "Claire, Rachel will have to be thirteen. You're not superstitious, are you?"

Trying to show her that I could not care less about her jersey number, I laughed. "Please, who believes in that nonsense?"

I stopped dead in my tracks. *Shit. Please tell me Raymond missed that comment.* He folded his arms across his chest and tapped his right foot with annoyance. "That's right, the ignorant black man and his Voodoo."

"I didn't mean—"

"If this team is unwelcoming to black folks, I'd just as soon know it now so we can—"

Mimi looked at me annoyed. "Raymond, we value our African-American players as an integral part of our multicultural, multiethnic, multi-ass-kicking team," she said, making sincere eyes at Leo and Raymond. "Can we please move on to team business, Claire?" Visibly irritated by me, Mimi flipped another page on her clipboard and continued.

ೞ ೲ

After an hour, Mimi finished outlining her expectations for the season as Gunther sat seemingly in a state of rigor mortis. "Okay, someone call the girls upstairs, so I can show them the DVD of last year's season highlights. Most of you know that Cara's grandfather owns a production company and put together this totally rockin' DVD for them. I'm sure even if you saw it at last year's end-of-season party, you won't mind watching it again, right?"

"A production company?" I whispered to Darcy.

"Shhh, you don't want to get in more trouble with the general, do you?"

I laughed quietly. "I thought she said the family business was importing."

"Oh, they import, all right."

"What does that mean?" I asked.

Lowering her voice almost inaudibly, Darcy confided, "The Shastas have *lots* of different businesses, but rumor has it that they're all just fronts to launder drug money." I made a horrified quizzical expression, begging her to continue. "There's no way you get *this* rich off importing wicker baskets."

"I bet the Pier One folks are pretty loaded," I whispered as I glanced around to make sure no one was eavesdropping.

"Trust me, the Shastas are on another pier altogether. The DEA could never get the evidence they needed to prosecute Freddy Shasta, but the IRS nailed him for tax evasion."

"Really?" I asked, incredulous.

"Yeah, he's doing two years in federal prison now. It's Santa Bella's dirty little secret. Even if anyone knew something that could hang Freddy, they'd never talk because he gives so much money to the community. You know that new playground?" I nodded. "Shasta money. The Shasta Eye Center at Santa Bella General, the New Globe Theatre, the Fine Arts Museum. This whole town is built with Shasta's dirty money."

I thought I was bringing Rachel to the land of milk and cookies, not the set of *The Sopranos*.

"Are you sure?" I asked, desperately hoping that Darcy's report was simply overblown rumors.

"Like I said, the DEA never proved anything, but at the very least, this family has a few unethical accounting practices."

"Wow." As I absorbed this, the girls trotted up the stairs and settled in. On a giant TV screen, a picture of last year's team appeared. The lights went down and the theme from *Chariots of Fire* began.

# Chapter Fourteen

The next morning, I noticed Rachel's goldfish, Jaws, was floating at the top of his bowl on the kitchen counter. Mentally, I went through my schedule to see when I could buy a replacement fish for Rachel before she got home from school. Even though it was just a fish, I preferred replacing it to having to tell Rachel that her pet died. Granted, it wasn't like she bonded with the slippery little bugger after a mere four weeks. I just thought it better to avoid any minor bumps in a road that was finally smoothing for her.

I looked at my watch and realized I was late to pick up Darcy for our shopping date. She was planning an "old fashioned" seventh birthday party for her Veronica, and asked me to join her to buy supplies at Party City. I found it amusing that "simple" birthday parties were now in vogue in Southern California. Darcy explained that, between Kelly and Veronica, she'd hosted every kind of birthday party from ice skating to rock climbing to scavenger hunts to laser tag. When Kelly was into princesses, Darcy hired Snow White, Cinderella *and* Sleeping Beauty, and transformed their home into a pink glittering castle. Every guest received a gown, wand and tiara. After three-year-old Veronica uttered, "Stars is pretty" one evening, Darcy threw her baby a birthday party at the planetarium. Now, the ultimate one-upsmomship was hosting a modest backyard party with Pin the Tail on the Donkey and a frosted white sheet cake with a single color of icing.

Last week, Darcy explained that she would buy plain pink paper products and a single candle with the number seven. I laughed at how much effort she was putting into her simplicity theme. "For entertainment, the kids can play old-fashioned games," Darcy said, beaming with pride. "I'm not hiring a single entertainer either." I swore her head sprang a little with pride. "What do you think?"

"You, my friend, are positively Amish," I told her.

I was enjoying having a best friend who lived next door. It reminded me of the sitcom childhood I never had.

I flushed Jaws and walked to Darcy's house, hoping she'd be ready to leave right away. If we got back before lunch, I could head over to Fish World and pick out a body double for Rachel's floater.

☙ ❧

For a guy who was always at the hospital, Ron seemed to cross my path often. Funny, but until soccer tryouts, I'd never seen him. Now he was my shadow. He opened the door wearing a charcoal gray Armani suit with a crisp periwinkle shirt and striking textured silk tie in an abstract pattern of bright yellow and red. It was a different—and completely appealing—look for him. "Come in," he snapped. It came across like, "Don't just stand there." Clearly, this man was not attracted to me or he would handle me a bit more gently than that. *Good*, I reminded myself. *I don't want him to be attracted to me. And I don't want to be attracted to him. This is a good thing. This is the right thing. This is the only thing that is good for everyone.*

I detested myself for my next thought, but couldn't help wondering *why* Ron didn't seem interested in me. I mean, not that anything was ever, ever going to happen between us. Never. Never, ever, ever. But why didn't he have a secret compartment in his heart with a shrine to me, complete with my photos, a lock of my hair and a sexy jazz tune playing in the background? Not that I had one for him. (I mean, really! Where am I going to get a lock of his hair?) But what was wrong with me that my lustful feelings were unrequited? Like I said, I hated myself for having these thoughts; nonetheless, they flooded my mind like an overflowing toilet—one with a dead goldfish in it.

"Is Darcy here?" I asked meekly.

Then I heard her voice from another room as she continued an argument with Ron. She sounded hard. "So are we in agreement? I'm not going to have another situation like we had at Kelly's party where I'm running around doing everything and you're sitting out back yucking it up with the dads, got it?"

Ron smiled at me in the same way he did that first time I saw him on the soccer field. It was inviting. But was he issuing an invitation? Or was he inviting in the same way, say, a slice of chocolate cake was—unknowingly, scrumptiously tempting without doing a single thing? "Claire's here, so you might want to tone down the nagging just a bit," he shouted upstairs. Then turning to me, he said, "I'm sorry."

Darcy rushed down the stairs, apologizing. "Why didn't you tell me she was here, Ron?!"

*She* was apologizing? Please. Last night I dreamt that her husband and I had sex every which way possible in locations I didn't know existed. Even in my dreams, I thought to myself, "Wait a minute, doesn't this guy have a wife?" Then the magnificent feeling of Ron's body enveloping mine was replaced with the self-loathing that came from seeing Darcy's weeping disembodied head floating through the sky. The dream ended with Mimi tackling me to the floor and throwing shorts over my face.

He snapped, "What part of 'Claire's here' didn't let you know that Claire's here?" The tone of his voice punctuated the sentence with a silent *dumb ass*. Now I knew what Rachel was talking about. These two were relentless.

I noticed myself backing toward the door, desperately hoping Darcy would cancel so I could exit immediately and head to Fish World. "Darcy, if this is not a good time, I have a couple—"

"It's a great time," Darcy said. "Let me grab my keys."

"Why don't you let her finish, Darc?" Ron said. He was bitter chocolate to be sure. Good thing for me, I don't find nastiness at all sexy. Ron's chocolate factor began to slip. The bad thing was that my friend Darcy was married to a bastard.

They both looked at me expectantly, so I spoke just to fill the silence. "It's just that, well, we could do this another time if you two want to, um, finish chatting because—"

"No, now is a good time," Darcy insisted. "The closer we go toward the weekend, the less stuff they've got, and everybody's doing simple this year."

"Jesus Christ, Darcy, why don't you let the woman finish her sentence?" Ron asked. "Go on, Claire. How come you want to go later?"

"Oh, nothing," I said, squirming to try to make my way out from between them. I hated being in the middle of another couple's fight. I hated conflict so much that I didn't like being in the middle of my own fights.

"It's not nothing," Ron said. I glanced past him at their kitchen clock, watching the morning slip away. "Tell me, what were you going to say?"

Now Darcy was looking at me expectantly. How embarrassed would I be when I revealed that my big agenda item for the day was replacing Jaws to protect my daughter from the horrors of goldfish death? "Go ahead, Claire," Darcy urged. "Tell us. If you have something else going on, it's okay."

I laughed, trying to show how ridiculous my original plan was. "You guys, it's nothing. I was going to buy a goldfish for Rachel because her old one died and I just don't want to deal with it. It's really very silly. Come on, let's go. I'll just tell her Jaws died and I flushed him, no big deal." Darcy assured me she could do the errand without me. "Of course you could, but it'll be fun. Let's go. Come on, let's go already." I felt like I was escaping from a burning building.

CR ℬ

When Darcy pulled her minivan into the lot at Party City, an identical one pulled up beside her with a redheaded woman in a pink alligator top. "Darcy Greer!" she screeched excitedly from her passenger seat to Darcy's. "What in the Sam hill are you doing here?"

"Jinx, have you met my friend, Claire?" Darcy asked.

She smiled curtly. "Not formally. I've seen her around. Tryouts."

"Oh, well then, Claire Emmett, this is Jinx Johansen. Jinx, Claire."

"Mmnnn," Jinx gave me a disapproving once-over as we all remained seated in our respective vehicles. "You're the one with the daughter from rec, right?" It took me a moment to realize that she was talking about soccer. I somehow heard it as Rachel had survived some sort of wreck, which, truth be told, she had.

Darcy answered for me. "Claire's daughter Rachel is one of our new girls. How's Sissy doing on Jillian's team?"

*Sissy, Sissy? Where have I heard that name?*

"Well, Darcy," Jinx said with a haughty tone. "She's doing as well as can be expected for a girl who was rejected by her soccer team."

*That's right! At tryouts, I remember hearing Mimi assuring a woman that Sissy would make the team. She was on her way to Starbucks with Gia, though, so I didn't turn around to see who she was speaking with. "Of course she'll make it," I remembered Mimi saying. "If I have anything to do with it, she'll be on the team again."*

Now, walking toward the store, Darcy said, "Jinx, you're not still upset about that, are you? Sissy's going to have a great year on the blue team."

"Don't patronize me, Darcy Greer!" she snapped, grabbing a shopping cart. "You know that if they ever put Kelly on the blue team, your husband would throw a fit. And he'd be right. Sissy is simply devastated by this. She feels like her friends have turned on her."

"Jinx, you know that's not true!" Darcy said, continuing this absurd conversation. I wondered why we couldn't just go to Target at the other end of the shopping center. Surely they had pink plates and napkins.

Jinx lifted her chin and turned away from us slightly. "Try explaining that to a twelve-year-old!"

I had to wonder how much of Sissy's devastation was nurtured by her mother. I know I was toeing the line of sanity there for a while, but I'd like to believe that if Rachel hadn't made the team, I would try to help her move forward instead of stagnating in bitterness.

Darcy reached toward Jinx's hand and placed hers on it. "I know it must be tough on her, but she'll be a star on that team and come back to tryouts next year even stronger."

*Oh please, I got less sympathy than this at Steve's funeral.*
"You're right," she sniffed.

"Maybe you'll hire a private trainer for her," Darcy suggested.
*A private trainer?*

Jinx glanced at me cautiously. "I don't think that will be necessary," she said. "I'm not one of those crazy parents who hires private coaches for their kids. That's plain insane." I got the definite feeling that Jinx was saying this solely for my benefit, but I couldn't, for the life of me, understand why. Why would she care if I thought she was a nutty parent?

"You're right, Jinx," said Darcy. "You always take things in stride."

*She does? She just told you she's all but medicating her rejection wounds.*

Jinx smiled placidly. "I try."

Darcy took the situation from simmering to room temperature in seconds. I wished she could do the same at home. "Tell me, dear," Darcy began. "When is your Spring Fling this year? Are you shopping for your supplies now?" Jinx nodded her head. "You are the most organized woman in all of Santa Bella. Would you believe I'm just now starting to shop for Veronica's party *this* Saturday?!"

Jinx looked aghast. "But it's—"

She could not finish her sentence. She could either not fathom or bear the thought of shopping for a party a mere four days beforehand.

"I know," Darcy said, feigning shame. "Would you help me prep for the big day?"

*Big day? I thought the theme was simplicity!*

As the three of us walked the aisles of Party City, Jinx's chatter revealed a lot. Although we didn't discuss soccer, it was very clear that the cause for Jinx's resentment of me was that she felt that Rachel had taken Sissy's spot as a midfielder on the squad. Perhaps if Rachel was selected as a defender, it wouldn't have stung so hard, but from her point of view my child had just stolen her child's heart. Although it was completely irrational, I sort of understood where she was coming from. If Rachel is still on the bubble next year, and the coach decides to move her to the blue team, I might very well feel betrayed by the club. My daughter would likely take the news hard and, as a result, I might see the replacement's mother through a lens that looked an awful lot like rifle sights.

After Jinx left, Darcy whipered, "Look, I like Jinx, but you should know that she and Mimi are best friends, so I wouldn't really trust her too much given your relationship with the general."

"Really?" I said. "I really thought we clicked there in Party City. You mean, you don't think I should tell her too much as we chitchat in her hot tub at the Spring Fling?"

"Okay, smart ass. Just trying to warn you."

❦ ❦

When we returned home, Darcy came inside with me for a quick bite. As we made our way to the kitchen, our eyes were immediately drawn to the fishbowl, where Jaws had been resurrected. Was he faking his death? Or were we bearing witness to the goldfish Messiah?

"He looks fatter," I said.

Darcy marched over to a piece of paper lain on the counter. She read aloud, "Claire, stop worrying about what other people want and take care of yourself." *What?* Placing the note back down, Darcy enlightened me. "It's Ron's handwriting."

The world froze. Jaws II stopped swimming. Darcy was motionless, and I couldn't breathe. Unfortunately, the world never came to a full stop for me, but rather resumed after a few seconds of sheer awkwardness. "Darcy, I'm, I don't know what to say."

Darcy's pace quickened. Her speech was fast and her movements bordering on jerky. "You don't have to say anything, Claire. It's nothing. Ron bought Rachel a fish, no big deal," she said.

"How did he get in?" I asked.

"We've got the spare key from when the Reynolds lived here."

"Darcy, stop, please. You don't need to wipe my counter."

"It's filthy," she said as she bent down to look under my sink for cleaning supplies. "He can be a real sweetheart sometimes. That's why I married him. We're not always fighting, you know. There's plenty of good in him."

"I know that, Darcy. I didn't say—"

"He's great with the kids and he's a great cook, did I ever tell you that?"

"Darcy, I—"

"And we have a lot of good times together. It's funny, Claire, people always think things are one way, but they don't see what the relationship is really like when no one else is looking."

I wanted to collapse into her arms and beg her forgiveness. I wanted to assure her that nothing would ever transpire between Ron and me. I also wanted her to stop squirting so much damned Fantastik on my stove top, but it didn't seem like a good time to bring up her nervous cleaning.

If I ever doubted that Ron felt something for me, the goldfish overture set me straight. There was something definitely there and, though I may have been walking away, he was running toward it.

I thought about how skillfully Darcy calmed Jinx today at Party City, and wondered why I couldn't do the same. Why couldn't I place my hand over Darcy's and give her peace of mind? Why couldn't I communicate to her that she had nothing to worry about with me? I looked at the tears building in Darcy's eyes and pretended not to notice them. "I know," I said. I wanted to say more, but these were not the sort of conversations people had aloud. Instead they talked around the issues. They wiped counters. They made their promises to each other in the guise of different gestures.

# Chapter Fifteen

On Friday after school, Rachel played piano in the background as I dialed the phone. It rang four times before an exhausted-sounding woman answered. "Kathy?" I asked.

Groggily, she replied, "Oh, hi Claire. What's up?"

"Not you, it sounds like. I was just calling to check in on you. How's the baby?"

"You mean my tormentor?" she said, perking up a bit with a laugh.

"I was thinking maybe I'd drive in tomorrow and give you a hand with him," I said. "Maybe a couple hours so you could take a nap?" I suggested, at the same time wondering what was showing at the LACMA. Maybe I would call Lil and the two of us could meet for lunch and a quick visit at the museum.

"Speaking of naps," Kathy said, "Duke's out right now, so I'm going to catch up on my sleep, okay?"

"Okay. How does three o'clock sound?"

"Like music," Kathy replied.

"See you then."

CR ⁊⁊

Rachel and I curled up in my bed that night and watched STivo, a collection of videos Steve shot of himself talking to Rachel and me. He left behind about forty hours of recordings so we wouldn't forget him. There were touching ones, like the message he left for Rachel on her wedding day. And there were the fun, everyday ones in which Steve offered his advice on dating. "Rachel, the answer is no," he said with a smile. "I don't care who he is or what the situation is, my answer is no. He's not good enough for you." In tonight's episode, Steve was recalling how I used to make necklaces with glass beads and sell them in Santa Monica on weekends. "I was finally starting to make money, and your mom decides it's time for her to start selling stuff on the street." I laughed, remembering the sight of my "boutique" under a palm tree near the Promenade. I set out a card table and strung beads as passers-by stopped and looked at my jewelry. Steve was at a nearby playground with Rachel and checked in on me every hour or so.

This evolved from Lil's motherly intervention. Shortly after Rachel's first birthday, she came over to babysit and plopped a copy of *The Learning Annex* catalog on our dining room table. "Pick one class you'd like to take and register for it right now," she said.

"Right now?" I asked.

"Right now, Claire," she said, hovering over me. "I have my checkbook and a stamped envelope with me and I'm mailing your registration on my way out this afternoon." There was no room for argument. I flipped through the pages and found a two-day beading class that was hosted at a jewelry shop on Fourth Street.

On my first day of class, the teacher talked about selecting beads that worked together, colors and textures that complemented each other rather than competed for attention. "You can have four gorgeous beads strung together and they'll look hideous," she explained, pronouncing the word *hid-jhis*.

"The trick is finding the right combinations, beads that help bring out the beauty in what's next to them."

As I watched my dozen classmates struggle with colors and shapes that fought each other, I put together patterns that "harmoniously sang with life" (the teacher's words, not mine). Soon after, I was making up to ten necklaces a day, which is no easy feat with a toddler. I loved the feeling of creating something that was alive with beauty. I made six for Lil, two for my mother, and one multi-stranded piece for Kathy. After a few weeks of this, it was clear I needed to find a way to get rid of these necklaces. It was Lil who suggested I start a small business, and if she was disappointed that it was located on the street, she never showed it. Every weekend I was greeted by a suspiciously high number of Junior Leaguers who just so happened to be passing through. When I was ticketed for selling without a license, Lil paid the fine and saw to it that I was legit by the next weekend.

Steve's voice grew weaker in his last recordings. "I took you to the playground and pushed you on the swing while Mommy did her thing. I bought you your first Popsicle there. I actually bought it for myself, but after I let you have a taste, it was yours. It was one of those red, white, and blue rockets and your eyes popped open when your lips hit the tip. I thought you were shocked by the cold, but then you grabbed my hand and said 'good' like thirty times while you ate that thing," Steve said, chuckling at the memory.

Rachel looked at me. "How come you don't make jewelry anymore?" she asked. She tilted her head ever so slightly and knit her brows, an expression she had since infancy. Her face had become that of a young woman, but her expressions were still my baby's.

"I don't know," I said.

"I love to bead," Rachel said. "Maybe we could do it together?"

"Sure," I promised. "I have to remember where I packed all of my supplies. They're probably still in the garage."

"Well, if you can't find them, there's a new bead shop that just opened up next to the Soccer Post."

CR ℘

Sunday was Veronica's seventh birthday party. As Darcy opened the front door, the sounds of kids' music, laughter, and horns burst out. Rachel's eyes shot past us as she spotted Kelly and Sapphire playing a video game. Cara was chatting with girls I'd seen at school. I scanned the room for Mimi and saw her in a heavy conversation with another mother from the team, one of the Jennifers, I believe. Surely it was about her physical fitness program she'd be implementing with the girls this year. We only heard about that for forty minutes at the meeting, so of course there must be more to tell.

Walking in, I saw an elderly woman with sagging knee highs and blue hair sitting in a rocker reading to a group of younger children. When I say blue hair, I don't mean that she dyed it so black that it had a blue shine, or that it was grey with a slight blue hue to it. She had full-on Cookie Monster-blue hair and wore a quilted robe that matched her slippers. I raised my eyebrows as if to ask who this senile old woman was who forgot to dress for Veronica's party.

"Aunt Betty," Darcy answered.

"Yours or Ron's?" I asked.

Darcy thought I was joking because she laughed. "I know I said no entertainers, but it's so hard to get Aunt Betty, and when I heard that Susie Atwater had to cancel Barclay's party, I knew I could snatch her up last-minute."

The family room was kiddie bedlam. I had hoped I wouldn't see Ron, but knew it was a ridiculous notion since I was in his home. I caught glances of him interacting with Veronica's friends and softened toward him. Okay, I'd never actually hardened, but I saw a gentler side of him, which, as luck would have it, I found incredibly sexy. He walked over to Mimi and told her something that made her nod affirmatively. Mimi looked as if she was excusing herself and the two walked off to the hallway. En route, he noticed me staring at him and gave a slight nod of his head and a smile. I loved the way his lips were full and uneven.

I needed an escape. When in the home of another woman, helping her in the kitchen is a perfect excuse to get away from the crowd. Quickening my pace, I walked toward Darcy, who was chatting with Gia and her boobs. "What do you need help with?" I asked.

"Thanks, Claire. We're all set," Darcy said. "Gia just finished setting out the juice boxes and Aunt Betty serves the sandwiches."

*Goddamn Gia and Aunt Betty!*

I saw Ron, who was now making his way toward us. Panicked, I shot, "What about milk?!"

"Milk?" Gia repeated as though she'd never heard of the stuff before.

"Darcy, you've got to offer them milk. What about the kids who are, um, fructose intolerant and can't drink juice? I'll go pour some milk in the kitchen."

I could see the thought bubble over Darcy's head. *Fructose intolerant?*

"Nancy told me about it," I lied. "It's very serious. A kid could get really sick."

"Okay," Darcy shrugged. "Thanks, Claire."

I scurried off to the kitchen just seconds before Ron arrived at our cluster. "Oh, hi," I said, breezing past him. "Nice party."

As I stood at the granite island, pouring milk into pink paper cups, Ron brushed past me. I felt the sparks of sexual electricity between us. "You're not avoiding me, are you, Claire?"

"Don't be silly," I said. "Why would I do that? Oh, thanks for the goldfish. Rachel really appreciated it."

"You're welcome," he said, the front of his body so close to the back of mine that we were touching. "Oh, excuse me, Claire." The feeling of his body coupled with the sound of his voice saying my name was almost too much. It was like cold liquid rushing over my hands. *Cold liquid rushing over my hands?* Shit! Shit, shit, shit!!! I was pouring milk over the top of a cup, onto my hands and all over their beautiful granite countertop.

"Oh my God!" I shrieked.

Ron rushed for a cloth from under the sink and tossed it onto the floor to begin absorbing my mess. "Don't worry about it, Claire. I'll help." As Ron knelt down to wipe the floor, I grabbed a handful of paper towels. I laid them on the countertop, never too far from the thought that Ron's lips were nine inches from my thighs. I wished I'd worn a skirt. *Stop thinking things like that!*

As one might expect, my cleaning efforts were about as fumbled as everything else I tried that day. My nervous energy caused me to wipe the milk from side to side without giving it time to absorb into the wad of paper towels. I wound up sending a waterfall of milk onto Ron's head and neck.

"Oh my God!" I shouted. "I'm so sorry." I knelt down to the floor where Ron was flicking milk from his hair. "I'm so sorry," I kept repeating.

"It's okay," he said, laughing slightly. "It's only milk."

"I'm such a klutz," I explained, as if *that* needed to be clarified.

"You're not much in the kitchen, are you?" Ron commented as our eyes locked. We both crouched behind the counter like soldiers in a foxhole. Okay, like secret lovers hiding from the world. God, I wished I was in a foxhole. I was positively the worst person alive. Uncomfortable silence flooded the space between us as the sound of cheering kids swinging at the piñata outside amplified.

"No," I said, meaning more than the concession that I was not a domestic goddess.

"That's okay," Ron said, never releasing me from his gaze. "You've got a lot of other things going for you." He finally looked away and started wiping the floor again, an obvious ploy to stay put.

"I'm really sorry," I said again, an obvious ploy to keep talking. "Can I, um, wash your shirt?" Thank goodness this offer made sense in the context of having just spilled milk on it because it was actually quite an independent thought. The idea of dancing around my laundry room with Ron's button-down top was my idea of a hot Saturday night.

"Nah, that's okay," Ron said, smirking as if he could see his loose shirt sleeves leading me in a tango. "I get laundry service here."

*Laundry service?* With those words, my heart broke for Darcy. I snapped back to reality.

"Oh. Well, thanks for helping me clean this mess."

He smiled. "You've already thanked me, Claire."

"Thanks for the goldfish," I said in the absence of anything else to say.

He smiled again, knowing he had me. "Anything for you, Claire."

The world stopped moving. This was the moment of truth. I had to put an end to this right now, but had to do it in a way that he could save face. I would make it a mutual thing that "we" had to end so he wouldn't feel foolish or rejected.

"Listen, Ron," I said, whispering as we remained tucked away from the rest of the world. My heart was pounding so loudly it was beating in my ears. As I moved closer to him, I contemplated changing my tack entirely and kissing him instead. Thankfully, my good sense returned before I lunged at him. "I think you're a great guy, but we've got to stop this."

"Stop what?" he asked suggestively.

"This little flirtation between us," I said. "I mean, if you weren't married it would be different, but I'm Darcy's best friend, so ..." I drifted off.

Ron scrunched his face as if he had no idea what I meant. "Claire, I'm really sorry if I gave you the wrong idea," he began. *Oh God, let me die right now.* "It was only a goldfish. Sorry if you thought it meant something more." With that, he offered, "No hard feelings, okay?"

*What?!* The world froze. Ron was still kneeling before me, his face cast in an expression of bewilderment. I searched aimlessly for life's rewind button. *How do I take back that whole exchange? How do I erase Sexy Dad saying, "No hard feelings. It was only a goldfish"?*

"Oh," slipped out softly. "Wow, I'm embarrassed." *Stop talking! Feelings of humiliation do not need to be shared with source of said humiliation.*

"Claire, don't worry about it. No big deal," Ron said, shrugging as he stood.

"There you are!" Mimi said as she appeared in the kitchen entryway. "I thought I lost you."

"Never," he said. *Oh, so now he's flirting with her?! Or is this just the way he interacts with women who aren't his wife? Oh God, let me die now, I've made such a colossal ass of myself.* "I was helping Claire clean up some spilled milk."

Mimi gave a little laugh that would sound like a giggle to a man, but any woman would know was really a cackle. "I hope you're not crying over it, Claire."

*Oh, hilarious. How long did it take you to come up with that nugget?*

"All right, you all set in here?" Ron asked me.

*Am I all set in here?*

"Yeah," I replied. "Thanks for your help."

"It was nothing," he said, walking away with Mimi.

*Okay, got it. Message received.*

I watched the two walk away in slow motion, then join the others outside as they beat the daylights out of a rainbow-colored jackass until its candy guts spilled onto the patio.

I mustered just enough gumption to find Rachel and told her that I was leaving. "Come home when the party's over. I have a headache," I said before slinking home to crawl under my duvet with the sincere hope that I would suffocate in bed and never have to face Ron, Darcy, or anyone in this neighborhood again.

I took three aspirins and decided to lie in bed and hyper-analyze every discussion I'd ever had with Ron. Every word, nuance, intonation and expression would be replayed, dissected and scrutinized the way only a woman could.

After about an hour of self-flagellation, I dragged myself out of bed and went online to check to see how much I could sell the house for and what housing prices were like in, say, Maine or New Hampshire. Before I could get an appraisal for our home, I heard the postal truck pull up to the front of my house and rushed to the mailbox. Steve always said that I had Cargo Cult syndrome because of my excitement over mail delivery. Apparently there is a group of Pacific Islanders who stand by the shore, convinced that their fortune will be delivered by an incoming ship. Hence the expression about someone's ship coming in. Whatever the reason, I unfailingly grew excited when I heard the rustling of mail being placed in my box.

Because absolutely nothing could go right today, the mail brought two disturbing notices. In today's delivery I received a fundraising letter from the Steve Emmet Foundation. (They still hadn't corrected the spelling of our name!) Under the logo —a set of winged lungs—Maggie Jennings pleaded for my tax-deductible donation to help her group find a cure for non-smoking-related lung cancer. Before I could tear up the letter, I noticed a faux-handwritten message reminding me to save the date for the first annual "Breath of Fresh Air" gala in September.

After tossing that into the trash I found a curious piece of mail—a MasterCard bill addressed to the treasurer of Kix GU13 White soccer team. Somehow, Mimi had guilted me into handling the accounting for the team. When I opened the bill, I found charges for the Marriott in La Perla and a pricey meal at Majorca Grill.

When I called Mimi that evening, she quickly told me I should just give her the bill and she'd take care of it. "How do I account for it on the books?" I asked.

"You don't. I said I'd take care of it," she replied curtly.

"But I don't understand why—"

"Claire, I said I'd take care of it. I need you to give me the bill at practice and I'll make sure it gets paid."

"But when did we—"

"Claire, you're obviously new to this, so let me explain how it works. You make sure everyone pays their registration and coaching fees. You write checks for tournaments and pizza parties, or anything else I tell you we need. I don't need to spend time justifying every little expense to you, got it?"

"Oh, I've got it," I said smugly. *Mimi was the recruiter of dads. Why didn't Darcy mention that it was our very own team manager who was taking one for the team?*

She sighed, sounding exasperated, but knowing that she had to provide some sort of explanation. "Claire, sometimes we recruit players from other parts of the state and we need to put their families up in a hotel and wine 'em and dine 'em a little. It's beyond the scope of what the club does, so I'm willing to pay for it out-of-pocket."

One might think that I'd have a little compassion for people who had just been caught in an embarrassing situation, but Mimi was so nasty to me at the team meeting that I took a little pleasure in twitting her a bit. "That is *so* generous of you, Mimi," I said, "but don't we already have a full team? Why are we recruiting new players at the beginning of the season? If a family lives so far from Santa Bella that they need to stay in a hotel, how are they ever going to make it to practices and games?"

I felt emboldened for exactly one second. Then Mimi launched into me and made it abundantly clear who would win the battle and the war. If I made Mimi my enemy, she wouldn't just tear a soccer jersey. "Listen here, Claire," she said with a mouth so tight I could see it through the phone. "I know you think you're really cute with your little innuendoes, but let me make myself clear. I am the manager of this team and will not take a half-ounce of bullshit from you. This family is moving to Santa Bella in September, and if our team can sign this girl, we'll be unstoppable at State Cup. Maybe no one explained this to you while you were busy worrying about team banners and the like, but after the regular season ends, we can add new players to our roster. The season is officially over so we can bring on new blood and cut the mistakes."

"Are you threatening my daughter?" I asked, outraged.

"I'm threatening *you*. Take me on and I guarantee you will lose. Be a good little treasurer and write the checks and shut up. I have no patience for you people who come to the club, know nothing about the way things work and waste my time making me explain it. Try a little humility and observe for a while before you come in and start running off at the mouth."

*Shit, this chick was scary! What happened to girl power?*

"Are you done?" I asked, feigning indignation. I thought it would come off better than the abject fear I really felt.

"I'm done and I hope this conversation is, too. If I have to talk to you again about this, I won't be as pleasant about it." Then Mimi hung up.

As I sat in a puddle of my own sweat, I looked at the clock, dismayed to see that this day was far from over. It wasn't even eight o'clock and I was ready to wave my white flag and surrender to the day. I changed into my pajamas, crawled into my bed and watched STivo tell me that I would be okay without him.

# Chapter Sixteen

After my exchange with Mimi, I faced a parenting dilemma. Did I still allow Rachel to attend pre-practice homework sessions at the Shasta Palace? Was the tax-evading, possibly drug-trafficking house a great place for Rachel to be? When I told Darcy about our phone conversation, she seemed completely unfazed. "Darcy, did you hear what I just told you?"

"She's a bitch," Darcy shrugged. "Everyone knows that. She's been like this since the girls were little, and I expect she'll keep it up till they're off to college. We've lost a few players because of her. Good players, too."

"Why does the club still let her manage teams?" I asked.

"Claire, her family completely funds the foundation. All of Shasta Imports' local clients are club sponsors. They think she's awesome. She's on their board and was the president of the organization for three years. Don't take this so personally. Mimi has issues with women, attractive women in particular." *Oh, thank you.* "Personally, I think she's awful, but the truth is she's terrific with the girls. She doesn't see them as competition."

"So you let Kelly go to her house unsupervised?" I asked.

"I'm telling you, Claire, she's amazing with the girls. Last year, Kelly came home with all of her homework done, her notebook organized, and an academic schedule that Mimi helped her put together."

"Really? Wow." Though I was happy to hear that Mimi would be a positive influence on Rachel, I had to admit to feeling more than a bit conflicted about the report. I wished Mimi were thoroughly evil, like the wicked queen who offers poison apples to fair-skinned lovelies. Now I wasn't sure who or what she was. A bitch with a soft spot for girls? A feminist athlete who was jealous of pretty women? Why did she have to be such an oxymoron?

## MEMORANDUM

TO:     The Team
FROM: Mimi Shasta
DATE: April 8
RE:     First Practice!

I hope you're all as excited as I am about our first practice this Tuesday afternoon! I will pick up the girls from Santa Bella Elementary after school, and my good friend Jinx has graciously agreed to pick up the girls who attend Our Lady of Forgiveness even though her daughter, Sissy, was cut from this year's team to make room for new girls! Since we only have two girls who go to Beth Israel Hebrew Day, I trust the parents will work out a carpool and get their kids to practice on time!

Our first tournament is right around the corner so we need to get busy! The Memorial Weekend Classic is in Santa Barbara and our team will be staying at the Crowne Plaza, the official hotel of the tournament! I will get you the schedules as soon as I can, but the club hasn't posted it yet (ugh!)!

Go Kix!!!

CR ℘

When I showed up at the practice field on Thursday, Mimi was leading the girls in laps. She was dressed in head-to-toe Nike gear from her wristbands to her socks. I suspect her underwear bore the swoosh as well. Rachel told me that Mimi bragged to the girls about her exclusive deal with Nike. Darcy said she highly doubted this was the case. The more likely scenario was that some old fart at Sports Chalet told her that she was "so purdy she oughta be the model for Nike." Mimi probably batted her extended lashes, pouted her collagen lips, and convinced the helpless schlep to give her a few free items. After all, who even knows about kids' soccer team managers? If no one was giving Gunther an exclusive deal, no one was giving Mimi one either. (Stellar college career notwithstanding.)

Rachel saw that I'd arrived and gave me a silly wave as she followed the pack. The girls then played leap frog, ran agility hoops and jumped hurdles. I was exhausted just watching for fifteen minutes.

Or maybe I was exhausted by listening to the dads. Paulo shouted directions in Italian to Giovanna constantly. I don't speak Italian, but he was clearly telling her to pick up her knees since this is what she started doing immediately upon hearing his commands.

Raymond told Violet to "work that hoop, girl!"

Dick, Bobby and Leo simply made a bunch of sounds that sounded like animal mating calls. How could they be *this* excited over fitness training?! I can see if we were at a game, but this was ridiculous.

Gia and her boobs were taking a *Cosmo* quiz, *Are You Discreet?* Nancy was knitting and the Jennifers decided to use their time to run. Only Jessica and Darcy were missing.

I was not looking forward to seeing Darcy again. I wondered how she reacted when Ron told her about what happened. Did she think me a presumptuous fool or a pathetic fool? God, I hoped pathetic.

Gunther blew his whistle and called the girls to him. Mimi pointed at her watch as if to tell him that her fitness training hadn't concluded. He returned the gesture with a dismissive wave. "They start practicing soccer now," he said.

Mimi smiled brightly, though anyone could see she was annoyed. "This is soccer, Gunther. It's fitness training *for* soccer."

"I start now," he said.

"Girls! Run a lap while I talk to the coach." As she walked over to Gunther, I swore I heard the Darth Vader music in the background. The two had a trial-like sidebar with Mimi's hands flailing about in protest and Gunther simply shaking his head.

"I am telling you no," he said, interrupting her tirade about their agreement.

"We have a lot of slow girls on this team!" she protested. *She couldn't be talking about Rachel.* "They need to be in shape or they'll never—"

"I am telling you no," Gunther repeated.

"I can hear that, but what I'm telling you is that—"

"We do my practicing, then we do yours if there is time."

*You go, Gunther. You da man!*

I have no idea what transpired between them in the weeks between our team meeting and the first practice, but clearly Gunther felt the need to assert himself and establish himself as the leader of this team. I, for one, couldn't have been happier.

"Gunther!" Mimi yelled.

"I am telling you to stop talking," Gunther said.

*Loving this! Why couldn't I tell Mimi, "I am telling you to shut up now"?*

When the girls came back around the track, Mimi announced that it was time for Gunther to take over. The group walked off to a small area offset by orange cones. Any reservations I had about our coach vanished when I saw him take control of the practice. For one, he spoke. He seemed to be stringing multiple sentences together and making facial expressions. Then the girls started laughing. "Yes, this is truth, girls," he said, admitting to something that Savannah said. "But you learn and work hard and you will do even better than I play soccer. I see you at tryout and you look like superstar." Good God, he was charming. And chatty. Who would have imagined?!

The four fat fathers stood like Mount Rushmore on the sideline. "Who to? Who to?" shouted Raymond when a plain-topped Violet passed to a girl wearing a neon yellow bib.

"Out wide, move to space, Savannah!" added Leo.

"Kylie, hustle! Mariah, on your toes! Tandy, you hang in there, stay tough!" shouted Dick.

"Turn and burn, turn and burn, Cayenne!" bellowed Bobby.

Paulo shouted more in Italian, which sounded like he just got in an accident with another motorist.

The worst part of it was that all of this voluminous instruction was dispensed simultaneously. It reminded me of traders at the New York Stock Exchange. If I were a child, I would have frozen in my tracks and cried. After a season of this, I would have been on kiddie Zoloft.

When Gunther moved onto the next exercise, the sideline coaching became sideline complaining. The dads started muttering, questioning the purpose of the drill. "What's Tandy working on shooting for?" Dick asked rhetorically. "She's a defender, she don't need no shooting drills."

"Like Cayenne needs to take shots on goal!" Bobby said of his goalkeeper daughter.

"Every girl taking a shot right now should have a sweeper on her ass, trying to shut her down, like in a real game," Raymond added.

"Nah, this ain't right," Leo said. "He can't be *sivious.*"

"Put Cayenne in at goal!" shouted Bobby. "Shooting on an open goal is never gonna happen in a game, Gunther!"

Gunther looked at the group, unsure of who shouted what. "Mimi, stop shouting," he pleaded.

"I'm not saying a word," she shouted, then followed up with a muttered "*Frankenschtein.*"

"Not *you* shouting," Gunther clarified. "Stop *the* shouting. I cannot concentration."

"Oh please," she said loudly enough for the parents on the sideline to hear, but not enough for Gunther and girls to catch wind of. "How many people were shouting during your World Cup games?"

Gunther turned his attention back to the girls and began another exercise.

Mimi ambled over to the Psych Ward. "I need you guys to be quiet."

"Ah snap, who let the dawgs out?" Leo said, laughing.

*What did that even mean?*

"What the hell's this guy doin'?" Dick demanded.

"I didn't drive no thirty minutes when I can get sucky-ass coaching at Conquistadors in my own backyard," Leo said.

"Guys, we need to put on a united front with these girls, got it?" Mimi said. "I wasn't exactly thrilled when my fitness session got cut in half, but you don't see me whining about it, do you?"

"We need to get the girls ready to play in game situations, y'see what I'm sayin'?" Bobby asked, sucking his teeth and adjusting his ExxonMobil cap. "Cayenne needs to be in the box blockin' shots, not learning how to shoot goals."

The group grumbled in agreement.

Gia stopped filling out her questionnaire and held her pen over the same spot on the magazine page. Clearly, she wouldn't need to score the quiz to find out that she was not in the least bit discreet. As the Jennifers jogged by, they noticed the escalating tension and slowed to listen. Nancy stopped at knit-one and stared as well, surely wondering if the gluten in their diets made them act so wacky. I imagined that she was going to suggest kava kava when she began walking toward them.

"Nancy, stop!" said Darcy.

*Uh oh. She's here. My moment of reckoning.*

"Oh hi, Darcy," Nancy said. "When did you get here?"

"Just now. You're not thinking of putting yourself in the middle of that cock fight, are you?"

Nancy laughed. "No, I was going to suggest that—"

"Do not disturb the animals!" Darcy warned. "Really, do yourself a favor and let them be."

Nancy laughed again. "That bad?"

"Worse," Darcy confirmed.

"You'd know best," she said, returning to her knitting bag.

"Hey, Claire," Darcy said. Funny, she didn't seem at all upset with me. "Haven't seen you in a while. Where've you been hiding?"

*Um, under a rock!*

"Oh, I've just been, I had to, we should—"

"Wanna catch up over lunch tomorrow? There's a new sushi place that's supposed to be great."

I waited for her to add, "Oh, by the way, you presumptuous little twit—it was just a goldfish." Instead she smiled expectantly.

"Sounds good," I replied.

Nodding her head toward the dads, Darcy said, "Looks like it's starting early this season."

"What's starting early?"

"The revolution," Darcy laughed.

"So this is normal?"

"Like I told you, Claire, it's club soccer," Darcy said. Waiting a beat, she finished, "Nothing's normal."

The familiar sound of my friend's voice was soothing. Ron spared me the wedge that would have come from our misunderstanding, and for that I was grateful.

Next came Dick's booming male voice, which didn't sound quite as comforting. "What the hell was that?! Give and go means go somewhere after the pass! It's not give and go to sleep!" Turning to Bobby, he continued, "That girl sucks. How the hell'd she make the team?"

Leo chimed in. "She got a little sister that's supposed to be *siviously* good, so the club don't want to piss off the family by cuttin' the older girl."

Dick seemed outraged. "So we have to suffer so some little peewee team doesn't lose a player?!"

"It ain't right, but you know how it is," Leo said, nodding at the injustice of it all.

"You said it, pal. Friggin' soccer politics," Dick huffed. "This deal stinks worse than shit."

# Chapter Seventeen

Rachel had no trouble getting to sleep the night of her first practice. As Darcy promised, Rachel showed up at Diablo Field with her homework done and her hair in neat French braids she hadn't left with that morning. Rachel said that Mimi even helped the girls with their geometry homework by showing them how angles relate to soccer. "She's way cool, Mom," Rachel told me as I tucked her in bed that night. "Cara's nice too. She's not stuck up at all even though they got like a bazillion dollars. Do you know they have *four* maids?" My daughter yawned and nestled her head in her favorite "mushy pillow."

"I'm glad," I said.

"Me too," Rachel said, fading.

And I was. Certainly, I'd prefer if the team manager didn't think of me as her personal target for lipstick darts, but she was kind to Rachel, and that was all that mattered. It was as if Rachel had been initiated into a sorority at a time in her life when she desperately needed sisterhood. And for that I could take a little nastiness from Mimi. Okay, a lot, but still, it was worth it.

After I heard the buzzing of Rachel asleep, I went to my computer to check email.

## MEMORANDUM

TO: The Team
FROM: Mimi Shasta
DATE: April 11
RE: Today's practice!

I'm blown away by the outpouring of support for my fitness trainings! Thank you so much for all of your calls and emails asking me to extend the fitness training to its full hour! It's sweet of you to suggest that we make it an entire practice session, but Gunther has a great curriculum for the girls and we really need to get to that too! I really appreciated—

**Ding!**

*What the?*

**You have an instant message from RGreer4@hotmail. com. Will you accept?**

*He* would *have an address at Hotmail!*

I deliberated for a moment, but then decided that refusing his instant message would show Ron just how mortified I was over the birthday party incident. I was determined to show him just how unbothered I was by the whole thing by acting as normal as possible. Of course, acting natural never works. Like, a few days earlier, I saw Ron filling his gas tank at the Shell station near our block, so I pulled in beside him and starting fueling my minivan just to show him that I would not be avoiding him. The problem was that I forgot that my tank was already full, and looked like an absolute fool as I stood beside him oh-so-casually for exactly thirty seconds. He smirked when he saw my pump stop dead at a half gallon, making that clanking sound like the slam of a metal door. Compassionate fucker that he is,

Ron made a snarky comment about how one can never be too careful about running low on fuel.

**RonGreer4: Claire, I need to apologize for what happened at Ronnie's party.**

*Exactly the conversation I never wanted to have. Why do people feel the need to rehash unpleasantness?*

**CEmmett: Okay, no problem.**

**RonGreer4: I embarrassed you and I didn't mean to.**

*And yet you continue to do so by bringing it up again!*

**CEmmett: No big deal. Thanks for the message.**

**RonGreer4: Did you say anything to Darcy?**

**CEmmett: Oh yeah, I told her all about it. It was a real special moment for us.**

**RonGreer4: LOL. Seriously, though, what happened was my fault and I'm very sorry.**

**CEmmett: Your fault?**

**RonGreer4: Sometimes my friendliness is misinterpreted and women think I'm flirting.**

**CEmmett: So this has happened before?**

**RonGreer4: Yes, and I regretted the misunderstanding just as much as I did at the party. I hope you'll forgive me and let this pass.**

*Somehow I did find this comforting. Idiocy loves company, I guess.*

**CEmmett: Okay, well, thanks for clearing that up.**

**RonGreer4: I want to make sure we're on the same page about Darcy. There's no need to hurt her feelings by telling her. Agreed?**

I stopped cold at the keyboard. This was no apology; it was damage control. He was simply covering his ass, which only made me wonder—from what?

**CEmmett: Sure thing. Good night.**

I signed off before he could reply.

# Chapter Eighteen

I only heard from Ron once more after that. About a week later while I was catching up on email, he chimed in again with an Instant Message, telling me about some move Rachel had mastered at practice. He knew I was there to see it, but correctly assumed I didn't understand what a great achievement this was. After the kitchen incident, Ron seemed determined to make a buddy of me, but how could I ever be pals with a guy who had to tell me that sometimes a goldfish was just a goldfish.

**RonGreer4: Hey there. Long time, no speak. What's up?**

**CEmmett: Oh hi. I've got to run. I'm super busy right now.**

**RonGreer4: No prob. What are you working on? Nice to see Rachel really perfect her wall pass at practice today. That's important for our mids.**

**CEmmett: Can't talk now. Rachel's calling me.**

**RonGreer4: Rachel's here.**

It was interactions like these that made me want fewer of them with Ron Greer. As I contemplated crawling under my kicky new duvet with poppies spread across it, I found a flier for carpet cleaning service. I hadn't given my thick, white carpet a good cleaning since Rachel and I moved in nearly a year ago. I must confess, in my effort to avoid dark, depressing colors like death black and mourning blue, I went the opposite extreme and decorated with too much white. My couch and love seat were fluffy white microfiber with tons of pillows strewn across them. The walls were crisp white; the entertainment center was birch wood with glass. If I was trying to avoid thinking of Steve's death, I might have considered something that looked less like the reception area of heaven. Last weekend I saw a duvet that sprang to life with its bright red flowers and knew I had to have it. From the moment I slipped it over my white down comforter, the whole room had vitality. Of course, one might comment that sleeping under a bed of flowers isn't exactly the strongest affirmation of life either. But it made me happy.

CB ∞

For the next several weeks, little happened that didn't involve Rachel's soccer team. The girls practiced twice a week with Mimi's fitness trainings getting shorter and shorter each time. Her fuse did the same, and I feared this woman would explode sometime soon, with the very real possibility of her tackling Gunther to the ground and biting him.

Loath as I was to admit it, Mimi's fitness trainings looked phenomenal. Of course, I didn't know anything about soccer, but she really seemed to have her program finely tuned. She set up obstacle courses that helped the girls develop different skills while keeping the activity fun. In the few weeks that Rachel had been working out with Mimi, I noticed that she looked faster and had more endurance. All of the girls seemed more muscular and sleek than they had at tryouts. Maybe it was the soccer practices. But to me, it appeared as though fitness training was quite effective.

Gunther, on the other hand, was less than positive about Mimi's sessions. He looked at his watch impatiently before blowing the whistle and announcing, "We are starting the real practicing now." By mid-May, we were down to eight-minute sessions.

Despite Mimi's claims that she'd received "overwhelming support" for her trainings, none of the parents seemed particularly outraged that Mimi's role as fitness trainer was diminishing as the season progressed. Her only real ally was Ron, who consoled her as they walked a few laps around the field whenever he was at practice. Her arms would flail in the air with exasperation, and he would gesture with his hands that she needed to take it down a notch. How I would have loved to have been a bird flying overhead so I could listen in on those conversations. Unfortunately for the general, Ron was in surgery more often than at soccer practice.

I also hated to concede that Rachel's homework never looked better. She did an impressive amount of work at Mimi's. Mimi even taught the girls to meditate and visualize their goals every morning. Mimi, the Zen general. I wished it was someone else—anyone else—but Mimi was turning out to be an incredibly positive influence in Rachel's life.

CR 80

In mid-May, I received a note from Lil, which made my heart pause with guilt. When was I going to call that woman?! This seemed to be her question as well, though she phrased it in her usual tactful fashion.

*Dearest Claire,*
*You and Rachel are always in my thoughts and prayers. I*
*do hope you'll call me soon. I'd love to see you both.*
*With much love and deep affection,*
*Lil*

It wasn't that I didn't want to see Lil. I did. More than that, I wanted her to see Rachel. But every time I looked at my mother-in-law, I saw Steve. And as long as I could never see Steve again, I couldn't bear to see him in her eyes, her cheekbones and her mouth. They even had the same laugh.

CR ℘

At practice two weeks before our first tournament, Gunther blew his whistle right as Mimi arrived at the field with the girls. "Bring in, girls," he shouted.

"Gunther," Mimi wailed, "We haven't even started."

"You run mile to get here," Gunther reminded her.

"That's nothing!" Mimi protested. "I brought—"

"Fitness training is finish. We have tournament soon and girls need to get serious."

I unfolded my chair, noticing the fragrance of spring blossoms in the air. I waved at Rachel, who smiled to say hello. *How was school?* I mouthed. She gave me two thumbs up.

"Fitness *is* serious, Gunther!" Mimi said with both hands on her hips. Parents began trickling in, mumbling about how they were at it again.

"You two oughta get married, you fight so much," Dick heckled from the sideline. Adjusting his umbrella, he turned his back to the coach and manager and began amusing Raymond, Bobby and Leo.

"*Sivious,* that's love if I ever seen it," Leo added.

Not one to be left out, Bobby shouted, "Get a room, you two."

The Normals sat quietly and took out their books, magazines, and running shoes as they waited for today's drama to resolve itself. Mimi and Gunther walked toward each other and came within inches of each other's face. Maybe they *were* in love. It certainly looked like they were moments away from a passionate kiss. It happened in movies all the time. The guy and the girl hate each other. They scream at each other, then suddenly they lock lips and hold a pose that looks like the movie poster for *Casablanca*.

"What are they fighting about now?" Nancy asked.

"What else? Fitness training. He cut it down to nothing today," I explained.

"For good or just for today?" Darcy chimed in.

"Don't know. He just told her that the girls need to get serious before the tournament, and she looked supremely insulted by that comment."

"Shhh, he's going to say something," Darcy said as we all watched Gunther grope for words.

"We have tournament soon!" Gunther said. "Girls need to play soccer."

Nancy, Darcy and I relaxed into our seats again, disappointed with Gunther's reply. "He already said that," Nancy noted.

"Well, I think it sucks in a major way," Gia piped in. "He promised her an assistant coaching position and he's so not keeping that promise. Mimi puts a lot of prep work into these trainings and cutting them is a total slap in the face."

"Please," Jennifer said. I wasn't even aware that she was listening to us as she laced up her running shoes a few feet away. "Gunther's the coach and he gets to set the agenda for the team."

"Hear, hear," Nancy said.

Gia looked around curiously. I could just see the thought bubble over her head wondering, *where, where?*

Mimi shouted, "Gunther, we agreed—"

"We have tournament soon. Girls need to play soccer."

"Not exactly a candidate for the debating team, is he?" Darcy said.

"Darcy Greer, you're bad," Jennifer teased before setting off on her run.

After a few minutes, Mimi gestured like she was throwing something to the ground, though her hands were empty. "Fine," she snapped, then stormed off to the sideline. When she joined the fat four and the Italian, it was a defining moment for our team.

In the first minutes of Gunther's drill, the wall of noise began.

"What the hell was that?!" Dick muttered just loud enough for the parents to hear.

"Time-wasting bullshit's what it is. He ain't *sivious* spending the last practices before the tourney doing this kind of crap," yelled Leo.

"Move, move, move it, Violet!" shouted Raymond. "No mercy, no mercy, girl!"

Paulo muttered unhappily in Italian.

"He's completely incompetent," Mimi added.

Loud Bobby just sighed. Loudly. Then he turned to Mimi, who stood watching with her hands on her hips and her eyes narrowed. "You played in college. They ever do drills like these with you?"

"No they did not," Mimi said, repeating the response while oscillating her head like a fan. Everyone needed to hear that during Mimi's glory days at Dartmouth, her precious time wasn't wasted with inferior Guntherian drills. "Of course, we were in *better shape* on my college team so we could do more advanced exercises!"

Darcy nudged me and laughed. "Aren't you mortified that our fifth graders don't measure up to Mimi's college soccer team? I could just die of shame."

*No, but I* am *mortified that despite the fact that your husband is an absolute ass, I still have wildly inappropriate dreams about him.*

CR SO

At the next practice, I watched Mimi pacing the sideline like an old-school father waiting in the maternity ward. "Mimi's getting wacky," I whispered to Darcy. "Rachel said that when she was at her place on Tuesday, Mimi was pushing these homemade Girl Power bars, saying that since fitness training was canceled they needed to make up for it with good nutrition."

"Is it canceled for good, or just before the tournament?" she asked.

"For good," I told her, my lips pressed together as if to say, *how do you like them apples?*

"Do tell," Darcy urged.

"Nothing to tell. I had to call Gunther about something, and while I had him on the line, I asked if he was just suspending fitness training or ending it altogether."

"You had to call him about something else?" Darcy asked suspiciously. "You little gossip whore," she teased.

"I did! Really. I needed to get Rachel new cleats and wanted to see if he recommended a certain brand or style."

"Oh," Darcy shrugged. "Well, does he?"

"He told me to get cleats that are comfortable and fit well."

"There's a hot tip."

"Yeah," I said. "He seems to communicate well with the girls, though. Anyway, he told me fitness training was a waste of time and that Mimi wasn't qualified to teach the girls how to use the equipment properly, blah, blah, blah."

"Really? Gosh, 'cause I heard somewhere that she played in college," Darcy said.

"Well, she didn't take very good notes because Gunther said Mimi was completely wasting their time, tiring them out for nothing. In any event, Rachel said Mimi was like June Cleaver Freakazoid, making them all eat her special high-octane cookies she baked."

"Kelly says they're quite tasty," Darcy said. "I guess when you make homemade treats, you can get pretty pushy about everyone trying them."

"I guess we should be thankful that she cares so much about their health," I said.

"Puh-lease!" Darcy snapped. "I'd believe Mother Earth over there cares about their health. Mimi cares about their performance on the soccer field. She cares about taking some sort of credit for their success. If she can't claim she made them the fittest team in Cal South, she'll say they win because of their superior nutrition."

"Who to? Who to, Violet?!" Raymond shouted.

"Get to the ball!" belted Loud Bobby. "You first, you first!"

"Savannah, you're hesitating!" Leo cried.

"You dented my new Fiat, you animal!" shouted Paulo. Or something like that. Did this guy even speak English?

"What was that?!" Mimi snapped at Cara. She was one of them now. May she pack on pounds and sprout facial hair.

The thing with club soccer parents was that they limited their public humiliation to their own kids. It was the unwritten code that no soccer dad should deny another his right to psychologically scar his own child. Still, there were plenty of mutterings. "How'd *she* make the team?" Raymond made the mistake of whispering about Tandy.

"Zip it, pal!" Dick snapped back. For a moment I was touched at Dick's loyalty. "You want to talk about sucky players, look no further than Debbie Does Defense. Or should I say *doesn't* do defense?" The group cracked up at that one.

"What about Sapphire?" said Loud Bobby.

*Shhhh, everyone can hear you!*

Nodding his head towards Gia, Bobby said, "Don't tell me Adolf didn't take that one so he can look at those tits on the sideline all season." Mercifully, Gia was reading *Cosmo* and listening to tunes through her iPod.

*Did her just refer to our coach as Adolf?*

"I think Katie's our weak link," said Mimi. "She's slow to the ball and can't finish."

"I don't even know which Katie you're talkin' about and I agree," Raymond said. "I'm not impressed with any of the Katies. And I tell you who else I don't like is Rachel. She don't do shit 'cept hog the dang ball and run it down the middle like she thinks she's bowling." The negativity was like lava flowing from Mount Vesuvius.

"Excuse me?" said Nancy. I admired her chutzpa.

"Yeah?" Dick replied, puffing out his chest, a somewhat ridiculous gesture when one's challenger is holding half of an angora scarf from a set of knitting needles.

"Did you just refer to one of the girls as a weak link?"

*Um, actually, he referred to several as weak links. Plural. And yes, both of our kids were included in that.*

"It's an expression. Don't get your panties in a wad," Dick huffed.

"My *panties* in a *wad?*"

"Also an expression."

"So is 'shut up'!" Nancy said.

*Oh. My. God! You go girl to the nth degree.*

"These are children you are talking about!" Nancy continued. "Calling any one of them a *weak link* confirms what I've long suspected of you, Dick! You are the weak link of humanity."

*Or the missing link,* I wish I had the gumption to say.

CR ∽

I was relieved that Mimi's lofty goal of having the girls play in eight tournaments over the summer didn't pan out. With family vacations and travel, parents could only come together for three weekends in the early summer: the Manchester United Memorial Day Cup in Santa Barbara, the Cooperstown Rebels' "School's Out for Summer" Cup, and the Patriots' Cup on July Fourth weekend.

As Rachel and I walked in the woods a few days before we left for Santa Barbara, I asked if she had any idea how much I loved her. She nodded, but I wanted more from the moment. "You are—"

"I know, I know, I'm all you have," Rachel said.

"No, Rachel. You're not all that I have. You're everything I have. Big difference."

"I don't really see the difference," Rachel said.

"You don't?" I asked, slightly disappointed that my daughter hadn't picked up the nuance.

"No, either way, it's like I'm it. I mean, I know you're saying it to be nice and all, but it's like I'm your basket with all the eggs in it, and what if I, um ... " Rachel groped for the words.

"Crack them?" I offered.

"Yeah! That's it. What if I crack them?"

I hardly ever told Rachel that she was everything I had. And on this occasion, she was the one who brought it up. Still, I remembered what our marriage counselor said when Steve and I would challenge each other's feelings: "Do you want to be right, or do you want to *do* right?" I wanted to do right by Rachel, so I accepted that this was her way of broaching a difficult topic with me, something I said I wanted from these walks.

"Rachel, first of all, you could never crack my eggs," I said.

"Can we drop the whole egg thing?" She laughed. "I think what you're saying is that one person can't be another person's whole world, right?" She nodded. "I bet it's a lot of pressure to feel like my happiness depends entirely on you."

"Yeah, sort of," Rachel said.

"So basically, you're telling me to get a life?"

She laughed, slightly uncomfortable with my interpretation. "Sort of."

I sighed like an exasperated teen. "Okay, if I have to."

Rachel giggled. "I love you, too."

 C&80

After several delays, Beadorable! finally opened its doors, which Rachel was more excited about than I. "Look, it's open, Mom! Let's go in! We can finally start beading again." I smiled because she'd never strung a bead in her life except for the big plastic ones they give kids in preschool. Nonetheless, I decided not to set her straight, and let her enjoy our imaginary shared history. I had to admit, it was exhilarating once we got inside and started looking through the precious stones and divider beads in so many different patterns. We could do fun and trendy pieces with rhinestone-trimmed dividers and chunky hammered silver, or more understated and elegant necklaces. It was when I approached the charm display that I knew what our first project together would be. Under the glass tabletop were delicate little silver soccer balls. We bought fifteen of them, along with different beads to reflect the personality of each member of the team. For Kelly, we bought pink, soft-shell pearls and tiny silver dividers. For Deborah, we bought unfinished crystals and black stones that looked like we might have found them on a hike. We got Cara beautiful blown-glass beads with different funky patterns on each separated by clear glass and silver discs. And guess what we got for precious Sapphire.

Rachel and I spent more than two hours picking beads for the team, and I wound up signing a MasterCard receipt promising to pay more than $300 for the beads and all of my new supplies like silver wire, crimping tools and a cutter. Oh well, I shrugged. I have money and this is what it's for.

For the next two nights, Rachel and stayed up late chatting, stringing beads at the kitchen table. She couldn't wait to give her gifts to her teammates after they finished their first tournament.

CR ∞

Before we hit the road for Rachel's first soccer tournament, we attended a different tournament of sorts. It was the Suburban Mothers Classic. It was billed as a party—a light-sounding "spring fling" at that—but make no mistake, this was the championship round in the battle of the moms.

As Rachel and I walked through the Johansen home, we passed a gauntlet of awards, framed certificates, and blue ribbons awarding Jinx for being the best mother ever. Of course, there were also the more subtle trophies like the framed photos with famous people and in front of well-known landmarks. Jinx definitely won the best-traveled family award, as I noticed shots of her in front of the pyramids, the Eiffel Tower and the Great Wall of China. We made our way to the backyard, where the first things I noticed were her topiary designs. There were bushes shaped like elephants, giraffes, and a gorilla. It looked like the entrance to the San Diego Zoo.

I expected the kids to run off on their own, but was surprised by the gender segregation. The men stood holding beer bottles, shifting their weight and nodding their heads as they engaged in sparse conversation about sports scores and home improvements. The women sat in tight clusters from which treble-clef laughter burst out in fits. At the center of the biggest congregation of estrogen was Mimi, regaling the group with a story about how Marla Bennett hired a show-and-tell coach for her first grader. "I am *not* making this up!" she defended against a playful accusation of exaggerating. "We were at the class publishing party when Marla gets up and starts making these crazy signals at Keiffer." Mimi then started imitating the woman wearing a painfully anxious expression, moving a rigid hand beside her head. "So I said to her, what in heaven's sake are you doing, loser?"

"You did not!" several mothers challenged, laughing.

"No, but that was my intonation. I asked what she was doing and she told me that she hired a show-and-tell coach for Keiffer to help him with volume, and get this, elocution." The group burst into laughter.

Jinx joined in as I passed the group and made my way to the snack table. "I can confirm this. Marla told me that when Keiffer got a 'good' on oral skills on his report card, she woke up in cold sweats with nightmares about her boy giving a presentation on his endocrinology research, but no one could hear him because he was mumbling."

"His endocrinology research?" a mom squealed.

"In twenty years," Jinx explained.

The group roared again. Jinx turned and saw me. "Oh, Claire. I'm glad you made it!" I was rather surprised when I received the invitation to her annual farewell to spring party, but Rachel insisted that we attend on the grounds that anyone who's anyone would be at the Johansen Spring Fling. Jinx reached her arm out and motioned for me to join the women. "Do you know everyone? You know Mimi, of course." We both smiled perfunctorily. "This is Kerrie, Gwenny, Olivia, Libby, Julia, and Wendy." The time passed pleasantly enough, though I really wanted to get home, put on some comfy clothes and climb into bed with a good book. Sometimes making conversation can be such work when I don't know people well.

I watched Ron from the corner of my eye. I wanted to see if I still quivered when I saw him, and I was very sorry to find that my knees did, in fact, shake at the sight of Darcy's husband. How could this be? I adored Darcy and would never do anything to hurt her. I also found Ron to be a jerk. So what gave? As I pondered the attraction, Mimi broke ranks with the moms and approached Ron. "You didn't text me back," she said playfully, but was clearly annoyed.

Ron's eyes shot around the garden as I began nodding absently at the story Libby was telling the group. "I was in surgery," he explained.

"I texted three days ago," Mimi said. "That's not very—"The gaggle of women began laughing at Libby's story. I joined in, though I hoped the laughter would stop soon because I wanted to hear the rest of what Mimi was saying. This Libby person better not be a real card.

"—now," Ron told Mimi. "What's so important?"

"If you don't care about Kelly's—"

The group of women burst into laughter again. "Oh my God, Libby, you are too hilarious!" Wendy cried. *My sentiments exactly!*

"—the manager, you'll handle it," Ron said. "No one ever gets over on you, Meem."

Mimi purred a laugh. "You are such a—"

"Lib-by!" shouted Darcy as she laughed hysterically. "There is no way this could have happened! I mean, it's a funny story, but come on, you're making it up! Claire, you don't buy this story, do you?" I looked at her and shook my head. "See, Libby, this never could've happened. Claire, what's the most you'd pay for that?"

"Me?" I stammered. They all looked expectantly. "Not much."

"Come on, Claire, give us a number. What's the most you'd ever pay for that?"

"Oh, um," I stammered. "Sure as hell not as much as Libby did."

With that the group exploded into laughter.

Wendy invited me to join the group for their next girls' night out. "We need someone like you to keep Libby in check," she said, winking at her pal. It was the single most successful social interaction I'd had since moving to Santa Bella, and I had no idea what I'd said.

Before Rachel and I left, Jinx said she wanted to have a word with me alone. Finally, her agenda would be revealed. We sat under a white canvas umbrella with sweating glasses of iced tea on a table before us. "I want to apologize for the way I acted that day at Party City," she began. "I was the worst kind of nasty and I really regret how I acted. Do you think you can forgive me?"

"Okay," I said. "It was a stressful time for everyone."

"Tell me about it. Sissy was just cut, so I was freaking out, but now that I have a little distance, I'm back to my old self again."

"I hear you," I said. "Been there, came back." I extended my hand and we shook.

"So how's it going on Gunther's dream team?" Jinx asked. "I hear he's thinking about dumping a few of the girls before the regular season starts."

"Really?! Can he do that?" *Not Rachel, not Rachel, please not Rachel!* "I hadn't heard that."

"Oh, probably just rumors. I mustn't get my hopes up."

"Oh," I said, squirming.

"I mean, of course Rachel's safe. I'm sure she's doing beautifully, right?"

"I guess so."

"Well, Gunther can make player changes anytime before the regular season starts, so Rachel will have all summer to shine. I'm sure her spot is secure."

"Oh, gee, thanks," I replied, looking around to see the crowd thinning. "How's Sissy doing? Is she enjoying her new team?"

Jinx leaned in conspiratorially. "No one was more upset than I was about Sissy being cut from the top team, but I have to tell you, it's been a real blessing. Sissy is a star! She's becoming so confident on the field. I have a feeling you may be seeing her again very soon, if you know what I mean. Gunther's been visiting our scrimmages, and I can see he's impressed with Sissy's progress."

"That's great," I faked. If Gunther was considering taking Sissy back on the team, would he then have to drop a girl from the existing roster?

"It would be wonderful. You never know what will happen. The Lord works in mysterious ways."

*God is involved in kids' soccer now? I thought he only answered the prayers of NFL players.*

Jinx's young son, McKendrick, ran up to us and started a panicked series of questions. The mother inhaled deeply to remind McKendrick to do this himself. "Calm down, count backwards and let's get to your peaceful place," she sang.

"We're gonna win the food drive this year, right, Mom?" he asked, breathing like he'd just finished a marathon—under water.

"Of course we are," she replied, Stepfordesque. Turning to me, Jinx explained, "Our Lady of Forgiveness has a food drive every year, and the class that brings in the most food wins a pizza party."

"Wrangler says his mom's bringing six hundred packages of Ramen noodles this year," McKendrick reported.

Jinx's back straightened in alarm. "Why would he say that? Did you tell him I plan to bring five hundred?" His eyes welled with tears and he nodded affirmatively. "McKendrick, I *told* you not to talk about how much food I'm bringing. The last thing I need is some crazy mother trying to outdo me."

"I'm sorry," he burst into tears.

Jinx hugged her son and in a moment of sheer maternal beauty, she added, "You're forgiven, but I hope you've learned a lesson from this. Mommy has a strategy. I bring in the food on the last hour of the last day when no one can run out and buy more." Turning to me, "Because believe me they would. Ramen noodles are a dime each at Costco." Directing her attention back to her fragile offspring, Jinx concluded, "McKendrick, you did the right thing by telling Mommy. I'll buy some more noodles on Monday, but *do not breathe a word of this, do you hear me?*"

"Okay," he sniffed, wiping his nose with his hand. "Now the poor people will get even more food!"

Handing him a napkin, Jinx asked, "What poor people?"

"I think the school probably gives the food to poor people," I told Jinx.

"Right, of course!"

"Thanks, Mommy. You're the best."

Smiling placidly, as if she were delivering the final line of a 1950s sitcom, Jinx said, "We're all the best in our own special way, McKendrick."

# Chapter Nineteen

Memorial Day weekend finally arrived and Rachel's team was ready for its first tournament. At least I thought they were ready, but the consensus among the malcontents was that we were prepared only for complete annihilation. Mimi told the four angry fathers that she'd try to do something to help the girls. I sincerely hoped it wouldn't be hiking up her pigtails and putting on a Kix jersey. I mean, she looked great for a thirty-five-year-old, but there was no way she'd pass for twelve. Her actions certainly were those of a spoiled adolescent, but like the rest of us, the years had chiseled their way onto Mimi's face.

As we pulled into the Crowne Plaza hotel in Santa Barbara, we saw dozens of minivans with team names painted on the back windows. "How totally exciting is this?! Rachel exclaimed, grabbing Kelly's arm. I volunteered to drive Kelly the night before so Darcy wouldn't have to schlep her whole crew for an overnight stay. I couldn't imagine how starting her day on the road at 5:30 a.m. was any easier, but she said it was. I figured since we had to spend Saturday and possibly Sunday night, we may as well make the hotel room our new home for a stint.

When we checked in, the man at the front desk seemed on edge. "It's like kid city here tonight," he said to no one. "Super planning, Pete." He shook his head and began tapping his keyboard. I guess he didn't like children.

"This is so awesome!" Rachel said to Kelly, ignoring the snub. A team of older girls from Turf walked through the sliding glass door in perfect cadence. In their red nylon sweat suits and soccer backpacks, they looked like a force to be reckoned with. As they passed, we all read the backs of their nylon jackets: *Turf Soccer Club—California State Champions.* "They won—" Rachel paused as if the words were too powerful for her to handle.

Kelly nodded her head, slowly, reverently affirming. "State Cup."

The next words I heard were from both girls, though I couldn't tell who was saying what. It sounded something like, "Oh my God ... so cool ... we could do it ... so awesome ... amazing!" Even I got a little giddy before realizing that a woman my age being impressed with a pack of teens was quite pathetic.

As the verbal popcorn settled, Rachel spoke again. "This is already the best weekend of my life!"

"This is nothing," the worldly Kelly advised. "Manchester puts on a ginormous carnival at the tournament, with a bungee trampoline thingy and a bazillion other cool things. It's seriously better than our county fair."

CR ∞

As it turned out, the live entertainment began long before we arrived at the tournament site. That evening, as we headed out for dinner, the hotel lobby transformed into a movie set—the kind of movie you don't take your fifth grader to see. Strutting past us was a frightful-looking geezer in black leather, from his Village People cap to his open-toe sandals. (And he *did* have yellow helmet toenails!) From each arm dangled a shop-worn woman who looked older than her age. I finally understood what my mother meant when she said that it wasn't the years, but the miles that took their greatest toll on a woman's looks. These over-processed blondes were frequent fliers who likely retired as Reno casino waitresses – in 1982. My eyes were immediately drawn to Lefty's tummy folds, which were clearly visible through her sheer burgundy dress. Righty flashed "muffin top" between her too-short leopard-print top and too-low matching leggings. Trailer Park Hefner in the center looked like the happiest old bird in the world, strutting with a bounce in his step that would make one think he had springs on his feet.

Following close behind was a full team that looked like it was also playing in the tournament of the skanks. Four men with bad teeth and stringy hair led in an assortment of bimbos, one more frightening than the next. The youngest one had choppy black hair reminiscent of Joan Jett, with facial piercings and a spiked dog collar around her neck. Two were going for the ethereal Wella Balsam girl look with long flowing hair and peasant skirts topping braless Grateful Dead t-shirts. One had no shoes and the dirtiest feet I'd ever seen. The last girl was definitely in character as a tight-laced librarian with watermelon-sized breasts brimming out of navy blue sweater set. A pearl chain held her reading glasses. Our actual librarian in Santa Bella had a *Friends* blowout, so this tramp's look was in dire need of a little updating. (As did our librarian's hair.)

Like waves in a storm, groups of sexed-up-looking characters kept coming into the hotel lobby, greeting each other with extremely friendly kisses. One guy who looked like Crocodile Dundee walked in shouting greetings to his "mates," went straight over to a silicone-enhanced playmate, grabbed her by the waist and nuzzled his head in her cleavage, while groaning with delight.

"Okay, let's get dinner!" I said to the girls.

"Oh my God, that lady's not wearing underwear!" Kelly whispered.

"Kelly," I said in my maternal scolding voice, "Don't be ridiculous!" *That's no lady!*

"No, Mom, she's right!" said Rachel.

"Hee haw!" a man shouted as a redhead entered with a boa constrictor around her neck.

"Don't be jealous, boys!" she shouted. *Do these people have any volume control?*

"Rachel, I'm sure the woman is wearing underwear in public!" I reassured them.

"Mom, look!"

I followed Rachel's eyes, which were bulging out of her head. Her neck showed every vein. Sure enough, I saw a woman whose baguette breasts and ass-tattoo showed plain as day through her dress. Honestly, I'd seen pantyhose that gave better coverage than that hideous nylon tube.

"Oh ma' goodness, won't you jest look what the cat dragged in?!" screeched a woman in a Naughty Dorothy costume, complete with a basket for Toto. Her shoulders were permanently shrugged, which made her look as though she had no neck.

"Man, you look good enough t'eat, sister!" a guy with a turquoise bolero told her.

This snapped me out of my state of agape paralysis. "Okay, girls, we need to get moving."

The congregation was now at about thirty with no sign of moving from the lobby. Dundee, the boob nuzzler, had "greeted" a half-dozen women, many of whom rubbed his limited hair around while he growled with delight.

"These people are gross!" Kelly said.

"Yeah, people in Santa Barbara are way ugly," Rachel added.

"Guys, they're not *from* Santa Barbara," I explained. "They're just visiting, like us."

This solicited a collective groan of protest. "Okay, not like us, but this is not a Santa Barbara thing. They're from all over, I'm sure."

As we walked through the doors, I saw a woman with a brown Dutch boy haircut and passel of seven-year-old girls in soccer team jackets. Before I could think of what to say, I held out my hand to stop her entrance. "No, no, no," I said. "You can't go in there."

She placed her hand on her hip and gave me an annoyed look. *Cute bracelet! No, Claire, focus.*

She huffed. "Let the bullying begin, I guess."

I laughed nervously. "Sorry, that didn't come out the way I meant it." I extended my hand to shake hers, and gestured her to lean in closer. "There's a swingers' convention in there," I whispered.

She raised her eyebrow. I nodded to confirm. "And they're staying at *this* hotel? I can't believe it. Does the hotel know?"

I looked at her sheepishly. "I think the guy just figured it out while checking us in."

"Are they going to do anything about it?" she said, a bit snappier than I thought necessary.

As if on cue, a glow-in-the-dark electric-pink school bus with the words "Hello, Kitty!" painted in metallic red pulled up to the entrance of the hotel. We all stood silently as the bus sighed and opened its doors. One by one, women who could have only been prostitutes flowed out of the bus to club music playing on a boom box. They all had different costumes with an ultra-slutty accent, like the cheerleader whose skirt was so short that her butt cheeks peeked out from the bottom, the naughty nurse whose red lacy bra was quite visible under her low-cut white uniform, and the dominatrix with a Cleopatra bob cut in black vinyl fishnets. There were kinky Girl Scouts with banners across their green uniforms that offered "Cookies?" There were cops with black leather shorts and boots, military hotties with ammo packs (of condoms) and a train conductor who held a suspiciously phallic whistle with "All Aboard" printed in neon pink. There were a dozen vacant-looking blondes who simply stared straight ahead, grinning placidly as they made their way down the steps. Following the zombie line, three burly men wearing dark sunglasses and headsets got off the bus and stood by the door with their arms folded over their Bluto chests. This was the porn version of the Secret Service. Last off was a platinum blonde twentysomething wearing red patent leather thigh-high boots and a pink marabou bikini.

"I have a Barbie like that," I heard a young soccer player whisper to her teammate.

"Yeah, she's pretty."

Porn Barbie raised her red-gloved hands in the air and screeched, "Special fucking delivery!"

"Okay, girls, we're going to check in at the Ramada," the woman said, hurrying her girls back to their van.

Rachel, Kelly and I followed. When we got to my minivan, Mimi pulled in to the spot next to us. "Hey Claire, you managed to find the place," she said. Directing her comments to the girls, she said, "Ready to whip some butt tomorrow?"

*Gee, Mimi, if you're really in the mood for butt whipping, you needn't wait till tomorrow.*

The girls said they were. Mimi asked, "Did you bring your swimsuits? I find a good swim so relaxing right before bed. Helps me get my best rest."

"Um, I think they may be having a, um, party at the pool tonight," I said, imagining the Plato's Retreat these people would turn the place into.

"Nonsense!" Mimi snapped. "When I made the reservations, I specifically told them that I need a facility with a heated swimming pool for my nightly laps, and they said it would be no problem. I don't care about some party, as long as they set off a lane for me."

My face cringed as I imagined the layer of oil that would sit on top of the water. I wondered if Chlamydia could travel through a swimming pool. I know the chlorine would kill a normal STD, but these folks probably have the super-resistant strains. "Have it your way," I said to Mimi.

Smiling brightly and winking at the girls, Mimi said, "I always do."

CR SO

It's amazing how thirty minutes and a change of scenery can transport you into an entirely different universe. We had returned to a place of innocence as we sat in Dairy Queen's orange vinyl chairs eating our Blizzards. Kelly looked at our match lineup in the tournament program that the check-in guy gave us at the hotel and shrugged. "Hmm, we've never played any of these teams before," she said. "I have zero info on them. Hmm, I wonder why we're playing Manchester's green team."

"Their green team?" Rachel asked. "Is that their B-team?"

"More like their C-team," Kelly said, scrunching her face. "At least that's how their colors have been in the past. Maybe they changed it or something." She shrugged again.

"So, can we ask you a sort of weird question?" Rachel asked me.

*Oh no, don't ask about our fellow hotel mates.* I had already dialed every hotel in town in a fruitless attempt to find another room. "Sure," I answered tentatively.

"What are swingers?" Rachel asked.

"Where did you hear that term?"

"You whispered it to that other team mom."

"It's, um, well, swingers are people, who, um. Well, when people get married they make a promise that they'll only dance with their husband or wife, but swingers make a different arrangement. They agree that it's okay to change dance partners throughout the evening."

"Oh, like square dancing?!" Kelly said.

"Sort of," I said, gulping. *But naked.*

### ‍ ‍ ‍ CR SO

Kelly Greer was right. The Manchester United Memorial Day Classic rivaled any county fair. Still, I had no idea one soccer tournament could be such a production. I stood at the entrance, awestruck by what was before me. As Kelly promised, there was a four-person bungee jump atop a trampoline, but there were also endless rows of games, food and merchandise. I could even have my blood pressure taken at a tent set up by a local hospital.

"Mimi said to meet her at the registration table," Darcy said, adjusting her visor to better shield the blinding sun as we walked. A seasoned soccer mom, she packed a rolling cooler with snacks and ice-cold washcloths for the girls to use during halftime. Ron kept trying to strike up a conversation in his usual chummy style, and I kept trying to demonstrate my casual indifference. Of course, devising a strategy to show how little I care proved the opposite, but only I had to know that.

We passed more families than we might see during peak season at Disney World. Well, maybe not quite that many, but it was packed. "How many teams are playing in this thing?" I asked Ron. *See, zero self-consciousness!*

"I dunno, a couple hundred, wouldn't you say, hon?"

*I just said that I didn't know. That's why I'm asking. Oh, right, hon meaning Darcy. Okay, no problem.*

"I'd say two hundred, maybe two-fifty," Darcy replied, staring absently onto a game field. "Come on, Ronnie, no dawdling." I thought the seven-year-old was remarkably well-behaved considering we'd just passed a booth where three guys with their shaved heads painted like soccer balls were juggling happy-face hacky sacks. Moments before, we had passed by cotton candy, hand-dipped ice cream, and a vitamin salesman. Granted, no self-respecting kid gives a hoot about dried wheatgrass tablets, but the guy held a green flower pinwheel and sang a cute little song about body parts working at "optimal performance." It was a bit hard even for me to stay focused walking past all of the displays.

When we finally reached the registration booth, Mimi purposefully looked at her watch, but thankfully directed her scolding at Ron and Darcy. She smiled broadly and wagged her finger, teasing. "I expect more from you old veterans," she said, winking at Ron. "Is our new mom a bad influence on you?" It was one of those things I dared not comment on, lest I be accused of lacking a sense of humor. "I need my players here an hour before kickoff, not forty-five minutes, not forty minutes."

*Her players?* I looked around for Gunther, but he was nowhere to be seen. As I scanned the group, I saw new faces I hadn't seen at practice. I'd almost forgotten that Tandy and Mariah had parents of their own. Two Katies had fathers; the other one had two moms, and Crazy Raymond found someone crazy enough to marry him. Crunchy Nancy brought a surprisingly corporate-looking husband and grandparents so stiff they looked like they belonged on coins. Paulo was in head-to-toe biking regalia, which made me wonder if he'd been out riding already so early on this sticky morning. His mother wore a full-length black skirt with a long-sleeved top that was slightly more oppressive than the rosary beads that hung from her neck. She reminded me of the old woman on the black-and-white personality tests—the one that could look like a big-nosed old woman with a babushka on her head or a young maiden wearing a feather cap.

"Okay parents, it looks like Gunther's going to be late *again*, so I need to take the reins here," Mimi said. *Again? Wasn't this our first game? Ten bucks says she told him the wrong time.* The girls and parents gathered around Mimi, who told us how "very proud" she was of *her* girls. "Girl power is all about supporting each other in our quest for excellence," she said. *Quest for excellence?* "I want everyone to remember our first tournament together, so I bought all the girls a little token of my deep admiration." Mimi began handing the girls small velvet pouches and waited expectantly as they opened them. "You know you're not allowed to wear jewelry on the field, so I need you to ask your parents to hold these."

One by one, out they came: silver necklaces with a "Girl Power" charm hanging in the center. Rachel's lips tightened and she looked at me unhappily. I shook my head, as if to tell her it was just a case of bad timing. "She didn't do it on purpose," I said as our group started walking toward the field.

"Duh, yeah she did," Kelly answered back.

"Do not talk that way to Claire!" Darcy scolded her daughter. "I am sure Mimi didn't mean to upstage Claire and Rachel. She didn't even know they were making necklaces for the team."

"Yeah she did," Kelly said. "Rachel told her about them when we were at her house doing homework. She totally stole the idea!" Kelly Greer's facial expressions were so much like her father's, I couldn't help simultaneously loathe and adore them. Ron walked and listened intently, his emerald green eyes translucent in the morning sunlight. I loved his unshaven weekend look with the ultra soft thick grey cotton t-shirt hanging loosely over his broad chest. And the way those jeans fit on his—pimply ass, focus on the pus-filled zits on his ass and the yellow helmet toenails capping his smelly feet! "She knew once she gave us necklaces, Rachel wouldn't be able to."

Darcy and I shot each other a look as if to say, *Let's toast this bitch later.*

"Says who?" I said in a maternal tone. "Who says the girls can't get two gifts this weekend?"

"Two necklaces?!"

"Rachel, I'm sure she had planned her gift long before you told her about yours."

Kelly snapped, "Then why didn't she say something when Rachel mentioned it?!" I looked at Darcy's daughter and realized that this was going to be my child's guide into a new age. "Seriously, do you guys really believe that Mimi didn't do this to be mean? I can't believe you people are the ones in charge of teaching us about how the world works." I sighed and looked at my future. It was a four-foot-eleven-inch freckle-faced kid with braces on her teeth. One who knew she was right and didn't second-guess it.

Darcy joined in. "I think what Claire is trying to say, girls, is that we should give Mimi the benefit of the doubt."

Part of me liked Darcy's parent-approved script, but another part wanted to give Kelly credit for seeing through Mimi's façade of girl power. I wondered what would happen if I replied, "You know, Kelly, you're right. Mimi is a bitch for what she did. Good for you for sniffing it out. That'll serve you well in life."

I almost said it when Darcy piped in with, "Mimi does a lot for you girls. Let's assume her intentions were good."

I started moving slower, weighed down by the sadness that comes from lying. This twelve-year-old cynic was right about Mimi, yet her mother and I basically told her not to trust her instincts. After a few minutes of silence, I inhaled deeply and said, "Maybe Kelly's right." Darcy, Ron, Kelly, and Rachel all looked at me in disbelief. (Ronnie couldn't have cared less what I was talking about.) "Yeah, if you say Mimi gave the girls gifts to upstage Rachel, maybe you're right. Maybe this was her pathetic way of asserting her dominance." I almost added the politically correct spin that she must feel insecure about her place in the world and blah blah blah, but I didn't have the energy. Part of it was that I didn't want to spew half-baked psycho-babble this early in the morning. The other part was pure pettiness. I didn't mind taking this bitch down a few notches in Rachel's and Kelly's esteem.

"Damned right I'm right," Kelly said. "I will say this, though. She makes awesome snacks when we're there for homework. These Girl Power bars are like baked in heaven or something."

"Well, that's positive!" Darcy said.

*Wait just a second here! What happened?* If I listed every one of Mimi's redeemable traits, I would have gotten nothing but sarcasm from Kelly. These damn kids were just plain contrary!

# Chapter Twenty

When we arrived at the field, Mimi hurried the girls into a circle where they passed the ball among themselves. Mimi wore a Nike headband and her official Kix manager's shirt, though I'm sure it killed her to wear the loose-fitting design. Everything I'd seen her in to date looked like it had been applied with a paint brush. She looked at her watch and scanned the field, pursing her lips and shaking her head. *She probably gave poor Gunther directions to another part of the state.*

A group of us unfolded our chairs and placed them behind the sideline where another bunch of parents were watching their boys play. Dick cracked open a can of beer wrapped in a red foam jacket, then reached into his cooler and distributed drinks to Crazy Raymond, Loud Bobby and Gangsta Leo. I understood that Leo shaved his head to keep him cooler in this smoldering heat, but couldn't understand why he chose summer as his time to grow a devil beard. Bobby was sunburned to the point where he looked like an angry tomato with all of his skin pulling toward the center of his face at his pug nose. Crazy Raymond's summer look was that of an ancient torture device. Rather than having cornrows sitting neatly against his head, his hair was twisted into dozens of short spikes. If we were friends, I might joke about playing a game of ring toss with his new do, but I dared not offend him any further than I unwittingly had already.

A ruler-straight line of girls dressed in Manchester green uniforms ran in perfect synchronicity to an area right beside the field. My God, these girls had better timing than the Rockettes. A coach with a thick English accent (though I'm not sure he was actually English) commanded the girls to "stop, drop, and give us ten." Our girls stood agape as the Manchester team loudly counted their perfectly timed push-ups. A little showy, I thought.

"What the heck is this?" I asked Darcy, who was nonchalantly looking in her bag.

"Pre-game head games," she answered. "Did you bring extra sunscreen?"

Handing her my sunblock, I asked her what she meant. "You know, the psychological warfare and intimidation that goes on before the games."

"Is this normal?" I asked.

"Claire, get used to it. Nothing's normal in competitive soccer."

I gulped at the sight of Ron's arms flexing as he planted an umbrella into the grass. "Don't do that now! We're gonna have to move it in ten minutes when the boys' game is over," Darcy said to Ron.

"So, I'll move it. What do you care?" he shot.

The Manchester team was now running around the periphery of the field in lock step. It was amazingly machine-like. "If these girls are this in tune with each other during warm-ups, what must they be like on the field?" I wondered.

"It's all showmanship, Claire," Ron told me. "Doesn't make any difference in how they play. They probably suck if this is what they spend their time working on."

Then an unfamiliar male voice added, "If they could balance the balls on their noses, that'd be different. Those are the really good teams." Darcy, Ron and a few others turned around and gave a collective greeting.

"Hey buddy," Ron said, grabbing hands and slapping backs. "Long time no see. How's it going?"

"It's going," the man said. He had an open, kind face that was handsome and humble with chiseled features and a neat patch of brown hair combed to the side. He looked at me and smiled.

"Hey, Dave, do you know Claire?" Ron asked. "Claire's our new halfback's mother." *Ah yes, just how every woman wants to be described.* "Dave is Katie's father."

Dave smiled as we shook hands and I sensed a glimmer of attraction between us, though I immediately reminded myself that if he was Katie's father, he was either Jessica's or straight Jennifer's husband. I put on my most professional voice and asked if his daughter was Katie the halfback, fullback or forward, impressed with my new vocabulary. "Katie Engle," he said. The fullback. Ah ha, so he was Jessica's husband. "Mind if I sit with you guys?" he asked, directing the question toward Ron.

"Jessica's over there," I told him, pointing to her, then shouting her name and waving.

She smiled and walked over to us. "Hey Dave," Jessica said, leaning in to kiss him on the cheek. "How's it going?"

*How's it going? Ahhhh, they were an amicably divorced couple. Jackpot!*

A silver-haired guy followed suit and came over to say hello. "Hi Dave."

"Hey Sam. You're looking well," Dave said.

*So civilized.*

Jessica asked what time Dave planned to return Katie on Monday, because she and Sam had a party to go to. As they hammered out the details, I turned to watch the boys' team wrap up their game and grinned. Darcy caught me and smiled back. Thankfully, she had the good sense not to say anything until later.

"There you are!" Mimi said to Gunther as he ambled onto the field, looking lost. "Nice of you to show up."

"We will talk about this after game," Gunther said, annoyed. I wondered if she told him to go to the wrong field or gave him the wrong kickoff time. Perhaps Mimi was infinitely more creative. I laughed at the vision of our coach handcuffed to the hotel bed headboard being whipped by a dominatrix that Mimi had hired.

"We'll have to," she snapped, looking at her watch.

ᘓ ᘔ

When the referee's whistle sounded for the girls' game, it was like the start of a horse race. Everyone leaned forward and several of the parents began rooting for their daughters. "Come on, Savannah, work the channel, *sivious*, work that channel," Leo said as a quiet woman with long black hair and humongous hoop earrings sat beside him. Every parent had a suggestion for the players.

"Look left!" one would shout.

"Find feet," said another.

"You've got time."

"Space!"

"One move and go!"

"Turn and burn."

"See Kelly, see Kelly right."

Then in the loudest voice I'd ever heard—louder than Bobby's even—Crazy Raymond started shouting, "No mercy!"

Repeatedly. It was a hoarse, drawn-out command that sounded like a general leading his troops into battle. Spit flew from his lips and he cried, "Nooooo mer-saaaaay!"

Gunther turned to Mimi and said, "I need them quiet!"

"You need to coach this game, Gunther!" she snapped. He was a rather hands-off coach, but he may have just been inhibited by all of the parental noise.

"I have train them in practicing. They know what to do at game. The shouting is no good," Gunther said.

Dave looked at me and raised his brows. "Whaddya think? Gunther one, Mimi zero?"

"I'd say she's less than zero," I said, smiling.

"Ah, an Elvis Costello fan?" Dave replied.

"More like a fan of anyone arguing with Mimi."

"I see Mimi's still picking on the pretty moms," Dave said.

*Two points for you, Dave!*

I smiled. "She's really got it out for me."

"I can see why," he said. Dave shook his nonexistent long hair and pouted his lips. "Don't hate me because I'm beautiful."

"Will you stop?!" I said, more than a little embarrassed.

I leaned my elbows onto my knees and continued watching the game as the girls skillfully passed the ball. Every pass made it to the player it was intended for. Girls looked around and planned their next move, accounting for the others on the field, moving the ball as if it were an extension of their own body. It looked like connect-the-dots rather than a swarm of bees buzzing around a hive. *So this is what soccer is supposed to look like.*

"Exciting, isn't it?" Dave asked. Darcy was smirking, trying to act as if she didn't notice the flirtation. Ron looked less amused.

"Very," I said. I liked the context of this interaction because I could keep my eyes fixed on the game, Rachel in particular.

She looked okay, but not her usual stellar self. It was almost as though she didn't know how to act when she had an entire team of competent players with her—and opposing her. Several times she should have passed the ball to an open teammate, but tried to make a move and go around a defender. These fullbacks were not falling on their butts. They snatched the ball away from her and regained possession.

"Pass the ball, Rachel!" Dick shouted, annoyed at her mistake. "That kid's a ball hog, man," he muttered to Crazy Raymond.

"Cracker's girl?" he asked. Dick nodded. Distracted by Katie's interception, he shouted, "That's right, girl. Work the channel."

Then the Italian started. Paulo shouted a series of instructions to Giovanna, who held the most intense expression on her face, her tongue clinging to the bottom corner of her lip. She dribbled with the ball until she passed the midline of the field, made a move that faked out the Manchester player, then released the ball before another player tried to strip her of it. Violet ran down the right channel of the field, then passed it to Kelly. My heart raced. Kelly looked as if she was going to shoot the ball, then quickly passed it to Violet who was now directly in front of the net. "Nooooo mer-saaaaay!" shouted Raymond as his daughter released a shot that went straight into the goalie's arms.

"What was that?!" Raymond screamed and his wife tried to quiet him. He paced the sidelines, sweating and flicking his hands as if he was trying to get paint off of them. "Why don't ya pick it up and *bring* it to her next time?! Maybe you want to wrap it up and put a bow on it? Girl, this ain't a birthday party, no gifts, no gifts!"

Paulo's mother started shaking her head and making a *tsk, tsk noise*. She said something to her son in Italian and he replied in kind. I had hoped it translated to, "Mama Mia, this man needs to settle down," with Paulo replying, "I know, Mama, these American parents are crazy." But in my short time in club soccer I came to expect less of people. She probably really said, "Stupid girl should shoot to the corners." Her son likely replied, "Americans know nothing about this game."

"No problems," Gunther told Violet. She smiled crookedly, as if to say, *You try going home with this freak tonight and you'll see that I DO have problems.*

Mimi chimed in. "Nice try, sweetheart. Not right to the keeper, next time, okay?"

*Gee, y'think?*

"Shoot it like you want it next time!" Crazy Raymond shouted.

Much to my surprise, Loud Bobby shouted, "Nice catch, Keep!"

I looked at Dave, who explained, "Everyone loves the goalkeeper, no matter what team they're rooting for."

"Good job, goalie!" I shouted.

Mimi turned around so quickly, she created a breeze. "Claire, sideline coaching is not cool," she snapped. "You're not in rec anymore."

I couldn't help laughing at the absurdity. Ron came to my defense. "Come on, Mimi. Have a little mer-saaaay on poor Claire."

Darcy giggled and nudged him.

Mimi narrowed her eyes at Ron, then turned her attention toward me. "Rachel needs to learn when to pass the ball," she snapped. "Who's she training with?"

"Training with?" I repeated, noticing the other parents start to look at us.

Repeating herself slowly for the benefit of my dim wits, Mimi said, "Yeah, *training with,* as in working with outside of regular soccer practices."

My heart pounded like the drum section of a virgin sacrifice. *Stay cool, stay cool.* "Gee, Mimi, that would be *you.*"

A collective laugh released from the sidelines. And one of the moms let out a "You go, girl." Though when Mimi turned to see who lent me support, they all acted like they weren't looking.

Walking close to me, hovering over my seat, Mimi growled, "Claire, trust me when I tell you that you do not want to be on my bad side."

*Okay! You're right. I'm sorry.* Instead of letting these internal thoughts escape from my lips, I stood to meet her gaze. "Really? Am I on your good side right now, Mimi? Because frankly a change of scenery would be quite nice."

Ron guffawed at this one, which gave the others permission to laugh aloud. She stormed away after telling me that she'd deal with me later. Ron shouted after her, "Come on, Mimi, lighten up!"

While the parents were embroiled in our drama, the girls moved the ball down the field and penetrated the other team's eighteen-yard box. (That's the area that's eighteen yards from the goal line. It's the outermost white lines. The little box around the goal net is called "the six," Dave explained. Ignorance had its benefits.) Like last time, Violet passed the ball to Kelly, who passed it back to her when she repositioned herself in front of the goal. "Noooooo mer-saaaaay!" shouted Raymond. This time, though, she shot it straight into the left corner of the net.

We all rose to our feet and I refrained from shouting, "No mercy!" The referee held his hands in the air and blew his whistle to indicate a goal.

"That is what I'm talkin' 'bout, girl!" Crazy Raymond said, shaking his head rabidly. "That's my girl. That's *my* girl!"

Bobby and Leo started shaking Ray's hands to congratulate him. "Nice job, man," Dick said.

I smiled at Dave and wondered aloud, "What did *he* do?"

"Living through your kids is one of the few socially acceptable forms of narcissism," he said.

*I could definitely like this guy.*

CR SO

During halftime, someone from the other team let his puppy run around on the field chasing a ball. The ball was the same size as the little guy, so his clumsy wrestling was utterly charming. Until he began humping the ball, that is.

By the middle of the second half, our girls were ahead by four goals and it looked as if we were headed toward a shutout. One might think that this would have a calming effect on parents, but the fat four continued shouting as if they were trapped in a burning building and all exits were blocked.

"Nooooo mer-saaaaay!" shouted Crazy Raymond as Kelly shot the team's fifth goal.

Later in the game, Manchester scored a goal, but Dick started screaming, "Offsides! That's offsides, ref, no goal!"

Dave looked at me and smiled. "Ron cracks me up, but if he keeps that up, one of these nut jobs is going to blow a gasket one of these days."

"What?" I asked.

"You haven't noticed?" Dave asked. I shook my head. "Keep an eye on Ron."

*Oh no, I don't think you understand what very bad advice that is.*

As the game continued, I saw that Ron was pacing behind Dick, provoking him by softly muttering things like, "Whoa, there's a slide tackle. Is this ref going to call anything?"

Within seconds, Dick would erupt, "Come on, ref! Call that slide tackle. Whaddya, blind, man?!"

*And I got reprimanded for lauding their goal keeper!*

Dave laughed at Ron and said, "You're a sick man, Greer!"

Ron nodded back and held his finger in front of his lips, looking toward Darcy as if to say, *Don't get me in trouble with the wife.*

"So, do you live near Ron and Darcy?" Dave asked.

"Very. We're next-door neighbors," I told him as I watched our girls score yet another goal. I enjoyed chatting with Dave in the context of a kids' soccer game because it allowed me to keep my eyes focused on something other than him. If we'd met in a coffee shop or an office, I'd have to face him straight-on, and that was something I was just not ready for. An occasional glance was about all I could handle without blushing. I was most grateful to have the action of the game to fix my gaze on.

In the final minutes of the game, the other team's parents started unraveling. I can understand that they didn't like seeing their girls lose, but a few of the fathers were downright unkind. "Come on, Chloe, you're faster than that pork chop," one shouted. His comment was only slightly mitigated by the fact that his wife swatted him. The truth was, though, that our team was looking kind of chunky lately—even Rachel, who inherited my string bean body and speedy metabolism. I hated to admit it, but maybe Mimi was right about the girls needing fitness training. In just the two weeks since Gunther discontinued fitness training, everyone but Cara looked as though she'd packed on a few pounds. Since Mimi was still doing fitness training with her daughter, Cara remained slender. The weight of our one-girl control group seemed to make a convincing case for resuming training, though Mimi had not made an advocate of me. If she had such overwhelming parent support, let her use it.

The non-pork chop from Manchester sped by our last defender and took a shot on our goal. As soon as the ball was released, Bobby shouted, "Nooooo mer-saaaaay!" *Oh God, now he was going to start saying it?*

As Cayenne tipped the ball away from the goal net, I asked Dave when mercy got such a bad rap. "I mean, why can't we let them have a pity goal? Would that be so terrible?" Ron jumped into the conversation and informed me that teams receive extra points for shutouts. "How sweet," I said.

"So their goal didn't count?" I asked.

"It was offsides, Claire," Ron said. "No goal."

During the final kickoff, Violet dribbled the ball downfield, where she was greeted by a behemoth defender from Manchester who clumsily reached her foot out to steal the ball. Sadly, she tripped Violet in such a way that the top of her leg went one way and the bottom went the other. *My knee hurt just watching.* She lay on the ground clutching her leg, crying as Gunther ran out onto the field. Raymond stood, devastated. Leesha placed her hand on her husband's shoulder. In this moment, I no longer thought of him as Crazy Raymond. I looked at his watery eyes and felt compassion for him as a fellow parent. He may have been a little out there, but at the crux of it, he was—

"Shake it off, baby!" he shouted. "On your feet, girl. Run through it!"

Violet wrapped her arm around Gunther's neck as he helped her hobble off the field.

The absolute maniacs on the other side of the field started clapping! I thought I had seen the lowest of parenting until this. These people were animals. Then *our* parents started clapping too.

"What is wrong with you people?" I couldn't hold back.

Dave reached for my arm and pulled me back down into my chair. "Claire, they're clapping because she's okay, not because she's hurt.

"Oh," I said, noticing Mimi smirking at my mistake. "Very good, then. Okay," I said as I clapped. "Brava, Violet!"

CB ED

After the game, Mimi jogged to an enormous white board where team managers with clipboards were all gathered taking notes. When we made our way to her, she reported, "Okay, we're in really good shape, but in order for us to win the tournament, Turf needs to shut out Conquistadors then lose to the Patriots, *or* Hot Shots needs to beat or tie Turf this afternoon *and* we need to win our next two games by at least two goals, unless we shut out one of the teams, in which case we'll only need a one-goal margin." *Huh?* The other parents just nodded their heads and started asking about games that were going on. Mimi instructed two dads to go to those games and report back to her with scores.

"You guys didn't get called on any of your fouls," one of the Manchester dads, their Loud Bobby, shouted to our group as he walked by. "You pay the ref or something?"

"It's your tournament, moron," Mimi quipped. "So actually, *you* paid the ref."

Their Normals stifled a laugh while ours looked mortified. "You got a smart mouth, lady," the Manchester Moron said, walking closer to Mimi.

"I suggest you step back right now," Ron said.

Darcy furrowed her brow quizzically.

"And you've got a dumb one," Mimi escalated.

"You want a piece of me?" the Manchester Moron snapped at Ron.

"God knows, there's enough to spare," Mimi shot back.

"How 'bout we take the girls to get a bite?" Dave asked me.

"Sure," I agreed. "Darcy, let's take the girls to one of the concession booths for lunch."

My friend nodded. "We need to be back at the field in an hour?" she reminded me. "Ronnie, Kelly, let's go," she said, leaving Ron and Mimi to fight this battle on their own.

Mimi must have bionic hearing, because although the Manchester Moron's friend, Drunk Roger, joined in the shouting match, she still managed to hear us making lunch plans. "No meat!" she shouted as we walked away. "I'm serious, no meat before games, Claire. Make sure they eat something healthy."

As we left the crowd by the white board, Gunther passed by us with a bratwurst fully loaded with toppings. "Good playing, girls," he said. "Very nice soccer."

CR ⁊Ͻ

Amazingly, we shut out the next two teams, beat another in the semifinals, then won the championship game on Monday morning. Even Preston showed up for the championship game, shaking hands with all of the dads and talking about other games being played at the tournament. "Did you come to watch us play, Preston?" Katie asked, tilting her head up at him like Cindy Lou Who in *How the Grinch Stole Christmas*.

"Oh, no," Preston said, laughing good-naturedly. "I'm recruiting players for next season." The parents who heard this looked at each other incredulously as Preston caught his faux pas. "But, of course my main reason for coming was to watch you girls play in the championship."

The impromptu team meeting seemed to be over until Mimi chimed in. "When does the window close for making roster changes for the regular season?" Preston appeared confused and looked to our coach for clarification. "Gunther?"

"I want no changes," he said.

"But if we did, when would those need to be done?" Mimi asked.

"Mimi," Preston said in a placating tone. "We've made a commitment to these players. If we've invited them on the team, they're on the team for the rest of the season." Three parents, including me, sighed with relief.

"Cal South allows roster changes until August," Mimi said. "Why would Kix put our team at a disadvantage by not allowing us to make changes when every other club in the regional league can? Come on, if we made mistakes in selection we should be able to correct them just like Conquistadors, Turf, and Hot Shots can!"

Preston answered. "We have to think about the integrity of the club." *I knew I liked him.* "We made a commitment to these girls." *That's what it's all about.* "Plus, we've cashed everyone's checks."

# Chapter Twenty-One

As we left Santa Barbara on Monday evening, Mimi congratulated the girls several times for winning "a fist full of medals" and bringing home the first tournament victory of the season. In her parking lot speech, she told the team that this was what girl power was all about. *Yep, one team of girls goes home happy, the rest go home disappointed, woo-hoo!* I didn't have any real issues with the competitive nature of tournaments, but Mimi's characterization of victory as some sort of feminist tenet seemed illogical. Mimi congratulated the girls as a group, then individually, then again with a thumbs-up as her minivan passed ours on the drive back to Santa Bella.

To the parents, however, Mimi sang a different tune. When I logged onto my email that evening, I received two notes from team parents. One pleasant, one not so much.

**Dear Claire,**

I enjoyed meeting you at the tournament. Looking forward to dinner this weekend. Wondering, do you like Chinese or is Thai better? Jess said the Thai place on Via Del Mar is under new management and the service is just as good as the food now. I don't know if you'd eaten there before, but you had to beg for your water, and you were SOL if you dropped your chopsticks. Wanna give it a try?

Dave

--------------------

## MEMORANDUM

TO:     Team Parents
FROM:   Mimi
DATE:   May 31
RE:     Manchester Tournament

First, let me congratulate the girls on their victory this weekend! Wins are always great confidence-builders, but all victories are not created equal! I want the girls to maintain that awesome feeling that comes from walking away from a tournament with a fist full of medals, so I ask that you keep this discussion among parents only! As the adults, there are some serious issues we need to address!

When Gunther killed my fitness trainings, I immediately noticed that the girls lost speed and endurance! If I may speak plainly, some are getting a bit chubby!!! I don't want anyone to have body issues! Girls need to love their bodies! Part of loving their bodies means treating them with respect! Exercise and nutrition are key components of health! We must start up fitness training again before this problem balloons, no pun intended!

Last week, I called Manchester United and requested that the girls be moved from the gold bracket to the bronze! Usually they don't accommodate last-minute requests like this, but the tournament director owes me more than one favor, so he moved the girls two full brackets down! Naturally we won! At the risk of sounding cruel, the girls essentially won the Special Olympics! There were even one or two rec teams that participated!

If we are going to be serious contenders for State Cup, we must resume fitness training NOW!!!

Go Kix!

I looked at the addressees and not surprisingly, Gunther was not receiving Mimi's email. I hit "reply all" then added his name to the recipients.

Hey Everyone:

Has anyone heard from Violet's parents? Leesha said that she and Raymond were taking her to their orthopedist when they got back. Does anyone know how that went? Do you think they got to see a doctor over the holiday weekend? I'm concerned. That fall looked seriously painful.

Claire

Hours later, Drunk Dick responded. I imagined him sitting at the keyboard baring his molars with his one biscuit eye bulging.

Team,

They did look sucky, those other teams. I looked them up online and Mimi's right, they're pretty bottom of the barrel. Two got knocked out of the last State Cup in the first weekend and the others didn't even go. I did find their records from last year and whoa, suck city. We should play real teams next time. I videotaped the game cause we always watch game tape. I attached the video file to this email so you can look at it too. We should bring the girls to my house and show them the games on my big TV. I got a thing where I can stop action and point stuff out. It's one thing to talk about the plays on the drive home but there's nothing like seeing it live on TV. I hear what Mimi's saying about getting the girls in shape to play real teams. We should do that. I always say to my girls no pasta except before games. That keeps them trimmed up.

Your Friend,
Dick

At the last practice before the tournament, when Dick offered to bring his camcorder and record the games, I thought he was nuts. After my weekend in Santa Barbara, I realized that making "game tape" for future analysis was part of the normal landscape of club soccer. There were the fresh white lines painted onto the grassy fields. There were the goal nets defining the ends. There were referees in yellow and black striped tops and their line assistants with matching uniforms and small flags to indicate when a ball was out of bounds. There were also fathers on the sidelines with video cameras focused on their kids' games. The camera-to-penis ratio was impressive, with one in four fathers sporting his own equipment.

When Darcy was near Nancy, she could convince her to stay out of Mimi's line of fire. But with Mother Earth home alone in front of her email, there was no stopping her from responding.

Dear Team,

The Special Olympics has been a meaningful and rewarding experience for my family for many years. We have volunteered as "huggers" at finish lines and have felt no greater joy than that which comes from a developmentally challenged youngster running into our arms. To dismiss less-skilled soccer players as "the Special Olympics" is insensitive and degrading to this entire team.

And yes, how is Violet? I must say it was heartening to see Leesha stand up to Ray and insist that they take her home at halftime of our second game. When that madman shouted to his injured daughter, "You can hop faster than that!" my faith in humanity dimmed.

I suggest that we parents work on our psychological and spiritual fitness a bit more as we go into our next tournament.

Respectfully,
Nancy and Roger Gilman

--------------------

## MEMORANDUM

TO:      The Team
FROM:  Mimi
DATE:  May 31
RE:Re: Re: Manchester Tournament

Thank goodness we have Claire to remind us of our obvious concern for Violet! As it happens, I had already placed several calls to Raymond and Leesha and was waiting for them to reply with the results of Violet's medical evaluation today! Sadly, Violet will be out for many months as her ACL heals — again! The doctor said she will not be able to play soccer again until November, or possibly even December! This means that until then we are down a player! Many of you already know

Sissy, who played on the team last year and is now the shining star of the blue team! She's been working with a private trainer (not a bad idea for all of the girls!) and is going to be a force to be reckoned with by State Cup! I suggest we snatch her up for the regular season!

*So, Sissy is working with a private coach after all. Why should I expect honesty from a woman who has a strategy for winning a food drive?*

Almost immediately, Dick responded.

Team,

I have the upmost respect for Mimi but got to disagree with her on the Sissy thing. If we only need eleven on the field, let's give our own girls more playing time. If this Sissy kid was so great, she wouldn't have got cut from the team this year. How many games have they played that she's such a shining star? This was the first weekend Cal South had any tournaments. I know she's your friend's kid, Mimi, but I got to speak my mind. Let her be the superstar with the B-team and let's shorten our bench a little.

Your Friend,
Dick

On behalf of the Richards and Jelineks too

--------------------

Dear Team!

I just wanted to say that I totally agree with what all of you are saying! Sapphy's dad and I had the best time this weekend. It's so nice to get away from real life and be part of the excitement of a tournament. The energy was so amazing! Sooo awesome to win too! Yay for the FFOM (that's fist full of medals)!

xoxo Gia

--------------------

Team,

Mimi and me will talk about team in privates. We are disgusting this later.

Coach Gunther

# Chapter Twenty-Two

"I feel a little guilty about going out with Dave," I confessed to Darcy as she stood above me pulling my hair through her flat iron. It was more than the sadness of going on living after Steve had died. I also felt guilty that the night earlier I had the most unbelievable dream sex with her husband. Let me be clear. I don't mean I had sex with Ron and it was surreal. I mean it happened after I fell asleep, when my subconscious mind took over and allowed my inner-marabou-wearing wild-child to evict the good girl in L.L. Bean. Intellectually, I knew I shouldn't feel guilty about my dreams, but I still did. Perhaps after I focused my attention on Dave, these inappropriate feelings would cease. God, I hoped so.

"Don't feel guilty," Darcy said, releasing a sheet of straightened red hair. "Don't you think Steve would want you to be happy?"

"Not with another man," I said, laughing because it was half true. Okay, ninety percent true. Because our eyes never met in the makeshift salon of my bathroom, I had the courage to pry into her marriage. "Would you want Ron to date after you died?"

Though she delivered it as a joke, she articulated what I also suspected. "What makes you think he's waiting till I'm dead?" Pulling my hair through the iron, Darcy's tone grew more serious. "I'm pretty sure he's having an affair with someone at the hospital." It was the first time I saw Darcy's eyes well with tears. It was the first time I wasn't expecting a flippant one-liner to follow.

"Have you done any investigating?" I asked.

"You mean like checking his cell phone bills, credit card receipts, deleted emails and all that?"

"I take it you've done this already?" I asked.

"Ron's a smart guy," Darcy said. "He's not going to leave a paper trail."

"Darcy, put your suspicions to rest and check!" I insisted. "If Ron's carrying on with someone, he's going to slip up somewhere."

I looked at Darcy through the mirror and she gave a perfunctory smile. "When you start handling your husband's pants like evidence on CSI, there's a certain line that you cross, do you know what I mean? It's like you're not who you thought you were and you don't have the marriage you thought you had. I guess I'm not ready to concede that yet," she said with a faint laugh. "He's always been a big flirt. I might just be imagining things because I'm so mad at him."

"What did he do this time?"

"Nothing," Darcy said. "That's the problem. We've got so much old shit that we don't even need to have a fight for me to be angry with him. He's got a shit credit with me."

CR ℘

Dave and I had the same low-key chemistry we had on the soccer field at the Manchester tournament. He was extremely handsome, smart and easy to talk to. He had such keen observations about club soccer, parenting in the modern age and the intensive cultivation of children. "I met this ten-year-old kid last week who can give this brilliant analysis of the book he's reading with all the cultural context and literary influences, but then that same kid doesn't know how to tie his shoes."

"Maybe he needs a private shoe tying coach," I suggested.

"Don't laugh, there's a potty training coach in San Paulo who's making a killing," Dave said.

I learned that he had two brothers and grew up in Lake Tahoe, where his parents ran a ski shop. He gave me an insightful and compassionate description of his family dynamics until I had to ask just how much therapy this man had gone through. "Plenty," he said with a laugh. "I'm a therapist. I thought you knew that."

"No, now I'm a little nervous."

"Think I'm analyzing you?" I nodded. "Everyone thinks that at first. It'll pass. I'm really not. I can clock out and enjoy time with a beautiful woman without needing to look through her baggage."

"I'm a widow," I blurted. "I just thought you should know that."

"I'm sorry," he said. He thought I was crazy. He had every right to. Here I said I didn't want to be a patient, he agreed to it, then I spring this tangential bomb on him.

"Thank you. I just didn't want to not tell you then have you wonder why I hadn't," I explained.

"Okay," he said.

I laughed. "I just had to get that out of the way. This is my first date since ... " I trailed off.

He smiled kindly. "I'm honored, Claire."

The evening went on comfortably from there. What we lacked in fireworks, we made up for with a natural ease around each other. Dave was one of the few people who didn't cut me off when I talked about Steve. It's not that others were being rude; they just couldn't stand the discomfort of knowing that I might cry at any moment. They'd always dismiss me by saying, "Let's talk about happier things," when the reality was that keeping Steve alive through stories made me quite happy. It was pretending that he never existed that killed me. For someone who was afraid of being viewed as a patient, I sure was acting like one.

Dave had "catch" written all over him, yet I couldn't stop thinking about women I'd like to fix him up with.

"Why do you think that Mimi asked Preston about roster changes?" I asked. "Be honest with me; you've been in club soccer for a long time. Did Rachel look like she wasn't cutting it?"

"No, she looked fine," Dave said.

"Really? Or are you just saying that to be nice?"

"She looked good. Not entirely sure of herself, but good. She's a natural athlete, and she's going to be great by the end of the season, I guarantee it."

"She was taken on the bubble," I said. "Do you know what that means?" He nodded. "It's just that we went through so much stress during tryouts, and now Mimi's talking like she wants to kick some girls off the team." I sighed. "I just want to know when I can stop worrying about this!"

Dave smiled sympathetically. "Whenever you choose to."

"You're not going to send me a bill for tonight, are you?"

"No, but I am hoping we can do this again."

"Really? Even though I really don't have it together yet?"

"Please," he dismissed with a wave. "I don't want to wait around forever for people to get it together. I like you, Claire. You're funny. And honest. I don't know about you, but I feel very comfortable around you."

"Oh my God, that's exactly the word I'd use."

"I actually used several," Dave said.

"Comfortable." I smiled.

CR ED

## MEMORANDUM

TO:      The Team
FROM:  Mimi
DATE:   June 15
RE:       The girls are getting fat!!!!

Two weeks ago another manager called our team the Chub Club when our girls were called up onto the stage to accept their medals at the Manchester tournament! I was mortified and was certainly relieved that none of our girls heard her cruel comment! As nasty as she was, this woman had a point! The girls are getting fat!!! I think they've gained 50 pounds collectively! I need parents to remind the girls that fruits and vegetables are healthy snacks! I also need your support in encouraging Gunther to resume fitness training! Let's all band together for the good of our daughters and get them back on the regimen of health and fitness!

Go Kix!

--------------------

TO:      Mimi
FROM:  Claire
RE:Re:  The girls are getting fat!!!!
DATE:   June 15

Rachel and I made some cute soccer necklaces for the girls that we plan on giving the team at the tournament. Just wanted to make sure this doesn't interfere with any gifts you're planning on giving the team.

--------------------

TO:    The Team
FROM: Mimi
DATE:  June 15
RE:FW: Re: The girls are getting fat!!!!

I gave the girls necklaces at the last tournament! I gave them a gift to commemorate their first tournament together as a team! If we give them something every time, it minimizes the significance of the gift, so I'd appreciate it if you did not give them anything more! They need to learn to feel pride internally, not by receiving trinkets! Recent studies on consumerism show that kids whose parents stress materialism wind up depressed!

Why did I even engage with this Queen Bee mom? I refrained from responding, but my buddy, Nancy could not hold back.

Dear Mimi,

I'm not sure if you realize that you're sending your emails to the entire team, but since you are, I thought I'd respond. While I fully agree that we live in an overly materialistic, consumer-oriented society, I might remind you that it was you who began giving the girls "trinkets" when you gave them "girl power" scrunchies at their first practice and necklaces for their first tournament. Lest we forget the team photo t-shirts and mugs you bought the girls at the tournament. It was also very generous of you to buy the girls "Chicks rock" shoelaces, but I think it somewhat undermines your credibility when espousing your belief that less is more.

Respectfully,
Nancy and Roger Gilman

I would really have to thank Nancy with a bouquet of pollen-free flowers when this season was over.

Hello Team,

Good luck this weekend. Kick some ass and show no mercy.

Violet's having another surgery, but she'll be back and that's a promise.

Raymond

℃℥℩

My mother and Blake could not have looked more out of place at the "School's Out for Summer" soccer tournament. She wore a silk scarf around her head and flung it dramatically over her shoulder. Mothers my age were competing through their children, but the women of the older generation were competing through sunglasses. Whoever could support the biggest pair won, and Barbara was a definite contender. The black, crystal-encrusted frames sat under the hood of her scarf, making her look like a chic strain of Unabomber—the type that sends you champagne with too many bubbles. Blake wore his usual yachting gear. Through his locked jaw, he told Darcy, Ron, and Dave how "spectacular" it was to meet them, then excused himself to "have a word" with Rachel.

"You can't do that, Blake," I told him.

Dick and Bobby sidled over to introduce themselves and explain that Mimi doesn't allow the girls to talk to anyone for an hour before games. "She says she's got 'em in some sort of zone," Loud Bobby shouted at a shocked-looking Blake. I don't think he was expecting to have his hair blown back by Bobby's voluminous explanation.

"That's absurd!" Blake said.

Never missing her cue, Darcy shot, "It's club soccer. Of course it's absurd."

### ‹З ᏜᎧ

As my mother and Blake chatted with some of the Normals before the game, I noticed Mimi arguing with the other team's manager. Her hands were placed firmly on her hips, her head jutted forward aggressively. The other manager held a panicked expression and slouched posture as she spoke with Mimi. She was a potato-fed woman of considerable girth with hair that extended past her bottom. If the setting were different, one might imagine that Mimi was a celebrity and the other manager was the schlubby assistant getting bawled out for having caffeinated Diet Coke in the movie set trailer. No one could make out exactly what they were saying, but Mimi seemed to be winning the argument.

"What did I miss?" Dave asked as he approached me.

"Hey," I greeted him. "Don't know. It just started. Stay here, I want to introduce you to my parents. My mom and her husband, rather."

Suddenly, the other manager stormed off to talk to Gunther, who was sitting on the sideline with the girls telling them who would be starting. "Excuse me, are you the coach?" she asked.

Dave stood by my side. "Let's wait till the commercial break," I said, gesturing toward the unfolding drama.

Mimi arrived seconds later. "Let's not have a scene, Trudy. You know the rules and you made a choice not to follow them. Accept the forfeit and move on."

"There is a problem?" Gunther asked. *This guy did not miss a trick.*

"What's the deal?" Dick demanded, his right eye bulging from his head like Rachel's old Mr. Whoozit.

"The deal is that we won," Mimi said. Parents started gathering to see what the commotion was about.

"My God!" Gia exclaimed, giggling. "I didn't even see the game start!"

"Girls, run a lap with Mimi," Gunther suggested.

"Oh, so now you want fitness training?" Mimi snapped. "You're not getting rid of me that easily."

Noting the wedge between our team manager and coach, Trudy immediately jumped in with her appeal to Gunther. "I meant to set my dryer for an hour but accidentally put the thing on auto-dry, so our white jerseys were in my dryer all night!"

No one understood why this woman was sharing her laundering woes with us, but she was clearly upset about her dryer working overtime.

Mimi gestured with her hands that Trudy should cut to the chase and said, "Bottom line, they forfeited."

"We did *not* forfeit!" Trudy said, growing two inches.

Gunther asked Jennifer to lead the girls in a lap around the field. "I don't understand the problem," he said as they took off. Now parents from the other team were walking over to see what was going on.

Mimi said, "We're the visiting team so we choose the jersey color, and they choose the side of the field. I told her we wanted to wear our whites and she freaked out!"

"You said you didn't care what color you wore until I told you I was relieved because I accidentally shrunk my white jerseys in the dryer last night! *Then* you insisted on wearing your blue tops so we'd have no other choice but white! Why can't you just wear *your* whites?!"

Gunther knit his brows, still confused.

Mimi escalated the argument. "We *can*. We choose not to, as we have the right to do as the visiting team. You choose the side; we choose the color! That's the way it works. It's not my fault that you ruined your white jerseys. If you don't have your whites, then you have to wear your blue tops! And since we chose to wear *our* blues, your team is not prepared to play by the tournament rules, thus you automatically forfeit this game to us!" She was quite satisfied with her cutting efficiency.

Turning to Gunther, Trudy begged, "Have a heart, coach. This could happen to you sometime."

"It would *never* happen to us!" Mimi screeched. "My housekeeper would never leave the dryer on all night!"

Gunther looked baffled. "Do we have white shirts with us?" he asked Mimi.

"Of course we do, Gunther!" Mimi said. "I always bring complete uniforms, both color tops. The point is that—"

"We use white tops and let them play in blue," Gunther said as Trudy sighed with relief.

"No we do *not!*" Mimi shouted so loud that a referee from an adjacent field looked over to see what the fuss was about. "A forfeit is worth seven points! Do you know what we have to do to earn seven points in this tournament? It's three for a win, a maximum of three for goals scored and a point for a shutout. The only way to earn seven points is to shut them out 3-0. Even if we shut them out 10-0, we still can't get more than seven points. This forfeit is their fault, not ours. I didn't ruin her white jerseys, did I?" *Did she?* "We'll let the girls save their strength and go into their next game fresher than the others who will have already played a game earlier!"

Dick looked at Mimi with deep admiration. "What a twat," he sighed.

"No, this is not nice," Gunther said. "We let them play in white."

"Thank you, coach," Trudy said. "I'm glad *you're* a reasonable person."

"Gunther, how can you—" Mimi shouted. He raised his hand. *So glad to see that "talk to the hand" translates to German.* "What-ever," Mimi said, rolling her eyes at Trudy. "We'll kick your asses just for practice. Since we gave you this break, we want the good side of the field. Move your stuff," she said, pointing at the sideline where her team had planted umbrellas, set up chairs and placed their bags. Trudy looked appalled.

After the other team's parents returned to their side of the field to begin their forced migration, Dick raised his beer can and gave a hearty cheer. "I think I'm in love with Mimi."

"Don't move," Mimi told our parents who were starting to collect their stuff for our move. As the other team's parents began crossing the field with their folded umbrellas and chairs, dragging coolers, backpacks and two baby strollers, Mimi smirked maliciously and turned to Dick. "Think you love me now? Watch this." When the disgruntled group arrived, she shifted her weight cutely and put her fingertip purposefully on her pretty little head. "You know, now that I think about it, we'll stay on this side after all." Mimi giggled and made a shooing motion with her hands. "Off with you. Back to your side of the field."

Mother leaned in toward me and asked, "Does this happen all the time?"

"No, Mom, that's the beauty of club soccer. There's fresh new bullshit at every game."

# Chapter Twenty-Three

I always root for the girls to win, but after they scored four unanswered goals, I'd had my fill of our success. I realized that these definitive victories were important for our ranking in the tournament, but the score of this game also reflected the score between our team managers, and it was more lopsided than I liked. Mimi strutted up and down the sideline, smirking at Trudy as if to say, *Bet you'd like to forfeit now.* Trudy averted her eyes, conceding defeat.

As much as I loathed the sight of Mimi gloating, the game held two pleasant surprises for me. First, Rachel grew into her uniform. She finally looked confident as a club player. Rachel always seemed happy playing soccer, but in the last tournament she was still playing rec-style breakaway soccer rather than working with her teammates. Today, in her sixth game with Kix, Rachel became a real club player.

"See, what did I tell you?" Dave said as he sat next to me, my mother and Blake. He was right. As center midfielder, Rachel was like the conductor of an orchestra. She brought the ball as far as she could, then passed to one of the forwards to shoot. She passed the ball back to defenders, which I thought was a mistake at first, but Dave explained that this was a smart strategic move when there was nothing but opposing players in front of her. "Good soccer players pass to space whether it's in front of them or behind them. You're right, though, it's a risky move because we're bringing the ball further into our own territory." I nodded. "But when we play easy teams, it's a good opportunity to practice doing this. We're not going to beat the premiere teams at State Cup if we don't know how to use the entire field."

On two occasions, Rachel even penetrated the eighteen (I loved saying that) herself. She passed the ball to Kelly, who was out wide. Kelly brought it back to Rachel, who shot it in the net! My heart grew two sizes when her teammates all fell to the ground and began bowing, doing the "we're not worthy" routine they always did when a player scored.

My second shock of the day was my mother. Much to her own surprise, Barbara was a closet soccer fanatic. As soon as Rachel got possession of the ball, she stood and began cheering hysterically. She didn't know a thing about soccer, but before long, she was urging players to work the channel, to find feet and to make one move and go. After Rachel's first goal, she wailed, "That's what I'm talking about, baby!"

Dave raised his eyebrows as if to say that this was not exactly how I had described my mother when we had dinner earlier that week. Our second date was less of a therapy session, but still had that platonic feel to it. Still, I wanted to hang in there and see if romantic feelings would develop. He was just the type of guy I'd always been attracted to in the past.

When Ron began pacing behind Dick trying to light his fuse, it was my mother's powder keg that exploded first. Barb stood, her heels sinking into the grass and shouted, "Come on, ref! Can we get a call on anything here?!"

Unfortunately, the referee took her words to heart and held up a yellow card, pointing at my mother. Blake began stroking Mother's wrist and urging her to sit before she started a soccer riot.

"Mother," I said, laughing, "I've never seen this side of you."

"Nor have I," she said, regaining her breath and composure. "My therapist said I needed to get in touch with the fun person inside waiting to get out."

"Dave's a therapist," I said, gesturing to him.

Barbara raised her eyebrows. "Really? Well, I certainly hope you haven't diagnosed me too harshly."

He smiled and gave me a look to say, *See, everyone thinks that.* Instead, he politely told my mother, "Rachel's having a great game. She's quite a little distributor." Blake and I looked confused but Mother nodded and agreed.

Ron paced behind the row of parents, stopping to consult with Mimi, who was taking judicious notes at the far end of the field. Darcy turned to me and said, "They never stop. She called last night to get Ron to go with her to the Kix board meeting to force Gunther to reinstate fitness practice." I rolled my eyes in solidarity.

"We should get your sister out here," Barbara said. "Maybe that would help her shake her mood."

"Awwww," the parents from our sideline shouted as Kelly Greer shot wide.

"What mood?" I asked. I hadn't spoken with Kathy in a few weeks. "Is she okay?"

Mother sighed, sounding a bit exasperated. "Baby blues," she explained. "I wish she'd get over it already. She's positively dreary around the office."

Loud Bobby filled the void that Crazy Raymond left and began shouting hoarsely, "Nooooo mer-saaaaay!"

"What do you mean baby blues?" I whispered.

"You know exactly what I'm talking about," Barbara said, now standing on her feet with her eyes locked on the field.

"Attack, attack!" she shouted at our defenders as a girl in blue approached our defensive third. Mother certainly was picking up the language quickly.

"Mom," I said, concerned. "What do you mean by baby blues? What's going on with Kathy?"

Shaking her hand loose from my grip, she shouted, "Offsides, ref!" There was no way my mother even knew what offsides was, much less had the ability to make the call. I glanced behind her and saw Ron pacing behind our chairs again. He mouthed an apology and pointed to Dick, trying to explain that our team drunk was his real target. How did I find this imbecile so attractive? What guy over the age of thirteen would purposely provoke the volatile team alcoholic?

"Mother, tell me what's going on with Kathy!"

"She's moping around, crying over the slightest little things, saying she's a bad mother. The same thing you went through with Rachel. It'll pass. It's rough in the beginning with all those hormones."

"Mother, I had post-partum depression and it didn't *just pass*! I went through months of therapy and anti-depressants. Why are you acting like she has a bad case of PMS and just needs to—"

"Shake it off, Macy!" a mother screamed at her flattened daughter in the blue uniform. The girl lay on her back, motionless. Her coach and the referee ran out to her and began asking a series of basic questions to determine whether or not Macy had a serious head injury.

"Hang tough!" her father shouted.

Two long braids rose from the ground and Macy hobbled to her feet. Her coach patted her on the back and said, "This body needs to last a lifetime, let's take a rest." Months ago, an interaction like this wouldn't have even registered with me. Now, moments of reason seemed remarkable.

As Macy hobbled off the field, I joined the others clapping for her. My mother whipped her head around at me, appalled. She looked at Dave, Darcy, Ron, Gia, Tom and the others and snapped, "You people are sick!"

Looking across the field at the other team parents was like holding up a mirror. They also had a wall of noisy dads who were interchangeably angry or arrogant, depending on the score of the game. Many of their parents shouted instructions that conflicted with their coach's. And, as with our Kix team, about half the parents looked absolutely normal and were simply there to support their kids.

Somewhere between the team's sixth and seventh goals, my mother noticed my latest experiment in beading. "What a darling necklace. Are those pence?"

I confirmed, pleased with both how the piece turned out and that my fashion-savvy mother noticed. I wasn't sure how the amber, turquoise and pewter would blend, but something about the unusual shape of the twenty-pence piece pulled it together. I made a nice garnet one for Darcy, sort of a "sorry for coveting your husband" present, and an Austrian crystal one for my sister, Kathy. I felt guilty that I hadn't thought to make one for my mother, but in fairness she'd never really cared for my designs before. She said she preferred classic elegance to my Bohemian mish-mash.

"I have a dozens of Italian coins left over from our trips before the euro," Barbara said. "Would you make a little jingly-jangly thing of lira for me?" *Jingly-jangly? Who was this woman?! Next thing you know, she might smile.*

"Sure," I said tentatively. "You'll need to give me some direction, though, because your taste is so—"

"Get that ball, Rachel!" Barbara interrupted as she stood to her feet. "That's it, that's it! Atta girl, move around her!"

The crowd cheered as Rachel scored another goal.

Leo came over and shook Blake's hand. "That girl's a *sivious playah* now."

"True player for real," Loud Bobby said, strutting over to Leo, then doing that fist gesture that is something between a handshake and a punch.

*Hey, where was my handshake?! I'm her mother.*

At halftime, Gunther told the girls that they were to work on their pass backs and foot skills in the second half of the game. "We need no more goals. I want practicing using our defenders more."

I looked to Darcy for translation. "Since we're up by five goals, we've already got the maximum number of points for this game, so he wants to use the second half to bone up on some of the things he's been working on in practice."

We tuned into Gunther again. "Kelly, you are goalkeeping this half." She nodded in agreement, but Mimi stormed over with loud protest.

"Kelly's our lead scorer, why put her in goal?" Mimi shouted. Trying to preserve her good reputation with the girls, she took it down a notch. "Cayenne is such a star keeper, why risk the shutout by taking her out of the box?" Gunther looked back at the girls and continued. "Gunther!" Mimi screeched. "I am speaking to you."

"Girls, I am explaining why I make the decision. Kelly, we no need any more goals to get maximum points."

"But what if they score on us?" Mimi demanded. "Then we lose the shutout point! Cayenne hasn't let a single goal go in. You're a star, girlfriend," she said, directing the compliment to Loud Bobby's offspring.

"They have not made any shots on goal," Gunther reminded her.

"But Kelly Greer in goal is such a waste."

"This talk is waste," Gunther said. Turning his attention back to the circle of girls, he continued. "In practice we work on plays I want to see using today. On three."

"One, two, three," the girls shouted in unison as they each held one hand into the center of the circle. "Go Kix!"

CR ℘

As was the case at the Manchester tournament, Mimi congratulated the girls Sunday evening for winning the "fist full of medals" at the School's Out for the Summer tournament, then promptly emailed the parents to remind us that our victory was a meager one.

**MEMORANDUM**

**TO:** The Team
**FROM:** Mimi
**DATE:** June 20
**RE:** We were in the lowest bracket again!

Congratulations to the girls on their second tournament win! I know it's exciting for some of our new players to have the opportunity to shine when we play marginal teams, but I encourage everyone to gently remind the girls that during our regular season we will not be playing inferior opponents like these! I blame myself! I hoped that these easy wins would be good for team morale, but now I see that I was wrong! We need to play our equals to really see how out of shape the girls are! We MUST resume fitness training if we are to have any chance at winning State Cup!

Also, Raymond keeps calling me to make sure we hold Violet's spot! He says her physical therapy is going well and that she will be back in time for State Cup! I adore Violet, but think her father is being overly optimistic! We really can't hold a spot for a girl who may very well never play soccer again! It is in the best interests of this team to replace Violet with Sissy so she can learn the plays in time for the regular season! Let's not dally on this! I have four votes in favor of this already and need to hear from the rest of you!

The phone rang as I was reading the email. "Did y'get Mimi's latest?" Dave asked before he even said hello. I loved our familiarity.

"Hang on," I told him, tiptoeing to Rachel's bedroom to make sure she was still asleep. One of the things I loved about soccer was that it completely cured Rachel's insomnia. I closed the bedroom door with my snoring daughter behind it, and clutched the phone receiver to my ear. "I know, she's a complete crackpot, isn't she?" Remembering his vocation, I urged Dave not to tell me that Mimi was simply misunderstood.

"No, she's wacky. I love all the exclamation points in her notes. That's diagnosable, you know?"

"Really?"

"Oh yes, it's a little-known condition, but a very serious one."

"Sad," I teased. "Poor thing."

"Did Rachel tell you about her conversation with Gunther?" Dave asked.

"No," I said, surprised that she hadn't mentioned every detail of her life with me.

"I overheard him telling her that she made him proud of his decision to take her on the team," Dave reported. Then, putting on his best German accent, Dave imitated our coach. "Soccer was my salivation when I was a boy."

"His *salivation?*" I asked, laughing.

"I shouldn't make fun of the guy," Dave said. "He was really being very sweet with Rachel, very big brotherly."

I loved my gossipy phone conversations with Dave, but dreaded telling him that I had to cancel our date because Kathy needed help with the baby. On the drive home from the tournament, I called and asked when the best time was to come and give her a hand. She snapped, "Now."

"How 'bout tomorrow?" I suggested, momentarily forgetting about my plans with Dave.

I knew I had to tell Dave about needing to take care of my sister, but decided to put it off for a few more minutes. The last time I canceled, he was a bit pouty. I hoped that as a therapist, he'd be more understanding.

I returned to my conversation with Dave. "What about that fight she picked over the jersey colors?"

"Hey, that's important stuff," Dave joked. "I hate to say she's right about anything, but the girls *are* getting chubby, don't y'think?"

"I'd like to stay in denial about it."

Dave laughed. "Good for you. So, tomorrow night—" He paused for me to continue. When I didn't, he said, "You're canceling again, aren't you?"

"Dave, I'm sorry. My sister has post-partum depression and she really needs me! She works for an insensitive beast who doesn't give her an ounce of compassion."

"You said she works for your mother," Dave said.

"Exactly." Thankfully, he laughed before telling me that he was beginning to take this personally. "Please don't. It's just bad timing."

"That's what I'm afraid of," Dave said.

We moved back into a conversation about the weekend's games, highlighting all of the things our daughters did brilliantly. In the championship game, Katie deflected a shot on goal with her head! She leapt into the air and bounced the shot off her forehead, blocking its path to the net. Cayenne was about to pick up the ball when an opposing player kicked it to her teammate in the center. When she shot the ball, everyone had accepted that the other team was going to score. The parents on the opposite sideline had already begun cheering when Katie jumped eleven feet in the air (wearing a cape and red boots that shot fire) and blocked the shot.

Cଃ ଅ

The only downside of winning tournaments was that the finals were always scheduled for late in the afternoon, which meant Dick had the whole day to get sauced. At the last tournament, he actually passed out on a grassy patch near a playground, despite the fact that a local rock band blasted Alice Cooper's "School's Out" at earth-shaking volume. I could barely hear Loud Bobby when Boiling Lead played its repertoire of heavy metal favorites and its original, "Rodent Pie." I loved watching people's facial expressions transform as they made out the words. The folks who were eating burgers were the best. "You taste so sweet, you make me wanna die," the mullet-headed singer screeched. "Lovin' you's like eating rodent pie."

"Yeah, exciting game," Dave said. "Listen, Claire, I'll understand if you're not ready to start dating again."

"I *am* ready!" I protested a bit too emphatically. "It's been a year and a half." *Five hundred thirty-four days to be exact.*

"It's really not an issue of time," Dave said, switching into a more professional tone.

"Let's reschedule right now," I insisted. I knew that Dave was exactly the kind of man I needed in my life and that my heart would eventually catch up with my head. In the meantime, I didn't want to let him slip away.

CR ƎO

The next morning, the electronic debate over Violet's future with the team began.

Dear Team,

Violet is part of our team and, as such, I feel it is callous to discuss replacing her. We bring our children to organized sports not only for the physical benefits, but to teach them the value of fairness, camaraderie and unity. I would personally feel very hurt if our team voted to abandon Violet. Let us honor her parents' request to hold her spot on the team. There is no need to fracture the team like this. It will dampen our spirit and make the girls feel insecure about their own place on the team. We mustn't send any child the message that he or she is expendable. Hence, my vote is no.

Respectfully,
Nancy and Roger Gilman

--------------------

Hi Everyone,

I like to remain on the sidelines of the soccer team politics, but I really need to speak up on this one. Violet is a part of our team and her parents are asking us to hold her spot. We have 14 healthy girls. There is absolutely no need to replace her. I am in agreement with Nancy.

Jennifer

--------------------

All right, I know emotions can get hot when we're talking about the team so let me remind everyone that what we should be thinking of is what is best for the team for the season and State Cup. Violet turned down other clubs to play for Kix, and if we don't stick by her when her chips are down Ray's gonna be pretty pissed and take her somewhere else once her knee's better. Why make an enemy when we don't have to? When she's back she'll remember how loyal we were and stick by us when recruiters start scouting her — which they will, believe you me. Bottom line here is less players means more field time. Sticking by Violet is smart for now and our future here. What's the problem?

Your Friend,
Dick
Representing the Jelineks and Richards.

--------------------

Bob here. I'm with Dick. Why alienize Violet when she might have a lot of good shots left in that foot? You see what I'm saying? If this Sissy sucked at tryouts, she sucks now. End of story.

--------------------

### MEMORANDUM

TO:     The Team
FROM: Mimi
DATE:  June 22
RE:Re:  We were in the lowest bracket again!!!!

So many misconceptions to correct, I'm not even sure where to begin! I'm not talking about replacing Violet permanently!

Of course she's welcome to join us again if and when her knee heals! Why pass up a star like Sissy for the season?!

Let's talk about fitness training! When I played in college, what separated the good and great teams was fitness! Do we want to be good or great?! In the history of State Cup, no team that was merely good has ever won, so what's the point of even going if we don't play to win?!

On a different note, I will miss having the girls at the house to do homework now that school is out! I'd like to organize a weekly book club meeting to make sure the girls are reading while school is out! Soccer is a thinking girl's sport, so let's keep our minds sharp!

Every time I thought I thoroughly hated Mimi, she'd do something positive like organize a book group. Every time I was prepared to keep my daughter far away from her, she'd shoot an email to me that offered an olive branch.

TO:     Claire
FROM: Mimi
DATE: June 22
RE:     Nice game, Rachel!

Please tell Rachel how proud I was of her amazing performance this weekend! She really had a breakthrough! Some people had their doubts about a girl coming from rec at eleven, but I always knew she'd prove them wrong! As a reward, she gets to select the first book for our summer reading group!

Go Kix and go Rachel!

# Chapter Twenty-Four

When I arrived at Kathy's place, the girls were visiting friends and George was still at the office. She opened the door and fell into my arms, sobbing. "I can't believe I named my baby Steve Emmett," she cried. "How horrible am I for not thinking that through?"

Standing in the doorway in her weekend sweats and dirty hair, I realized we had a very big problem on our hands. Kathy followed my mother's philosophy of never being seen anything less than cover-ready. She took this to the extreme by scheduling a bikini wax one week before her scheduled Cesarean delivery. This new, unshowered Kathy was a new low. I don't even think she had lip gloss on.

"Kathy, have you been to a psychiatrist for an evaluation?" I asked, walking in and taking baby Duke from her arms. My God, I'd be depressed too if I had a child who wasn't going to be able to wipe his nose for four years. Gross, a bubble had just come out of his nostril.

"I've got an appointment with my regular doctor next Thursday and she'll give me a shrink referral then," Kathy said listlessly.

"Are you kidding?! Did you tell them how awful you feel?! This is urgent, Kath."

"George made the appointment," she said. "They said it was the soonest they could see me."

"Give me the phone number," I said, reminding myself of Lil ten years ago. I am quite certain that if she hadn't come along to rescue me, I would have still been crouched behind my hamper, begging for a quick and merciful death. Poor Steve would have had no one to help him through any of his treatments. Rachel would've essentially been an orphan with a dead father and a shell of a mother. "No, I'm sorry, I cannot hold," I said to the receptionist.

"Excuse me?" she replied, bewildered.

"You asked if I'd mind holding, so as long as you're asking, yes, I do mind. My sister's been scheduled to see the doctor nearly two weeks from now and that's far too long a wait. We have an emergency situation here."

"If it's life-threatening, hang up and dial 9-1-1," the receptionist said.

"Are the calls ahead of me life-threatening?" I asked.

"I most certainly hope not."

I laughed. "Okay, fair enough." I listened to Muzak for the next seven minutes while I paced the room bouncing Duke.

"Okay, what's the emergency?" the receptionist snapped when she returned.

"My sister has post-partum depression and the doctor scheduled her for a visit two weeks from now. *Then* he's going to give her a referral to a therapist. We need her on medication tonight."

"How do you know it's post-partum depression?" she asked.

"It runs in the family. Only my mother never took care of hers and she's still pissy after thirty-eight years."

Finally, the ice cracked. "I've got one of those too," the receptionist said. "If you promise not to tell anyone I'm doing this—" She paused. I assured her my lips were sealed. "Call Dr. Lampert and tell him Angie said to get your sister in right away. He doesn't book patients after four so he's able to take urgent calls—or go home early. In any event, if you say Angie sent you, he'll make sure you get in today."

"You are the best!" I screeched. "Thank you so much, Angie!"

"Oh, I'm not Angie, but you're welcome."

෬ ෪

"I wish I had a sister like you," Darcy said when I recalled the story the next day.

"My mother-in-law did the same for me after Rachel was born," I explained.

"Ah, mama karma."

"Exactly," I said. "Did you ever have post-partum depression?"

"More like post-partum oppression. Still have it. Apparently, there's no cure."

There was an awkward silence as we both avoided the topic of Ron's straying. A few days after Darcy first mentioned it, I broached the topic again. She seemed uncomfortable and asked me to forget she ever mentioned it. For weeks, we pretended we never discussed her suspicions of Ron's infidelity, but today she brought it up again. "I'm pretty sure it's someone he works with," she said. "He's been at the hospital a lot lately, more than usual, but when I call it just rolls over to voice mail. Of course, he has to turn off his cell phone when he's there."

"Have you asked him?"

"Claire, men who cheat on their wives usually don't have much of a problem lying to cover their asses."

"Why don't you just talk to him, Darcy?"

"I want to know the answer before I confront him," she said, though I suspected there was more to it than that. The reality is that once you set the ball in motion, you need to be ready to get in the game. She had no plays, no moves, and no goal yet, so she remained on the sidelines until she was ready to take the field and kick some balls.

CR SO

Dave and I had one more date and four more cancellations after I went to Kathy's place that day. I felt about him the way I did about Darcy: immediate intimacy, but no desire to have a romantic relationship. He sat across the table telling me about the hoops he was currently jumping through to adopt a St. Bernard from the full-breed rescue mission, and how he was ready to just settle for a mutt from the pound. "I had to provide *six* references and answer a questionnaire about what type of environment I intend to provide for the dog," he said. "I mean, I'm all for them making sure that dogs go to good homes, but I don't know what my 'discipline style' will be, or who will take care of the dog if I die. Would you believe they asked where the dog will sleep? How do I know where he'll sleep? Let him move in, sniff around a bit and figure it out. Am I supposed to have a bedroom set up for him?"

I laughed. "I think they just want to be sure you're not going to beat him or make him sleep outside on a slab of cement."

"No, Claire, they also asked who I planned to use as a vet and if they incorporated canine massage as part of their routine care."

"Dog massage?!"

"You heard right."

"Man, I want to be a St. Bernard," I said.

"You are."

I blushed. I know it sounds utterly ridiculous to be charmed by a man calling me a dog, but it was endearing. I sighed internally at how wrong Dave was about me, though. He deserved the St. Bernard he thought I was, but he was really getting an old flea bag that probably was not going to learn any new tricks.

I think he may have realized this after I canceled our last date. On Friday night, Rachel complained that she felt sick, so I emailed Dave to apologize for rescheduling again and explained why. He shot back a note right away saying that he was trying to be patient, but had to wonder whether or not I was really interested in him. The tone was light, with a subject line reading "She's just not that into you?" But clearly he had doubts about my intentions. This made two of us.

Rachel woke up late Saturday morning and said she felt fine. As I was picking up the phone to see if Dave was still available that night, I stepped outside because I thought I heard a noise in my backyard. The sound was actually coming from Darcy's yard. The clanking was a watering can that was accidentally kicked by Ron as he paced the far side of his yard, which also happened to be the fence that separated our properties. "No, I'm not saying that," he whispered into his cell phone. "Of course I do, don't be so dramatic." There was a long pause. "I don't know, maybe later." Pause. Then his voice softened. "Okay, I'm sorry. I know. I know. Okay, okay. I have to go in to the hospital this evening so we can ... Oh, I don't know. What? No, it's not that ... All right, I already said yes, let's leave it at that."

As he walked back in the house, I remained hidden behind my neighbor's fence, unable to move. Darcy was right. Ron was carrying on with someone at the hospital. I started trying to imagine whether he was having an affair with another surgeon, a nurse, or maybe a billing clerk. I don't know why any of this mattered, but I wanted to have a clear picture of who he was cozying up to in the linen closet of Santa Bella General Hospital.

If Darcy didn't have it in her to investigate her husband's activities, then I would do it for her. If she needed evidence, I was hot on the trail to getting it. I knew he was meeting someone tonight at the hospital, and I would be there with my digital camera to document it for her. Then when we found out what a louse Ron really was, we could both evict him from our hearts once and for all.

That was the plan anyway.

As I sat crouched in the driver's seat of my minivan, I watched Ron get out of his car and walk in the door at a fast clip. *Now what?* I wondered. I hadn't thought this through very well. *Do I go in and follow him around the hospital corridors, ducking into doorways every now and then? Do I suit up in scrubs and a mask and try to sneak into the operating room?* I imagined that his lover would simply strut out into the parking lot in her naughty nurse costume and the two of them would lose themselves in an illicit embrace. I got out of the car and started walking toward the door, afraid he'd escape from my sight. I saw another doctor approach him, hand him a chart and lead him out of the lobby. Was that it? Was his earlier phone conversation an innocent chat with another doctor who wanted him to cover the night shift after he finished his evening surgery? Who scheduled surgery for the evening anyway?

Before I could ponder that question, I heard a familiar male voice behind me. "Claire?" Dave said. I turned around to see that he and Katie were also standing in the waiting room. "Claire, what are you doing here? Is Rachel okay? Did she get worse?"

"Oh, um, hi guys," I stammered. "No, she's fine, I'm just ... What are you doing here?"

"Jess spilled boiling water on her hand, so I gave her a ride over here. I was dropping off Katie and Sam's not home, I gave her a ride. Jess is in getting patched up right now. What about you? What's with the camera?"

"The camera?"

"Yeah," Katie added, pointing. "Hanging from your neck."

"Oh, this?" I said, hoping a little laughter would dismiss the question.

It didn't.

*When was I going to learn to use the camera on my cell phone?!*

"Yeah, the camera." His expression was clear: *You canceled a date with me so you could hang around a hospital emergency room taking pictures?*

"This?" I said, waving my hand. "It's just, I just, I volunteer here sometimes. You know, a lot of people think they're not going to want pictures of their hospital stay, but it turns out they really regret not bringing a camera along. I mean, it's a part of their lives, right? Why not put it in your scrapbook alongside vacations and graduations and other big events?" Getting softer, I finished, "It's an experimental program. We're going to see how it goes."

"You take pictures of people while they're in the hospital?" Katie asked as if she'd just met a mother even weirder than her own.

"Um, yeah, it really brightens some people's days," I said, hoping to hell that Dave was buying this.

"You told me Rachel was sick," he reminded me.

"She was," I replied. "She absolutely was. But now she's better, and then the hospital called and said that they really needed me to come in tonight, so how could I say no?"

Mercifully, Jessica appeared. A nurse pushed her in a wheelchair as she smiled at her daughter and ex-husband, holding up her bandaged hand for them to see. "Hey, Claire," she greeted me brightly. "What are you doing here?"

"Hi Jessica," I said sheepishly. "I'm, um, a volunteer here. Want a picture of that hand? Make the memory last?"

ଓ ଯ

Kathy was a new person by Rachel's twelfth birthday party at our house weeks later. I was thrilled that the whole family could make our impromptu celebration. These things don't always come together the day before a long holiday weekend. I was especially pleased to hear the familiar lilt in Kathy's voice as she accepted the invitation. "Sure, sounds fun," she said. Yes to fun means medication is working.

Rachel and I were traveling to San Luis Obispo for the Fourth of July weekend for the Patriots Freedom Cup, but still wanted to have a family gathering to mark Rachel's birthday. Darcy popped in for a few minutes and told Rachel and me what to expect this weekend while the rest listened with rapt attention. The league created a colonial theme park with cobblers and blacksmiths who gave demonstrations right there on the cobblestone roads in front of their Main Street shops. The street was lined with façade shops, a bank, a saloon, and a post office. Women with long skirts and bonnets sold homemade chocolate fudge, while others sheared wool from live sheep, then spun it into nubby wool thread. On the first evening of the tournament, after the games ended, the Patriots typically hosted a reenactment of the Revolutionary War, providing red coats and muskets for participants. Thankfully, they weeded out nut jobs like Drunk Dick and Loud Bobby by making people go through a two-hour safety and history class. The Patriots took their tournaments even more seriously than Manchester did, which, ridiculously, filled me with a bit of American pride.

Darcy continued to fill us in. "They kick off the tournament with a morning parade where historical characters march down the street waving flags and ringing the Liberty Bell."

"Oh, that reminds me," my mother interrupted. "I brought the lira for my necklace. Put them close so they jingle when I get a little trot going."

"She has a fist full of lira!" Rachel said in a voice resembling the evil Natasha from *Rocky and Bullwinkle*. Despite the fact that Mimi was as American as apple pie, Rachel and I found it befitting to use this accent whenever we brought up the oft-mentioned "fist full of medals."

I added a maniacal laugh, "We will take this fist full of lira and rule the world!"

Everyone looked at us as if we were out of our minds, but we laughed hysterically. As much as I resented Mimi, it was fun for Rachel and me to share a common enemy. And I had to admit, Rachel was reading more than ever in order to keep up with Mimi's book group. Mimi's rule was that you couldn't attend if you hadn't read the book, and both Rachel and Kelly agreed that Mimi's snacks were too good to miss. "Seriously, I'd sell my sister for one of those Girl Power bars right now," Kelly recently told me as she and Rachel described in delicious detail how much they loved snack time at Mimi's.

"Happy birthday, Rachel," Darcy said after leaning in to kiss me goodbye. "Nice to meet you all." With that final word, my heart dropped. This was not "all." Aside from Steve, someone from my family was most definitely missing from Rachel's party: her grandmother, Lil.

My mother reached into her purse and pulled out three autographed photos of Mia Hamm for her granddaughter. "You'd be amazed at all the soccer paraphernalia they sell on eBay," she explained. "Rachel, I bought you a jersey from the Mexican National Team. I've got one too. We can be twins!"

Blake chimed in. "She watches soccer games on Telemundo now."

"Viva Mexico!" she said, raising her glass of sparkling water.

*We can be twins? Viva Mexico? How I wished I'd discovered soccer thirty years ago.*

CR ED

That night my heart raced as I dialed Lil's number. She would have had every right to greet me with a chill after more than a year of avoiding her. Worse, I kept her from Rachel. I did return some of her calls, but only during times I knew she wouldn't be there. If the tables were turned, I'm not sure how forgiving I would've been. "Hello Lil? It's Claire."

"Claire," she said softly, extending the word like a mother's stroke against a child's cheek. "How are you, sweetheart? How have you been?"

"Okay," I said, ashamed of how selfish I'd been. "How are you?"

"Okay, too." After a moment thick with silence, she spoke again. "There isn't a day I don't think of him. Whoever said time heals all wounds never lost a child."

"I'm sorry I haven't called. I just—"

"I know, sweetheart. You tried to call. It just so happened to always be at the exact same time I've been volunteering at Children's Hospital for the past thirty-four years." (And she was really volunteering, not on some flubbed stakeout.)

"Lil, I'm—" *busted.*

"Claire, I understand. I have to tease you a little, though. You deserve that much."

"It was just too hard to—" I started before a lump formed in my throat.

"It's all right, sweetheart. You're calling now and I'm so glad you did. Tell me something happy before we get each other going. How is your new home? Is Rachel adjusting?"

"She discovered soccer and life hasn't been the same," I said. Lil laughed, coaxing me to tell her more. "The team is quite good, but some of the parents seem to think the girls are training for the World Cup. Some kids have their own private coaches, one's already had two knee surgeries, and the manager ... " I paused. "Don't even get me started on that nut."

"Is Rachel on a travel team?" Lil asked.

"Yes, how did you know?!"

"You remember all of Stevie's trophies? If you want to hear some crazy stories, I have a few of my own from Little League. One of the parents on Stevie's team sued the coach for malpractice." She laughed at the memory, though clearly it couldn't have been funny at the time.

"I didn't realize there was such a thing as coaching malpractice."

"There isn't. This father was trying to set a legal precedent to spare future children from being the victims of bad coaching."

"Wow, was the guy abusive or something?"

"Have you ever heard of a child suffering long-term emotional trauma over losing a Little League championship?"

"A child, no," I said. "A father, I can see it. I can't imagine a lawsuit over it, though."

Sounding like a damsel in a film noir, Lil said, "Stick around, sweetheart. You'll see it all by the time Rachel gets to high school.

The case was dismissed on summary judgment. Thankfully, the judge once played varsity football and understood how crazy parents can get."

"What have I gotten us into?" I said, laughing.

"I'd love to see her play sometime," Lil said. "When's Rachel's next game?"

"Tomorrow, actually, but it's up in San Luis Obispo. Our first game isn't until two, so we're driving up in the morning. The next time we're in L.A. is—"

"Claire!" Lil cried with the joy of discovering a fortunate coincidence. "My sister lives in that area and I'm going to visit her for the holiday weekend! I'm driving up in the morning. I was packing my travel case when you called."

"I was packing too!" I matched her excitement level.

CR Ж

A drum roll marked the start of the Patriots Freedom Cup Parade. A male voice that sounded like the guy who narrates movie trailers welcomed us to the official kickoff of California's oldest and largest kids' soccer tournament. Though I wore a tank top and white shorts, the humidity made me sluggish as I stood with Lil and Darcy on the "Old Town" sidewalk. If a sheep hadn't pooped three feet away from us, I would have been in better spirits. There was nowhere to relocate as thousands of parents stood shoulder-to-shoulder, moist arms smearing against each other. I spotted Leo and Bobby chatting with Dick about our team's lineup. With his freshly-shaved face, Leo told the guys, "Nah, if we keep Savannah as sweeper, it don't matter who they put up top. *Sivious*, nothin's getting by my girl."

Dick set them straight. "That bitch Mimi put us in the gold bracket, so we're up against three teams that made it to the semifinals of State Cup last year, and one that *won* it. We're getting our lunch handed to us, and she knows it."

Bobby disagreed, saying that he wasn't impressed with the Piranhas' new team. "I watched them last week in the Turf Cup and they're not so hot. They may have been a factor last season, but they lost half their girls when the coach went over to Corinthians. They're nothin' now."

Leo asked, "Why you was at Turf Cup? You got another kid?"

"Checkin' 'em out," Bobby said. "I knew we'd face 'em here so I wanted to scope 'em out."

"Dude, you sick," Leo said while high-fiving Bobby, who had also shaved his head.

I leaned in to Lil and whispered, "Those are dads on our team." She nodded. Lil wore a floral pattern sundress that reached all the way down to her wedge sandals, and held a lacy white fan that she occasionally waved in an attempt to battle the heat. Darcy waved to us and pushed her way through the crowd to stand beside us. "Darcy, this is Lil. Rachel's grandmother," I said.

After they exchanged greetings, I asked where the rest of her posse was. Okay, I wanted to see where Ron was. "Helping Mimi get the girls warmed up," she said, rolling her eyes. "Tough job in this weather, right?" Darcy wore her hair in a bun, but sweat formed around the crown. She stroked her throat often. I wasn't exactly sure what it was supposed to accomplish, but she seemed committed to it, so I didn't question her.

Trailer Guy's voice boomed importantly. "We enjoy our freedoms and liberties today because of the fearless sacrifices made by those who came before us. It all began when a brave band of Pilgrims set forth on the *Mayflower* to seek a better life in the New World." With this, a giant *Mayflower* float sailed by the cheering crowd. Pilgrims on board waved their fifty-star flags with unbridled enthusiasm not typically associated with Puritans.

"A fifty-star flag," Lil whispered. "Ah, the fruits of the California educational system."

One long-haired teenage boy in a black Puritan hat and large white collar gave the crowd a hang-ten gesture and threw his head back and forth as though he were listening to Boiling Lead on his iPod. A middle-aged couple in the same get-up did the bump seventies-style, while one sexy little thing clad in black-and-white blew kisses at the crowd very suggestively. It wasn't a friendly "love ya!" gesture. It was more like something from *Puritans Gone Wild.*

"The slutty one looks like Gia," I whispered to Darcy.

Darcy gasped. "It is Gia!"

"How did Gia get on the *Mayflower*?!" I shrieked.

Lil smiled and quipped, "Now, now, she's obviously seeking religious freedom like the rest of them."

Gia spotted us and began jumping up and down excitedly, which was never a good idea on a float. Tom chuckled and waved at us, "Hello, ladies!" That man disgusted me.

"My goodness, you can see quite a bit of cleavage through that bib," Lil remarked. We all looked more closely and realized that Gia had a slightly different costume than the rest. While most of the Pilgrims wore the traditional white bibs over black smocks, Gia had white fishnet covering the scoop neck of her black leotard. I thought I'd escaped the porn costumes at soccer tournaments in Manchester. Thankfully, Rachel was with her team and nowhere near this site, lest I have to explain to my fresh-faced twelve-year-old why Miles Standish had a boner.

Trailer Guy continued. "After years of living under English tyranny, the settlers revolted against the king and declared their independence." A dozen men wearing bright blue jackets and white wigs marched by, playing "Yankee Doodle Dandy" on their flutes. Behind them were two drummers and a flock of Founding Fathers displaying a replica of the Declaration of Independence. The voice dropped an octave and proclaimed, "Let freedom reign!"

The next voice I heard was a familiar slur. "What the —?!"

All heads in our area turned to Drunk Dick, who was standing agape pointing at Thomas Jefferson. "That's friggin' Danny Cartwright!"

Dave found us and asked, "What did I miss?" He leaned in to kiss me hello, but I quickly turned my head down to look for nothing in my purse. Nervously, I introduced Lil to Dave, stressing her status.

I turned to Dave and provided an update. "Dick's had a bit too much to drink."

Dick bellowed, "Danny Cartwright, you thought you saw the last of me, didn't you?! You're gonna pay this time!"

Danny Cartwright looked terrified, his eyebrows like parentheses. He pointed at himself and mouthed, *Me?*

"Don't you play dumb!" Dick shouted. All of the Founding Fathers and the Pilgrims on the stern of the *Mayflower* were now watching the drama unfold. "I'd know your ugly mug anywhere, wig or no wig! Yer nothing but a two-bit cheater."

Darcy wiped her brow. "I've never really trusted Thomas Jefferson. Did you know he had slaves?"

As Lil, Dave, and I laughed, Dick lunged into the parade and grabbed Jefferson/Cartwright by the collar and started shaking him. Soon, a blue jacket lay on the ground with the jackhammer of Dick's fist thrusting into it. The Founding Fathers shouted for help but nary a one of them jumped in to break up the fight. Okay, the ass-kicking.

The crowd screamed when Dick picked up Jefferson and threw him through a drum. Lil gasped, "Claire! Do something!" Without thinking, I jumped into the brawl, grabbing George Washington's ax on my way.

"Dick, get off him!" I demanded, holding the ax.

Dick looked up at me and informed me, "The ax is plastic, Claire!" and continued beating this poor soul. "He deserves it anyhow for cheatin' me!"

Weakly, pleadingly, the bloody-faced man uttered, "I have no idea who—"

"You think I'm stupid, Cartwright?! You think you can walk outta a poker game and screw Dick Merrick outta forty bucks and get away with it?! No sir, sooner or later, I'm gonna catch up with you and kick your fuckin' ass, buddy!"

*Hardly a time to be calling another person "buddy."*

"Please," Jefferson said weakly. My God, Dick was out of his mind! He was actually going to kill this man over a forty-dollar poker dispute. Finally, John Hancock came to Jefferson's rescue, running toward Dick wielding his quill pen overhead.

A man of many fights, Dick knew what to do when someone came at him. He flew out of the way like a matador's red cape and left Hancock plunging toward—me! My right thigh to be exact. And while George Washington's ax was plastic, John Hancock's quill was very real and very sharp. Whoever said that the pen was mightier than the sword had obviously been stabbed with one. The cut required eight stitches at the local hospital.

The upside of my stabbing was that I won the Emergency Room Injury of the Day. Apparently, the staff awards the most bizarre accident of each day and posts a photo of the patient on its wall of fame.

I realized that in my short time as a club soccer parent, I'd grown more competitive. I felt a bit of pride as I held the shining trophy with the wings supporting a Beanie Baby of Eeyore. (I suppose the message was that this was the jackass award.) I was a little disappointed to learn that the trophy stayed at the hospital. "The glory is yours forever," my doctor said, stitching me up. "You have stiff competition on holidays too, with all your barbecues and fireworks and the like. So what did you do to piss off John Hancock so bad, anyway?"

"She did a very brave deed," Lil told him. When the doctor excused himself, she said, "Claire, I cannot get over your actions today!"

"You told me to do something," I replied.

"I meant something like calling security." We laughed. "It wasn't exactly what I had in mind, but I must say it was good to see you running toward a problem rather than away from it." After an awkward silence during which Lil seemed to be deciding whether or not to continue, she went on. "Remember when Rachel was born and you wanted to move to Bali because California had too many earthquakes?"

"I believe it was Bora Bora," I said, feigning indignation.

"Well, wherever it was, it was good to see a different side of you today, though I must say, you might have chosen a safer forum." She kissed my forehead. "You're a braver person than you once were, Claire Emmett."

As Lil and I left the hospital, I posted my photo on the corkboard and smiled. It wasn't a fist full of medals, but a soccer mom had to take her victories where she could.

# Chapter Twenty-Five

Lil and I made it back to the field in time to watch the last few minutes of Rachel's second game. While I was the most bizarre injury at the hospital emergency room, I certainly wasn't the most serious, which meant a long wait for treatment. Every time I grew impatient and asked Lil to step outside and call Darcy for a score, the giant double doors would swing open and bring in another cracked skull or broken arm. It was late in the day, and all the parents we passed on our way back to the field seemed at their wit's end. Fathers were lecturing their sons about what they could've done better, and one mother had gone totally Joan Crawford on her daughter. "You made me sick the way you played today," she barked. *Are you sure it's not the portrait-sized piece of funnel cake you're scarfing down?* The daughter hung her head. "You don't deserve to wear that jersey. Take it off right now!" The girl looked incredulous. "I said take it off!"

"I'm not wearing anything underneath," the girl squeaked.

"Gimme a break," the mother snapped. "You're eight. There's nothing to cover up anyway."

Lil and I looked at each other in shock. "Touching, isn't it?" I said.

"Excuse me, ma'am," Lil said to the mother. The mother's and child's heads whipped around to see what the stranger wanted. "That child needs sunscreen if she's going to walk around without a shirt. She'll burn to a crisp on a day like this."

"Why don't you mind your own business, lady?!" the mother snapped. "I know how to handle my own kid."

"Have it your way," Lil said. "For the record, that's what Lizzie Borden's mother used to say too."

I muffled a laugh while the mother stood dumbfounded for a few seconds. "Put your shirt back on," the mother said, tossing the jersey at her daughter.

"Who's Lizzie Borden?" the girl asked.

"Never you mind about Lizzie Borden. Put the shirt on."

After they were well out of earshot, Lil said, "That's what I call pulling a Claire."

"Oh please," I teased. "All she was armed with was funnel cake, and it didn't look like she was about to give that up."

Lil pouted playfully. "She had a fork. We can't all put ourselves in the path of dangerous signatories."

◠◡

When we reached the field, even the Normals were shouting zealously. I knew we'd lost the first game and were down two goals at halftime of this one. "What's the score?" I asked Darcy, setting our seats next to her.

"Three-zero, we're losing," she said, shoveling spiral pasta salad into her mouth. "You have got to try some of this. Giovanna's grandmother brought like seven different pasta salads for lunch. We've got tons of leftovers," she said, nodding over in Paulo's and his mother's direction. "She said the girls are too skinny and need some meat on their bones." Needless to say, it's a good thing that Mimi doesn't speak Italian and Carla doesn't speak English because there was a definite difference of opinion on that one.

"I miss all the good stuff," I said.

Darcy protested with her mouth full. After she finished her bite, she said, "The pen thing was still the highlight of the day, but it's been a day of drama." Lil leaned in to hear the gossip. "Mimi's now on the warpath saying that Gunther's the cause of our poor performance."

"Why would she say that?" Lil asked.

"Because we're losing," Darcy explained.

Dave walked over and asked how my leg was doing. "It'll heal," I dismissed.

"I need to talk to you," he said in that *we need to talk* way.

"Um, okay," I said.

As we walked away from the crowd, Dave inquired about my prognosis. Then about my sister. Then finally, he cut to the chase. "Claire, you know I like you." I nodded and assured that I felt the same. "Yeah, well, I think we need to hold off on any sort of, you know, relationship."

He froze mid-word. I looked around the field. Fathers' mouths hung open mid-scream and players stood still on the field. In an instant, action resumed. "You do?" I asked.

"I do."

"Why?"

"Claire, I don't think you're ready to date yet," he said. "Or maybe it's me, I don't know. In any case, all the cancellations, the whole hospital photography thing. It's a hint and a half for a guy."

"No, no!" I said, panicked. "I'm just playing hard to get, that's all."

He laughed slightly. "I wish that were true, Claire. We're still friends, right?"

"Of course," I said, devastated by the thought of losing him as a friend.

"So, let's keep it that way and stay in touch, and who knows what'll happen later."

Lil turned from her chair to see what was going on between Dave and me. *Just getting dumped. Be back with you in a moment, Lil!*

"Okay," I said, holding back tears. "I'm sorry that—I wish I was more together right now."

Dave smiled. This man was more pure-hearted than anyone I'd ever known. "Don't lose my number. I'll take you back in a New York minute."

"But I'm not dumping *you*!"

"Claire," he said, correcting me with his tone. "You dumped me weeks ago. I'm only saying the words aloud. It's okay. I understand."

CR ℬ

The girls returned to Santa Bella without a single victory, much less a fist full of medals. Still, they were giddy with tales of Rachel's mother being stabbed in the butt with John Hancock's pen. The pen never made it anywhere near my butt, but the girls liked this visual far too much to let accuracy interfere with a good story.

As we made our way back to my minivan, Gunther called out to me. He jogged up and said that Rachel had played well at the tournament. "You didn't see last game. She play a smart game. I have high hopes for Rachel Emmett," he said in his Germanic clip. I thanked him, not only for the tournament, but for the special interest he seemed to be taking in my daughter. At practice, he often used her as a demonstrator and seemed to soften when he spoke to her. I wanted to ask him why he'd taken Rachel under his wing, but it wasn't the sort of thing you asked without sounding suspicious of his motives, which I was not. Instead, I just told him how much being on the team meant to Rachel. "I know," he said. "I was Rachel once." Thinking Gunther really had bumbled his English this time, I started to correct him, but he continued before I could do so. "I was seven years old when my mother died in the car crash. I play soccer all day every time I could. Instead of crying, I practice penalty kick. Instead of feeling mad at driver, I kick ball. By time I am ten, I am so good with ball that I can go anywhere on field with it, and no one can take it away from me. In soccer, I am in charge of what happens," Gunther explained. "My father cry all the time until he come to my futbol game. Then he see me play and he is happy again. Futbol give me life. Soccer make my father put his shoes on and come out of the house to see me play."

I smiled. Soccer is life. I get it now.

∞

Dick was banned from all future Patriots Cups. As it turned out, Thomas Jefferson was not Danny Cartwright and never cheated Drunk Dick out of his meager poker winnings. Jefferson, also known as Philip Oberholtzer, filed assault and battery charges and has a permanent restraining order against Dick. "My mistake" was Dick's big concession as he told a group of parents about the incident at practice the following week. "The guy looked exactly like this fucker who screwed me outta forty bucks."

Gia told the group that she had "*the* best time" at the tournament. "I missed spring break this year, so this totally helped me blow off steam."

*Spring break? Is Gia still in college?*

"Gia, how old are you?" Nancy asked.

"Twenty-four," she said.

"And you're a student?" I asked.

"Yeah," Gia said, fidgeting with her ring. "I took some time off to deal with family stuff though, so I'm not sure when I'll finish."

*Deal with family stuff! Oh, please, is that what they're calling blowing your geezer groom these days?*

Without an ounce of sarcasm, Darcy added, "Well, if anyone deserves a break, it's you, Gia. Tell us, how did you wind up on the *Mayflower*?"

"We didn't want to drive in the morning, so we got to San Luis Obispo the night before. When we were checking in, there was a big fundraiser for the Patriots right there in the grand ballroom, so we were like, there! Anyway, they had this live auction, and I went a little crazy so I could get the super cute Pilgrim costume."

Before our resident trophy bride could regale us with tales from the *Mayflower*, Mimi stormed over to the cluster of parents. "Parent meeting, now!" she demanded. Darcy and I tried to contain our snickers. There was no need for such a grand proclamation. We were already assembled in the requisite half-moon formation, ready for her to turn our sideline chat into an emergency summit. "We need to get a handle on what's going on with the team," she snapped. Sadly, I knew she was referring to the girls' fitness rather than the need to control alcohol consumption at games. "Gunther's zoned out during games! He has no clue when to make substitutions and which players have chemistry together."

I turned to watch Gunther as he led the girls in soccer drills. He looked coherent to me. He was no rousing Knute Rockne, that was for sure, but he seemed to know what he was doing. More importantly, Rachel adored and respected him.

"Hear, hear!" Dick agreed with Mimi.

Gia searched the field.

"She's right," Loud Bobby blasted. "Those were some kick-ass teams, but we didn't have to get shut down as bad as we did."

Leo added, "That dude's got his head up his ass." I almost felt incomplete until he punctuated the sentence with "*Sivious.*"

Nancy's willingness to speak up always amazed me. "Let's not forget that the girls were playing in the gold bracket at the Patriots Cup. Of course, they're not going to fare as well as they did in the bronze."

"You mean the retard league?" Dick taunted.

Nancy stood straight. "You are vile."

"I need everyone to focus on our discussion about fitness," Mimi barked.

*We were having a discussion about fitness?*

"As manager of this team, I need to start asserting my authority a bit around here!" Mimi told us. *Shit, what exactly had we been experiencing?* "The girls are to meet at my house at 7 a.m. on Mondays, Wednesdays, and Fridays where I will resume fitness training with them."

"Does Gunther know about this?" Jessica asked. Her hand was still wrapped in white gauze bandages.

"I don't need to tell Gunther everything," Mimi defended. "What I need to do is make decisions that are in the best interest of these girls."

As I looked at my feet, I remembered Lil's comment about my running away from uncomfortable situations. It's not that I hadn't already made this self-observation. I just didn't realize how liberating it was to do the opposite. In the moment when I ran into the parade of patriots, and the last time I stood up to Mimi, I felt like the Claire I was when I was Rachel's age. I felt like the me who hadn't learned to hide. "Mimi," I heard my own voice say, "exactly how is scheduling double-secret practices in the best interest of the girls?"

"Right on, double-secret practice. *Animal House!*" Bobby said.

Nancy added her two cents, then Darcy chimed in with her objections. Twenty minutes later, no one was on board with Mimi's clandestine plan. We all had our different reasons, but the bottom line was that no one was bringing their daughters to an early morning secret fitness training with Mimi.

"How much fatter do these girls need to get before you people start taking this problem seriously?!" Mimi asked as she stormed off.

When practice was over, Cara was left looking around the field for her mother. "Mrs. Emmett, have you seen my mom?"

Heads began scanning the area.

"Don't worry, Cara," I assured her. "I'm sure she's fine."

"Oh, I'm sure she's fine too, but I need to get home."

"I'll give you a ride, honey," I told her.

## ○8 ○○

When Rachel and I returned home from soccer practice, I popped dinner in the oven and pressed the flashing light on the answering machine. "Claire, it's me," my mother said with an uncharacteristic lilt in her voice. "I have some zippy news for you! We were shooting the cover for the November issue today and made a last-minute change to the model's top—a fabulous looking V-neck thing, but that's beside the point. We needed a necklace that would pull the look together, and guess what happened to be around my neck? You guessed it!" *I did? I was still stuck on the fact that some poor older women had to don autumn clothing in the height of this sweltering summer heat.* "My lira necklace—the one you made for me—is going to be on the cover of *Garb*. Isn't that fun?!" *Who was this woman using words like "fun" and "zippy" in one thirty-second message?* "We'll be up late tonight if you want to call us back. Mexico is taking on France at eleven, so you can call till around two."

Beep.

"Hi Claire. Hi Rachel. It's Grandma Lil," she said, masking fear with levity. "I have nothing to say really, just that I enjoyed watching you play soccer last weekend and I hope we see each other again. Soon." I could hear a quiet desperation in her voice, one that begged me to return her call and assure her that we weren't going to disappear again. After a momentary pause, she continued. "Claire, I got a very unusual invitation in the mail today that I'd like to speak with you about. Please do call."

After Rachel went to bed that night, I returned Lil's call. "I'm glad you called," she said with thinly disguised relief. "Have you ever heard of the Steve Emmet—one t—Foundation?"

"Oh boy," I sighed.

"They say they're funding research for lung cancer," Lil said.

"Non-smoking-related lung cancer," I corrected.

"So you've heard of these people?"

"One of Steve's partners from the firm. He has this, well, very enthusiastic wife who started a foundation in his name."

After a moment of silence, Lil reminded me, "Stevie had lymphoma."

"I know, Lil."

"Then why is this woman ..." she trailed off. "We're going to this dinner," Lil said emphatically. "I'm buying a table and we're going to see what this foundation is all about. I'm inviting your mother and Blake. If there's anyone you'd like to bring, please let me know."

"Like a date?" I asked.

"I suppose it would be a little awkward, wouldn't it?" Lil said, laughing for the first time. "Though I hope you know that if there were anyone you were dating, he would be welcome at my table."

"Oh, I, um."

"You don't have to discuss it with me," she said. "I suppose what I'm trying to say is that I expect you to meet someone nice someday, Claire. And when you do, I hope you won't feel funny about it with me."

I laughed ruefully. "I think that someday is quite a ways off."

"You haven't met anyone interesting?" Lil asked. "I thought there might be something between you and that fellow at Rachel's soccer game."

*How mortifying! Could everyone see through me as easily as Lil?*

"Absolutely not!" I protested vehemently. "He's married to my best friend. I would *never* betray her!"

"Dave is married to Darcy?" Lil asked. "He told me he was Jessica's *ex*-husband."

"Oh, um, you're right, he is," I fumbled. "So, you're telling me that if I met someone, you'd be okay with that?"

"Someone special," Lil clarified. "Before Stevie's father died, he told me that the highest praise I could have for our marriage would be to remarry."

"And you think Steve would have felt this way?"

"I think he would have wanted to challenge the young man to a few arm wrestling contests first, but yes, I think he'd want you to be happy with someone else."

"Can I tell you something I've never told anyone, Lil?"

"You fancy Darcy's husband," she said.

"Guess I kind of let the cat out of the bag on that one," I said. "Do you think I'm just awful?"

"No, it makes complete sense to me," Lil said.

"I swear to you, nothing has ever happened."

"Oh, I'm certain of that, Claire." Lil continued. "Sweetheart, I've known you for a long time, and if someone asked me to bet on whether you'd have an affair with a married man, I'd put my money on no, and rest easy. You're just not the type, which is why it makes perfect sense that you'd find yourself attracted to your best friend's husband. You know he's unavailable, so you can be too. It's like wanting to marry George Clooney. It's completely safe. Now, let me guess at another thing. You're less interested in the real prospect, Dave. Am I right?" I made some sort of meager acknowledgment, like a mousy grunt. "If you had feelings for Dave, he might return them, and you two might find yourselves in a real relationship. That has benefits, but risks too. That's a frightening prospect for a girl who wants to run off to Timbuktu every time there's a tremor. Am I overstepping?"

"No, it's okay," I said, holding my chest, reminding myself to breathe.

"Can I give you some advice, sweetheart? You need to end the relationship with your imaginary boyfriend next door and start dating real men."

"Lil," I said, sniffing, "where would I be without you?"

# Chapter Twenty-Six

The remainder of the summer was fairly uneventful, which was exactly what I'd hoped it would be. Though Mimi had aspirations of the team playing in eight tournaments, the three were plenty for me. Rachel may have enjoyed more soccer-filled weekends, but I needed a few solid days of lazing by the Santa Bella pool. I was never fully relaxed because there was always a chance of Mimi showing up in her bikini and strutting around the deck like she owned the place, which she probably did. Even if I was buried behind a book, she never missed the opportunity to cast a shadow over me until I had no choice but to look up and acknowledge her. Then she'd make a face as if she were repulsed by the sight of my body.

The regular soccer season started the weekend after school began, which I thought was particularly poor planning by the Pico League. Learning the names of the various leagues was an education in its own right. The California Youth Soccer Association had a Southern California branch called, not so creatively, Cal South. Then there were various regional bodies that oversaw entire counties. San Diego had the Presidio League. Santa Bella had the Pico League, which covered forty soccer clubs, like Conquistadors, Turf, and Kix. During the regular season, we would play other teams in the Pico League. During tournaments, we'd mostly see teams from Cal South. But during the coveted four-weekend State Cup, we would meet up with our counterparts from Chula Vista to Eureka, the most southern and northern tips of the state.

Just to make the weekend even busier for us, the Steve Emmet Foundation "Breath of Fresh Air" dinner was also scheduled for that first Saturday night in September.

Mimi emailed the parents letting us know that we were playing in the triple-A bracket, the highest level. She explained that although we might lose some games, the girls would develop fastest playing against premiere teams. Wonder of wonders, Gunther agreed and there were no disputes between them. He simply emailed back a note to everyone, saying, "This is good idea."

Both Kix and the Conquistadors were skillful in their footwork, passing and shooting. The fact that the score was zero-zero for more than thirty minutes said a lot about each team's defense as well. Rachel played beautifully, though she was a bit distracted by the sight of my mother's bullhorn being confiscated by the referee after she ignored his repeated requests to stop shouting "Viva, Rachel!" Most parents were amused by Barbara, but Mimi, of course, did her fair share of eye rolling. I thought that after an entire summer of Dick's drunkenness, Bobby's volume, Leo's sideline rantings, and Paulo's Italian tirades, my mother made for a refreshing change.

"Lady!" the referee shouted, holding a yellow card. "If I have to tell you to hold it down one more time, you're getting red carded." A few minutes later, he kept his promise. The Psycho Dads hooted with admiration for my mother, who waltzed off the field with her head held high.

"Yo' mama's the bomb!" Leo told me. "*Sivious.*"

"Don't let the bastards get y'down, Barb!" shouted Drunk Dick, who was immediately given a warning by the referee.

"I shall return," she said dramatically as she held her hand overhead, waving like the queen. Blake followed, saying he'd meet us back at the house.

In the end, the girls lost to the Conquistadors in the final moments of the first game.

Though I would never admit this to Mimi, I was pleased that she'd placed the girls in lower brackets for our first two tournaments. It was a good opportunity for them to learn to take the ball to open space. With tougher teams we'd face in the regular season, there was so much pressure that the players didn't have time to try out new strategies. Today, it was clear that practicing those plays in the early tournaments paid off. Rachel looked to her three forwards, who were blanketed by Conquistadors defenders. She passed the ball back to our sweeper, who shot the ball thirty yards up the field, slightly farther and wider than where our left forward was. The pass gave Kelly just enough time to collect the ball, then cross it in front of the net, where Mariah slammed it in definitively. We thought the game was won, but Conquistadors were determined to, well, conquer, and came back with two equally beautifully executed goals, the final one scored with less than a minute left on the clock.

Losing wasn't a big deal for me. (It was for Rachel, though, who sobbed for about five minutes after every loss.) I just enjoyed watching the girls play well. Of course, the highlight of this game for me had nothing to do with soccer. Cara kept shouting to Mimi that her shin guard felt funny. Mother-of-the-Year belted back that she should focus on the game. Finally, right before the whistle blew for a kickoff, Cara reached down under her sock and pulled a lacy black thong from underneath her shin guard. Both sidelines of parents burst into laughter.

Apparently, the Velcro from Cara's shin guard trapped Mimi's underwear in the clothes dryer and hung on persistently. "The housekeeper is so dead when we get home," Mimi muttered, running onto the field and collecting her tiny slingshot.

I glanced at Darcy, who was nodding her head. "Now, that was a first," she laughed, poking Ron beside her. He laughed along, seeming to enjoy the game with his wife and younger daughter.

"You ought to get panties like that, hon," he said to Darcy.

Even Preston, who had showed up at halftime, got in on the joke. "Atta girl, Mimi. Distract 'em however you can!"

Dave and I managed to remain quite friendly, which was a relief. I really enjoyed his friendship, but things can get so sticky after a breakup. Though he was the official dumper, we both knew it was he who would likely feel the sting. Thankfully, there was none of that weirdness between us.

There was plenty of awkwardness, however, between Ron and me, despite the fact that we never had any romantic involvement. Well, he didn't. A few days earlier, he caught me eavesdropping on another of his clandestine cell phone conversations. I couldn't help myself. All that whispering sounded so secretive, I just had to listen. Disastrously, my cell phone rang as I was huddled behind a bush. He barked "Who's there?" several times, but the answer was pretty clear since the ringing was coming from my hedge.

CR ∞

As Rachel practiced her piano in her sweaty jersey, shin guards and socks, I checked my email and saw that Mimi was back on the warpath.

## MEMORANDUM

TO:     The Team
FROM: Mimi
DATE: August 29
RE:     Today's fiasco

I'm sure I don't need to point out the myriad of tactical errors the girls made today! The game should have been ours by two goals, and if we had had a competent coach that's what would have happened!

It is also abundantly apparent that the girls are not getting enough exercise! Some are horrendously chunky! This is not a vanity issue! They move slowly on the field when they are fat! Players can feel our girls approaching from behind as the ground shakes like it did with those damned dinosaurs in Jurassic Freaking Park! We need to get serious about this!

Please ask your guests to refrain from classless behavior when visiting our games! Enthusiasm is great, but we need to set an example for our girls! I'm sure we would not want any of our daughters to behave in a way that would warrant a red card at a game! Let's not send them the message that this is okay!

Go Kix!

That was it! The only people who got to criticize my mother were Kathy and me. I hit "reply all" and began typing.

Dear Team:

I couldn't agree more with Mimi about sideline behavior. I will ask my mother to refrain from making such scathing comments as "Go Rachel!" and "Yippee!" It must have been devastating for the girls to hear such language, especially when they are used to the sober wisdom of some of the fathers on the team. Mimi, frankly, I was embarrassed by your note. Not only because you have a valid point about my mother's overzealousness, but because I've been silent for too long about the blatant consumption of alcohol at games and practices. Three fathers on this team regularly bring beer and flasks of hard liquor. One has been banned from a tournament because of his drunken assault on another parent! I cannot believe that your first mention of poor behavior from the sidelines is about my mother, a senior citizen with a passion for soccer. Admittedly, the bullhorn was a bit much and I will speak to her about it, but I challenge this team to take a good, hard look at what we are teaching our daughters when we turn a blind eye to the alcohol abuse. Let's all support Mimi in enforcing the Kix guidelines that prohibit alcohol consumption from practices and games.

I thought the girls did a terrific job against a very tough team today. I did not play soccer when I was in college, but if I had, I certainly would not find these degrading emails in the least bit motivating. Our coach and players did a fine job today. Unfortunately, our opponents played a little better. Let's get 'em next time!

Go Kix!!!!!
Claire Emmett

I hit send before I could change my mind. The one thing that bothered me a tad was that Mimi was right about the girls' fitness. Okay, fatness. I couldn't understand what was going on with them. They played soccer three times a week and every player except Cara was porking out, and I'll bet her mother didn't allow her to eat anything but celery sticks and Fiber One cereal with no milk. Ever since school started, the girls really ballooned. Mimi said that because the girls were sitting at desks for six hours a day, they weren't burning as many calories as they were during break, but I was starting to wonder.

CR 80

I looked at my watch and saw that there was a little time before I had to jump in the shower. When I called Violet's house last week, her father simply said he had nothing to say to me. Still, I couldn't help wanting to know how Violet's knee was healing. Mimi simply told us that Violet wouldn't be returning until State Cup, but I felt like there was more to the story. With Mimi, there always was.

"Hello, Violet?" I asked when I heard a female voice. The television was blasting in the background so it was difficult to determine whether it was her or Leesha.

"Yes."

"Hi, honey. It's Claire Emmett, Rachel's mom. I'm calling to see how your knee is doing. Is your mother around?"

"Daddy says my knee is real good, but the doctor says I can't play for a few more months."

In the background, I heard an angry male voice. "Who you talkin' to, girl?"

Uh-oh. Noooo mer-saaaaay!

"It's for Mama," Violet said, then put me on the phone with Leesha.

I heard voices garbled as Violet explained that it was me. "Hello," she said impatiently. I could hear a door close behind her.

"Hi Leesha, it's Claire from the team. I was—"

"I know what you was," she snapped. "An' I'll tell you what I told Mimi last time she called. Violet can't play soccer till her doctor says it's okay. I don't care who you give her spot to, this is my baby!"

"Oh," I said, taken aback. "I'm not calling to get her to play. I just wanted to see how she's doing."

"Uh-huh," she said with a tone of skepticism. "You tell that Mimi she can stop callin' on us. She can stop havin' other people call on us. My baby don't play till the doctor says she's okay."

"Leesha, you don't understand. I—"

"You can give her spot to little Pissy for all I care!"

"Who you talkin' to in there?!" I heard Ray shout through the door. "Don't let them give Violet's spot away, woman!"

"Leesha!" I said, fighting for a voice in the conversation that now became one between Angry Leesha and Crazy Ray. "I'm just calling to see how Violet's doing! That's all."

"That's all?" I could see her eyebrow raised and her lips stuck out to one side. "Nothin' more?"

"Well, if you need anything like a prescription filled or a ride to physical therapy ..."

Silence.

"Hello? Are you still there, Leesha?"

"Yeah."

"Okay, well then, is there, um, anything you need?"

"I do need some Comet."

"Comet?"

"The cleanser," she explained.

"No, I understand what Comet is, but what does that have to do with Violet's knee?"

"If I take her to the doctor, I don't have a whole lot a time left to buy Comet."

I laughed to myself. How did I always get stuck with these assignments? "Okay, Comet it is. Anything else?"

"Paper towels, Brillo, and Windex."

"Okay, anything else?"

"I could use a carton of Lucky Strikes."

CR SO

As I was getting ready to step into the shower, I heard Dave's voice blasting through the house through the answering machine.

"Rachel!" I called to her hoping she'd pick up the phone. I peeked my head down the staircase and looked at her, still in her soccer uniform, doing Sudoku at the kitchen counter.

"What?" she asked.

"Did you want to get the phone?"

"It's for you," she replied.

Dave's voice continued, "Anyway, I know it's late notice, but I thought I'd check and—"

"Hello," I answered.

"Oh hey, Claire. Screening?"

"Just getting ready for this fundraising dinner tonight."

"That's actually why I'm calling. Lil just called—"

"Lil, my mother-in-law, Lil?"

"Yeah, she's got an extra seat at her table for this thing tonight and asked if I'd like to come as her guest," Dave explained.

I paused, tackling questions from the trivial to important. *How did she get Dave's phone number? Why did she invite him to the bogus Steve Emmet Foundation dinner? Why didn't she check with me first?* "Oh," was all I could muster.

"I'm wondering if it's going to be awkward if I go," he said. "If it's something you'd rather I sit out, I understand."

"Oh," I said again, dumbly. "What did you tell Lil?"

"I said I'd check with you and get back to her. Claire, I haven't pulled any punches with you and I'm not about to start now. I'm looking for any excuse to spend time with you, but this isn't exactly your typical rubber chicken benefit, so I want to check in and see what you think of me tagging along. I mean, I want to be respectful of your wishes."

"Respectful of my wishes?" I repeated.

"Well, your boundaries," he said.

"You sound like such a therapist," I teased.

"That doesn't sound like a compliment."

"It's not. I feel like I'm going to have to turn in an invoice to my HMO after this conversation."

"My God, that's exactly what Jessica used to say," he laughed.

"She was right. Treat me like a woman, not a patient."

"A woman?"

"A woman friend," I clarified, though as I said that I wondered about my position. Might that have been a flutter in my heart as we bantered?

"Claire, I'm really concerned about you," he said.

"Please, Dave. I'm sure I'll be fine whether you attend tonight's event or not."

"No, it's not that. Do you really have an HMO?"

# Chapter Twenty-Seven

I was stunned by the volume of chatter at the cocktail reception before the event. I'd expected maybe a hundred people to show up at this thing, but before we even entered the lobby, we could hear that there were far more in attendance. When Dave and I turned the corner, I stopped dead in my tracks at the sight of nearly a thousand people mingling at four separate bars. In my black wrap dress, I was painfully underdressed as women sashayed about, each gown more glittering than the next. Half of the men were in tuxedos, while the others were in suits. I felt like a waitress. My rhinestone barrette pulling back my low ponytail paled in comparison to the flowered-up dos and braided masterpieces. Maggie Jennings wore a rhinestone tiara. Good Lord, let there be a podcast of this in heaven.

A few minutes after our arrival, I found Lil, Barbara, and Blake. Steve's brother and his wife were running late. As we chatted, we noticed the pianist was wearing small angel wings as he played cheesy eighties pop songs at the keyboard. Upon further inspection, I was aghast to see that they were actually model lungs thinly covered with white feathers! My jaw dropped, but before I could say a word, the group turned and politely began clapping. The pianist stood, placed his hands in a prayer position, and bowed. *Blech!* He sat again, then began playing "Lost in Love" by Air Supply. Come to think of it, the last song he played was "Every Woman in the World." Oh. My. God. The song before that was "Even the Nights Are Better." Was Maggie Jennings really hosting a reception for non-smoking-related lung cancer where the musical repertoire consists solely of music by Air Supply?

"You look like a ghost, sweetheart," Lil said, touching my arm. I closed my eyes and took in the delicious scent of White Shoulders, the perfume she wore at my wedding, family gatherings, and her son's funeral.

"Why shouldn't I?" I shrieked. "The piano player's dressed like an angel, and the hostess looks like the Queen of England. This is clearly a masquerade ball. Why shouldn't I look like a ghost?"

"Shhhh," she said, stroking my arm. "Relax, sweetheart." Mother and Blake milled about chatting with guests. Dave was getting us drinks at the bar. Soon the ballroom doors opened and it was time to be seated. Now, admittedly Lil spelled her last name differently than the Steve Emmet Foundation, but one would think they'd notice the similarity and check to see if she was related. No such luck. Our table was in the outer region of Siberia.

After dinner plates were cleared, the lights dimmed and Maggie floated onto the stage. "That dress is awful!" my mother said, a bit too loudly.

"Good evening, friends," Maggie began. Looking dramatically to the left, then right, then up toward the heavens (or her spotlight), she continued. "Friends. Family. We are here tonight to honor the memory of a beautiful soul who left us far before his time."

Lil's eyes glazed. While this was no more than a performance for Maggie, Lil and I really felt the sting of Steve's death. Behind

Maggie was a screen that read, "Welcome to the first annual Steve Emmet Foundation Dinner." As Maggie continued, a studio portrait of the Jennings family appeared on the screen. It was the same one they had used on last year's holiday letter. "When Steve came to the firm, it was with big dreams and even more drive." Lil looked at me, smiling at the memory. The screen flashed a new photo of Steve's back as he tossed a football to Jimmy Jennings. "At the annual picnic, no one spent more time with the kids than our Steve." The picture changed to a meeting where Ed Jennings was speaking and sixteen partners sat around the mahogany table and listened. *Is that Steve or Zack Winston? Oh, there he is in the red tie! I bought him that tie.* "Having Steve at the firm made us all richer, and I don't just mean because of his savvy business sense," she said with a cheesy laugh. "We were blessed by his spirit, his vitality, his joie de vivre." The image changed again to Steve and his friend, Elaine Chin, after they finished the Los Angeles Marathon. They held water bottles with the firm logo emblazoned on them. "Steve worked hard and played hard with his beautiful, athletic wife, Clara."

Everyone at our table looked at me in shock. "Did she just call you Clara?" Lil asked.

"That doesn't look like you," Dave added. *Well, no, considering Elaine Chin was Chinese.*

My head dropped into my hands in horror. This horrid woman hadn't bothered to get a single fact straight about Steve. She was almost defiant in her inaccuracy.

The photo now changed to one of Ed Jennings holding six-month-old Rachel at the firm picnic. It actually was Rachel, which was a relief. Maggie continued, "And how Steve loved his son."

I almost laughed until I caught a glimpse of Lil accepting a handkerchief from Dave. "Lil, are you okay?"

"This is too much," she sniffed. "This woman is making a mockery of my son's life."

My mother placed her hand on top of Lil's and mouthed for me to *do something!*

I looked at Dave for guidance. He nodded his head in agreement, then added, "Someone needs to set this woman straight."

I felt as though I had strings on my shoulders and someone was lifting them up. I had no intention of standing, but suddenly I was on my feet. "Excuse me," I said loudly. Maggie continued, oblivious. A few tables in front of us heard me and started mumbling curiously. "Excuse me, Maggie," I said louder. More tables began buzzing as Maggie chattered still unaware of my interruption.

Rarely does life come with such recognizable moments of self-definition. I knew that how I handled the next few seconds would determine who I was from this day forward. I could sit down quietly and hide, or I could demand to be heard. "Excuse me!" I shouted so loud that nothing but the sound of my voice filled the room.

Unfazed, Maggie remained smiling, squinting into the crowd to address the silhouette in the back. "I'll be happy to answer questions from the audience after the presentation," she said sweetly. *Audience?!* "When our friend Steve was diagnosed with lung cancer, we were shocked. He didn't even—"

"No!" I shouted so loudly I shocked Maggie into silence. Lil grabbed my hand to bolster me. "Answer my question right now." The crowd began murmuring, asking who I was and what I wanted. Only one person recognized me as Steve's wife, but he was quickly corrected by another, who pointed out that I wasn't Chinese.

"As I said, I will be happy to entertain all questions after—"

"*Entertain* my question?! You'll *entertain* my question?! That is the most accurate thing you've said all night, Maggie Jennings! This whole event is about entertainment and the glorification of you and your self-important family!" There was another gasp and a few muffled giggles. Maggie stood frozen at her podium, holding her hand to her chest in horror. "Don't you even recognize me, Maggie? It's Claire. Claire, Steve's wife. Not Clara. *Claire.* Claire Emmett with two T's, Steve's widow. And this is his family," I said, gesturing to the people around our table. My outrage was mounting as I had the rapt attention of everyone in the room. "We came here to see why you started a foundation in Steve's name without checking with any of us first. We wanted to let you know that Steve didn't die of lung cancer. He died of lymphoma!" The crowd began murmuring quite loudly now. "I would have told you this if you'd bothered to call us—even once—over the last two years to see how we were doing. So you can stand up there like the almighty lung princess and pretend you cared about my husband, but I'm here to tell everyone that you are a complete and total fraud!" The crowd gasped. "Really, do any of you believe this ruse?!"

I heard a squeaky voice at another table comment, "I didn't know Maggie was Russian."

I laughed. "Listen, you're all here because you care about finding cures to serious illness. Please give money to the Cancer Society or the Lung Association because the family of Steve Emmett is completely hurt and appalled by this sham foundation."

Though the guests muffled their responses, I could tell they were with me. So could Maggie, which is why she began her sugary protest. "Claire, honey, I know this has been a difficult time for you, but please let's not lash out at those who love you most." *What?! Until three minutes ago, she thought I was a Chinese woman named Clara.*

"Grab your coats," I demanded of the table. Lil and Dave stood first and the rest followed suit.

"Please, honey, let's not let grief divide us when we need each other," Maggie said.

"Save it, Maggie!" I said, reaching for my wrap. "I've got bigger idiots than you to deal with. My kid plays club soccer."

As we all exited toward the lobby, Dave broke the tension. "I hate those charity dinners," he said. "Same old thing every time."

"You told me to say something!" I said to them.

Lil smiled. "I didn't mean right that second. Sweetheart, you've got a lot of gumption these days, but we really do need to work on your timing."

# Chapter Twenty-Eight

September brought the team two wins and two losses in the regular season games. Mimi blamed the girls' weight and sluggishness on the field, and continued urging parents to demand fitness training. She even brought a petition to practice, which half of the parents signed. This brought Preston to the field to have a parent meeting at the following practice. He explained that Gunther was the coach and whether or not to have additional fitness training was his call. "Nothing is stopping you from running laps with your kids on your own time, but the coach makes the decisions for the team," he said lightly. "By the way, does anyone know about the nine-year-old goalie at Turf? Natalie Something. I heard her family isn't happy over there. Anyone know those folks?"

The girls ran their plays, worked hard and looked good in their first four games. The Normals were satisfied, but the angry dads and their flame fanner were livid with Gunther's alleged incompetence. They were at their worst when we were down a goal or two in a game. When we were ahead, things were okay, celebrative even. While we no longer had Raymond on the sidelines shouting, "Nooooo mer-saaaaay!" Leo recycled an old hip-hop lyric and sang, "Whoop, dere it is!" whenever our girls scored.

"That's what I'm talking about!" my mother added.

Blake nodded approvingly as if the only thing he might add would be, "Jolly good."

Ron stopped provoking Dick after the last game in September, when our inebriated soccer dad charged the field and jumped on the referee's back, wrestling him to the ground. His counterpart from the other team ran out onto the field, which everyone assumed was to pull Dick off of the ref, but then he began kicking Dick. Really hard. I had mixed feelings about this.

Obviously, they were both ejected from the game, but oddly Mimi did not feel compelled to address this in her post-game email. I would have thought this was worth at least three exclamation points.

What also became part of the regular season routine were the sideline pep talks from the dads. Anytime a girl was on the bench, her father would kneel beside her and start telling her everything she did wrong. Of course, none of the Normals did this, but Dick, Bobby, Leo, and Paulo could always be counted on to deliver to his daughter a bottle of water and an utterly uninspiring discussion about how she was blowing the game for the team. Paulo's were the most tolerable because I couldn't understand what he was saying, but I didn't need to speak Italian to get the gist of it. I'd just watch Giovanna's posture deflate as her father's words drained her expression of every ounce of joy. Often, pools of tears collected in the girls' eyes right before they had to go back on the field. Sometimes these dads wouldn't even wait until the girls were off the field to criticize them. After Kylie missed a penalty kick, Dick shouted, "That's what you get for hesitating!"

CR ЯD

I don't know how I managed to turn into a Girl Friday for Raymond and Leesha, but I seemed to be visiting Target with two shopping lists a lot in the fall. Once, Rachel and I made our delivery at around dinnertime, so Leesha invited us to join them for the most succulent pot roast with sweet potatoes and corn I'd ever tasted. With every visit, Raymond softened a little toward me, but the day I won him over was when I brought Leesha a box of nicotine patches instead of her usual carton of Lucky Strikes. "You're sweet, Claire!" she said, visibly moved as she looked at the smoking cessation kit. "Look Ray, she got the patches in brown."

"What do you want?" Raymond asked me.

"I'd like Leesha to stop smoking. I don't know if you've heard the new Surgeon General's report, but they say that smoking may be related to lung cancer." Raymond smiled and nodded. "Listen, some people aren't all that sympathetic when smokers get lung cancer, that's all I'm saying." I filled them in on the Maggie Jennings dinner after Violet and Rachel left the table to play a video game. They listened agape.

CR ℘

By October, the team parents had divided like the Red Sea. There was the Dick camp, who wanted to overthrow Gunther and replace him with Mimi. Then there was the other half of the soccer team parents, who just wanted to show up at games, cheer for the girls and be done with it until the next Saturday. Unlike the Soccer Freak faction, the Normals had other activities scheduled on Saturdays before and after games. Lo and behold, they felt no need to return home immediately and review game tape with their child's private trainer. We appreciated soccer for what it was and had absolutely no desire to stage a coup d'état and instate a new regime. Frankly, I liked Gunther. Rachel's soccer skills had improved immeasurably, and most importantly, she belonged to a team at a time in her life when she needed it most. She had a place where she belonged, and I had zero interest in upsetting it.

Not only did this team bring Rachel the purpose and confidence she so desperately needed, it offered me a lot too. Parents' lives can get so busy that developing and sustaining adult friendships can be tough. Through the team, I had a standing date with Darcy and Dave, which was time I treasured. I enjoyed chatting with Nancy, Jessica, and the Jennifers; loath as I am to admit it, I found Gia surprisingly enjoyable to have around. She was like a little pink buoy in a stormy sea. Soccer also brought together my family in a way I hadn't expected. "Red Card Barb" was at every single game and didn't flinch when the alcoholic fathers gave her the nickname. Heaven help me, they liked her.

The team's October games looked a lot like September's. They won some, they lost some, and most could have gone either way because both teams fielded excellent players who seemed to be improving every week. Just as our girls perfected a set play, so did the other team. Each game was a nail-biter as opposed to the easy road to the medals we had in our first two summer tournaments. The regular season games were also unlike the pummeling we took from the teams we met at the Patriots Cup. Our girls looked solid, but it seemed unlikely that we were going to win the state championship this year. The clearer that became, the crazier Mimi got.

CR ♂

"This is so cool!" Rachel said as she held the December edition of *Garb* featuring my "fist full of lira" necklace on the cover. "When does it hit the newsstands?"

"Mid-November," I replied, trying to sound nonchalant. Secretly, I was thrilled that the following week my design would hang from the neck of an ultra-hip senior. More than the cachet of having made a necklace that would be seen by millions of women was the seal of approval from one in particular.

"So, next week every grandmother in America's going to be looking at your necklace?" Rachel asked.

Letting down my guard, I smiled coyly and said, "Only the ones with taste."

"That's so cool, Mom. You should do jewelry for teens." Ah, the ultimate compliment—acceptance by a group of Justin Bieber fans.

The following week, my mother called. "You are never going to believe what's going on here this morning!"

"Becks and Posh broke up?!"

She laughed. "Really, guess whose phone is ringing off the hook this morning?"

"Wow, I've got to hand it to you, Mom. Whoever thought your phone sex for old folks would take off?"

"Oh, you are just full of hilarity this morning, aren't you? Be serious for one moment."

"Just tell me, Mother!"

"Subscribers are calling to find out where they can get lira necklaces. Apparently, quite a few women have good memories of pre-euro Italy."

"Wow, that's amazing. I'll bet you feel pretty special having the only one."

"I'll be wearing it every day for the next few weeks," Barbara said.

"That's good."

"Claire, aren't you going to ask me what happens in a few weeks?"

"You'll get sick of it?"

"I certainly will," my mother said gleefully. "And ask me why I'll grow weary of it in a few weeks."

"Because you're a fickle fashionista who'll have moved on to setting the next trend by then."

"You're partly right," she said. "It will be a trend by then because everyone will be wearing one. Your lira necklaces are going to be the 'it' item of the holiday season. Kathy's assistant has been taking orders all morning. I finally had to remind her that she works for *Garb*, not you, so she set up a domain name and all the orders are rolling over to your email address."

"What!" I said, hoping to stop time. "Back up and tell me what you're talking about."

"We've been getting calls all day. At first we took orders, but finally had to start telling people to order through your website tomorrow morning."

"My website? Mother, I don't have a website."

"Which is why I'm calling, Claire. You need to set up a website, *tout de suite,* or should I say *pronto*?"

"Mother, back up. Kathy took orders for lira necklaces? How did she do that? What did she charge people? How did they pay?"

"You know your sister," Mother said. "She set up a PayPal account and, I'm sorry, but we had to guess how much to charge people. We couldn't reach you by cell."

"Rachel's class had a field trip," I explained. "How much did you charge?"

I could see her bony spine curve with trepidation. "Two-twenty, is that enough?"

"Two hundred twenty dollars?" I said, laughing. "No one's going to pay that for my lira necklace." I was both disappointed and relieved. There was a part of me that was looking forward to stringing together a few dozen necklaces and starting a net-based business. Since Mother was completely out of touch and priced me out of the market, it looked like that wasn't about to happen. Another part of me was grateful that I wouldn't have to hassle with a new venture. Honestly, it seemed as if Rachel's schedule was enough to fill my days.

Barbara replied haughtily, "They most certainly will. We took more than a thousand calls this morning. Check your email account."

I gasped as I logged on and the email guy said, "You've got a shitload of mail."

"Mother, I'm not set up for this!"

"Claire, get set up for it, then. You can do this. Sit down this afternoon and put together a plan. We guaranteed delivery by the holidays. Be thankful Hanukkah's late this year."

"What?!" I shrieked, scrolling down to peruse my inbox.

"Hanukkah, the Jewish holiday," Barbara explained. "Sometimes it's quite early in the season, but this year—"

"Mother! I know about Hanukkah. I've got over a thousand orders here. There's no way I can do this."

Barbara paused. "Not alone, but you'll get help. Hire some women from the neighborhood, put out a nice cake and some coffee and it'll all work out."

"You want me to set up a sweatshop at my house for suburban housewives?!"

"I said to set out a cake!" Barbara snapped.

The thought was daunting, but also exciting. In my mind I was working out the details. I'd need lira. I'd have to buy crimping beads and tools. Beads wouldn't be a problem. The more I thought about it, the more it seemed doable if I hired a dozen neighborhood women. The only part of the equation that was missing was a business manager. There was no way I could handle packaging, shipping, and billing without screwing things up royally.

As I hung up the phone, the doorbell rang. Darcy stood at the door holding a box of cereal and snacks. "Can you help me?" she began. "We're getting exterminated tomorrow and I need a place to park this stuff."

My response to her question was taking the box from her arms. "I need you to run my business for the next few weeks," I said urgently.

"I didn't know you had a business," she responded. "Everyone and their secret lives."

"It's just a temporary thing. I know this sounds bizarre, but my mother just put me in business a few hours ago," I said as I began explaining. About twenty minutes later, Darcy was my business manager, already vetoing my first decision. I wanted to post signs with the headline, "Need Holiday Cash?"

Darcy shook her head emphatically. "Thank God I'm here. Look, no self-respecting suburban mom is going to admit she needs holiday *cash*." Darcy said the word as if it were covered with vomit. "What we need to do is get on the phone and explain to people that you're in a crisis and need help."

"But I'm going to pay them."

"Doesn't matter," Darcy explained. "They need to feel like they're helping you out. Otherwise there's no reason to do it."

"Why don't we just hire women who actually need the money?"

"Do you really want a dozen strangers in your house for the next three weeks?" Darcy asked, raising her brows. For the first time since I'd known her, her presence was commandingly energetic instead of nervous.

"Darcy, can we really do this?" I asked. "I mean, we could just email these people and tell them never mind."

"Never mind? Why would we do that?"

CR SO

That afternoon at practice, Mimi called another emergency meeting of the parents. "I have it on good information that Gunther was booted off the German team because he was busted for steroids," she said, scanning for our reactions.

"Get there first!" shouted Leo, not especially interested in Mimi's charges. "Leo!" Mimi snapped. "I need everyone paying attention."

Feeling a little restless myself, I raised my hand and asked if parents still needed to attend every practice. "The season's over in a few weeks and the holidays are hectic for everyone," I said to a group that seemed to be in agreement.

Darcy added, "Yeah, come on, Mimi, no other team makes their parents sit through practices."

"If we want to be a serious soccer team, I need every parent on board. If you can't make it, Darcy, you can always send Ron. Back to the drugs. Preston told me that Gunther's career was ended by a head injury, but someone's lying because right here it says he tested positive for steroids."

Loud Bobby scrunched his face to the side. "Steroids for soccer?" I reached for Mimi's notes, but she snatched them back.

"Let me see that paper," I demanded. "For all we know, it's a recipe for angel food cake."

Ignoring me, she continued. "We need to get rid of him and I mean yesterday! We're talking about our daughters' safety."

Darcy rolled her eyes. "Are you afraid he's going to punt the girls across the field while amped up on steroids?"

"I need you all to take this seriously. If we're going to have any chance whatsoever of taking State Cup, we need to cut the dead weight from this team after next week's game."

"No fucking way!" the newly renamed Dry Drunk Dick bellowed. A judge ordered him to attend Alcoholics Anonymous meetings, but he refused to do Step One, claiming that he just had to show up, not admit he was an alcoholic. "She paid her dues like every other player on this team."

All heads turned to him quizzically. Nancy whispered, "How no one has checked *this* guy for a head injury is beyond me."

"What are you talking about?" Mimi asked.

"Tandy. You can't dump Tandy right before State Cup. I'll fight you to the death, lady!" Dick said. "Don't think I won't jest 'cause yer a chick, either."

"I'm not talking about Tandy, you fat head! I'm talking about Gunther," Mimi said. "What's wrong with you, we talked about this on the phone last night?!"

"Oh, right," he quieted.

"After the last game, we'll all thank him for his efforts this season and tell him no one wants to go to State Cup because the girls are all so fat," Mimi said.

"We're not goin' to State Cup?" Bobby shouted.

Mimi sighed, exasperated. "That's what we *tell* him. Then, I'll enroll us in the tournament with a new coach."

"And that would be you?" Darcy asked.

Mimi nodded. "I have the license. And I did play in college. Give me two months with these girls and they'll be warriors."

*Shit, I have necklaces to string.*

Jessica said she didn't like the sound of this. The Jennifers agreed. Gia said she thought it sounded sneaky. *Nothing got by that girl.*

Mimi crossed her arms. "It's what needs to be done," she explained. "Our girls did horribly this season. We've got nineteen points, and unless something dramatic happens in the next two weekends, we'll place seventh or eighth in our division for the season." Looking at me, she concluded, "Surely, even you can see that sucks, right, Claire?"

I sighed with exasperation. "So is this a safety issue, or are you just upset that the girls aren't winning every game?"

"And if the team's so terrible, what makes you think they'll do well in State Cup?" Darcy asked.

"The difference is the coaching," Mimi explained. "Gunther's pissed away a season for the girls, but we can make up for it if we start training hard for State Cup now."

"I'm sorry, Mimi," Nancy said, "but is anyone else thinking, *so what?* I mean, so what if we place seventh or, God forbid, eighth? So what if we don't win State Cup? Is the world going to come to a screeching halt?"

Several parents stared incredulously. Leo examined this strange creature before him and asked, "She *sivious?* This is State Cup we talkin''bout."

"You can sing your freakin' Kumbaya shit all day long, but I'm with Mimi," said Dick. "What's the point if they don't get in there and at least fight like hell to bring home the State Cup?"

"Are you *sivious?!*" I shouted. "I mean, serious. Are you serious? What's the point? My daughter lost her father and had a gaping hole in her life until this team—these girls and this coach—came into her life. She talks about her teammates and practices, Gunther and tournaments constantly! And God help me, she talks about you, Mimi. She talks about your amazing Girl Power bars, and how you played soccer in college, and how even the milk at your house tastes better than ours. That's what the point is, Dick! The point is that my daughter has found a place in the world at her most vulnerable phase of life. The point is that my insanely rigid mother is watching Telemundo at midnight and recently hung a Mexican flag in her office. The point is that my mother-in-law is back in our lives and we have something to talk about other than how much we miss my husband, her son. That's what the point is! I don't give a rat's ass about winning the State Cup. I don't care what bracket we play in or what place we come in at the end of the season. From where I'm sitting, having your daughters be a part of Rachel's life is enough for me. My family has won. I don't need another thing from this season. We've already won!"

There was a long silence. Finally Mimi spoke. "Well, Claire, you certainly have brought more than your fair share of drama to the team this season."

"Shut up, Mimi," said Loud Bobby of all people.

The group was still. "I was kidding!" Mimi said. "Of course, we've all loved having Rachel and Claire on the team. And of course, there's more to the season than winning the State Cup, but let's face it, winning wouldn't suck, would it?" I could feel the fathers shifting their allegiance back to her. Or maybe I was kidding myself and it had never left her. In any case, she had them. "Let's all give ourselves time to cool off and talk about this after Saturday's game."

# Chapter Twenty-Nine

The girls won their next game, but Dick lost fifty dollars because he bet a two-point spread with one of the dads on the other team. I hadn't known it until this game, but Dick had a small-time gambling ring going with some of the fathers in our bracket.

In the meantime, Darcy had transformed my family room into a necklace factory with folding tables set up in a horseshoe formation as if we were at a wedding banquet. She had me set up with a temporary license, and had the UPS guy scheduled to pick up orders every day at 4 p.m. And she was right about our employees. Each showed up with a placid smile and told me she was so happy she could help. That didn't stop a single one from accepting a paycheck at the end of the day, though, Darcy noted as we cleaned up.

Darcy scheduled four-hour shifts that were as informative as they were productive. I learned that the soccer mom who had sex with a player's father was not in fact Mimi Shasta, but a woman named Irene Shaston, whose kids now both play at Stanford. Another woman advised her friend to eat omega-3-enriched eggs to enhance her flagging libido. And one cluster of moms launched accusations that Debbony Wright bought a black market copy of the Gifted and Talented Education test from an illegal exam dealer she found in Chinatown in Los Angeles.

Another set of women ripped into a teacher for her insistence on using a red pen for grading tests after they'd shown her a study on how doing so was deleterious to children's mental health. "She said 'thank you for sharing' like I was some sort of ninny," the woman with the short curls, pale skin, and two enormous moles complained.

"That's so like her," an over-processed teen wannabe mother replied. "She does whatever she wants in that classroom. It's as if none of us has any right to say boo." The mother wore too much base makeup that didn't quite match the color of her skin, and her hair had been bleached so many times, it had a haggard Rod Stewart look to it.

Darcy walked by them and inspected their clasps. We'd found that this was the weak link of our production line and had to redo a few. If this kept up, we'd never meet our deadline, especially since the website accepted another several hundred orders between the day the magazine hit the streets and the weekend. Still, Darcy couldn't help getting in on the conversation. "It *is* her classroom," she reminded the women.

"They're *our* kids!" the mothers said in unison.

"Darcy!" said the blonde. "I know you like to tease us, but Miss Lortel is being difficult just to be difficult. All she has to do is grade papers with a purple or green pen so the kids aren't jarred by the sight of red all over their tests." It took all of my self-restraint not to attack her face with a Wet One. Who wears chalky pink lipstick? It looked as though she'd taken a swig of Pepto-Bismol and hadn't bothered wiping her mouth afterward. The ad caption should read, "Got Gas?" And what was the deal with the green eye shadow? It looked like two parakeets had crash-landed on her face.

Darcy asked, "You're afraid the kids will think it's blood?"

"Very funny," the helmet of curls said. Her fashion statement was that forty was the new fifty. "Darcy, be serious, what's so hard about switching ink colors? The study said that some kids were very traumatized by the sight of red ink."

"Why?" I couldn't help inserting myself into the conversation.

Neither woman being a devotee of Botox, their foreheads compressed like accordions. Parakeet Eyes said, "They feel as if they're wrong."

"Aren't they?" I asked. "I mean, doesn't this Miss Lortel only red-mark the wrong answers?"

"You're missing the point, Claire," Helmet Curls said. "Their answers may be incorrect—"

"I think the term is validity-challenged," Darcy interjected.

"Darcy's the neighborhood comedienne, in case you haven't noticed," Helmet Curls told me.

And on and on our debate went about whether Miss Lortel should stand by her red pen or succumb to the pressures of mothers who read an article in *Psychology Today*. At the end of the shift, Darcy wrote their checks in red ink, and smiled as she handed them to the women. "I hope this will help you form positive associations with red ink, ladies."

How was it that Darcy always ended her disagreements with women with double-cheeked kisses and plans for lunch? I, on the other hand, had been tackled over a jersey, stabbed by John Hancock, and abused by the team manager.

"We'll see you tomorrow, dear," a mom said, leaving.

The next group was one I recognized from Rachel's days in recreational soccer. Kim, the über soccer mom, shocked me when she went R-rated within five minutes of walking in the door. She asked how I was surviving the season with Loud Bobby.

"He's actually not the worst of them," I told her.

"Really?"

"He's not in the normal faction by any means, but there are two or three dads who have him topped."

"Well, you know what they say?" she asked with a wink. I looked blankly. She finished, "The bigger the mouth, the smaller the pecker."

Darcy walked by just as that line was being delivered and laughed. "Kim McNamara! Get you away from your kids and you're a regular potty mouth."

"How is it on the dark side?" Kim asked.

"Oh, it's dark," I replied.

"Are you guys done yet? When does the season even end?" Kim pulled out a chair and seated herself at the center of the table, where the bride would sit if this were her rehearsal dinner.

Darcy placed a plate of beads in front of Kim and answered the question. "It never ends. Season is a misnomer. We're lifers."

"Well, Rachel loves it," I added. "So it's worth it, but Darcy's right, it is a huge commitment."

A few more mothers from the old team trickled in, and after I looked at the table I asked, "Is this the soccer moms shift?"

Darcy nodded. "Also known as opposition research."

"What?"

"We hear a bunch of stuff on our end, and they've got their own rumor mill on rec, so I figured we'd get the two camps together and see what comes up," Darcy explained.

After about an hour, I realized Darcy was right. We learned not only about soccer, but who had affairs, who had cosmetic surgery, and who was still holding grudges over bidding wars at last year's school auction. It was all done very skillfully. The women knew that gossip was unseemly, so they packaged it with the pretty paper and bows of concern. As in: "I am so concerned about Felicity's butt implants. When Petra had them done, they got infected and it was a nightmare."

Response: "What really concerns me is *why* she's doing it. I mean, I am totally supportive of a woman's right to choose, but if she thinks it's going to keep that dog of a husband home at night, she's got another think coming."

New concerned woman: "He really ought to focus on finding a new job already! It's been a year since he was laid off, and if they don't get back on their feet soon, they might have to sell the house. My Reeba would be devastated if Uma left Santa Bella."

Finally, someone suggested they bring casseroles over to the house to help Felicity during her recovery. Ninety-five percent of the people who bring meals to the grieving and recovering do so with only the purest intentions. There are, however, those who use their casserole as a Trojan horse. They stand at the door in a floral print dress, smiling brightly, then they walk into the kitchen, taking copious mental notes to be stockpiled as ammunition.

I also learned that when Drunk Dick told me he was an agent for Tandy and Mariah, he wasn't kidding. Tandy's parents paid Dick to get her on the top team at a club. Dick, in turn, gave Mariah's parents a cut as an incentive to be part of the package deal.

Months ago, Darcy warned me that half of everything one hears about other people is bullshit, but on this day I also discovered that half of what you think about them is also false. "I am so concerned about Tom," a mom said. "How is he going to manage once Gia starts school again in the fall?"

"He'll have to get help, that's all. It's such a shame, though. I really thought Anne was going to beat this thing, but she's gotten worse."

As it turned out, Gia was not Tom's trophy wife after all. She was his daughter who had taken time off from college to help care for Sapphire and her mother, Anne, as Anne fought her second bout of breast cancer. I felt as if my body were going down a giant drain. All season I'd been sneering at Gia's ever-present boobs and her ever-absent husband. As it turned out, she had a fiancé who was patiently waiting for her at Long Beach State. And a mother who was at home dying.

CR&CO

Ten days later, Claire Emmett Designs had shipped more than four thousand lira necklaces. And Claire Emmett had learned that there was a lot more going on in Santa Bella than she had originally thought, or given credit for. I wasn't the only one who had dealt with family loss. I wasn't the only one who'd come to blows with another mother (though Mimi and I were still legendary at the Soccer Post).

In the height of production, we had a cameo from Barbara, who came wearing her oversized, belted Real Madrid jersey hanging over black knit leggings and black boots. Lil took over as den mother, cooking for us and taking Rachel to her last practices. Even Dave stopped by after he dropped Katie back at her mother's. He tried to help, but his beefy fingers couldn't manage the beads or petite cutters. I found it endearing the way he tried to win over my mother, as if he somehow needed her permission to take me to the prom.

"Mother," I said, rushing past her. "I love you for doing this, but next time you put one of my necklaces on your front cover, you need to give me some advance warning."

"Consider this it," Barbara said.

"Consider what *what?*" I asked.

"This. Consider this your warning. I thought since my readers liked your lira necklace so well, we'd go ahead and feature another one this spring. It's going to have to be something very bold. Bold, colorful, and alive is the new—"

"The new black?" I asked.

"Awww, I was going to say that!" Darcy said, pouting.

I startled, realizing that I'd entirely missed what my mother had said. "You're putting another one of my necklaces on the *Garb* cover?!"

She nodded. "Make it your best, Claire."

I lunged into her arms, not realizing how much I needed this. By this, I don't mean getting back into jewelry design, though that had certainly fulfilled me more than I'd expected. The *this* I needed was my mother's help. Never before had she used her position at *Garb*—or anywhere—to give me a leg-up in life. She once told me that parents who over-assisted their children were giving them a zero-confidence vote. Though I think she firmly believed it, there was also an element of selfish laziness to it. Even at my age, a little maternal coddling was incredibly comforting.

CR ∽

I managed to make it to the team's last practice just before winter break. Darcy had things so well under control that we were actually ahead of schedule. For all of their drama, I'd missed attending practices. Since this was the last of the regular season, I wanted to be there. Mostly because I wanted to see everyone and wish them a happy holiday, but also because Darcy and I had been out of the loop of Mimi's discussions of her Wall Street-style hostile takeover of the team. I was dropped from her email list, and Darcy said she was getting her information from Ron, who was actually able to reconfigure much of his hospital schedule so he could attend practices more regularly. I was hopeful that he was doing this to help Darcy manage Claire Emmett Designs, but she told me not to be naïve. He was doing it to help Ron Greer Self Interests, Inc.

At practice, Mimi didn't say a word to either Darcy or me as she whisked by the sidelines barking orders at the girls. Gunther glared at her a few times, but this was hardly a deterrent. "Drop, drop!!!" Mimi shouted at Katie. "To who? To who?!" she cried. It was exhausting just listening to her.

"I cannot hear my thinking," Gunther barked, looking genuinely flustered. He held his temples with his hands and knit his brow as if to trap thoughts from escaping.

"That's because you're *not* thinking!" she shot back.

"Oh, snap," Leo said, nudging the other fathers.

"Give it a rest, Mimi," I muttered. Unfortunately, it wasn't quite as inaudible as I'd expected.

"Excuse me?" Mimi growled as flames shot from her mouth.

"You just might want to give them a break, that's all," I said.

"They've basically lost an entire season at the hands of this moron. This is the first real coaching they've gotten. If you were around more, you'd know that, Claire."

Darcy opened her mouth to defend me, but I got the words out first. "I've been at most practices, Mimi, and my mother-in-law has brought Rachel to the others, so I don't know what you're complaining about. I've done your books all season, which is no easy task, let me tell you, with all those hotel room charges and fancy meals."

Mimi's eyes shot nervously toward Darcy before she regained her steely composure. "Okay, you're right. You've been helpful, Claire. I apologize. Managing this team has been more stressful than I bargained for. Sorry I took it out on you."

Darcy and I looked at each other dumbfounded.

"Um, okay, no problem," I said.

Now smiling at us conspiratorially, Mimi leaned in as if we were all the best of friends. "I do have a special treat for the girls after practice today. I'm taking them all to the Mustang Diner in style," she reported as if she needn't bother with getting our consent. The Mustang Diner is one of those cutesy fifties-theme restaurants where the burgers are big and the waitresses' hair is even bigger. A character reminiscent of Divine roller-skates across the dining room floor. Another Hula Hoops or flashes her ruffled pantaloons while cartwheeling. The cashier has a slicked-back ducktail, wears a black leather jacket and calls customers Daddy-O and Sugar Mama.

When practice ended, a stretch limousine pulled up to the practice field and a chauffeur got out and stood by the door. "Girls! Your chariot awaits you," Mimi announced grandly. The girls screamed with excitement and started running past the parents toward the limo. Apparently all of the others had been asked beforehand and had agreed because even Darcy seemed to know about the surprise post-practice dinner. No one knew what Mimi had planned—just that it was something special.

As the car pulled away, Darcy stood frozen watching the spot where the limo was parked. "It's her," she said to no one in particular.

"What?" I asked as I packed Rachel's things. Gunther and the other parents packed soccer gear and started trickling into their cars.

"Mimi. That's who Ron's having an affair with," Darcy said, still staring at the blank parking spot.

Dropping Rachel's bag, I asked, "Why do you think that?"

"Did you see how she looked at me when you mentioned the hotel charges and restaurant bills? It was just, I don't know, I could just tell."

"Darcy, you can't know from—"

"Oh, I know. I've known for awhile there was someone, but I finally figured out who. Come on, when has she ever apologized to you? *You*, Claire! She said she was sorry because it was *that* important to shut you up."

Part of me felt kicked in the stomach by the idea of Ron having an affair with Mimi. *I* felt betrayed, and couldn't imagine what Darcy was going through. Part of me ached for Darcy, and as much as I hate to admit it, a smaller part of me felt jealous. I'd struggled hard with my feelings toward Ron while he was busy sniffing around town for anyone who would have him. I wasn't so special after all.

The more I thought about it, the more I was convinced that Darcy was right. Mimi began lashing out at me right from the start. I was just a random hit at the Soccer Post, but after that it got personal. It went from a petty jersey battle to a full-on war when Ron and I had our first glimmer of attraction at soccer tryouts. I always assumed that she despised me because Rachel replaced Jinx's daughter, Sissy, but I should have known that for Mimi to really, truly care about something, it needed to somehow affect her.

Darcy and I sat on the empty field, completely oblivious to the plummeting chill in the evening air. "Do you want to know for sure?" I asked.

"I already do," she said as we walked to my car.

"Do you want to confirm your suspicions once and for all?"

We sat in the front seats of my car and turned on the heat. "Does your home phone have caller ID?" I asked.

"Please," Darcy said, shaking her head. "Ron's not even listed in the phone book, and gee, I wonder why."

*Oh boy.* Just as I'd resolved to drop it, Darcy pressed. "Why, what do you want to do?"

"If you really want to know, I can find out. Are you sure?"

"I'm sure."

I dialed the Greer house and turned on my cell phone speaker. "Hello," Ron said.

In my best English accent I replicated a gag I'd heard on the radio a few years ago. "Hello, sir, good evening. This is, um, Poppy from Romantic Roses Dot Com. I'm not trying to sell you anything, but since we're new to the area, we're doing a special promotion where we're giving away free roses and delivering them to your special lady absolutely free."

"Not interested," Ron said.

"Sir, there is absolutely no charge for these roses. We're going to deliver one dozen gorgeous long-stem roses to the special lady in your life at no cost to you. All we ask is that when you're thinking about sending flowers in the future you think of us here at Romantic Roses Dot Com. Sound fair?"

"I don't have to give you any money?" Ron asked.

"Nothing, sir. This is our way of getting out the word about the great service and quality of Romantic Roses Dot Com."

"I don't have to join any club that I have to quit after thirty days?" he asked.

"No sir, you just—"

"You don't need my credit card number?"

*Just shut up and let me finish, you cynical jerk!* I thought, before remembering that I was, indeed, trying to scam him, just not in the way he thought. "No sir, you simply give me the name and address of your special lady friend—or male as the case may be, nothing wrong with that," I added.

"No, no, she's a lady," Ron chuckled good-naturedly.

"And her name is?" I asked.

My heart was pounding fiercely as Darcy and I looked at each other for the moment of truth. *Say Darcy, say Darcy. Please, if there is a God in heaven, let this man say Darcy!*

"All right. It's free, right?"

"Totally free."

"No catches?" Ron asked. Darcy looked at me as if she were thinking the same thing: *Say the name already!*

"No sir. No catches, no hidden fees. This is just our way of helping spread the word about Romantic Roses Dot Com. Now, who's the lucky lady who will receive a dozen gorgeous roses from you this evening?"

"Mimi," he said.

I looked at Darcy, who was clutching her chest, her mouth agape. Though we were parked in my minivan on a cold December evening, I suddenly knew how Thelma and Louise must've felt as their car started its descent, plummeting them into certain death. This was worse, though, because after hearing that awful name, I had to continue the charade.

"And what would you like your card to Mimi to say?" I asked, trying to maintain my chipper tone.

*Please dear God, have him say, "Thanks for a great season, pal" or "From the Team."*

"Let's see," Ron pondered. "Write, 'Remember Jamaica.' "

Darcy's and my heads snapped toward each other. *Remember Jamaica?! What the hell did that mean? Had they actually been to Jamaica together? Were they planning on going and he was telling her to be patient and keep her eyes on the prize of Jamaica? Jamaica, Jamaica? Jamaica the restaurant?! Jamaica the punch line to a joke?* Whichever way you sliced it, "Remember Jamaica" had more intimacy than what was acceptable between a soccer team manager and the married father of a player.

*Remember Jamaica?!* Darcy mouthed, gesturing with her hands that I should try to get more out of him.

"Is that all, sir? We've got plenty of room on our cards at Romantic Roses Dot Com. You could write an entire poem if you'd like."

"No thanks," he said. Desperately, pathetically trying to lessen the blow, I gave Darcy a facial expression as if to say, *See, he doesn't care enough about her to write a poem.*

Getting through the rest of the phone call without blowing it was a challenge. I wanted to scream at him for being such a lousy piece of shit to Darcy. Still, I continued with my happy little Brit routine, asking for Mimi's address and nearest cross street. I couldn't help myself, though. "Hmmmm, is this Mimi Shasta by any chance?" I asked.

"Uhh, yeah, it is. Why?"

"Oh, it's just that she's a very popular girl. This is the third bouquet we've sent to her on this promotion. Would you like to include your last name on the card so she can be sure who these are from?"

I finished taking his order and hung up the phone. Darcy and I sat in still silence, which slowly transitioned into her tears.

# Chapter Thirty

Rachel returned home that night proclaiming I would never believe what Mimi told the team at dinner. *That she's having an affair with one of the team dads?* I didn't say, and hoped to God that Mimi didn't either. One could never be sure what that woman would share with the girls. "Gunther's going back to Germany and left her with the team," Rachel said. "Doesn't that totally suck of him? He didn't say a thing to us about it. He is so lame."

"What do you mean he's going back to Germany?" I asked.

"Uh, what part of he's going back to Germany and ditched his team did you not understand?" Rachel asked, sounding more like Kelly Greer—and Mimi—than I cared for.

"Rachel, I think you'd better understand that speaking to me this way is getting you nowhere you want to be," I told her.

"Sorry," she said.

"Let's start over. What exactly did Mimi tell you guys?"

"Gunther's gone. He leaving for Germany tomorrow morning, and she's got to take over the team if we're going to go to State Cup."

"Wow, I'm shocked he didn't say anything to anyone."

"You are?" Rachel said, laughing. "This doesn't surprise me at all. It's so typical. Anyway, I'm kind of excited that Mimi's coaching us. She said we're going to be in amazing shape for the games and will totally rock."

Rachel then spent the next two hours rehashing the situation on the phone with the teammates she'd just shared dinner with. They all seemed to be in agreement that Gunther was a traitor and Mimi was their salvation. "Oh yeah, Mom," Rachel said as an afterthought. "Mimi's going to email all the parents tonight and let you know what's up."

It was tough to absorb anything more this evening. I was still reeling from the fact that Darcy confirmed that Ron and Mimi were having an affair, and everything else seemed trivial. "Okay," I said lifelessly.

I wondered what was going on next door at the Greers. Darcy said she wanted some time to "sit on" her discovery while she figured out what she wanted to do. Her plan was to neither do nor say a thing to Ron that would let him know she was on to his philandering. This was the plan, at least. With all of Darcy's nervous energy, I wasn't sure she'd be able to contain herself for longer than a few seconds. I wouldn't. If Steve had cheated on me, Maggie Jennings would've had to start a foundation to help stop the decapitation of cheating husbands.

"So make sure you check," Rachel added, "because Mimi said all the parents need to know about the new training schedule that starts tomorrow."

"Tomorrow?"

"Mom, Mimi says if we do everything she tells us, we have a real shot at State Cup. We're having practice on Christmas Eve. That's how serious she is about us, unlike Gunther who just took off. Did you know she played in college? She says I remind her of herself at my age," Rachel said proudly. Shifting gears, she said wistfully, "The only thing I'm bummed about is no more of those amazing Girl Power bars."

"So she's not going to make those for you anymore now that she's taken over the team?"

"No time," Rachel said, shrugging. "Did you know that she runs the club foundation *and* is on the board of directors at Shasta Imports? Plus, she teaches aerobics to old people at the senior center. Her plate is, like, way full. Anyway, she wants us to stick to this athletes' diet." Rachel reached into her soccer bag and pulled out three pages of pink paper. I looked at Mimi's directive to load up on vegetables and protein, and saw that the diet came from the Sports Medicine Department of our local hospital. At the very bottom of the last sheet was a promise that this diet would increase an athlete's strength and reduce fat faster than any other program available. On the surface, this statement seemed innocuous, but something about the need for fast fat loss struck me as odd.

"Rachel, what was in Mimi's Girl Power bars?"

"Oh my God, Mom, don't even tempt me. Mimi said we can't eat any more of those until State Cup is over."

*Oh no. She didn't.*

"But what's in them? I mean, did she ever give you the recipe?"

"Nah, she said they're a family secret, but it's like this peanut butter goop, but better. Kelly said it tasted like macadamia nuts, but Mimi said it was some special seed from a fruit tree. Anyway, there's that stuff on a graham cracker with a chocolate bar and coconut shavings. Then another cracker to hold it all together. Oh right, and some special powder that makes girls strong."

"Special powder?" I asked, terrified.

"Yeah, it comes in this big jar with muscle men on it."

*Oh my God!!!*

"But no more for awhile," Rachel reported. "We even have to start drinking skim milk. Blah!"

I was afraid to ask the next question, but did anyway. "What kind of milk has Mimi been giving you?"

Rachel shrugged. "I don't know. She always puts it out in a big glass pitcher. She's so fancy." Then remembering a time when she saw the milk carton in the garbage can, she startled. "Oh right, it's called half-and-half."

"Half-and-half?!" I cried. "She serves you all half-and-half?"

Rachel said, "Except for Cara and Sissy. They're dietetic so they can't drink half-and-half. Or have Girl Power bars."

"*Diabetic?* Cara is diabetic? And what's Sissy doing there?"

"Dietetic," Rachel clarified. "I've never heard of it either, but I'm glad I don't have it 'cause Girl Power bars rock!"

"Rachel," I said hesitantly. "Do you happen to have any of these bars?" Her eyes popped wide and she looked as guilty as I'd ever seen her. She shook her head no, unable to lie to me with words. That was positive, at least. "Boy, I really, really wish you did because if I could taste one myself, I'm sure I could figure out the recipe and make them once State Cup is over."

Rachel looked down at her shoes, then shifted her weight uncomfortably. "Promise you won't be mad?" I nodded my head to encourage her. "It was totally Kelly's idea."

"Go on," I urged.

"Well, last week Mimi said this was the last batch of Girl Power bars she was making, so we, um—"

"Yes," I pulled.

"We sort of stole some," she said quickly, sealing her lips when she finished.

"You *stole* them?"

"You said you wouldn't be mad!"

"Rachel, I'm not angry, but this is so unlike you."

"It was totally Kelly's idea," Rachel defended.

"An idea that you went along with."

"You're mad."

"Do you have any more of these stolen bars?" I asked. Rachel nodded sheepishly. "Bring me one."

Minutes later Rachel slinked back into the kitchen with an open tin of Girl Power bars, which looked more like cookies. "You stole them in a cookie tin?" She scrunched her mouth to the side and shrugged her shoulders.

I popped one of Mimi's treats into my mouth and could see why the girls were reduced to a life of crime. They were beyond delicious. They were beyond three thousand calories each. And later that night, I discovered that they were beyond groovy.

At about ten that night, I was lying in bed thinking about how much I loved the world and everyone in it. Even Mimi. She was troubled and misunderstood to be sure, but underneath it all, weren't we all beautiful creatures of divine spirit?

I reached for the phone to call Darcy before remembering that she had bigger problems to deal with at the moment. I looked at the clock and realized it was a half-hour past Lil's bedtime. I dialed Dave's cell phone, but it rolled directly over to voice mail. *Where was he at 10:30?* I wondered with a pinch of jealousy. Realizing that there weren't many people who would welcome a late-night phone call about soccer drama, I decided to just lie back and write poetry in my head.

The next morning I woke up and all I could think about was having another cookie. I rushed downstairs where Rachel was dipping one into a glass of milk. She shrugged. "One more before they go stale."

"I thought you weren't supposed to eat these anymore?" I said between bites.

"Mimi said she doesn't have time to make 'em anymore," Rachel said with a full mouth. She gulped her milk as if merely to wash away the thick macadamia nut butter so she had room for the next bite. "But why let these go to waste?"

"You are so right!"

"You forgive me for, you know?" Rachel asked, trailing off.

"For stealing them?!" I asked, cookie crumbs flying from my mouth. "Are you kidding? I want you to go back and steal some more."

The phone rang. "Huh-ro," I answered, not taking a break from chewing.

"Claire? Is that you?"

"Uh, huh Rave. Huh y'dung?"

"Fine," Dave replied. "What's wrong with your voice? You sound like you've got your mouth full."

Swallowing, I said, "Sorry. Rachel and I were just having breakfast." Suddenly, it all came rushing back to me. Mimi was taking over the team. Gunther was fleeing for Germany. The team would have Christmas Eve training sessions in preparation for State Cup.

"So, what's up, Claire?" Dave asked, interrupting my panic attack. "I have nine missed calls from you last night. I figured it must be pretty important."

"Oh, right," I said. "I just wanted to—" *tell you that I love you. But I also loved Mimi and Ron and my nasty seventh grade teacher, Mrs. Markowski at the time, so never mind. No need to lead you on.* "I just wanted to say hi, that's all."

"Claire, your last call was at a quarter to two."

*Oh right. Where the hell were you, anyway?*

Mercifully changing the topic, he asked if I'd heard the news about Mimi taking over the team. We chatted for awhile before he asked if he could come over for a quick visit. "I mean, since you're so eager to say hello to me," he teased.

"Are you in Santa Bella?"

"Yeah, I just dropped Katie off at her mom's and don't need to be at work today."

Rachel asked if she could go to Kelly's, and I waited for Dave's arrival. The fluid motion of my computer screensaver caught my attention, so I decided to check my email to see if there was anything from Mimi. And maybe have another cookie.

## MEMORANDUM

TO: The Team
FROM: Mimi
DATE: December 23
RE: Gunther's gone

As you know, Gunther has opted to spend the next three weeks in Germany rather than getting the team ready for State Cup! According to the club bylaws, teams can fire their coaches after the regular season if there is a majority vote! I polled parents last week and we've got the eight votes we need to replace Gunther! As you know, I played in college and have my "E" coaching license, which is why the majority of parents want me to take the girls to State Cup!

I need you to understand that this was not an easy decision! But after watching Gunther squander away an entire season, I had to step up and do something! We have so few points that we are in jeopardy of losing our triple-A status next year! If we advance far enough in State Cup, we will gain the points to stay a premiere team _and_ gain seeded-team status! This means that we get to choose our coach for the season, rather than depending on the league to assign us another brain-dead idiot to run our team into the ground!

Please join me in welcoming our newest player, Sissy, who will replace Violet for State Cup! I know Roy and Lisa seem to feel

**Violet's 100%, but I'm not ready to take that risk! We have a lot depending on this game and she has missed an entire season! There's no way she's going to be effective!**

"Hello, Mimi," I said into the phone. I felt she was a lamb who'd simply lost her way. If only I could be there to hug her.

"Claire," she said, sounding annoyed.

"I got your note. You told the girls Gunther was leaving for Germany, but he's not going for good. He's just visiting family for the holidays."

"It's a critical three weeks, Claire. I knew you wouldn't understand."

I twirled my hair around my finger, noticing how very pretty it was. "Is that why you didn't call me and get my vote?" I asked.

"How would you have voted?"

"Against firing Gunther!" I said too loudly.

"That's what I figured. I didn't ask Nancy either. I figured why take her away from her busy day of composting when I can cast a no ballot for her. I still have the majority without you two."

"What about Darcy?"

"One vote per family and Ron completely gets what I'm trying to do with the girls."

*No, I meant what about the fact that you've carried on an affair with her husband for more than a year?*

"I see," I managed to say. "And what did the league say about all of this?"

"They'll get my email right when Gunther gets his copy."

"You fired him by email?" She didn't reply. "Mimi, are you still there?"

"I'm here. How should I respond to that? I told you I emailed him, so you already know the answer."

"Well, you can count us out. Rachel will be going to State Cup with Coach Gunther," I said firmly.

Mimi cackled. "Claire, you are so dense. I don't know what part of this you're having trouble understanding. Gunther isn't our coach anymore. According to the bylaws, if a team—"

"I know, I know, if the majority votes to oust the coach in the post-season, they can go do it. So, you've basically just pulled off a Wall Street-style hostile takeover of a twelve-year-old girls' soccer team?"

"I wouldn't call it hostile," Mimi said. I could see her rolling her eyes and checking her watch.

"Subversive then," I said.

"I did what was best for the girls. If one lame coach gets his feelings hurt along the way, so be it. As for Rachel dropping off the team, that's your choice. Be sure you tell your daughter that this was your decision, not mine. There were plenty of parents who wanted me to dump her, but I fought to keep Rachel on the team. I'm loyal to my girls, and I said there was no way I would turn my back on her."

"Rachel's the leading scorer," I reminded her. "Who would want to cut her from the team?"

"The voting is confidential, but if you must know, Rachel is not the problem—it's you. You've alienated more than a few parents this season."

*I have?* I thought as a lump formed in my throat. I knew that demanding alcohol-free practices and games wasn't going to win me any points with the dads formerly known as "the saloon," but who else disliked me? Who hated me enough to punish Rachel for it? Maybe it wouldn't be such a bad idea if Rachel sat out of the State Cup. If parents were going to be unwelcoming to her, maybe it was best if we just took off until … until … until she reappeared at tryouts in a few months? How would it look if she didn't play with her team in the State Cup? Maybe she didn't *want* to sit out of State Cup.

My God, I wish Steve were here for this one.

"Claire, I don't have time for this."

"Nor do I," I said, hanging up.

The next phone call I made was to Preston, who once told me to call him "anytime" with concerns about club soccer. "I'm facing a weird situation," I told him.

"Yes," he said, sounding bored already.

I explained that Mimi fired Gunther by email and planned to take the team to State Cup as their coach. I expected him to gasp and tell me he'd put a stop to this right away. "Preston? Are you there?"

"Yes," he said.

"Did you hear what I said?"

"Yes, Mimi is up to her old tricks again. She does something crazy like this every year. Mrs. Emmett, if she has a majority of the parents voting to replace Gunther, my hands are tied. Parents pay a lot of money to play in Kix. If they're not happy with the coach, they have a right to replace him after the regular season's over."

"That's it?"

"He's still under contract," Preston said. "He'll get paid. Mrs. Emmett, maybe this is for the best. Gunther gets a paid vacation and you get a chance with a new coach."

"I don't want a chance with a new coach! Gunther is great. Plus, what am I teaching her about how to treat people? I don't trust Mimi! Did you know she's been giving the girls high-fat cookies and half-and-half ever since Gunther canceled her fitness trainings?!"

"That doesn't sound like a good idea," Preston said dumbly.

"Preston, it's an awful idea! It's completely unhealthy, and they all gained a ton of weight."

"I don't understand how that is fitness training," he pondered aloud.

"Preston! She fattened them up to prove that it was a mistake to cancel fitness training. Like, 'See what happens when we don't do my fitness training?'"

I could see the light bulb over Preston's head. "Oh, that's bad, even for Mimi."

*Plus she's having an affair with a team dad!*

"Why do you let her get away with stuff like this?" I asked, not expecting an answer. It was simple. She paid, she played.

"I'll have a talk with her," Preston said. *Oh thank God!* "See what type of system she's planning on using."

"What?! You'll see what system she's planning on using?! I don't want my daughter playing for this maniac!"

"Oh, well, that solves the problem then," he said. "If Rachel doesn't want to play in the State Cup, she doesn't have to."

Seeing that this conversation was going absolutely nowhere, I hung up the phone and spent the longest ten minutes of solitude as I waited for Dave to arrive.

When the doorbell rang, I almost ran to answer it. I rushed him inside, high on the adrenaline I felt after my argument with Mimi. "She is so evil!" I said, seating him with urgency. "Great cook, though. Want a cookie? High fat, but so worth the calories." I reminded myself of Darcy when I first went to her house to ask about club soccer. *Oh God, poor Darcy! I wonder how she's doing.* I stood before Dave, extending a cookie toward him, and began to sob.

"Claire, what's wrong?" he asked, standing to comfort me. "You're acting weird, even for you."

CR ℘

After a half-hour of crying, laughing and espousing random Tibetan philosophy, Dave asked me what was in Mimi's cookies. I shrugged, but moved toward the cookie tin to devour my seventh of the morning. Dave reached for my hand and said, "Claire, put down the cookie."

"Can we share it?" I squeaked.

"I have a buddy who works at the UCLA Nutrition Lab. I want to have her take a look at this."

I nodded emphatically. "I already know it's super fatty, but look at me," I gestured to my body. "All my life, everyone has always said that I need to eat more. If anyone can afford the calories, it's me."

"It's not the calories," he began, staring at me in shock.

"What then?"

"Claire, stop licking crumbs off the table!"

"Then give me the cookie!" I demanded. "You can take her a piece. A little piece should do the job, right?"

"No, Claire, I need the cookie."

"So do I!"

CR ℘

Later that day, Dave called me. "Claire, I got the results," he said. "Are you ready for this?"

"Girl Power cookies are high fat," I said dully. "Amazing. You must be so proud of your breakthrough." I hated that bastard.

"Have you ever heard of OxyContin?" Dave asked.

"The pimple medicine?"

"No, not the pimple medicine, Claire," Dave replied, as if he were losing patience with me. I admit I may have gone a bit overboard when I jumped on his windshield as he drove off to

Los Angeles with my last cookie. "It's an addictive painkiller, and this cookie's got a pretty good dose of it."

"What?" I gasped. "Mimi's been putting painkillers in the Girl Power cookies? Why?"

"To keep them hooked," Dave explained. "It's not a dangerous amount, just enough to create a team of addicts."

"So I'm—"

"A junkie? Yes, Claire, I'm afraid you are. Thankfully, the girls never ate a dozen cookies in a twenty-four-hour period, or they also may have treated their friends to a performance of kitchen chair rodeo."

"Oh, I forgot about that," I said, recalling the great pleasure I took in watching my kitchen clock travel across the wall like Halley's Comet as I bucked on a backward chair.

"Are you mad at me?" I asked.

"I'm mad as hell at Mimi," he said to my great relief.

I looked at the phone and smiled. "Dave, you're my best friend. I mean it. It's not just the drugs talking."

# Chapter Thirty-One

That evening I had the conversation I was dreading. Rachel sat at the table, flipping through *Garb* with an expression of horror on her face. When she saw me, she launched, "Do you have any idea what women do to get rid of those blue veins on their legs?!"

"Rachel, we need to talk," I began. Knowing what I did about Mimi's questionable ethics, there was no way I could have my daughter play for her renegade team. She turned the girls into fat little drug addicts, had an affair with a player's father and fired the coach in a subversive takeover. What good could come of Rachel's involvement with this woman? I gave Rachel the PG-rated version of the story and hoped that she would understand. I knew she would be disappointed, but I prayed she'd take it in stride. And truth be told, I was terrified that she would be angry with me. I could stand Mimi's hatred, Dick's animosity and Preston's indifference, but I was truly frightened that Rachel would despise me for this. I realize that all parents of adolescents have moments when their kids think they're ogres. In fact, it's probably a promising sign that I'm doing something right. Still, I feared that this would be the point of no return—the moment our relationship began to unravel. "So the bottom line is that I really can't let you go to State Cup with Mimi's break-off team," I concluded.

"You're joking, right?!"

"No, I'm not, Rachel. I wish there was a way for you to go to State Cup, but under the circumstances, our only option is to sit out."

She stood enraged. "Why is that the only option?! Another option is going with Mimi like everyone else. This is State Cup, Mom. I don't think you understand what a big deal it is."

"Rachel, I have been hearing about State Cup since before tryouts last year. I get it. What you don't get is that I'm not looking to guide you through one soccer season. I'm in this for life, and I can't condone what Mimi did to Gunther. If I let you go with her, I'm saying what she did was okay, and it's not."

"Mom!!!" Rachel screamed. "I know she can sometimes be bossy, but she really knows what she's doing. She played in—"

"I know, Rachel. I think we're all well aware that Mimi played soccer in college."

"You're jealous of her! You don't want me to go because you hate her. That's so unfair!"

"Rachel, I am not jealous of Mimi Shasta!" *Okay, maybe a little.* "I wish I could let you go, but—"

"You can! All you have to do is say, 'Rachel, go to State Cup.' That's all. No other parents are making a big deal of this. Why do you have to be the nice police about this?!"

My tone and intensity escalated. "It's not about being nice, Rachel. It's about doing what's right. Where is your loyalty to your coach? The coach who took a chance on a rookie! The coach who taught you everything you know! Mimi just fired that coach—by email! She took a secret vote and ousted him. She put painkillers in your cookies! This is who you want to play for?!"

"Maybe she just didn't want us to be sore after practice," Rachel shouted. "I don't care who I play for, I just want to play."

"You know what, Rachel? I knew this was going to be an unpopular decision, but I'm sticking to it because I know it's the right thing to do. You're twelve. You don't get a say in every decision, even if it involves you!"

"I can do what I want! You can't control me!" Rachel screamed before trotting up the stairs.

Shouting at her back, I shouted, "If you make your choices simply to defy me, I *am* controlling you, Rachel!" The door slammed. *Well, that went swimmingly.*

CR & SO

I decided to give Rachel some time to cool off before I tried to make peace. I dialed Darcy's house, checking first to see that Ron's car was gone. "Darcy?" I asked of the faint voice that answered the phone. "How are you doing?"

"Meh, been better," she said with the tiniest laugh.

"Did you say anything?"

"Not yet," Darcy said. "I need to figure out what I'm doing first, and if Ron knows that I know, it'll complicate things. Better to just get through the holidays letting him think everything is normal."

"What do you mean, it'll complicate things?"

"Claire, he'll start hiding money so I can't get it in a divorce."

"So, that's what you've decided?" Before I thought it through, I asked, "Do you really think he'd hide money from you?"

This annoyed Darcy. "Gee, Claire, I don't know. He's been hiding his dick in the team manager all season. Speaking of that crazy bitch, did you get her last email? Can you believe she fired Gunther?"

I couldn't believe that in the height of her marital crisis, she was still concerned about soccer politics. "There's no way I'm letting her take Kelly to State Cup," she said.

"I'm not letting her take Rachel either. You're never going to believe what I found out," I said. Darcy didn't seem all that shocked when I told her about the Girl Power bars. In fact, she gave the faintest acknowledgment of it and moved on to ask if I'd spoken with anyone else from the team. I told her I hadn't.

"Do you have time this morning?" she asked.

"What do you have in mind?"

"Let's get on the phone and see just how much support Mimi really has. I'll bet if we refused to let our daughters play for Mimi, we could get Nancy on board with that. Let me talk to Gia and Tom and see where they stand. I'll call the Psycho Dads and you talk to the Normals and the Italian and let's touch base this afternoon. Maybe we can undo this takeover."

"Do you think we can?"

Sounding energized, Darcy said, "Claire, I can't turn back the clock on the affair Ron had with her, but I can mess up her stupid plan to take over the world of girls' soccer." I smiled. "I'll tell you this, Claire, I'd like to take a fist full of medals and stick them straight up her ass!"

"Then so you shall, my friend," I said.

෨ ෬

Hours later, Rachel still had not come out of her room, answering my knocks only with, "Go away!" It was a shame she had to be such a snot considering she was missing out on news that she would quite like. As it turned out, all three Katies' parents, Deborah's parents and Sapphire's parents had voted not to overthrow Gunther, which meant Mimi only had the support of the Psycho Dads, Ron, Giovanna's father and, of course, herself. Paulo put an older cousin of Giovanna's on the telephone, who explained that he spoke English "more good than Uncle Paulo."

I explained the situation as I heard young Gianni translate for his uncle. Paulo sounded flustered and began repeating the word "no." "My uncle he is very sorry he did not understand what the lady saying. He no want to get a new coach than Gunther."

"Really?! That's wonderful news. Grazie, molto grazie," I said.

As it turned out, Mimi never bothered to call Violet's parents, but when I called, Ray and Leesha said that they would vote however I thought they should. "I never trusted that rich bitch with her fancy-ass house," Raymond said.

"You didn't trust me either," I reminded him.

"Don't make a proud man say he's sorry, Claire."

"I think you just did," I teased.

"Good 'nuff then. Let's do to this team what you did to that lung dinner."

By the next morning, Darcy and I had chipped away at Mimi's team until it was only Cara, Cayenne, Tandy, Mariah, Kylie and Savannah. Oh, and of course, Sissy. There was a part of me that hated tearing the team down the middle like this, but as they say in kindergarten, she started it. The larger part of me knew that Darcy and I were doing the right thing. Mimi had been operating like this throughout her entire life, and it was high time someone put a stop to it.

# Chapter Thirty-Two

After the New Year, Gunther returned to Santa Bella and seven phone messages from me. "We've got half the team back, and Preston said we could borrow players from the B-team for State Cup," I said in my fourth message. When he finally called me back and I filled him in on Mimi's plan, he laughed with more vitality than I'd ever heard.

"This woman is cuckoo," Gunther said. "All season she tell me girls are fat, and now you say she feeding them fat food? Then she fire me?"

"Yeah, um, I know, it's hard to believe."

ᘓᘔ

A week before State Cup, Darcy still hadn't told Ron that she knew about his affair with Mimi. As far as he knew, he was happily married, and his daughter would be playing on his girlfriend's team at the state championship. Darcy told me she'd been doing some digging and, with what she discovered, there was no way Ron would stop her from switching Kelly's allegiance. "Trust me on this one, Claire. Ron's going to be extremely cooperative with me next week, and my lawyer the week after that," she said coyly, still absolutely refusing to let me in on her secret. "I promise everything will become very clear next weekend."

With Mimi now coaching the other team, I volunteered to take over as manager for what was left of Gunther's team. Strangely enough, it was in the few weeks that I stood in as team manager that I gained appreciation for Mimi's contribution. Sure, she was a vicious, lying, cheating scoundrel. But she did handle quite a bit of paperwork for the team. I had no idea how many forms, phone calls, and emails this job entailed. Still, all things considered, I wasn't about to drop her a thank-you note.

CR ∞

Because my mother had called in a few favors in the magazine world, several of my designs were scheduled to appear in the glossy pages of women's monthlies in the spring. This was just the kick in the ass I needed to get back to work. Claire Emmett Designs was my mother's first true gift to me and was scheduled to officially open its doors in February. Mother had bought me clothing and jewelry throughout my life, but in spoon-feeding my upstart business to me, it was the first time she had really thought about who I was and what I needed most at that point in my life. I found a great space that had room for about twenty workstations in the back where people could string beads. And there was a small shop in the front—just large enough to hold a few designs and tiny enough to feel like a chic boutique. Adding to the character of the shop would be my ritzy sales clerk, Lil, who volunteered to work for me once a week. Afterward, she'd have dinner and take the train home the next morning. It would be good to have her around on a regular basis again.

Last week, when I told Lil about Ron straying, she nodded her head as if she already knew. "He seemed the type," she said.

*Holy crap, did he hit on her too?!*

"Can I tell you something awful?" I asked.

"You just did, sweetheart."

"No, I mean, something awful about myself, about my reaction to Ron's affair with Mimi."

"You were jealous," Lil said.

"Yes!" I exclaimed. "I mean, I really put myself through the wringer over this. I felt horribly guilty over my thoughts. And once, oh God, I can't even believe I'm going to say this aloud, but once I wondered if it would be so terrible to follow through on my feelings because what Ron and I had together was so clearly special," I said, laughing at the absurdity.

"But you didn't," Lil said forgivingly. I shook my head emphatically. "And you wouldn't have. Claire, you're not the first woman to feel hurt when she learns that the neighborhood lothario views her as no more than a fungible unit of sex." I giggled as Lil brushed the hair from my face.

"A fungible unit of sex?"

Lil smiled. "Should I have said 'booty'?"

I raised my eyebrows.

"Lil, you're the best," I said, resting my head on her shoulder.

"What you must always remember, Claire, is that you are special. Not because some handsome cad pays attention to you. Why give that jerk so much importance? You're special because *I* love you."

CR ED

It was a new year and time for the battle of our lives. When we saw the sign reading "Welcome to the California State Cup," my heart was beating in my throat. Every pore was open and I felt like my innards were going to drop through my pants. Kelly and Rachel carried on in the back seat, a blend of nerves and excitement.

An hour earlier, as the girls watched *Bend It Like Beckham* (or as Darcy called it, *My Big Fat Sikh Wedding*), I whispered, "How did you get Ron to agree to let Kelly play for Gunther again?"

Darcy glanced back at the girls, who were fully immersed in the movie, and whispered, "It's in Ron's best interest to disassociate himself from Mimi."

"Did you confront him?" I begged.

"I did," she said. "I've done my homework on Miss Shasta, and my husband's not the only one she's been screwing."

Peeking back at the girls again, I whispered, "Do tell."

"Oh, you'll find out. But you know Mimi's stellar college soccer career she always reminds us of?" I nodded. "She played intramural."

"No!"

"Yep, the biggest game she's ever been in was a rivalry match between the Tri Delts and Kappa Kappa Gammas."

"I'm loving this!"

"It gets so much better, Claire."

"Why do you tease me like this?!" I said, swatting her.

"Claire, you will not leave this tournament this weekend without knowing everything."

"Do you think we have any shot of advancing to the next weekend?" I asked.

"Honestly, no," Darcy said before reconsidering. "Maybe next week, but no further than that. You know I love our girls and I think our patchwork team is pretty darned solid, but the teams that go on to the semifinals and finals of State Cup are amazing. The good news is that Mimi's team won't advance either."

"Yeah, she had to take half of the B-team just like us. Basically, we both have A-minus teams."

"Pretty much," Darcy said. "But Mimi wouldn't advance to next week if she had Mia Hamm and the Women's National Team playing for her." She smiled mischievously.

CR ∞

Shockingly, we won both of our first two games in tight, hard-fought battles. The girls from the B-team were far better in games than they looked in practice. And the parents were so much more pleasant on the sidelines than I'd expected. There was no sideline coaching, no disparaging other players and no secret pow-wows second-guessing Gunther's plays. We had a sudden infusion of Normals, including, I'm happy to say, Raymond. After his first "Noooo mer-saaaaay!" Leesha placed her hand on her husband's leg and said, "Mercy is a good thing, honey." He looked at her and nodded in agreement. It was a private reference that quieted him instantly.

When we faced Mimi's team on Sunday, the mood became decidedly tense. This was no longer just a soccer game; it was a battle between good and evil. Then I looked across the field and saw Tandy's bony arm waving at Rachel. She called back, "Good luck, you guys!"

Okay, maybe it was just a soccer game.

As we watched the game, I was filled with pride over how much the girls had improved over the season. Sure, girls like Violet and Kelly came to the team with superstar status, but Rachel had really grown this season. And Tandy—wow! At the beginning of the season, she tripped over the ball. Now she was doing scissors and crossovers as if they were second nature to her. The sideline was awkward with Darcy and Ron sitting beside each other as Dave and I shared a canvas bench with a soccer ball pattern. Their conversation was clipped, and that's when they spoke to each other. Thankfully, Paulo came to sit with us and struggled through an apology in broken English. He was almost weeping with remorse as he explained that he had no idea what Mimi was doing when he agreed to let Giovanna play for her break-off team. Looking at his rosary-clad mother, I wondered what his penance was for this transgression.

Gia and her boobs—and her fiancé—were at the State Cup jumping around wildly like, well, kids. Sadly, Tom couldn't make it, as Anne had taken a turn for the worse and he wanted to be by her bedside. I made a mental note to call him when we got back to Santa Bella. I had a list of the top ten worst things to say to the spouse of a terminally ill person, and promised not to utter a single one of them. Unless, that is, Tom was the type of person who found comfort in humor. If that were the case, the two of us could share war stories. I didn't know, but would make a point of finding out who Tom really was, instead of assuming I already knew.

Nancy and her CFO husband huddled together under a wool blanket, while some of the Normals showed us seat warmers they bought earlier that day. Everyone clutched a cup of hot chocolate, coffee, or cider.

I watched Ron as he averted his eyes from Darcy, me— and Mimi, which was actually quite challenging since she was directly across the field from us.

Dick, Bobby, and Leo looked absolutely hammered, which wasn't surprising since it was the last game of the day. We could always count on them to start the party early and keep it going till the cleanup crew broke down the goal nets.

When it was time for me to bring the girls out to the referee, I walked out to the center of the field, where I was met by Dry Drunk Dick, who, I guess, was Mimi's team manager. "We're taking the kickoff," he snapped.

"Team captains flip a coin," I reminded him.

*How many games have you been to now, Loser?*

As if he heard my thoughts, Dick's head snapped up from its limp state and he shot at me, "D'unt matter cause we're gonna kick yer friggin' asses no matter who kicks off."

When the whistle blew, everyone moved forward in their seats a few inches. Despite their marital issues, despite family illness, despite language barriers, we all had one thing bonding us. We wanted our girls to leave this tournament with a victory. As much as we may have liked individual girls on Mimi's team, we still wanted to beat them. Not because we were competitive, but because we wanted all of the girls to see that right always wins in the end. We wanted to have our Disney ending, then have a meaningful chat about it on the drive home in the minivan. It wasn't that we wanted to stick it to that pigtailed bitch in Nike sweats. It was about teachable moments.

ॐ ೞ

In the final minutes of the game, the score was tied at one, and as luck would have it, my daughter fouled Cara in the box. Just in case anyone missed the implications of this—or might have had to wait a whole thirty seconds to see it—Mimi started shouting, "Right on! Penalty kick! Mariah, take the kick."

*Uh-oh.* I'd seen Mariah's boot. And I'd seen our goalkeeper. McKenzie was doing a lovely job, but was no match for Mariah's precision bombs into an unreachable corner of the net. "This is not going to be pretty," I said to Dave.

Dave nodded his head and pursed his lips as if he were about to agree, but also added an optimistic twist. He looked as if he were going to tell me that kids grow emotionally from losing "the big game." I thought he might also share a statistic about the low percentage of penalty kicks that make it. (God, I hoped it was a low percentage!) Instead, he leaned in and whispered, "She'll choke under pressure." I looked at him in mock horror, and he winked. "Ten bucks says it's wide."

Unfortunately, thanks to psychologists like Dave, kids like Mariah were unflappable, mentally balanced, grace-under-pressure little buggers. I got to watch the whole thing in slow motion, frame by frame. First, the young Jodie Foster look-alike sniffed while shrugging her shoulders to loosen them. Already, I was intimidated by her and the way she paced around, scouting the spot from which she would begin her approach. A year ago I would have thought the kicker simply stood in front of the ball and took a single chip at it. Through the intense faces of twelve-year-old strikers, I learned that there was a whole technique to this. And an entire psychological dance that goes on between the shooter and the goalkeeper. In the match-up between Mariah and McKenzie, the winner was pretty clear. McKenzie probably peed.

At the sound of the whistle, Mariah ran toward the ball from an angle and reached her right leg back. With the slow-motion effect, I could see the ropy definition of her quads. It was like something from a biology classroom poster. I was also struck by the tension in Mariah's neck as she contorted her face with determination.

When Mariah's foot connected with the ball, the impact sounded like thunder. I've seen her shoot beautiful arches where the ball drops down into the corner of the net, and I've watched Mariah shoot straight, fast, hard shots into the upper corners of the net. Today she was shooting arches, which reminded me of Cupid's arrow being released from his bow. There was no way any goalie could have caught Mariah's shot. I almost wish she hadn't tried because it was embarrassing for everyone when McKenzie fell back and got her arms tangled in the back of the net. She appeared almost Christ-like when her head dropped to her chest as her hands splayed in the ropes.

With the referee having blown the two-minute warning whistle just before the foul, Mariah's goal had probably ended the game. "There's still time," Dave said, patting my hand as if he had been reading my mind.

"It's over," I said.

"I've got a good feeling about this game," he said.

"Me too," Darcy chimed in. Ron sneered at her as if he had something to be angry about.

Looking at Dave, I said, "Look how your last prediction worked out."

As we were talking, Rachel stripped the ball from Sissy and passed it to Kelly. *Oh my God, they're going to do this!* The referee looked at his stopwatch, then looked up at the field. A girl I only knew as the Scab Defender approached Kelly, who made a move around her and then passed the ball to Violet, who was out wide, just outside of the eighteen. "If they tie this game, we're still in," I said to Dave.

As the theme to *Chariots of Fire* began playing in my head, Rachel ran in slow motion to the center of the box. The girl was in perfect position to score. In the movie version of my life, Violet would give Rachel the perfect pass, and she would lob it into the net.

The reality went somewhat differently. Violet did indeed pass a beautiful ball to Rachel, who wound up and took a nice shot on goal. Unfortunately, it was not quite nice enough, and hit the post and bounced back.

All of the formerly sane parents from our side were on their feet, shouting, "It's still live! Shoot, shoot the ball!" Violet, who was now in front of the net, kicked the rebound, which rolled slightly left of where Cayenne was standing. "Oh my God! It's going in!" I cried. "We're gonna score!"

Like the sound effect of a closing vault, I heard Cayenne's body fall to the ground with the ball underneath her. As she lay on the goal line, I wondered why I was the only parent cheering.

There was a collective gasp from both sidelines as the referee began walking toward Cayenne.

"Dave, why is everyone silent?" I asked, noticing that the only sounds I now heard were coming from another game. Cayenne's body was perfectly placed on the goal line, which meant the ball under her had to have inched over the line, I explained urgently, as if my telling him this would set everyone straight.

Darcy leaned toward me, but never took her eyes off the field. The referee continued walking toward Cayenne after instructing her not to move a muscle. "Claire, the ball needs to fully cross the line."

"It did cross the line!" I said.

"Maybe," Dave said.

"Not maybe, it's over the line."

"Claire, the ref needs to see if the back end of the ball made it completely past the line," Dave explained.

"Oh my God! Is he serious?!" I said, panicking as I watched him inspect Cayenne's catch of the game. "That thing is so clearly in, it's got to be a—"

"No goal!" the referee shouted, seeming a little too happy about it for my taste. Wasn't he supposed to be impartial? I wanted to swat that bumblebee clear across the field, no goal. That was such a goal. That was absolutely, positively—

The whistle blew in a series of three. The game was over. Mimi and her girls began screaming and running onto the field. They lifted Cayenne and started cheering "hip hip hooray!" *Oh please. It's just a soccer game, you man-eating bitch.*

Speaking his first words of the game, Ron sighed at Darcy and me and said, "Guess that's what happens when you tear the team apart, ladies."

Darcy turned to him and said, "Ron, the depth of your idiocy makes me wonder why I ever married you in the first place."

"You were pregnant," he snapped back.

I squelched my first impulse to say, "Oh my God, Rachel was a shotgun baby too!" and just glared at him instead.

Dave said, "At least we've got our weekends free now."

"I wouldn't make plans just yet, Dave," Darcy said.

"Oh boy," Ron said. "I'm outta here. Darc, you taking Kelly back to Santa Bella or am I?"

Darcy smiled a saccharine grin and looked at her watch. "Closing ceremonies are in an hour. I wanna be a good sport and watch Mimi's team take their fist full of medals at the podium."

"Suit yourself," Ron said before changing his demeanor and approaching Kelly with his swell-dad persona.

"Well, Darcy, we're going to hit the road too," I said of Dave, the girls and me.

"No, no, stay. I insist," Darcy implored.

Dave explained that he needed to get Katie back to Santa Bella, but Darcy assured him that there would be plenty of time to watch the closing ceremony, catch a bite and be home well in time for a good school night's sleep. "Okay," he shrugged, giving me a look as if to ask why it was so important for her to stay and watch her nemesis receive accolades.

I shrugged. "She's got something up her sleeve."

♋ ♋

A plump MC with a wrap-around hairline looked off to the side at Mimi and winked before announcing the results of our age group. Darcy looked around, frantically searching the crowd. "Where the hell is he?" she muttered several times. Dave and I exchanged glances as the team from Group A was called onto the stage and Darcy became more panicked. As the MC called Mimi's team, the winners of Group B, up to the stage, a pimple-faced lanky boy trotted onto the stage and handed the older gentleman a note. He unfolded the paper, read it and grimaced. Darcy sighed. "Yes, perfect timing, Oscar."

"Oscar? Who's Oscar?" I asked.

Before she could answer, the MC turned to Mimi discreetly and showed her the note. She began shaking her head in denial.

"Who's Oscar?" I asked again.

Darcy smiled. "My knight in shining armor. One of them, at least."

After a few minutes of quiet discussion between Mimi and the MC, she threw down her hands in exasperation and stormed off the stage, taking the girls off with her.

"I'm sorry for the delay, folks," the MC said, smiling uncomfortably. "Because of administrative issues, the Kix Under Thirteen team has been disqualified."

The crowd gasped collectively. Murmurs of "What happened? What is he talking about? Why are they disqualified?" fluttered about the audience.

"The team from Group B that will now advance instead ... " the MC began, consulting his clipboard, "Ha! Well, wouldn't you know, it's the *other* Kix Girls Under Thirteen team."

Technically, they were the other team, but this was the least of my concerns. As Mimi descended the steps of the stage, she caught Darcy's eye. My friend smiled brightly and mouthed *girl power*, giving Mimi two thumbs up.

"What the heck's going on, Darcy?" I asked.

"Mimi needs to have a valid coach's license *and* renew her risk management every three years to coach a team."

"Risk management?" I asked.

Dave leaned in to me and whispered, "A perv card." God, his breath against my hair suddenly felt so inviting. I scrunched my face to query the term. He clarified, "It means she's okay to be around kids."

Darcy continued, "I did a little digging and little Miss Nike forgot to get hers renewed this January. Since she doesn't have the risk management, her coaching license isn't valid. You can't *ever* coach a club team without a license, and you most certainly can't do it at State Cup. If the coach isn't licensed, the team is not valid. If the team isn't valid, it can't play in State Cup, much less advance to the next level."

The girls stared agape as Mimi stood by the side of the stage quietly arguing with a gentleman with the CYSA logo on his shirt. Dave whispered to the kids that they should come over and stand with us.

Darcy said, "You know who I have to thank for this? Kelly was smarter than all of us at Manchester. She knew that Mimi ripped off Claire's idea about the necklaces, but we were all too thick-headed to listen."

"I told you she was a bitch!" Kelly whispered.

"Kelly!" Darcy scolded. "Watch your language. Mimi *is* a bitch, not *was* a bitch. Present tense. Honey, you've got great instincts about people. I'm sorry I doubted you. Listen to your gut, Kelly. You'll go far in this world."

Dave looked at me and smiled. I cannot say what it was about that moment that made me want to kiss him. Certainly we weren't under a starry, moonlit sky sharing a bottle of wine and a lazy night. He hadn't said or done anything special in that moment, but it was the Sunday evening after the first weekend of State Cup when I began my slow descent into falling in love with Dave.

"Oh, here comes the good part!" Darcy said as two men in dark suits approached Mimi and asked if she was indeed Mimi

Shasta. When she confirmed, one flashed a badge and slapped handcuffs on her. The other began reading Mimi her rights.

"You can get arrested for coaching without a license?!" I gasped.

Darcy laughed. "No, but you can for certain types of *importing*," she said, shifting her eyes toward the kids.

"The rumors are true?" I asked.

"That's for the DEA to decide, but I have a feeling we won't be seeing Mimi Shasta for another ten to fifteen years."

"Really?" I asked.

"No, not really," Darcy said. "I'm sure the Shastas have enough people paid off to keep Mimi out of prison. Plus, she's a mom and first-time offender. She'll probably get a slap on the wrist and some community service. I'll tell you, if it weren't for Cara, I'd really fight to see justice done, but how can you do that to a kid, right?"

"Yeah, I'm sure seeing her mother arrested at a soccer tournament is going to be a wonderful memory for her, Darcy," I said.

"Claire, that child has seen worse, and will continue to as long as her mother chooses to be a drug-smuggling, husband-stealing slut who stages coup d'états of soccer teams. She made her choices, and I'm sorry if her daughter has to learn the hard way that actions do actually have consequences," Darcy said haughtily.

Awkwardly, the MC continued, "So if we could have a representative from the Kix Girls Under Thirteen Team—"

"Claire, go," Darcy urged. "You're the manager. You go up there."

"Yeah, Mom, go! We get medals for this round. Go get 'em for us."

"Come with me, girls," I said to Katie, Kelly, and Rachel.

"Is there a representative from the team here?" the MC asked.

As I looked at the dumbfounded group of girls, I knew what I had to do. "Cayenne, Tandy, Mariah, Kylie, Cara, Sissy," I said. "Come with us."

"What are you going to do to us?!" Tandy asked, terrified.

"Tandy!" I said. "Just come up on the stage with us. The girls looked at each other and consulted with glances. In a moment, they agreed.

As I stood on the stage, I looked out into the audience and saw Dave and Darcy. As they smiled giddily at us, the MC handed me—of all things—a fist full of medals. "Um, excuse me," I whispered to the gentleman, looking at the team surrounding me. "I hope I don't seem totally ungracious here, but I'm going to need a few more medals." He looked baffled. "Our team just got a lot bigger." The girls smiled. Cayenne, of all people, had tears in her eyes.

"You want more medals?" he asked.

"Yeah, is that okay?"

"I don't know. I've never been asked for more medals before. I'm sorry, but I don't think we have enough to give one team more medals."

"It's okay, Mrs. Emmett," said Mariah. "Your team won, you guys take the medals." Tandy and Kylie concurred vocally while the others simply nodded.

"No, that's okay," Kelly said. "You guys would've won if your coach hadn't been arrested and all. You take 'em."

"Okay, so shall I just give the medals to you?" the MC asked, hurrying us along.

"No," said Rachel. "I hope I'm not out of line or anything, but I don't want my medal if the other girls aren't getting one too."

"Me neither," said Katie. Kelly agreed.

"Okay, so now none of you want the medals?" the MC asked.

"I'm sorry," I said. "We're going to pass on the medals. Thank you, though. They're lovely. See you next weekend."

The girls giggled victoriously and cheered as we trotted off the stage. Last off stage, I saw Dave at the bottom, waiting for me. He opened his mouth to speak, but before he could get out the words, I wrapped my arms around his neck and kissed him. Hollywood style.

The girls all stopped what they were doing and turned to watch. The giggling and cheering increased in volume. It ended only when Dave came up for air and asked, "What was *that* for?"

"I'm ready," I told him.

"You are?"

"I am."

Darcy clapped her hands and said, "Leave it to Claire to upstage Mimi's grand exit."

Our team was in a gigantic huddle with Dave, Katie, Darcy, Kelly, Rachel, and me at the center. "Hey, should we call Gunther to give him the news?!" shouted Kelly, euphorically.

I snorted a laugh. "I hardly think he cares about my kissing Dave."

"Oh my God!" Rachel said, laughing. "Of course he doesn't, Mom! She means, do we want to call him to tell him the news about the team?"

"That we turned down the medals?" I asked.

Rachel laughed. "No, Mom, that we're back in the game!"

*Sneak Peek!*

Read the opening chapter of Jennifer Coburn's novel

# *Brownie Points*

# Chapter One

*August*

"**D**amn, this place is sweet!" Maya exclaimed, her face pressed against the back window of our car. "Gucci, Hermes, Chanel, Juicy!" Continuing her inventory, she gasped, "Look how cute! That bakery is called the Cookie Cutter."

"Wait till you see the school you and Logan are starting at next week," Jason said, pleased that Maya approved of her first sight of Los Corderos. "The field is bigger than Golden Gate Park." Glancing in the rearview mirror, he asked Logan, "What do you think, buddy?"

"It's very clean," he answered. I had to suppress a laugh because that was my first thought when Jason and I first came to look at Los Corderos last month. Logan's delivery was neutral, so I couldn't tell if he was pleased by or aghast at the immaculate appearance of the town. My son then shuddered as he saw a shiny white Nissan Armada pass our car. "I can smell that guy's cologne from here," Logan said of the driver, a young Turk conducting a seemingly very important cell phone conversation.

"The windows are closed," Jason scolded with thinning jocularity.

The sidewalks of El Camino Real looked as if they were made from sand-colored granite; the roads were paved with virgin tar. A pristine mega-mall anchored the community with hundreds of high-end shops and chain restaurants. The only hint of regional flavor was the neat row of thirty-foot palm trees that lined the main drag.

Logan perked up. "Look, they've got a Williams-Sonoma here!" This wasn't the first hint that our son would very likely return to San Francisco in his adult life. We didn't think much of it when Logan was three years old and referred to the evening skyline as "jewels." A few years later, my friend Jorge raised an eyebrow after Logan told him that he was making canapés in his sister's Easy-Bake Oven. When the twins were eight, there was no getting around the fact that our son was as queer as folk. Maya finished a make-up application on Barbie's Dream Head in which Mattel's trophy blonde wound up looking like Tammy Faye Bakker after a week-long bender. Logan shook his head in disgust, lightly shoved aside his sister and worked with a team of imaginary assistants. Twenty minutes later, the parakeet blue eye shadow was replaced with a nude shimmer directly above smoky liner smudged to perfection. Barbie's disembodied head had what my third grader labeled a perfect day-to-night look, a term he must have picked up from one of my friends.

As the retail landscape of Los Corderos scrolled by us, my eyes welled with tears at the sight of a road sign letting us know we were 98 miles from San Francisco. Moments later, another sign informed us that this stretch of El Camino Real was kept tidy by Dolce and Gabbana. I imagined the store's well-heeled staff strutting down the sidewalk disdainfully jabbing candy wrappers with sterling litter sticks. No doubt they'd do something kicky with the trash bags.

I know our culture has become more consumer-oriented and that this trend is nationwide, but Los Corderos seemed Bed Bath and way Beyond the norm. Silently I assured myself that there had to be more to the community than the commercial strip with its army of SUVs and late-model tanks. I inhaled deeply and reminded myself to give Los Corderos a chance. Who was I to be so judgmental anyway? I was just another failed artist exiled from the city because her career couldn't pay the mortgage. If Jason had the opportunity to serve as the first African-American fire captain in Los Corderos, the least I could do was go in with a decent attitude.

My feeling of optimism lasted all of thirty seconds. It quickly deflated when I saw one of the new boutiques inspired by the mega bestseller, *The Answer*. In these orange-blossom scented Answer shops, youthful bindi-wearing salesgirls languished on bamboo counters, providing their expert opinion on healing elixirs, body oils and inspirational tea. They wore organic cotton tank tops with the word "Bliss" in Hindi. Answer stores sold these in several colors, with various spiritual aspirations like Forgiveness, Truth and Balance. Inner peace didn't come cheap either. The rhinestone encrusted "Namaste" ribbed tank was $98 on the clearance rack.

"Almost home, kids," Jason said through the rear view mirror, his chest slightly puffed. My husband agreed that he would have liked to buy a place with more individuality than what the 600-home Utopia luxury housing development offered, but long held a philosophy that environment was internal. Home was where we made it, he said. At least one of us was centered. Maybe I needed a t-shirt that said "Bitter" in a different language, preferably Hebrew so no one around here could read it.

When we were house-hunting earlier this summer, we asked the realtor where the Black-Jewish neighborhood was. She smiled sweetly and told us, "Wherever you two buy a home." Jason laughed, but a nervous giggle escaped my lips. Sensing my discomfort, the realtor gave us a warm honey smile and assured me that Utopia was a veritable United Nations. There was a

Pakistani anesthesiologist, a Japanese-American landscape architect, and "one of those strict Jewish families." I later learned that the only reason Anna Stein wore a wig was that she was undergoing chemo.

When we signed the papers to purchase our home the month before, Jason placed his arm around my waist and said that he couldn't wait till his parents saw our new place. I nodded, and a tear fell on the papers, smudging my signature.

As much as I loved our life in San Francisco, I loved my husband more, and could never deny him this opportunity. Jason rose quickly through the ranks of the fire department, but there was no way he'd become a captain for at least another ten years. We needed to move to a small, growing community where there weren't a dozen senior firefighters standing in line ahead of him. Plus, Jason had already made so many sacrifices for me that I couldn't say no to the move. Loving him more than my home didn't make leaving San Francisco any easier, though. I'd convinced myself that it would ease the pain, but as we pulled into Los Corderos that first day, I realized I was sadly mistaken.

☙ ❧

"Welcome to Utopia," Logan said as we approached the gates of our new home.

"We can all read the sign," Maya told him. "Are those gates real gold?"

Jason pointed to the gate posts. "Check out the angels up top there."

"Maybe we're in one of those freaky movies where the family's actually dead, but they don't know it yet, and we're really driving into heaven," Logan suggested.

*Or hell,* I thought but did not say.

"The gates of heaven are pearly, duh," Maya corrected her brother.

He snorted. "Yeah, sorry to get my facts wrong on the oh-so-realistic scenario of us driving into the great beyond, Glamour Don't." Logan then pointed to the guard at the booth. "Oh, look! St. Peter's got a stun gun." He shook his wavy hair in a brief, unconscious gesture that he always did when he'd beaten his sister in the battle of wits.

I suppose all kids are a blend of their parents, not quite a copy of one or the other. But it is strikingly so with mixed race kids. Their mocha skin is neither like Jason's chocolate brown hue nor my pale tone. Twins, Logan and Maya both have my build and their dad's intense brown eyes, which are so dark they can swallow you whole. By the grace of God, they have Jason's full lips and not the measly licorice shoelaces that frame my mouth. Everyone says that the kids look Latino, though their preschool teacher insisted they looked Korean. This only made sense when one considered that she was Korean and adored my children.

As we drove through the gates, Jason wanted feedback from the kids on every square inch of Utopia. He'd already gotten mine, and he was eager to hear something positive about our new residence. "These are some fancy houses," Maya commented. "Pretty fresh grass," she said of the lawns that bore a suspicious resemblance to Astroturf. The labyrinthine streets of Utopia were rimmed with uniformly manicured square bushes, and the sky looked as if someone had stirred in a bit of blue food coloring. At one point, I swore I saw a formation of doves circling a bicycling child the way they might accompany Snow White at the wishing well.

"Were these houses all done by the same architect or something?" Logan asked.

"Yeah, they all totally match," Maya noted.

It was bad enough that there were only three models of brick McMansion behind the gates of Utopia, but the Homeowners Association had a book of Codes, Covenants and Restrictions so oppressive, it not only dictated the accent paint colors we could use on the outside of our home, it actually had a short list of shades we could use on the inside. We were informed that there was a CC&R Enforcement Committee that restricted the number and type of flowers we were allowed to plant in our front and back yards.

Jason and I bought a home in Utopia because it was the only place to live in Los Corderos except for a mobile home park or a few houses that looked like dilapidated red barns or mint green shoe boxes. Our little Victorian three-bedroom in the city sold for more than twice what we needed for a ridiculously large Model-A sitting on a full acre in Utopia. We made enough from the sale of the place in San Francisco to retire our debt to Jason's parents and buy the place in Utopia outright. For the first time in my life I had a decorating budget.

When money got tight for us last year, I suggested we sell the house and rent an apartment, but we'd been priced out of that market too. Moving to Los Corderos made too much sense.

Jason wanted the promotion more than the move, but he wasn't heartbroken about leaving the city either. He had lived in Baltimore for most of his childhood, then the Bay Area for his adult life, and said that some time in the country might be a nice change. The reality was twofold. First and foremost, my husband was eager to finally put to rest the lingering assumption that dropping out of medical school meant he would never have real earning power, as his father predicted. Second, Jason was a more adventurous person than I. San Francisco was our home, so I saw no reason to ever live anywhere else. My childhood was transient, with an artist mother who moved us from city to city whenever the moon was in the seventh house or Jupiter aligned with Mars. My father vanished for months, sometimes years, at a time. I was only in three schools long enough to ever see how the class photo turned out. While this upbringing might make some people adaptable and free-spirited, it made me crave stability and community. The life Jason and I had created in San Francisco was the happily-ever-after I'd been waiting for since I was Logan and Maya's age.

It wasn't just Jason and I who would miss the city. The kids' school took field trips to opera dress rehearsals, fringe theatre and the Exploratorium. Maya studied karate with two-time kata champion Rob Kanazawa, whose father brought Shotokan to the United States in the seventies. Logan's best friend Josh went trick-or-treating dressed as René Magritte's headless man in a bowler with a green apple. After a cursory search for a fencing academy for Logan, I came up with nothing in Los Corderos. Maya would continue her karate lessons with a guy named Dave Anderson, who ran a martial arts studio called Chop Kix.

As we rounded our street, Jason turned to me. "I got an email from the Los Corderos police chief."

"Let me guess, you fit the profile of a suspect they're hunting," I said.

"You are a funny one, baby. Listen, he's got a kid around Logan's age and they're having a birthday party this weekend. He's invited. They thought it would be a good way to meet some of the guys before school starts up next week." Glancing in the rear view mirror again, Jason added, "It's a sword fighting party. What d'ya think of that, bud?"

"A sword fighting party?" I asked, incredulous. "For thirteen-year-old boys?"

"Not real swords, I'm sure," Jason said, squinting his eyes to read the road sign. The need for reading glasses was his only sign of aging so far, something I simultaneously loved and envied. Gravity had not taken its toll on his body as it had mine. Driving into Los Corderos, he wore a gray cotton t-shirt with our alma mater stretching across his broad chest. Gripping the steering wheel showed off his defined arms and protective hands.

"What are they going to do, have plastic swords?" I asked.

"I don't know," Jason replied with a shrug. "I didn't quiz him. He said his wife was gonna drop off an invite at the house and there'd be kids from Los Corderos Middle. Said they were gonna do some sort of sword fighting theme. Knights of the Round Table or something."

"Isn't thirteen a little old for a theme party?" I whispered.

"Whatever," Jason dismissed. Looking back at Logan through the rearview mirror, he said. "You wanna go meet some of the guys from school?"

"Nah," Logan said, shrugging.

"What do you mean, 'nah'?" Jason asked.

Logan corrected himself. "I'm sorry, I mean, no thank you."

"Am I talking to the youth champion of the City by the Blade tournament?" Jason asked. "Come on, it'll be a good chance for you to meet some of the guys from school."

This seemed to push Logan further in the opposite direction. "I thought I'd help Mom with the—"

"Your mother will be fine," Jason interrupted. "Tell him, Lisa."

"Your father's right," I said. "Meet some of the boys from school so it's not all new faces when you start classes."

"It'll be new faces at the party," Logan said.

"If he's not going, I will," Maya chimed in.

"It'll be all boys," I explained.

"Awesome."

"Not happening, Maya," said Jason.

CR SO

"Home sweet home," Jason burst out proudly as our car pulled into the driveway. He placed his hand on my leg and looked at me tentatively. "It'll be good, I promise." Turning around to the kids, his volume grew. "So what do you guys think?"

"Oh. My. God," Maya said, dragging out each word to properly express her shock. She really knew how to play her father. There was no way that Maya could possibly be so stunned by the exterior of our home. She had just driven by a few hundred exact duplicates. "We're like *Real Housewives of the Sticks!*"

"What do you think, Logan?" I asked.

"Nice," he shrugged. Then Logan flashed the charming crooked smile he inherited from his father and assured us that he liked the new house. "I love colonials."

"That's the spirit," Jason said, not absorbing the fact that, until that moment, even he hadn't known our home was colonial style. When we were house-hunting, Jason told the realtor he liked these "old school" designs.

Logan smiled. "I guess I can go to that stupid party, too."

"It sounds pretty gay, but go, suck it up and be polite, and you'll get the lay of the land. You got nothin' to lose, buddy," said Jason. He took the key out of the ignition and opened the door to get out.

Pretty *gay?!* I mouthed.

Jason shrugged and gave me a look as if to say what he'd told me the last time we had this conversation: "The word has different meanings. I mean 'dorky,' not 'homosexual.' Don't make a big deal of it."

The kids were already running up the brick path to our home. "Just say 'dorky' next time, okay?"

CR ЄΟ

It wasn't a bad house. In fact, it would be nice to have so much open space and ceilings that rivaled a planetarium. There were certainly worse places to live than Utopia. We could live in the hood and face gang violence. We could live in an area where the Klan is alive and well. We could live in a country where we weren't allowed to vote or educate our kids. There were far worse places for our family to live, I thought as I stared at the white lacquered banister that looked as though it was made from a Home Depot kit. I looked up at the equally generic lighting fixture and down at the plush beige carpet and sighed deeply.

Yes, there were worse places to live, but there were better ones too. One of them was the sweet little gingerbread Victorian on the hilly street where we knew our neighbors, I walked to work at the Four Circles Gallery blocks away, and the barista at Tea and Sympathy knew exactly how much milk to put in my chai latte.

After we closed escrow a few weeks earlier, Jason and I drove up for an orientation for new parents at the middle school and met a few of our new neighbors. One of the dads patted Jason on the back and asked if he was "jacked about his sweet new crib." Jason gave the guy a perfunctory smile, then shot me a look I'd seen before. It wasn't every white guy who tried to cram as much MTV lingo into one sentence as possible. In fact, it wasn't even very many. Still, it was enough to remind Jason that there were some people who would see his skin and write his life story in a moment. It was always the same history, too. Poor, black Jason was the first in his family to graduate from college and leave behind his gangsta life thanks to a killer jump shot and affirmative action. They never drew the conclusion that was Jason's true story: that his choice to pursue firefighting was a huge disappointment to his father, a surgeon at the Johns

Hopkins Burn Center. Jason's family paid full freight at his boarding school and college, and used the same affirmative action program that the rich white kids did, a father who golfed. I was always the one who wanted to set the record straight, and it was always Jason who told me not to bother.

At the school orientation, the Utopian fathers exchanged a round of thinly veiled self-congratulations about living in an upscale community. Their blowup-doll wives agreed dutifully.

Jorge, my Puerto Rican Yoda, once told me that we were most critical of other people's shortcomings when we saw them in ourselves. In the privacy of my own thoughts, I had to confess that he was right. I might have had an air of self-satisfaction too. Back when I had high hopes for my career, things like chain restaurants and Prada backpacks didn't bother me in the least. It was only when I realized I'd failed at my own artistic dream that I began rolling my eyes at other people's lifestyles.

As we crossed the threshold of our new home for the first time as a family, I tried to take my eyes off the assembly-line construction of the house and focus on how much this meant to Jason. Ten years ago, when I was miserable in my job in advertising, Jason suggested I pursue sculpting full time. "This ain't a dress rehearsal, baby," he told me. "Chase the dream 'cause it's not coming after you." Now it was my turn.

I looked around the empty foyer. *Positive, positive, I can do positive.* "There are four bathrooms so we can all poop at the same time."

Jason smiled and put his hand across my waist. "I appreciate that, baby."

When I looked back at him, I silently promised myself I'd really give this place a chance.

Maya shouted hello to see if she could get an echo in the empty foyer. "Where's my room?"

"Top of the staircase, turn right," Jason answered, giving my butt a light swat the way he always did when the kids were about to leave us alone. He started doing that at Berkeley when his roommates were on their way out of the house. It still makes me smile. "Yours is up there too, buddy." Logan and Maya trotted up the stairs to inspect their new digs. I felt a smidge guilty that their first time seeing the new place was the day we moved in, but everything happened so fast. The kids were in San Diego with my mother while we were house-hunting, then flew to Baltimore to visit Jason's family while we were closing escrow. This didn't seem to bother them in the least. We heard both kids hoot with satisfaction and high-five each other over the size of their rooms.

"You'll like it, baby," Jason said. He kept repeating this promise so many times, I wondered who he was trying to convince.

"I know," I said, forcing a smile as we walked into the kitchen. I noticed a toy trumpet resting on the unblemished granite countertop. "What's this?" I picked up a small brass horn with a scroll stuffed inside. Unrolling the parchment, I read aloud, "Hear ye, hear ye! Your presence is requested for games and feasting to celebrate Sir Max's birthday."

"Sir Max?"

"Must be the police chief's boy."

"Oh right, the sword fighting thing," Jason said as he leaned against the granite countertop, amused.

"He lucked out with that invitation, right?" I asked. "With all of the years he's been fencing, I'll bet he'll really impress the kids."

"Who said he was too young to start lessons at six?" Jason asked, moving closer so we could drink in our new surroundings together.

I laughed. "Uh, I believe it was the fencing school."

"And look how wrong they were," Jason said. "They thought a little boy and a sword would equal trouble, but he proved them wrong."

"Well, Logan's hardly your typical boy, is he?"

"Nope," Jason said looking past the kitchen counter and into the family room. "Both he and Maya are pretty damn special."

"Jason," I said, my tone more serious. "You know what I'm talking about. When are you going to listen to me about him?"

"Baby, let's not start on that today. This is a day to celebrate."

Trying to reintroduce the dismissed subject, I joked. "We could make this his coming-out party."

Jason sighed, annoyed that I wouldn't let this go. "How many times do I have to tell you, it's too soon to tell on that sort of thing."

"I can tell," I said.

"He's thirteen. Lots of boys his age are —"

"Gay, Jason," I interrupted. "Gay, gay, gay. Get used to it already. The kid is gay and the sooner you accept it, the better off we'll all be."

"Has he ever told you he's gay?"

"Don't you remember the hat he made for Opening Day at the races?" I said, recalling his creation — the wide rim decorated as a horse track complete with plastic model thoroughbreds and jockeys. The center of the hat was made from silk red roses and blue first-place ribbons. It was the height of gaudy chic. He won the award for best hat, and a tight-faced socialite paid him a hundred dollars for it.

"He's a businessman," Jason dismissed. "Look, baby, you're an artist. Of course our kids are going to be creative. There are plenty of straight —"

"Straight male hat makers?"

"I was going to say straight artists," Jason corrected me.

He pulled me in to lean against him. "He's not a hat maker. He made one hat, one time."

"Trust me, Jason, there will be more hats in our future," I said, laughing.

"Don't be so quick to slap a label on the kid," Jason said. "A boy doesn't need his own mother calling him gay."

"It's not an insult, you know."

"I know that," Jason snapped. "Come on, today's a day to celebrate. We got a new life here. A fresh start."

I imagined Jason starring in a Windex commercial where fathers could wipe away the gay from their sons.

"Since when do you have a problem with gay people?" I asked.

"I don't," Jason dismissed. "Some of your best friends are gay."

I surrendered for the moment, but felt the emptiness that came every time Jason failed to admit the reality of our son's orientation. I needed the closure of Jason knowing, acknowledging and accepting. I needed him to say, "Of course he's gay and that's cool with me." Jorge once accused me of "shoving Logan out of the closet," a criticism that stung the way only truth could.

"Okay," I told Jason, quietly reminding myself to relax and let life unfold on its own.

With that, Maya came running down the stairs as Logan slid down the banister next to her, sitting on the rail with his hands outstretched as if to say, *ta-da!* "Look what we found in your bedroom," Maya said, handing Jason and me a booklet of swatches entitled "The Fabric of Utopia."

# About the Author

Jennifer Coburn is a *USA Today* bestselling author who has written six novels and contributed to several literary anthologies.

Over the past two decades, Jennifer has won numerous awards from the San Diego Press Club, and Society for Professional Journalists for articles that appeared in *Mothering, Big Apple Baby, The Miami Herald, The San Diego Union-Tribune* and dozens of national and regional publications. She has also written for *Salon.com, Creators News Syndicate* and *The Huffington Post*.

Jennifer lives with her husband William and their daughter Katie in San Diego, California.